Praise for
USA TODAY bestselling author
Lynne Graham

"While the idea of marrying for revenge is not novel, she manages to make it fresh with strong characterization and technical skill."
—*RT Book Reviews* on Lynne Graham's 100th book, *Bought for the Greek's Revenge*

"The second-chance romance is a heartbreaking page-turner. Graham's ritzy settings are ideal, her little-boy co-star coaxes smiles and her couple's tumultuous relationship enthralls."
—*RT Book Reviews* on *The Secret His Mistress Carried*

"Graham's desert romance is superb. [The] tongue-lashings are spectacular, the lovemaking is as hot as the desert at midday and her exotic locales give the read a modern *Arabian Nights* feel."
—*RT Book Reviews* on *Zarif's Convenient Queen*

"The romance was filled with seductions, interesting conversations, secrets, confrontations and sizzling sexual tension. There was never a dull moment."
—*HarlequinJunkie.com* on *Challenging Dante*

P9-DUV-653

Lynne Graham was born in Northern Ireland and has been a keen romance reader since her teens. She is very happily married to an understanding husband who has learned to cook since she started to write! Her five children keep her on her toes. She has a very large dog who knocks everything over, a very small terrier who barks a lot and two cats. When time allows, Lynne is a keen gardener.

Books by Lynne Graham

Harlequin Presents

Bought for the Greek's Revenge
The Sicilian's Stolen Son
Leonetti's Housekeeper Bride
The Secret His Mistress Carried
The Dimitrakos Proposition
A Ring to Secure His Heir
Unlocking Her Innocence

Christmas with a Tycoon

The Greek's Christmas Bride
The Italian's Christmas Child

The Notorious Greeks

The Greek Demands His Heir
The Greek Commands His Mistress

Bound by Gold

The Sheikh's Secret Babies
The Billionaire's Bridal Bargain

The Legacies of Powerful Men

Ravelli's Defiant Bride
Christakis's Rebellious Wife
Zarif's Convenient Queen

Visit the Author Profile page
at Harlequin.com for more titles.

LYNNE GRAHAM

The
BRIDE'S SECRET

HARLEQUIN PRESENTS® EPICS

Recycling programs
for this product may
not exist in your area.

ISBN-13: 978-0-373-20836-4

The Bride's Secret

Copyright © 2017 by Harlequin Books S.A.

The publisher acknowledges the copyright holder
of the individual works as follows:

The Pregnancy Shock
Copyright © 2010 by Lynne Graham

A Stormy Greek Marriage
Copyright © 2010 by Lynne Graham

Printed in U.S.A.

CONTENTS

THE BRIDE'S SECRET

Part One

CHAPTER ONE

ALEXEI DRAKOS BROODINGLY surveyed the crowded Port Vauban marina from the deck of his yacht, *Sea Queen*. There were paparazzi everywhere. As a man who set a high value on privacy, he was not impressed. He was even less impressed with the topless sunbathers on the vessel moored beside his who were calling out to him and making inviting gestures. *As if,* Alexei thought with all the disdain of an aristocrat for rotten meat. As a teenager he had sampled many female bodies without the need to make dates or chit-chat, but he had grown up since then.

If Calisto had not begged him to bring her to Cannes, he would have been miles away from the noise, the poseurs and the fuss. *Sea Queen* was easily the biggest, sleekest and most expensive yacht there but, as he was a fourth generation Drakos, and possessed of fabulous wealth and privilege from birth, such petty comparisons were beneath Alexei's arrogant notice.

Standing six feet four inches in his bare feet, Alexei was built with the lean muscular power of a trained athlete and surprisingly fit for a noted workaholic. Half Russian and half Greek, he was a dazzlingly handsome man with a formidable reputation as a womaniser. Yet for the past few months there had been only *one* woman in his life: Calisto, the ex-wife of the Swiss electronics tycoon, Xavier Bethune. Keen to get back to work and aware that his business team awaited him indoors, Alexei strode back into his on-board office, which was as streamlined and technologically advanced as any on shore.

Some minutes later, Calisto stalked into the crowded room without warning. Alexei was surprised, for he had sent her down the coast to tour his magnificent villa in an effort to get some peace. An echoing silence spread even before Calisto burst into staccato speech. 'You won't believe what I've discovered at your villa!'

'Nothing short of the Loch Ness monster in the bath tub would excuse this intrusion when I am working,' Alexei drawled, and he was not entirely joking as he glanced up from his laptop to survey the irate blonde.

'The place is a disgrace! The swimming pool hasn't been serviced in months, the garden is overgrown and the house isn't even stocked for our stay next week,' Calisto raged, her bright blue eyes full of indignation. 'And when I asked the housekeeper to explain herself, all she would say was that Billie always dealt with that stuff and that she had received no instructions.'

Calisto Bethune was a six-foot tall beauty and former model, quite capable of stopping traffic with her stunning face and shapely body. She was Greek-born, she was gorgeous and, now that she was free of her husband, the woman whom Alexei had loved and lost as a teenager was finally his again.

'Did you hear anything I just said, Alexei?' Calisto prompted impatiently. 'Last month the refit on *Sea Queen* overran and we couldn't use her. Who was responsible for that? Every place I go in your life things are going wrong and I discover that this Billie creature is at fault!'

'Until a couple of months ago, Billie took care of all my properties as well as my social calendar and travel arrangements. Unfortunately, she insisted on taking a career break and her replacement was so inept, I sacked her after a month—'

Calisto studied him wide-eyed, a frown building on her face. 'This Billie that everybody talks about is a... *woman*?'

'Why not?' Alexei returned to his laptop with renewed energy as he was hotwired to the pursuit of profit and in no mood to hear any more about boring domestic problems. No Drakos male he had ever known had concerned himself with such trivialities. In even listening to Calisto's tirade, he believed he was being very tolerant, offering the listening ear that all women were supposed to crave.

'And this Billie, this woman *insisted* on taking time off? Since when do you allow your employees to insist on anything?' Calisto demanded.

Alexei frowned and straightened before he rose to his full height and urged the gorgeous blonde across the hallway outside the office into the opulent and spacious salon. 'I've known Billie since she was a child growing up on Speros. She has a little more licence than the rest of my team—'

A frozen look stiffened Calisto's wide cheekbones. 'Does she indeed?'

'Until now Billie has always been available when I want her. *Usually* she doesn't take vacations or even days off. Day or night, she has worked extremely hard for me,' Alexei volunteered, but his tone was flat because in spite of what he was saying he too blamed Billie for the many annoying developments that had taken the edge off his comfort in recent months.

Billie Foster, his most trusted aide and gofer, his right-hand woman, had insisted on taking an eight-month-long career break to look after her recently widowed but pregnant aunt in England. His even white teeth clenched as he mentally shifted through the aggravations he'd had to tolerate during Billie's prolonged absence. Impersonal and personal matters that he had once taken for granted as being taken care of were suddenly rolling up in front of him undone and causing him *considerable* inconvenience.

He had never dreamt that Billie might act in so selfish a manner. Even though she knew he disagreed with her taking such a lengthy break, she had gone ahead regardless. He had been too soft with her. He should have told her *no*. He should have told her that if she left she would have no job to return to. After all, for what did he pay her such a handsome salary? To go running off to England whenever she took the fancy? Alexei had expected a lot more from a young woman whom he had known since childhood and who owed more than she knew to his family's generosity.

'A wife would take charge of your properties and

your social calendar. It would be no big deal,' Calisto remarked softly. 'Then you wouldn't need a Billie in your life.'

Alexei was too clever and wary of feminine manipulation to respond. He shrugged a broad shoulder and signalled a steward to bring coffee. Calisto might be the first woman to spend more than a few weeks with him, but marriage was another step altogether in his book. He was all too well aware of how expensive a bad marriage could be: his late father had endured three very nasty and costly divorces. No, Alexei was in no hurry to name the day. Although Calisto was the first to even consider that the altar might be within her sights, she might also yet reveal a deal-breaking flaw. In his experience, women were rarely predictable and even more rarely truthful.

Turning her nose up at the coffee that powered Alexei through his long working day, Calisto put on some music and began to dance, twisting and working her hips in movements as suggestive as any lap dancer's. Recognising that she was trying to use sex to get his attention, Alexei studiously ignored her while wondering why she thought a lap-dancing impression might get her up the aisle. If anything the demonstration repelled him. Outside the bedroom a wife should have a certain dignity, he reflected seriously, adding that quality to the mental list he cherished. Under the influence of a few drinks at a party, Calisto could well become an embarrassment.

A brilliantly coloured print scarf lying on a bar stool caught his attention. Black brows pleating, he lifted it up. It belonged to Billie, who had little sense of colour coordination. A faint old-fashioned peachy scent that was familiar assailed him and his nostrils flared. Just as quickly, his penetrating dark eyes took on a frowning expression of bewilderment. The sense of something erotic skimmed indistinctly through his mind and his body reacted with primal male hunger, hardening with instant lust. Bemused by that powerful reaction and unable to find a logical connection, Alexei registered that he was still holding the scarf. Filled with distaste at the tenor of his thoughts, for there could be no woman more sexually naïve than Billie, he tossed the material down again...

'You'll miss all the options here...' As the two women emerged from the public library Billie waved a hand to encompass the busy London street, full of shops, restaurants and bustling traffic. 'That you should return to Greece with me seemed such a great idea after John died, but now I feel horribly guilty for getting you involved in all this. The island is very quiet—'

'You're just tired and feeling down again,' Hilary scolded, a tall, slender blonde with gentle brown eyes in her late thirties. She bore little resemblance to her diminutive red-headed niece with her emerald-green gaze, whose heavily pregnant state made her seem almost as wide as she was tall. She urged the younger woman onto the bus and passed the journey with a cheerful monologue about how much she hated the damp English climate and how much she was looking forward to having the peace to write the book she had long been planning.

Billie, who was more tired than she was prepared to admit, remained unconvinced. In an attempt to do the best she could for her own future and her baby's she had ensnared Hilary in her plans but she felt increasingly guilty about that fact. It was a relief, however, to return to her aunt's comfortable semi-detached house and sit down with a cup of tea.

'You just don't appreciate how desperate I am for a change of scene and direction and I couldn't afford either without your support,' the blonde woman declared ruefully. 'Without your financial assistance during John's illness, I wouldn't even still be living in this house. Your generosity made it possible for us to stay here until he had to go into care; being able to be somewhere familiar helped John a good deal because he couldn't cope with change.'

Hilary's voice cracked up a little because her husband had only passed away some months earlier. As a result of early-onset dementia, the essence of John's personality had gone long before he'd died at the age of forty-three in a care home. Towards the end, as his condition had worsened, he had become too difficult for his wife to look after alone. Prior to that, Hilary had supported her husband for several years and had had to give up working as a teacher to do so. The welfare benefits the couple were entitled to had been too meagre to meet their mortgage payments and Billie had come willingly to the rescue to ease their plight.

'I was glad to help,' Billie told the woman who had often been the only voice of sanity during her childhood, even though they had lived so far part.

Billie's mother, Lauren, had moved to the Greek island of Speros when Billie was only eight years old. Lauren had always been an irresponsible parent, who'd put the latest man in her life ahead of her child's needs. More often than Billie cared to remember, a visit or a phone call from her flighty parent's sensible sister, Hilary, had persuaded Lauren to behave more like a normal mother.

Hilary groaned, 'Unfortunately you helped all of us too much for your own good. You bought a house for your mother, you gave John and I an allowance—'

'And, all on my own, I spent a foolish fortune building my own house on Speros too,' Billie cut in, uncomfortable with the other woman's gratitude. 'If only I had thought ahead to a time when I might not want to work for Alexei any more. If only I had just put all that money in the bank instead...'

'Nobody has a crystal ball. You may not feel it right now but you are still very young at twenty-six,' Hilary reasoned soothingly. 'You had a great job and you were earning a small fortune, so you had no reason to fear the future.'

Billie's delicate features shadowed. She would not be comforted on that score for she blamed herself bitterly for her extravagance. She had grown up in poverty, had lived through the experience of going hungry at mealtimes and of hiding from view when the landlord called for his rent. With those memories behind her, she believed she should have saved up for the proverbial rainy day.

'Nor should you have any reason to fear the future

now. Your baby's father is a very rich man,' Hilary pointed out firmly.

Billie's hands clenched into the tissue she was holding. 'I think I'd rather be dead than face Alexei like this. Thank heaven I was out at a hospital appointment the day he called here at the house to see me!'

'Yes, we weren't expecting that. Fortunately he wouldn't come in, so I doubt if he had the time or the presence of mind to notice that I didn't actually look very pregnant,' Hilary remarked wryly.

Billie was still engaged in recalling her shock on learning that Alexei, over in London on business, had decided to visit her without so much as a phone call to forewarn her of his plans. How shocked he would have been had she answered the door to him with an obviously pregnant stomach! It was pure luck that the deception she had entered into with Hilary—the planned pretence that her aunt was the one having the baby—had not been exposed on the spot. Afterwards, she had phoned him to ask if there was something he had needed her assistance with and he had laughed and said that his visit had been a last minute idea, taken when he had some time to use up before heading to the airport and his flight home.

'If you ever feel in need of courage to face Alexei Drakos, I would face him for you.' Hilary said this softly but the light of battle was in her usually placid gaze.

Billie lifted her chin. 'It's not a matter of being too scared—'

'Oh, I know you're not scared of Alexei Drakos. But you're still madly in love with him and determined to protect him from the consequences of his own behaviour.'

Her colour fluctuating, Billie said sharply, 'It's not like that. I have my pride and my plans. I don't need him in any way. If I continue to work for Alexei for at least a year after my baby's born, I'll be able to save up enough capital to start up my own business back here.'

Hilary gritted her teeth on a tart retort because she didn't want to upset Billie. Her niece, after all, had already suffered the considerable trauma of watching the father of her child—and the man she loved—fall for an old flame from his past. Even so, Billie's reasons for remaining silent were insufficient to satisfy Hilary's hunger for natural justice. So Alexei Drakos had bedded Billie, an employee, one dark night, had recklessly ignored the need to use protection and had conveniently contrived to forget the entire episode by the next day? Did pigs fly too? Hilary's only loyalty was to Billie and she was a cynic who would, had the decision been up to her, have happily destroyed Alexei's latest liaison with a public announcement of Billie's fecund state.

That same evening Billie went into labour. She was a week early and, in spite of all the prenatal classes she had diligently attended, she almost panicked when she awakened and realised what was happening to her. Her case was packed, everything prepared for the big event. She was thoroughly fed up with hauling round her huge bump and trying to sleep while a very lively baby seemed to be trying to kick its way out during the night. But there was also a great wellspring of hungry tenderness inside her, eager and ready for the birth of her child. Her baby might not be planned but it was already very much loved.

The first few hours she was in hospital Billie was given gas and air to cope with the contractions but nothing seemed to be happening very fast. By noon the next day the contractions were coming closer together and were more painful. Billie was getting exhausted and it was at that point that the doctor realised that the baby was in a posterior position with its head stuck in her pelvis.

'You're carrying a big baby for a woman of your size and I don't think you can deliver without help. I believe the possibility of a C-section was discussed during your antenatal visits?' the doctor questioned, while the midwife urged Billie not to push any more.

Billie nodded anxious affirmation, too out of breath to speak.

Hilary gripped her hand. 'You'll be fine and so will the baby be—'

Everything moved very fast from that point. The procedure had to be explained to Billie and she had to sign consent papers before she was moved out of the labour room to the operating theatre. She was given an epidural and while her lower body went numb a little curtain was erected midway down her body so that she couldn't see anything. Time became a little blurred and there was a feeling of pressure and then suddenly Hilary was whooping with excitement.

'It's a boy, Billie!'

'A whopping great boy,' the doctor added.

The cry of a baby intervened and Billie's heart

lurched. She was so eager to see him she could hardly contain herself while the staff took care of measuring him and making him presentable for his first meeting with his mum. He weighed ten pounds and he was very long, exactly what she might have expected with his father's genes; Alexei's family was one of tall, well-built men. At last her son was placed in her arms.

Tears stung Billie's eyes as she looked down into that adorable little face and carefully tracked her gaze over his big dark eyes and the shock of black hair that proclaimed his paternity. 'He's…gorgeous,' she whispered chokily, smoothing a wondering fingertip over his baby-soft cheek.

At that moment everything she had undergone to have him seemed worthwhile. In the early stages of her pregnancy, Hilary had talked her through every option from termination to adoption, yet nobody loved babies more than Hilary, who had never had the opportunity to have one of her own.

'Any idea what you'll call him?' her aunt prompted, stepping back to let the nurse reclaim the baby, for Billie's eyes were very definitely sliding shut.

'Nik—'

'What?' Hilary queried.

'Nikolos.' Billie spelled out the letters through lips that barely moved.

'Isn't giving him a Greek name a little revealing?'

'I've lived in Greece since I was eight,' her niece reminded her, and on that thought she drifted asleep while her mind swept her back seventeen years to her very first meeting with Alexei Nikolos Drakos…

THE BOYS SHOUTED rude words at Bliss when she followed them onto the beach. She knew the words were wrong but she didn't understand their meaning and refused to let their attitude bother her. At least the boys talked to her in some way, recognising her actual existence. The girls in the village school, on the other hand, shunned her, whispering behind her back and shooting disapproving looks at her while excluding her from their games and conversations. It was very similar to the way her mother was treated by the local women. After a year, Bliss had discovered that life on the Greek island of Speros could be very lonely for a little girl who didn't fit in.

Bliss hated everything about herself: her lack of height, her fiery red head of hair and skinny body, even her pale skin, which burned horribly in the sun. The fact she had no father meant yet more mortification on an island where single parents were frowned upon. And although Bliss would never have admitted it to anyone in those days, her mother embarrassed her most of all.

As Lauren often reminded her daughter, she was only thirty years old and couldn't be expected to live as if she were a 'dried-up old hag'. An artist, Lauren rented a small house in the village and sold watercolours to the well-off tourists who patronised the exclusive resort spa at the other end of the island. None of the local women dressed as her mother did. Lauren was most often to be found clad in skimpy bikini bottoms with her full braless breasts bouncing in a cut-off T-shirt. Bliss believed that her mother, with her lovely long blonde hair, jewelled tummy button and endless tanned legs, was very beautiful, but she was beginning to think that only men liked that fact, for Lauren only ever had male friends.

That particular day, Alexei had come off one of the fishing boats being dragged up the sand so she hadn't known who he was at first. He was a tall, rangy boy in his early teens, and she initially mistook him for an adult when he frowned in her direction and waded in among the jeering boys and demanded to know what was going on. Silence fell, the same sort of silence that the village priest could command. Shame-faced glances were exchanged and Alexei asked her name. One of the boys supplied it with a suggestive laugh and a gesture that set all the boys off again.

'Bliss,' Alexei repeated deadpan, strolling over to her. 'You're the little English girl. Bliss is a stupid name. I would call you Billie—'

'That's a boy's name,' she argued.

'It suits you better,' he told her with a shrug, lazy dark golden eyes resting on her with only the most fleeting interest before he turned away to address one of the older boys in the group, Damon Marios, the doctor's son, and said something to him in Greek too fast for her to follow as she was still learning the language. Damon flushed and kicked the sand.

'Who is he?' she asked Damon when Alexei had climbed into the car waiting for him at the harbour and was driven off.

'Alexei Drakos.'

And that was all he had to say to her even then for her to understand. The Drakos family lived in feudal splendour in a huge villa overlooking a beautiful bay at the quiet end of the island. For more than a hundred years the Drakos family had owned the island and they also owned the resort, the businesses and most of the houses in the village. The family controlled everything that related to Speros from the planning laws to who lived and worked on the island. Speros was the Drakos fiefdom and it was ruled with a rod of iron. The locals, however, were perfectly happy with that state of affairs because there were well-paid jobs at the resort and the village businesses opening up only added to their prosperity. Alexei's father had also built a new school and a small hospital and, at a time when other islands were losing their young people to the mainland, the population on Speros was steadily increasing.

'Mum, is the Drakos family very rich?' she asked when her mother was cooking a meal that evening, a rare event as Billie was often left to fend for herself when it came to food and generally lived on sandwiches and fruit.

'They're loaded,' Lauren volunteered with a grimace. 'But they don't impress me at all. They're not one whit better than we are, for all their cash. The old man, Constantine, was married three times and he never managed to have any children. Then his Russian mistress, Natasha—who's half his age—fell pregnant with Alexei, his only child. Constantine divorced his third wife and married Natasha two days before she gave birth to Alexei—'

'What's a mistress?' Billie asked her mother.

'You'd never understand,' Lauren replied, already tiring of the subject.

School became a little less unbearable for her after that night. Everyone started calling her Billie. The boys stopped teasing her and Damon's sister, Marika, spoke to her in passing. But nobody was ever allowed to come and play at her house and she was never invited into anyone else's home. Her mother's boyfriends came in a continual stream from the resort where Lauren often made extra money working as a waitress. Usually back-packers, some only stayed for a night or two, while others ended up living with Lauren and her daughter for weeks on end. By the time she was eleven years old, Billie, who had abandoned her birth name entirely to avoid the sniggers it invited, understood that it was Lauren's free and easy lifestyle with her lovers that scandalised the locals and that had led to her own exclusion from island life. Other mothers were afraid that she would grow up to live like Lauren and act as a bad influence on their daughters.

Two days after her eleventh birthday, Billie met Alexei Drakos for the second time. She was out exploring when a sudden thunderstorm sent her running along the harbour road for the shelter of home. Alexei stopped his beach buggy to give her a lift and insisted on going right to the door with her.

'Where's your mother?' he asked, scanning the empty silent little house.

'In Athens,' she told him innocently. 'She got the ferry on Friday—'

'That's four days ago,' Alexei incised harshly. 'Where is she staying in Athens?'

'She has friends there.'

'Do you have their name or phone number?' Alexei pressed while the thunder boomed out in loud cracks beyond the house walls and made her pale and flinch.

'No. Why would I need it?' she asked. 'There's nothing wrong. I can manage fine on my own.'

'When will she be back?'

'She said this Friday.'

With a bitten-off exclamation, Alexei strode across the room to the refrigerator and flung the door open to study the bare shelves within. 'What are you eating?'

'There are tins in the cupboard,' she answered stiffly, feeling threatened by his mood and his behaviour. 'Not that it's any of your business.'

'You will have to come home with me.'

'No, of course I won't—why would I? I'm perfectly happy here in my own home,' she protested.

And Alexei being Alexei, and having no patience whatsoever, simply lifted her off her feet and dropped her back in the buggy before speeding back to his home. Ignoring her protests, he dragged her inside and explained the situation to his parents in rapid Greek. His father shrugged and went back into his office, complaining at the interruption. His glamorous mother studied Billie as if she were something the cat had brought in and had asked if there were any neighbours prepared to help out. As assured and decisive as any adult, even at the age of sixteen, Alexei handed Billie over to the housekeeper and she spent that night and the two that followed housed in staff accommodation. There she was well fed and well looked after for the first time in more years than she could recall. Lauren had always lacked the maternal gene. Before that day only Billie's aunt, Hilary, had ever paid that much heed to the little girl's comfort.

Of course, had she been a more normal girl perhaps she would have formed a crush on Alexei as she grew up. After all, he was the island pin-up, worshipped by every girl between ten and twenty-five on Speros. From his film-star looks to his growing bad-boy reputation and the sexual exploits diligently reported by the gossip magazines, Alexei made headlines almost from the moment he hit puberty and followed faithfully in the lusty footsteps of his father and his grandfather. But after the terrible row Billie had with her mother because she'd admitted to others that she'd been left alone for a week, and a subsequent, very embarrassing visit from the island priest, who had been tasked with the challenge of telling Lauren that leaving her daughter for so long was unacceptable, Billie's main impression of Alexei was of a frighteningly dominant and interfering personality who did exactly as he liked at all times, regardless of the damage he might do to anyone else.

While Billie boarded in Athens during the week and attended secondary school, it was Damon Marios she fell for while they travelled back and forth on the ferries at weekends, he to his private school, she to her far less fancy state institution. By then she was seventeen years old and, for quite a few weeks, believed her feelings were reciprocated for she and Damon met secretly for coffee, going for walks, talking a mile-a-minute to each other and discovering similar interests.

Of course, she should have known better than to believe that dreams came true or that she could ever be seen as anything other than shameless Lauren's illegitimate daughter, a murky step below the other girls on the island. She still remembered the cold hard fear that gripped her one evening at the ferry terminal when Damon suddenly dropped her hand and turned away from her. Looking up, she saw Alexei strolling towards them. Already a qualified pilot, Alexei had had to ditch his plane in the sea the previous month and the shock of his son's near-death experience had traumatised his father, who had grounded him. Now in his last year at university, Alexei was very much an adult. For the rest of the journey, Damon ignored Billie as studiously as if she had been a stranger.

'I'll drop you off,' Alexei declared at the harbour while Damon hurried off homeward with a down-bent head.

'I don't need a lift.' Sixth sense warned her and she didn't want to get into the sports car but she did anyway.

'Don't be stupid,' Alexei said drily. 'I'm only trying to protect you from making a big mistake. Your mother won't bother.'

'I don't know what you're talking about—'

'Damon, the leading light of the Marios family. He'll screw you but he'll never take you seriously or take you home with him. Didn't you get that message today when he acted like he didn't know you around me?'

Like a knife cutting through tender flesh, his blunt forecast tore through Billie and she looked back at him, focusing on the lean bronzed beauty of his features with furious condemnation. 'You don't know him!'

'I know Damon very well. His family will never accept you and he hasn't got the backbone to fight for you. He's a *nice* guy but he does as he's told. Cut your losses and ditch him now before you get in any deeper—'

'I don't want your advice!' she shrieked at him in Greek.

'Suit yourself,' Alexei drawled silkily. 'But whatever you do, keep your knickers on. All Greek men fantasise about having a virgin in the marriage bed.'

'That is a disgusting thing to say!' Billie launched back at him in a positive rage. 'I love Damon—'

'You're seventeen. You're not old enough to love anyone,' Alexei derided, stopping outside her house and leaning across her to throw open the door as if he couldn't wait to be rid of her. The male scent of his skin tinged by some expensive cologne wafted across her. She froze, rigid at that first taste of intimacy with a man, a fleeting intimacy that had the miraculous power to make her body prickle all over with uneasy awareness. That response shook her up because she had never reacted that way to Damon.

'I don't think I've ever disliked anyone quite so much,' Billie snapped in as cold and controlled a voice as she could manage.

'I'm always knee-deep in women who are crazy about me,' Alexei countered with amusement. 'I doubt if I'll notice the absence of one little girl from my hordes of fans—'

'You're so incredibly bigheaded!' Billie flung, stepping out of the car in one electrified movement of rejection, her cheeks still burning hotly from that crack about keeping her underwear on.

A shockingly charismatic smile slanted across Alexei's wide sensual mouth and his stunning dark golden eyes gleamed. 'But still much more of a man than Damon will ever be…'

CHAPTER TWO

A YEAR LATER, Billie finished school and fought her mother hard for the freedom to go to university to study for a business degree. To survive, she had to work endless hours in a student bar where, mercifully, the low pay was matched with free meals. Aged twenty-one, she took her first job in a small import firm in Piraeus where, no matter how hard she worked, her male colleagues got the recognition and she got all the routine administrative tasks. When she saw Drakos Industries advertising a well-paid PA post on the Internet the following year, she wasted no time in applying.

Alexei Drakos had quickly tired of working for his billionaire father in the family shipping line. Breaking away, he had set up Drakos Industries at the age of twenty-four, had made millions and was already well on the way to becoming a formidable tycoon in his own right. 'The Shark,' *Time* magazine had labelled him in an article marvelling at the speed with which he'd shaken off his reputation as a jet set playboy to demonstrate his worth as a shrewd entrepreneur.

As part of the application process for the job, Billie was one of the lucky few allotted a place in a day-long assessment. It was a gruelling experience comprised of working against the clock and handling difficult personalities but, forty-eight hours later, she learned that she had passed this first stage and had won an interview with Alexei. She was surprised he took so active a part in recruitment.

By the time she walked into his big fancy office in Athens clad in her smartest clothes, she was high on nerves. Sleek as a jungle predator in his black designer suit, Alexei surveyed her. 'I was surprised to see your name on the shortlist.'

Billie looked steadily back at him, noting the toughness that time had added to his lean strong face. 'I just want someone to give me a chance to do a proper job where I can use my brain—'

'And you think I might?' His brilliant dark eyes were nailed to her, his wide sensual mouth cool, discouraging.

'I don't think you will mark me down because I was born in England—'

'A positive panoply of praise from someone who doesn't like me,' Alexei mocked lazily. 'But you're right. I don't care where you came from, I'm only interested in who you are now. What could you offer me as an employee?'

'I'm very discreet and I work fast and hard. I also have good ideas—'

'Everyone's got ideas. I don't always want to hear them…'

'I'm a great organiser and I can think on my feet.'

Alexei rested his unsettling gaze on her and she shifted uneasily, suddenly alarmingly conscious of her every physical flaw. It was as though his very masculine perfection highlighted her deficiencies. Her vibrant mane of hair was restrained in a French plait, her green eyes bright against her pale skin. Full as she was at breast and hip, she felt she lacked the height to successfully carry off her curves. Her waist was small though and her legs slim. Lauren had always refused to tell her daughter who her father was and Billie had wondered cynically if her mother even knew. Certainly, she had signally failed to inherit any of her mother's leggy blonde assets.

'The position on offer would entail working directly for me.'

Belatedly, Billie understood why she was receiving an interview from the boss himself. 'I'd like to know exactly what the job is.'

'The successful candidate will take care of everything I don't have time for. He or she will often travel with me and the hours will be long. The job will cover everything from setting up appointments with my tailor to buying gifts on my behalf and barring women I don't want to see or hear from any more,' Alexei spelt out bluntly. 'It is a post which demands considerable trust on my part. A confidentiality agreement will be included in the contract of employment, making it illegal to share any revelations about me or my lifestyle with the press.'

In truth, Billie was totally taken aback by the extent of what was being offered to her. Even if it didn't sound like her role would have much of a business angle to it, any position working directly for Alexei would still add kudos to her CV.

'I want to hire someone willing to turn their hand to anything I ask at any time of day—'

'A slave?' Billie quipped and then wished she could bite off her facetious tongue when his superb bone structure tensed and cooled.

'A very well-paid one. I don't work by the clock. Neither do I want someone who counts the hours or excludes certain tasks.'

Billie nodded, tantalised by the prospect of travelling and reasoning that she was free as a bird and well able to cope with such a demanding role. The following week, she was informed that she had got the job. The salary took her breath away being, even at a conservative estimate, twice what she had expected. On her first day she arrived neatly attired in her newest suit.

'You need to smarten up your work wardrobe,' Alexei informed her at the first glimpse he had of her. Seemingly impervious to the flush of mortification warming her face, he handed her a business card. 'And this first time, you can do it at my expense—'

Billie stiffened. 'That's not necessary—'

'Look in the mirror. You are a frump,' Alexei countered bluntly, 'and I always decide what's necessary.'

Feeling cut off at the knees, Billie took the card and went that same afternoon to an upmarket store, where she was kitted out with the sort of figure-hugging clothing and high heels that she had always deemed unsuitable in a working environment. On the third day she wore a skirt well above her knees that outlined the curve of her hips and a jacket that nipped in at her waist, accentuating the shape and size of her breasts. She didn't like her reflection; she thought it was unprofessional.

'Turn round,' Alexei instructed casually during his morning coffee break and he studied her with assessing cool, oblivious to her blushing discomfiture. 'That's a major improvement.'

'I prefer a more formal look,' she told him starchily.

Dark golden eyes alight with amusement as he absorbed her rigid stance and tight mouth, Alexei laughed out loud. 'You're young and pretty. Make the most of it while you can.'

As Billie looked at his vibrantly handsome features she felt the sensual buzz of his compelling attraction right down to the centre of her bones and it unnerved her, for she did not want to feel that way around her boss. But even though she fought it, she was flattered by the simple fact that this man, who kept company with some of the world's most beautiful women, could deem her 'pretty'. Suddenly the high heels and the short skirt no longer felt like such a bad idea.

Alexei's business team was all male and she was assiduously ignored until the first time Alexei phoned her in the middle of the night to help him handle a minor crisis and the team then discovered that they had to liaise with Alexei through her. Later that week, with the ice broken, she took the opportunity to ask one of the men why she was excluded to such an extent.

Panos gave her an uneasy glance. 'Sooner or later the female staff on the team end up in bed with Alexei,' he told her reluctantly. 'And that makes us all uncomfortable. After a week or so, Alexei always transfers that person out of the main office to another job. We know the score. Four women have already come and gone in your particular role in a short time.'

Billie managed a calm smile. 'It's not going to happen that way with me. I'm here for the long haul.'

But that warning also put her on her guard around Alexei, even though she soon appreciated that the fault was rarely his. A phenomenal number of women, exposed to Alexei's charismatic good looks and wealth, literally threw themselves at him the first opportunity they got. His sex life frequently shocked her, for the very nature of her job and her need to work closely to him meant that she saw virtually every woman he had in his life. During the second month after employing her, he spent the night on his yacht with twin blonde models, Katia and Kerry, who could barely string an intelligent sentence between them.

'Take them out shopping,' Alexei instructed Billie the next morning, tossing her a credit card. 'And don't look at the price tags. I'm not on a budget.'

Billie travelled to shore in the launch with the two giggling blondes, who seemed not to have a care in the world. Indeed, acting as Alexei's entertainment for one night only appeared to have energised their spirits. While she escorted the twins round the exclusive boutiques on shore, she was forced to listen to a great deal of sexual banter about what Alexei was like in bed. Her every attempt to change the subject was turned aside and by the time she thankfully parted from his effervescent lovers she was very angry and determined never to have to repeat the experience. She wasted no time in tackling the subject when she found Alexei out on deck on her return to *Sea Queen*.

'Please don't put me in a position again where I have to escort your lady friends around while they discuss your sexual performance during the night before,' Billie framed in a tone of tremulous rage, her green eyes as bright as emeralds, her face pink and set in censorious lines.

Alexei dealt her a startled glance and then burst out laughing, astonishing her with his reaction almost as much as she had astonished him with her verbal attack. 'How did I rate? Did I figure as a hero or a zero?'

'That is not something I would wish to discuss with my employer,' Billie assured him thinly, rigidly unamused by his attitude for he was refusing to take her objection seriously.

'You're a real prude.' Alexei lounged back against the rail, a darkly handsome and graceful presence in a lightweight beige summer suit. 'I'm surprised. We both have liberal parents in that regard and yet the experience seems to have affected us very differently. A good time was had by all and sex was not a serious subject when I was growing up. I prefer to keep it that way now—'

'I'm not a prude,' Billie proclaimed sharply, her voice rising a little because she was deeply embarrassed by his reference to her mother's promiscuous lifestyle. That was part of the past she had left behind her and she very much resented any reminder of it.

'Billie...the sight of me having breakfast with two women this morning offended you,' Alexei countered drily. 'But you are not required to exercise your moral convictions while you work for me. I'm not interested in what you think. My private life is just that—*mine*. My sole expectation of you is that you do your job—'

Her slim shoulders straight as a ruler, growing tension bubbling through her small frame, Billie breathed, 'And I've told you that I have limits. This morning, Katia and Kerry crossed them. I was embarrassed to be out in public with them. They dress, behave and talk like hookers—'

'I don't sleep with hookers,' Alexei cut in, his rich dark drawl harsh in reproof. 'One more suggestion along those lines and you're fired.'

Outraged by his attitude and white hot with resentment, Billie snapped, 'Because I've got standards? Because I expect to be treated like a professional during my working day?'

'You don't have standards, you have a narrow mind. I warned you before I hired you that I would expect you to cope with everything I throw at you—'

Determined not to be intimidated by the anger in his scorching dark golden eyes, Billie lifted her chin. 'Katia and Kerry were a step too far—'

'If I can't count on you to follow orders, you're no use to me. I will not tolerate any member of my staff telling me what I can and can't do, or complaining about the responsibilities I give them,' Alexei delivered coldly. 'So, if that is how it is, clear your desk and I'll have you flown back to Athens.'

Billie had gone too far to back down and, her head held high, she went indoors to pack her belongings.

How dared Alexei Drakos christen her a prude? Just because he slept around and looked for nothing more than beauty and sex from his partners!

Lauren's habit of bedding every man she met had made Billie very cautious in her dealings with the opposite sex. How could she not have been influenced by the distaste and contempt that Lauren's lifestyle had roused in so many people? In every way possible Billie drew a clear boundary line between her life and her mother's. She never wore revealing clothes. She didn't flirt with other women's men. Casual uncommitted sex was anathema to her. She'd only ever had three relationships—Damon, and two at university that had come to nothing after her boyfriends sought easier conquests. A highly sexed and very handsome philanderer like Alexei Drakos was Billie's worst nightmare in the partnership stakes.

Billie returned via Athens to the island of Speros, where Lauren soon dragged the story of her dismissal out of her daughter.

'Why didn't you just laugh at those women? Why do you take everything so seriously?' Lauren demanded, her incomprehension patent. 'You're your own worst enemy—you land the job of a lifetime and straight away you screw it up!'

'I don't need this, Mum,' Billie breathed tautly. 'But don't worry. I can still cover your rent for the next couple of months and by then I should have found another job.'

'You certainly won't find one as well paid. What got into you?' Lauren snapped. 'Alexei Drakos is a young, good-looking single guy and all he is doing is what comes naturally. Of course he doesn't want to be tied down at his age or with his opportunities. What does it have to do with you?'

'I just don't like his lifestyle or his attitudes and I'm with him so much I can't avoid either.'

Lauren dealt her smaller daughter a scornful look. 'You've got the hots for him and you're jealous—'

'No, I haven't!' Billie argued, incensed and shaken by that accusation.

'He's gorgeous. *I* wouldn't say no,' Lauren replied with a voluptuous pout and a toss of her blonde head.

Billie resisted a shrewish urge to agree that no wasn't a word that came easily to her mother's lips. In her forties, Lauren was no longer the siren she had once been and there were fewer men in her life. Eighteen months had passed since Billie had last come home to find that she was sharing her mother's house with a resident toy boy. But the very suggestion of Alexei and Lauren together made her feel physically sick and this knowledge worked on her that night while she tossed and turned and failed to find restful sleep.

Was she attracted to Alexei more than she was prepared to admit? Had she been mortally offended by Katia and Kerry because they had shared Alexei's bed? Was that because in some dim dark corner of her mind she was jealous of the carefree and sexually confident twins? She shuddered at the suspicion. Alexei was as bronzed, beautiful and flawless in feature and physique as a Greek god and she was a flesh and blood ordinary woman who could hardly be impervious to that reality.

But being aware that he was a very good-looking guy did not mean that she was physically attracted to him, did it? And even if it did, what did it matter? Nothing was ever likely to come of the fact. Alexei only went for gorgeous women and she was much too sensible to be tempted even if he should have a weak moment in her radius. Mortified by her growing suspicion that she might not be as unprejudiced or as principled as she had fondly believed, Billie lay awake until dawn.

The following day, she returned to Athens and the apartment she shared with two other women. She needed to be on the spot to job-hunt. She put her short-lived job with Alexei into a mental box and hammered it shut, but she soon discovered that the very brevity of her employment with him had harmed her standing in the eyes of others. A month later, she was less angry with Alexei and angrier with herself for damaging her career prospects. By then her proud and impulsive walk-out on a matter of principle was beginning to strike her as more foolish than brave.

That was the mood she was in when the doorbell went one evening and she answered it to find one of Alexei's security team facing her. 'Mr Drakos would like to speak to you. I have a car waiting outside for you,' he volunteered before swinging away and heading downstairs, it not even crossing his mind that she might dare to refuse such an invitation.

Billie stepped back into the apartment, glancing at herself in the hall mirror. Her hair, freshly washed, lay in vibrant waves across her shoulders. She was wearing cropped jeans, a sleeveless cotton top and canvas pumps. She lifted her chin. What did Alexei want? She could just say no to the offer of a meeting and then she would burn with curiosity ever after, she completed ruefully. He could just want to see her about something she had dealt with while she still worked for him. Grabbing her bag, she slammed the door behind her.

Alexei had a ritzy apartment in Athens, just one of the many properties scattered round the world that he owned, since he had already inherited several from his father's side of the family. She recalled his town house in Venice, a chateau in the south of France, a house in New York, a ski lodge in Switzerland and a ranch in Australia. Taking care of those properties and their staff had been her responsibility and she had been looking forward to visiting each and every one of them at some stage.

Alexei was on the phone chattering in French when she was shown into a massive living area with bold designer furniture and an array of modern art and sculpture. A wide-shouldered, lean-hipped figure clad in linen trousers and an open shirt, Alexei was barefoot and clearly fresh out of the shower. His black hair was still spiky and shiny with moisture, his aggressive jawline rough with the shadow of blue-black stubble that accentuated the wide sensual allure of his masculine mouth.

Just looking at him, she felt his impact like a thud in her ears and a kick in her stomach. He was all rogue male, from his dark-as-midnight eyes heavily fringed by lashes to the slice of torso visible between the unbuttoned edges of his shirt, which revealed a matt of dark curls sprinkled across his bronzed chest and the six-pack stomach that Katia and Kerry had raved about…among other things. Her mouth dry and feeling oddly breathless, Billie squashed those inappropriate thoughts—but not in time to stop her disobedient gaze dropping to the distinctive masculine bulge at his crotch.

Reddening to the roots of her hair as fully as only a woman of her complexion could, Billie yanked her eyes upward and said jerkily, 'You wanted to see me?'

He shifted a hand, which urged her to wait until he had finished his phone call and, that fast, she wanted to shout at him again. Her spine stiffened, her full soft mouth compressing, for he had summoned her like a minion across the city at seven in the evening and he was still putting his own wishes first. And it would always be like that, she acknowledged tautly. He was poised there, more beautiful than any mortal male had any right to be, and the world was his oyster because he was a blue-blooded filthy-rich Drakos. In *his* life, people always dropped everything to run and do his bidding. It had been that way for him since he was born.

Constantine Drakos had truly idolised his one and only child. Every cough and sniffle Alexei had suffered had been a major episode for his father. Alexei had had a bodyguard before he could even walk. A weaker child would have been indelibly scarred by such a protected upbringing but Constantine had found that he had a fight on his hands as Alexei had fought his ultra-safe regime every step of the way. He had taken part in dangerous sports at school; he had gone out fishing on the elderly boats of the village fleet; he had learned to sail alone; he had even learned to fly. Full of restive boundless energy, he had always challenged himself and those around him. He'd let nothing and nobody hold him back from what he wanted to be.

'Sorry about that.' Alexei sighed, tossing aside the phone. 'Take a seat.'

Billie sank down onto the sofa behind her, closed her hands together neatly on her lap and sent him an enquiring look.

'I've tried out two personal assistants since you left and rejected both. They couldn't handle your job—'

'At the end I couldn't handle it either,' she pointed out, and then wondered why she was drawing that failing to his attention again.

'It is important to me that I don't have to deal with all the hassle of being a Drakos—the properties, the social invitations, my relatives. I need to concentrate on business,' he breathed impatiently. 'When I'm not working, I like a smooth peaceful life. For the six weeks that you were in charge I enjoyed perfect peace. I want you to come back and work for me again.'

Billie was tense: she was flattered and troubled at one and the same time. 'I'm not sure that would be a good idea—we didn't gel.'

'From my point of view, I barely noticed you were around most of the time,' Alexei volunteered. 'You're very quiet.'

Not best pleased to hear that she was just part of the wallpaper as far as he was concerned, Billie met his stunning dark eyes unwarily and her tummy performed a somersault. 'I assumed that that was what you would want.'

'Why are you always so tense?' Alexei demanded with a sudden frown. 'You were like that around me even when you were a kid. Look at you now—sitting there as frozen as if you're waiting to be tipped into a pool of hungry sharks!'

In a defensive move, Billie folded her arms. 'I never know what you're going to do or say next. It's...unnerving.'

'You could learn to live with it. If you start back to work tomorrow, I'll double your salary,' Alexei murmured silkily, watching the sunshine play across the gold and copper shades in her auburn hair, which was much longer than he had appreciated and surprisingly attractive. He went for blondes, not for redheads, but for the first time ever he could see the draw of her striking colouring, particularly in the contrast between her hair and her pale, flawless skin.

'But I haven't even said I'll come back yet and offering to double my salary is just crazy and extravagant!'

His expressive mouth took on a humorous quirk. 'I can afford to be. If having to occasionally deal with the women in my life is a sticking point, you can hire an assistant to deal with them on your behalf. I don't care.'

It was a compliment to her efficiency that he should be so keen to have her working for him again. As he smiled that lazy smile and remained poised there in the sunshine pouring through the windows she was, for the first time, hugely conscious of his compelling charm. He was offering her an amazing salary to do a job she enjoyed. With that amount of money coming in, she would no longer need to worry about Lauren falling behind with the rent or not being able to buy her own property.

'All right,' Billie said gruffly. 'I'll start back tomorrow.'

'You didn't get another job, did you?'

'I couldn't come up with a good enough excuse for leaving your employ after only six weeks!' Billie responded with spirit.

Alexei laughed. 'Where were your wits? You should've said I made a pass at you. With my reputation everyone would have believed it.'

Billie turned a slow hot pink and evaded his keen gaze. 'That idea never occurred to me.'

Probably because it would never have occurred to her either that anyone would *believe* she had actually found his attentions unwelcome and turned him down, Billie acknowledged ruefully...

CHAPTER THREE

'THAT SHOULD WRAP it up,' Alexei pronounced, stabbing a final button on the keyboard before pushing away his laptop in a rare gesture of rejection. Rising up, he stretched like a lion, flexing strong muscles bunched up by the constraint of sitting at a desk before shrugging back his sleeve to check the slender gold Rolex on his wrist. It was after one in the morning. 'You should have told me how late it was.'

Blinking, Billie stifled a yawn. 'I *did*.'

That quiet rejoinder made his handsome mouth quirk. Billie was the only employee who ever answered him back. He studied her with narrowed eyes, taking in the white sleeveless top she wore and the full rounded thrust of her breasts against the fine cotton that was pulling at the pearl buttons. More than a lush handful, he calculated, pressure building at his groin as he instinctively pictured the baring of her firm pink-tipped flesh. He was startled by his reaction. Evidently, it had been too long since he had been with a woman, he reflected in exasperation.

Even as he looked, Billie was reaching for the jacket she had removed. In the past two years during which Billie had been on his staff, she was always covered up, buttoned up, zipped up, just as her hair was always clipped, plaited or tied—everything held in tight restraint. In an age when other women were happy to reveal as much flesh as possible, Billie's modesty made her stand out from the crowd. Even when she went swimming she donned a modest black swimsuit that would not have shamed a nun. Yet the feminine mystique she was careful to preserve was strangely and powerfully sexy, Alexei acknowledged. Odd, too, how he felt guilty even thinking about her in such a way. But then he was almost certain that, rare as it would be, Billie was still a virgin.

'You'll have to stay here tonight. You can't disturb your mother this late,' he commented, lifting the house phone to issue instructions to the housekeeper, Anatalya.

'I'm sure it won't bother her if I wake her up,' Billie protested, uneasy at the prospect of spending the night at the Drakos villa where she generally felt like a peasant-born intruder.

'Don't make a fuss,' Alexei groaned in all-male irritation, silencing her.

Behind his back, Billie flushed at the reproof. The door opened, revealing not the maid she had expected, but Alexei's mother, Natasha.

'I'll show you upstairs,' the tall, still-beautiful brunette said with an artificial smile. Billie was never more conscious of her humble little-island-girl beginnings than she was in the radius of Alexei's glamorous and patronising mother.

Alexei said something in Russian to the older

woman. Dark eyes warming only as they rested on her
only child, Natasha left the room to escort Billie up
the palatial staircase. 'Do you often work this late for
my son?'

'Not that often. But I'm very well paid, Mrs Drakos. Occasional long hours go with the territory,' Billie pointed out.

A door was pressed open. Rather stiff and taut, Billie
walked in. She was always aware that Alexei's mother
didn't approve of her working for Alexei. She had no
idea why, only the vague suspicion that Natasha didn't
think Lauren Foster's daughter was good enough to
work in so trusted a position.

Her reluctant hostess was already turning to leave
when Billie noticed the man's shirt lying discarded on
the carpet and put two and two together fast. 'Is this…
Alexei's room?' she breathed in dismay.

'Why, yes, I assumed that…' Natasha Drakos gave a
little suggestive shrug of her slim shoulders.

'You assumed wrong.' It was Alexei's assured drawl
from behind the older woman that broke the tension and
the brief, awkward silence that had fallen.

Billie's face was drenched with colour and she could
barely bring herself to look at him or his parent. 'I really think I should go home—'

'I'm sorry,' Natasha Drakos murmured. 'I misunderstood.'

Rather than make more of a scene, Billie allowed
herself to be shown into the room next door but she felt
humiliated. She was well qualified and she performed
her job to the highest standards, for no Drakos had yet

been born capable of accepting shoddy work. Why did Alexei's mother have to assume that her role automatically extended to warming her son's bed? That was a very demeaning supposition. Locked in that thought, she was then nonplussed by the discovery that her hostess had yet to leave her alone.

'You probably think you're very clever getting so close to Alexei and worming your way into his confidence,' the older woman breathed with cold dark eyes, her angry hostility laid bare now that her son was no longer within hearing. 'But you're wasting your time. He's a Drakos and, although he'll think nothing of sleeping with you when there's not a more attractive prospect available, he'll never marry beneath him.'

Billie did momentarily toy with the idea of responding with the simple fact that Alexei's father had done exactly that when he chose to wed his pregnant mistress, a little-known fashion model from a poverty-stricken home in some obscure industrial town in Russia. But Billie had never been bitchy and she was reluctant to rattle Natasha's cage when she was an increasingly frequent visitor to the villa.

With that acid condemnation, Natasha mercifully departed and Billie exhaled. At least she now knew why Alexei's mother didn't like her. She thought Billie was too close to her son and in spite of Alexei's denial that he and his PA were intimate, Natasha remained unconvinced. Initially, Billie was vaguely amused to think she could figure as a clever, calculating gold-digger in Natasha's eyes, but she was not at all amused by the comment that Alexei would only sleep with her if she was the only woman available to slake his high-voltage libido.

How much more hurtful and wounding could one woman be to another? Billie wondered once she had got into the comfortable bed. She was already very much aware that she was not good looking. After all, she had grown up in the shadow of a handsome mother and Alexei's women were always noted beauties. Billie knew her best points and her worst ones. She was now also wondering if it had been a mistake not to date at least one of the men who had asked her out since she started working for Alexei. Perhaps if, at some stage, she had had a boyfriend Alexei's mother would not have regarded her with such poisonous suspicion.

Billie lay in the moonlit room and mulled over the awful truth that daily exposure to Alexei had made other men pale by comparison. Alexei had more sex appeal than any man she had ever met. Although she tried not to think about her employer on those terms, he was gorgeous to look at and usually very entertaining to be with, because he was clever, witty and dynamic while also being amazingly attuned to what women liked. Only Alexei would order her a hot chocolate topped with melted marshmallows at the end of a particularly long or difficult day, or send her for a relaxing hot stone massage when she got headaches at that certain time of the month. Times without number he'd picked up on things other men would have failed to notice.

Maybe, Billie began thinking anxiously, it was her own fault that Alexei's mother had thought it necessary to warn Billie off her son. Maybe her own behaviour was to blame for Natasha's belief that she shared Alexei's bed. Just at that moment it suddenly struck Billie that, for a mere employee, she was far too attached to Alexei. Somewhere down the line her protective barriers had crumbled. Alexei was brilliant in business and working for him was exciting. But she admired him too much, she conceded grudgingly. When once she had disapproved of his energetic sex life, now she turned her head away from the evidence of it, reasoning that his lovers were experienced women who knew the score. When had she started making excuses for his lifestyle?

Just when had she started falling in love with her boss?

Shattered by that belated glimpse into her innermost heart, Billie was furious that she could have been so blind to the feelings she was developing. More than a few of the women Alexei had had affairs with had descended into sobbing heartbreak in front of Billie when his interest had waned. Billie had offered tissues and platitudes in response, protecting Alexei from such aggravations, guarding his privacy as best she could. Why had it taken Natasha's taunts to make her appreciate that, over the past couple of years, she had got too close to the sun and got burned without even realising it? Was her attachment to Alexei equally obvious to others? Billie cringed, resolving that she needed a little space, time to get a grip on herself and her emotions again. She did not want to turn into one of those sad women who worked for the man they'd loved for years without ever being noticed by him, because being close to him was better than being without him entirely.

When she got up the next day, heavy-eyed from her lack of sleep, it was to be greeted with the news that she had the day off because Alexei had gone out fishing with his father around dawn. One of the security guards gave her a lift to the village house she had bought for her mother six months earlier. The purchase had not been as straightforward as she had hoped, for at least one local had complained to the Drakos family about a foreigner like Billie being allowed to buy property on Speros and she had little doubt that allegations about Lauren's morals had also been part of the argument. Thankfully, Constantine Drakos had squashed the protests and approved the sale.

'My father believes that you and your mother have lived on the island long enough to be viewed as part of the community,' Alexei had told her.

'I'm grateful. I just want Lauren to have a secure home that no one can take away from her,' Billie had confided, not bothering to add that, from her point of view, buying a small house outright was cheaper and safer than trusting Lauren to use the money Billie gave her to pay the rent.

Lauren was delighted with her new home and had gone to unusual effort to furnish and decorate it.

Smiling at the window box of bright geraniums ornamenting the blue-painted front sill, Billie knocked on the rough-wood front door of the tumbledown whitewashed house at the end of a crumbling terrace. Her smile slid away a little when the door was opened by a strange man. Around thirty years old with long brown hair and an unshaven face that made him look more unkempt than trendy, he sported shorts and a T-shirt.

'You can only be Billie,' he said cheerfully. 'Lauren's in her studio.'

The tiny sunroom at the back of the house had become her mother's workplace. Her deeply tanned, leggy parent turned from her easel to say, 'When I saw the yacht had docked in the bay last night I expected you home.'

'I had to work late. If I'd known you were expecting me I'd have phoned.' Billie stretched up to dab a kiss on Lauren's cheek. 'Who's your guest?'

'Dean? He was a deckhand on a boat that called in a few weeks back. We met at the taverna and he decided he'd like to stay a while. I'm enjoying the company. You know how it is,' her mother told her, shooting a flirtatious glance at Dean, who was stationed in the doorway, denying Billie the privacy she would have preferred with her parent.

'I'll just go upstairs and change.' Billie came to a halt and had to say, 'Excuse me, Dean...' before her mother's boyfriend let her pass.

And, as Lauren had commented, Billie did indeed know how it was when it came to Lauren's boyfriends. They were usually backpackers, dropouts or seasonal workers, happy to latch onto the chance of free board and lodgings on an idyllic Greek island. Billie could not recall when her mother had last had a guest who contributed in any way to the household budget. But she was determined not to let Dean's presence spoil her brief stay.

Billie made a salad lunch for the three of them in the kitchen, coolly clad in a pair of shorts teamed with a tankini top. She glanced up while she was setting the table and noticed that Dean was staring lasciviously at her cleavage. A hot flush marking her cheeks, she looked hurriedly away again. After they had eaten, she said she was going down to the beach and went upstairs to put on a T-shirt. When she came back down again Lauren and Dean were whispering and kissing on the sofa and she couldn't get out of the house quickly enough.

Not for the first time she wished she had her own bolthole on Speros. If she moved out it would be yet another nail in her mother's coffin as far as the locals were concerned but after so many years did that really matter? On the other hand, she had very little time off and was usually staying on the yacht or in one of Alexei's other properties when she was free. How much use would she get out of an independent home on the island? It would not be much of an investment either as privately owned houses on the island had to be offered to the locals first for sale, which kept prices artificially low.

That evening, they dined at the taverna—Billie's treat, of course. By then she was noticing that her easy-come, easy-go mother seemed unusually keen on Dean, and that Dean drank too much and talked too loudly. Billie was revolted by the way he kept on staring at her breasts and the jokes he began to crack about busty women. She went to bed early and stirred only when her door opened some hours later.

'Mum?' she mumbled, drowsily trying to unclog her

lashes to open her eyes when the side of the bed gave as someone came down on the mattress and tilted it.

The smell of beer and male sweat assailed her in warning a split second before a bristly jaw line made scratchy contact with her cheek. 'It's Dean,' her mother's boyfriend whispered thickly. 'Keep your voice down or you'll wake your ma, and we don't want to do that, do we?'

The instant he made physical contact her eyes flew wide in panic and her arms flailed wildly to push him away from her while her body frantically squirmed and heaved up to escape the weighty imprisonment of his body lying half over hers. 'Get off me! *Get out!*' she screamed at the top of her voice.

Within thirty seconds Lauren was in the room demanding to know why her boyfriend was falling off the end of her daughter's bed. Her mother had had a great deal to drink as well and the older woman lost no time in accusing Billie of trying to steal her man. In the midst of the resulting madness, in which her mother slapped her face hard, Billie got out of bed, gathered up her clothes, fought past Lauren's hysterical attempt to hold on to her and escaped into the bathroom to get dressed. By the time she emerged, her mother was shouting at her to get out of her house and never come back and the neighbours were banging on the party wall in complaint. Billie paused only long enough to grab up her bag, which she had not unpacked, and her phone.

Tearstained and trembling, she sat on a bollard down by the harbour, wondering what to do next. The sun was slowly rising in a crimson glow on the horizon. Nothing

would make her go to the Drakos villa in such a state
to ask for shelter, but *Sea Queen* was anchored out in
the bay and she had no reservations about calling the
yacht and asking for the launch to be sent out to pick
her up. The crew would think little of her request since
she often went on board at odd hours without Alexei.
The launch came quickly and she climbed in, her heart
thudding fast as the boat drew closer to the giant white
yacht that towered above them like a skyscraper. She
was embarrassed when she realised that Captain Mc-
Gregor had got out of bed to greet her. She thought he
looked at her a little suspiciously and, after apologising for interrupting his sleep, took her leave of him as
soon as she could.

Still shell-shocked by her ordeal at Dean's and Lauren's hands, Billie felt dizzy and she kicked off her
shoes and lay down on the bed in the opulent cabin
Alexei had long since assigned to her in the guest—
rather than in the crew—quarters. Her head was aching, her face was sore where she had been slapped and
her hands were shaking so badly she had to set down
the glass of water she was trying to drink. How could
her mother have believed that she might welcome her
boyfriend into her bed?

A loud rat-a-tat-tat on the door made her sit up with a
start against the headboard. 'Come in!' she called with
a frown; even that movement of her face hurt.

She was shocked when Alexei strode through the
door looking rather less elegant and laid-back than was
his wont. His black hair was tousled, he needed a shave

and he was wearing jeans and a half-buttoned white dress shirt below a dinner jacket.

'What are you doing on board?' Billie burst out.

'McGregor phoned me.' His probing gaze a clear hot gold, Alexei came down on the bed on his knees beside her, suddenly, disturbingly close. But where Dean had brought her out in a cold sweat of fear and disgust, Alexei sent her heart racing in an all-out sprint.

'Why did the Captain phone you?' Billie dragged in a feverish breath, a bubble of heat bursting low in her tummy when she collided with his level golden gaze.

'My goodness, I'm so sorry you were disturbed, Alexei. I seem to be causing an awful lot of trouble, but I only needed a bed for the night and I couldn't face your mother. I'm sure she would've thought I was being cheeky turning up at the villa,' Billie gabbled, embarrassed and scarcely knowing what she was saying

His brilliant scrutiny oddly intent, Alexei lifted a bronzed long-fingered hand to turn her face into the pool of light shed by the lamp. His sleek ebony brows pleated and a stifled Greek curse escaped his taut mouth. 'McGregor phoned me because he could see that you had been attacked and naturally he was concerned.'

'Attacked?' she echoed in consternation.

'You have a long scratch and blood on your cheekbone and I suspect you may have a black eye by morning,' Alexei enumerated in curt explanation. 'Have you any other injuries?'

Billie lifted a tremulous hand and let the pads of her fingers brush the swelling soreness of her cheekbone.

She had not even looked in a mirror since boarding. 'No. I'm perfectly fine.'

'You'd tell me that if you were lying here dying!' Alexei vented, unimpressed by that assurance. 'What happened? Who did this to you? Get over the idea that it's not done to admit to being hurt!'

'I really appreciate your concern but I'd prefer not to talk about it,' Billie mumbled, her eyes stinging like mad beneath her lowered lashes, because his concern on her behalf was more than she could bear while the thought of sharing such a kitchen-sink family drama with him just made her want to cringe in humiliation.

'Save the nonsense for fools. *Talk*,' Alexei instructed in an emphatic growl of threat that ratcheted up her tension and widened her gaze to focus on the harsh set of his darkly handsome features.

'Storm in a teacup,' she said shakily. 'Mum's boyfriend made a pass at me. He'd been drinking and he came into my room and lay down on my bed while I was sleeping—'

'He…did…*what*?' Alexei roared, springing back upright and glowering down at her in angry disbelief. 'You could have been raped!'

'But I wasn't. He gave me such a fright I screamed at him, and that woke Lauren up and she stormed in and misread the situation…' Billie was becoming too uncomfortable to hold his gaze. 'She slapped me—'

'Blamed you as well, no doubt,' Alexei incised with a gritty lack of hesitation. 'Why on earth did you waste your money buying her a house?'

'She's my mother and I know she's not perfect, but

she's the only one I'll ever have,' Billie proffered, tight-mouthed.

'She's no mother at all when there's a man in the equation,' Alexei derided. 'If you had been more aware of your own interests you would have bought that house for your own use. You shouldn't be under the same roof as her.'

After Lauren's attack and abuse, Billie wondered if she ever would be under the same roof again. That violent response from her mother had gouged a big hole in Billie's heart. She knew alcohol had probably had a lot to do with her mother losing her head but it still hurt that Lauren could trust a man she had only met a few weeks ago more than she trusted her daughter.

'Well, it's too late now,' she muttered ruefully.

His attention still nailed to her swollen face and reddened eyes, Alexei breathed grimly. 'We'll see.'

Another knock sounded on the door and Alexei opened it to reveal the familiar, careworn face of the island doctor. The older man was taken aback by the state of Billie's face and, with all the assurance of someone who had known her as a child, he told her not to be silly when she insisted that an examination was unnecessary. He checked her eye and a steward brought a cold pack to help reduce the swelling. The doctor's probing revealed no further injury and the cut was minor enough to require no further attention.

'Now go to sleep,' Alexei instructed, leaving the cabin in the older man's company as soon as Billie had swallowed the painkillers she had been given. 'We'll talk tomorrow.'

Billie could not think what they could possibly have left to discuss. She lay curled up in the bed, tears seeping from below her lowered eyelids and stinging her sore face. She heard the doctor leave on the launch and its return when the sun was high in the sky because sleep had evaded her once again. A cup of tea was brought to her and she peered at her reflection in the mirror in horror: she looked a sight with one eye half shut by purple bruising and swelling that had destroyed the symmetry of her face. The phone by her bed buzzed.

Sunglasses firmly attached to her nose, she went up to the main deck to join Alexei for breakfast. He was on the phone and, sketching a movement with an imperious brown hand, he indicated that she go ahead and eat without waiting for him to join her. There were a couple of faces at the windows of his office and she reddened, knowing that the breakfast invite would be viewed as a sign of favouritism by the rest of the team, while anxiously wondering if word of her sudden arrival on board the yacht in the middle of the night had spread among the crew.

Alexei's dark rich masculine drawl took on the subtle change that warned her that he was talking to a woman. In Spanish? She had learned to recognise a number of the languages he spoke even if she couldn't speak them herself. He could well be talking to the actress, Lola Rodriquez, whom he had recently met in London. It was none of her business, Billie told herself urgently, squashing the beginnings of an envious daydream in which she, got up in a fabulous dress, dined out with

Alexei, leaving him open-mouthed in admiration over her looks, her wit and her sex appeal.

'Let me see you,' Alexei urged, bending down to filch the sunglasses off her nose and inspect her battered face in the full unforgiving light of day.

Mercifully unaware of the heights her imagination could take her to, Alexei grimaced. 'Nasty. It'll be a few days before you look normal again.'

Billie snatched back her sunglasses and replaced them on her nose with a shaking hand. His input on how she looked was overkill, for wasn't she already wincing over the rainbow bruising round her eye and the swelling distorting her face?

'Your mother's boyfriend is gone,' Alexei informed her.

Her brow furrowed. 'Gone? *Where?* What are you talking about?'

'I dealt with him.'

'And what's that supposed to mean?' Billie queried nervously.

'I took the launch back to the harbour with the doctor last night and confronted the man to tell him to leave.'

Billie rammed back her chair to stand up. 'You had no right to interfere!'

'Your mother is full of apologies but she caught the ferry with him this morning. The neighbours are up in arms and I think she decided that a short break from island life was in order.'

'Oh, my goodness!' With a groan of protest, Billie flung herself back down in her chair. 'What on earth did you say to Mum?'

'That if she ever hurt you again she would be charged with assault—'

A whimper of dammed-up fury and frustration escaped Billie. 'It was none of your business!' she bawled back at him. 'How dare you?'

'It's how we deal with problems on Speros—you know it is. Every community must have rules. Lauren's boyfriend could have raped you, although the neighbours are so nosy I think you would have been rescued before he got very far,' Alexei conceded with a gleam of dark sardonic humour in his unrepentant gaze. 'All that matters is that he is no longer on the island and he won't dare to come back.'

'But Lauren's gone as well, driven out of her own home!' Billie condemned emotively.

'Your mother will be back, don't worry. She's too clever to abandon the easy life she has here, thanks to you,' Alexei countered carelessly, his interest in the subject patently on the wane. 'However, I've come up with a solution to your problems.'

'I don't have any problems,' Billie told him stonily, abandoning the table and turning on her heel to head back at speed to her cabin.

'Billie!' Alexei breathed rawly. 'Get back here right now!'

Trembling with fury over his meddling in her private life, Billie was outraged by that glossy impenetrable Drakos assurance that made Alexei believe that he could do whatever he wanted to do, particularly on Speros. But the particular note of command in his strong voice stopped her dead. She could storm off but where to and why? They had gone toe to toe once before and, though she might have got her job back, she knew her tycoon boss well enough to know that it had been a one-chance-only deal. Slowly, as if every movement physically hurt, Billie turned round again.

'Finish your breakfast,' Alexei told her harshly, his exasperation unconcealed. 'We're leaving the ship in ten minutes.'

Clashing with the warning in his hard dark eyes, Billie breathed in slow and deep, suddenly aware that the exchange was taking place right outside the office windows and marvelling that she could have forgotten the fact that they had an audience. Her spine as stiff as a steel pole, she took her seat again. A steward poured her tea and Alexei's coffee. She had to force herself to eat as all appetite had fled...

CHAPTER FOUR

A FOUR-WHEEL-DRIVE vehicle collected Alexei and Billie at the harbour. Billie was observing a rigorous silence.

'I've never known you to sulk before,' Alexei murmured with withering bite.

Her teeth were clenched together so hard that she was surprised they didn't chip. 'As far as I'm concerned you invaded my private life last night in a way that you had no right to do,' Billie responded brittlely.

Alexei closed a hard hand over hers and pulled on it to make her turn round and look at him. His heavily lashed golden eyes struck hers boldly head-on. 'I did what had to be done. You have no father, no brother, no other male relative or boyfriend, who can protect your interests. In their absence I count myself a friend as well as an employer. I took care of Dean Evans in a way that he understood.'

'And what's that supposed to mean?' A suspicion belatedly occurred to Billie and she gave him a shocked appraisal. 'Surely you didn't hit him?'

'Did you think that I would shake hands with him for what he did?' Alexei flung his handsome dark head back, his stunning bone structure full of proud challenge. 'Yes, I hit him.'

In mute despair, Billie shook her vibrant head, the bright hair she had left loose to hide her swollen face behind rippling round her cheekbones. She said nothing, knew there was no point saying anything, and that any local man witnessing such an act the night before would have heartily applauded Alexei's violence. On every primitive masculine level, Alexei had been raised to react with the raw aggression of a caveman. Crossed in business, he hit back hard and his enmity was feared in the marketplace since he never forgot a slight. He would never turn the other cheek. He would find it impossible to forgive without having first meted out punishment.

'Well, I wish you hadn't got involved. I don't need anyone but myself to look after my interests.'

'You are very fortunate to have me,' Alexei responded as if she hadn't spoken and he gave her a glance of such fierce conviction and confidence in that statement that he left her bereft of speech.

When the four-wheel-drive turned off the road that followed the shoreline up a rough grassy lane, Billie frowned. 'Where are we going?'

The security guard driving them stopped the car and got out to open the door beside her, forcing her to climb out.

'I want to show you something…'

Billie swallowed a weary sigh, knowing better than to question a male whose every thought and idea seemed embedded in a driven need to make another fortune on top of the many he had already acquired. Walking into the sloping field, sheep scattering at their every step,

Billie glanced in bemusement at Alexei. 'Isn't this too close to your family home for a tourist development?'

'I own this plot and I'm not planning a development here personally,' Alexei said drily. 'I'm offering it to you to enable you to build a house.'

Her green eyes opened very wide and she stared at him. 'I couldn't afford to buy this—'

'The plot would be a gift. From my point of view it would be convenient to have you living close by.'

'A gift? For goodness' sake, what would your family think?' Billie lifted an arm to indicate the fabulous view of the bay where the turquoise ocean below washed a long crescent of pale sand. 'A site like this must be worth a fortune!'

'I could give you a house in the village. Of course it would mean chucking out the existing tenants first.'

'Don't even think about it!' Billie shot back at him in horror.

'And a village house, even if there was one currently available, wouldn't address your problems.'

'For the last time, I don't *have* any problems!'

'You're too loyal to acknowledge the strife your mother creates for you, and as long as you live in the village you will still be dragged into Lauren's messy life. But if you have your own home at this end of the island, you will be left in peace,' Alexei pronounced.

There was a good deal of truth in what he had said and the idea of a private base where she would be far removed from Lauren's adventurous love life was a huge draw. 'I couldn't possibly accept a site from you. Your mother is already suspicious of me.'

Alexei laughed. 'So what? Live the life *you* want, not the life other people would lay out for you.'

'If only life were that simple…'

Alexei closed a strong hand over hers before she could walk away. Glittering golden eyes assailed hers in stubborn challenge. 'It is you who makes it complicated. I have more wealth than I could spend in a score of lifetimes. You need an independent home outside the village. You can build a house here and pay for it in stages. If you require finance I will give it to you. Your only other option will be to take up permanent residence in one of my family's guest suites.'

'But I'm hardly ever here!' she protested.

'That situation is about to change radically. My father is feeling his age and I have agreed to assume control of Drakos Shipping. I will be spending much more time on the island and you are my most trusted employee. So, cease this argument right now,' Alexei advised impatiently. 'You could make a proper home in this place. You know it makes sense.'

Her slender fingers flexed in the hold of his. His expectant gaze was on her, his domineering will bearing down on her like a powerful weight. She made a last ditch attempt to regain equality. 'If I accept the site, you will have to accept part ownership of any house that I build. That would be the only fair solution.'

Gazing down at her with deceptively indolent eyes of dark gold, a wicked slanting grin slowly slashed Alexei's wide sensual mouth. 'If I were to own a share of your house, it would give my mother sleepless nights!'

'But it would give me peace. I just couldn't accept

the site as a gift. It's too valuable,' Billie told him in an urgent rush. 'You could explain the situation to her.'

'It is no business of hers.' Alexei stared down intently into the vivid little face so familiar to him that he could instantly discard any awareness of her bruises. Sincerity shone in her clear green eyes while her coppery hair snaked in bold strands across her cheekbones. No woman had ever fought to come up with a way of accepting a gift from him while returning the value of it. He wondered why money had less of a hold on her than on others of her sex. He wondered why he had never noticed before that she had a soft pink mouth as firm and luscious as a ripe peach. Hunger stirred arousal and a familiar delicious heaviness formed at his groin.

Billie felt the change in atmosphere with every fibre of her being but could no more have stepped away than she could have stopped breathing. His gilded gaze was mesmeric in its power to hold her. Her mouth ran dry, frantic tension holding her fast. The pool of liquid heat forming in her belly was sending an electrifying surge of responsiveness through her entire body, pinching her sensitive nipples taut, creating heat and dampness at the secret heart of her.

Alexei closed his arms round her. Cupping her hips with an intimacy that shocked her, he drew her up against his hard muscular length and kissed her. It was a kiss full of a passionate demand that rocked her where she stood. It was like being hit by lightning as she sizzled like meat under a grill and her knees almost crumpled beneath her weight.

It was Alexei's strong arms that kept her upright

while he lightened the pressure of his intoxicating mouth and teased her reddened lips with tiny provocative caresses. Having reduced all resistance to rubble, he finally went in for the kill, dipping his tongue between her lips in a piercingly sweet invasion of her unbearably sensitive mouth and provoked a series of whimpering shivering gasps from somewhere inside her. It was the very first time she had experienced true sexual hunger and it was a raw need so powerful it rolled through her like thunder, blanking out all thought and control. For those split seconds she was both defenceless and aggressive, clinging to his lean hard physique, angling her head back to enable him, her entire body yearning for much more of the same.

'Will I be the first?' Alexei prompted in a roughened undertone.

'Yes,' she answered before she retrieved her wits and intelligence came back in a floodtide of anxiety and anger and regret. As she pulled free in response to those promptings the slivering pain of sudden separation from him cut through her as sharply as a knife.

Retaining a controlling grip on her slender hand, Alexei walked her back towards the car.

Billie hauled her fingers free of his. *'No!'* she protested strickenly. 'I don't want this!'

Alexei stilled and sent her a frowning look of incomprehension. 'What don't you want?'

'I don't want to be another notch on your bedpost. Just roll back time a few minutes, *please*! The kiss didn't happen, forget it. You're my boss. I work for you... Neither of us wants to change that relationship!'

'You sound almost hysterical.' Hot golden eyes semi-screened by luxuriant black lashes, Alexei squared his aggressive jawline. 'Everything changes, nothing stays static—that's life and you can't control it. You can't turn the clock back either. I want to take this attraction to its natural conclusion, *moraki mou.*'

'Only because you're not accustomed to any woman calling a halt…but I *am* calling a halt. I'm not like your other women… I don't do casual,' Billie proclaimed with proud vehemence.

'The spark we fired between us is too hot to douse,' Alexei delivered thickly, dark golden eyes locked to her like an incoming missile attack, making it clear that nothing she had said had impressed him.

'It was just sex,' she argued. 'And sex you can get anywhere with women far more beautiful than I am, so forget it and me in that line!'

'While I can still taste you in my mouth,' Alexei murmured huskily, shooting her a shockingly sensual appraisal that burned through her like a hot burning coal. 'I won't forget how you made me ache.'

'Stop it…' Billie raised her hands to silence him in a rare physical show of eloquence. '*Stop it!* It was a stupid kiss, a mistake, but it's not important and it's never going to happen again.'

Alexei stretched out his arms without warning and hauled her back to him, reconnecting her to the lean, tensile power of his muscular thighs and the potent thrust of his erection. Holding her entrapped, he stared down at her with all the cool of a predator stalking prey who knew he had all the time in the world. 'You can't tell me it's not going to happen again—that will only make me want you more.'

Awesomely conscious of the deep desperate longing still whirling inside her and crying out for satisfaction, Billie rested pleading green eyes on him. 'You know this is wrong. You know you would much rather have me working for you than having sex with you,' she told him feverishly.

'But having you fulfil both functions could well be an amazing tour de force,' Alexei countered with single-minded conviction. 'I would cut down on the other women.'

Billie almost screamed in frustration because no statement could have told her more clearly how out of alignment they both were. He was not only not getting her message, but also stubbornly refusing to listen to it.

'And that statement just shows how ill-suited we would be, because I wouldn't accept you having *any* other women! I wouldn't share you. No matter how many diamonds and treats you flung my way it wouldn't buy you back your freedom at the same time as you were with me.'

Alexei dealt her a lingering appraisal, searching her still-dilated pupils and the revealing redness of her lips while a rueful smile shadowed his beautiful sexy mouth. 'You're trying to scare me off—it's kind of sweet. But you know me better than that. When I want something I keep going until I get it. I don't switch off to order.'

'Was this all one big set-up, then? Is this why you're offering me this magnificent site to build on? Were you *trying* to buy me?' Billie flung at him in an emotional surge of accusation.

'You know me better than that, *moraki mou*. In any case, I'm more likely to give a reward to a lover at the *end* of the affair rather than at the beginning,' Alexei pointed out without an ounce of discomfiture.

Standing there in the sunshine, daring her censure, his lean bronzed features breathtakingly handsome, he could still take her breath away. Billie dropped her gaze and got into the car, wondering if the driver had seen that embrace, praying that he had not. If he had seen it, every member of Alexei's staff would know about it within twenty-four hours. The Drakos employee grapevine was terrifyingly efficient and the slightest hint that she was more intimate with Alexei than she ought to be would be sufficient to destroy the respect of her co-workers and her reputation.

'I've always been curious about you,' Alexei volunteered as the car took them back to the harbour. 'But I didn't suspect that we might be dynamite together.'

Curious? Would he make love to her out of curiosity alone? Sadly Billie thought that, yes, he would, for novelty attracted Alexei, who with every passing year became more bored with the myriad choices he enjoyed. Why the heck had she admitted that she was still a virgin? It was like whetting the appetite of a big game hunter with the offer of the ultimate quarry. After all, she was different and his lovers, strung across every continent, were almost interchangeable, she reflected tautly. They were actresses, models or socialites, usually tall and blonde, always beautiful, sophisticated and aware that no woman held Alexei's interest for very long. They entered his life and left it again without causing a single ripple in his routine.

Only one woman had ever dented Alexei's ego and it had been Lauren who shared that story with Billie. According to island gossip, Alexei had fallen for Calisto Kolovos, the daughter of a rich manufacturer, when he was twenty-one years old. But all along Calisto had had another boyfriend: Xavier Bethune, a much older man who had been a good deal richer and more powerful than Alexei who, in those days, was still dependent on his father. Calisto was said to have married Xavier for his money and, ever since then, Alexei had had a heart of stone when it came to women. Billie was not naïve enough to believe that she could change him. She wanted more than sex from him and, if that was not forthcoming, valued her job more than any short-lived sexual fling that would only last long enough to satisfy his curiosity.

They boarded the yacht together. Tension was simmering like a hissing, boiling pot between them. 'Alexei…don't do this,' Billie urged half under her breath as they crossed the deck.

'Don't do what?' he drawled smooth as glass.

'It's not fair to put me in a position like this.'

His bold profile froze.

'I'm damned if I do and damned if I don't,' she continued awkwardly. 'I like my job. I want my life to stay the same.'

No woman had ever made a plea to his sense of honour on such terms and it infuriated him that Billie had done so; he felt she should somehow sense that the innate sense of integrity he possessed had the power to make him back off. Dark deep anger burning below the surface, for he was a man very much accustomed to getting his own way, Alexei murmured icily, 'I find it hard to believe that that is what you want.'

Billie looked towards the sun and wondered how much it resembled the male ego in size and brilliance. Alexei was a hugely powerful and wealthy man, made irresistible by his Greek-god looks and notorious reputation. Women had always wanted Alexei Drakos and it was a truth he had learned so young that her surrender could only seem inevitable to him. 'In the circumstances—my working for you,' she extended with care. 'I don't want anything to change.'

'So, if I sack you, I can have you,' Alexei pronounced flatly.

'You don't really want me, you know you don't. I'm not your type,' Billie reasoned in a feverish undertone.

'Make arrangements for a flight to Monaco for me and then take the next couple of days off,' Alexei instructed just outside the office, startling her. 'You were assaulted last night. You need recovery time. Naturally you can stay on board *Sea Queen*.'

And, that fast, she registered that he had listened to her at last. The strangest and most contrary sense of disappointment washed through Billie's taut figure. The excitement of the chase was over. He had loads of eager female connections in Monaco. Quickly, Alexei would move on, find a more willing woman and forget that he had ever thought she might be worthy of a fling. Her

heart felt as if it were being hurled from a cliff down
onto jagged rocks. She ignored that fact, her weakness;
she had done what had to be done and it was time that
she lived a more full life and found a man of her own
to be with. In the course of her work, she had turned
down many invitations because she had yet to meet
anyone who could equal Alexei. But she would have
to stop being so picky. By turning away from Alexei,
she reminded herself firmly, she kept her excellent job
and would hopefully also retain a good working relationship with him.

Alexei was less content. Since when had he, a Drakos male, allowed himself to be upstaged and outma-
noeuvred by a female? But she had appealed to his
conscience and, although it went against the grain to
admit it, she had talked a good deal of sense. Wasn't
that why he employed her? Common sense and calm
distinguished Billie and until he had taken that kiss
he would have sworn that nothing would faze her. But
sex had splintered the calm and put her into retreat.
She wasn't his type, he reminded himself impatiently
while he showered later that day on board his private
jet. She was just an employee and only in the very early
days of creating his empire had he slept with women
he employed. There were excellent reasons for respecting boundaries and, even as it was, Billie was always
breaking through them and crossing the line. Was that
why Billie was the only person in his life who had the
power to make him feel human and real? She wasn't in
awe of him, or his wealth or his status. When he had
watched her eyes close in dreamy receipt of his mouth

he had got a kick out of that susceptibility. At that moment, she had been with him every step of the way.

His brow furrowed. Why the hell was he even still thinking about her? His common sense and practicality did not seem to be the equal of hers, he registered grimly. His libido had him over a barrel. He would have sacrificed their working relationship in a second, had she been waiting in the cabin bed for him…and to hell with the immorality, inconvenience and poor long-term outlook of it all!

THREE MONTHS AFTER that day, Billie went out on a date with a charming Italian businessman called Pietro Castronovo. He took her out to dinner in a very fancy Florentine restaurant where she toyed with food that was too rich for her taste and tried to respond to his flirtatious chatter.

At ten o'clock, Alexei rang her and wrecked the evening. 'You should have checked with me before you went out. Pietro is a married man with two kids.'

'Thank you, sir,' Billie murmured flatly.

'I've got some work for you to do.'

'Right now, I'm on an evening out,' she responded thinly.

'Surely you're not planning on spending any more time with a married man?' Alexei enquired sardonically.

Billie came off her phone and apologised to Pietro for having answered it. 'I always take Alexei's calls.'

'You stand very high in his regard,' Pietro commented.

Billie breathed in deep. 'Are you married?'

Her companion's thin, good-looking face tightened and she knew the answer before he even parted his lips and acknowledged that he was. 'I should have asked,' she said ruefully. 'I wouldn't be here if I had known.'

Pietro tried to dissuade her from cutting the evening short, but Billie stood firm and wondered why she was so much angrier with Alexei than with Pietro. After all, Alexei's warning had been a timely one, coming as it did before she could get any more involved with the handsome Italian. But, somehow, being saved at the eleventh hour from a mistake by a male who had very few morals of his own simply incensed Billie.

When she returned to the penthouse hotel suite Alexei was occupying, Alexei was at work with the rest of the team. She sent him an accusing glance but would not have dreamt of telling him how she felt about his previous phone call in front of an audience. When the business was dealt with, he called her back before she could leave.

'Did you shake Castronovo off? He was born with the gift of the gab,' Alexei said very drily. 'I should have warned you about him.'

'I am able to look after myself,' Billie told him starchily. 'Thank you for the warning on this occasion, but please don't interfere like that again.'

'Naturally I interfered. I knew that you wouldn't intentionally date a married man.'

There was a little devil inside Billie's head and it deeply resented his assumption that she would never do anything untoward. 'Actually, that's not necessarily one hundred per cent true.'

'You were back at the hotel within thirty minutes of my phone call,' Alexei countered with dark amusement. 'Don't be ashamed of your principles. Too many people have none at all.'

And still she had wanted to slap him. Her long-overdue venture onto the dating scene had gone belly-up and left her with egg on her face. The person she most hated for his interference was, without a shadow of a doubt, Alexei. She would never choose to date another woman's husband, but Alexei had once again managed to make her feel a fool.

EIGHT MONTHS AFTER that mortifying evening, Billie was in a better mood. She was sitting in her office in the Drakos villa on Speros, watching beautiful people through the windows. Got up in their fabulous evening outfits, the guests were laughing and drinking on the terrace outside the entertainment suite. The party she had arranged for Constantine's eightieth birthday was a huge success. Having made an appearance as instructed and stayed around long enough to check that the party schedule was running smoothly, Billie had bowed out to finish off some work.

In recent months her working hours had been very long, even though she now enjoyed the services of an assistant because her duties currently stretched to taking charge of Alexei's parents' social and travel arrangements as well. At the same time, she was making a hundred and one decisions about the building of her new house, which was currently two-thirds of the way towards being completed. She had picked the doors, the door handles, the bathroom and kitchen fittings and tiles. By spring the following year, she would be living under her own roof and could still hardly believe it.

In the planning stage the house had been a nightmare. Since anyone doing anything on Speros always looked first to the local community to supply services and skills, she had hired the island architect, Damon Marios, to design her new home. Damon, long since married and the father of two sturdy children, was still a friend. Alexei, however, had insisted on seeing the plans and changing things, pointing out that if he had an interest in the house, he also had the right to voice his viewpoint and ensure that the property was worthy of the site.

'I wanted something that fitted in with the island architectural style,' Billie had argued, fighting for the simple little cottage that Damon had designed.

'There is no style here. A century ago, dirt-poor people built dwellings that were the cheapest of the cheap,' Alexei had derided, urging Damon to use a little creativity and open up windows and doors to the fabulous views in a much more contemporary—and expensive— approach.

'Plain can be stylish,' Billie had said sharply.

'No wonder people talk about you and Alexei,' Damon had remarked in the aftermath of hearing that rough-edged exchange of views between them. 'I can't believe the way you argue with him.'

'It may be an unconventional working relationship but it works well for us,' Billie declared lightly.

It had been easy to silence Damon, make him cloak

the curiosity she saw in his eyes, for he was too polite to persist. She was accustomed to being questioned about Alexei and her relationship with him. Just about everyone was madly curious about Alexei: how he lived, what made him tick, his women, his houses, his yachts and his sporting prowess. He provided an endless stream of fascination for others. Since he had taken the helm of Drakos Shipping, he had become a hugely powerful tycoon. The richer he became, the more the media wanted to know about him and the less they found out, because Alexei didn't grant interviews. Paparazzi lay in wait for his every public appearance but his brutally efficient security team barred and evaded their invasions. Some of his lovers had, of course, gone to the press to sell stories, acts of betrayal that had only increased the level of interest in him and his lifestyle.

'Billie!' A voice intervened, separating Billie from her thoughts and making her look up from her computer screen to smile in some dismay at the slender brunette in her fifties framed in the doorway. 'I knew you would sneak off to work!' Natasha Drakos scolded. 'Come back to the party, *please.*'

Billie surrendered gracefully; Alexei's mother was a strong-willed woman. From the moment Alexei had taken over the family shipping business, Billie had started working long hours in the office suite at the Drakos villa and inevitably the two women had got to know each other better. While her son flew one woman after another out to Speros for entertainment during his hours of leisure, Natasha had soon realised that she had nothing to fear from Billie and had been considerably more concerned about some of the wilder females in her son's incomparable little black book.

Billie, a slim, vibrant figure in an apple-green dress, reflected that she had had to build an armour-plated shell to cope with the heartache of constantly seeing Alexei with other women. Her sole consolation was that none of them seemed to have the power to hold on to him for very long. But constantly controlling her thoughts, reactions and expressions in Alexei's radius was a strain. Even now when she was chatting to his mother about the party, Billie was already bracing herself for a glimpse of Alexei with his current love, the English socialite Tia Flint.

Alexei was so tall that it was the work of a moment to pick him and Tia out of the crowd. Tia, an eye-catching blonde in a black glistening sheath dress, was wound round him like a vine. Billie studied Alexei, noting the stubborn angle of his strong jaw and the distance in his brilliant dark eyes. Tia was giggling and gesticulating with her hands to a bunch of friends nearby. In his tailored dinner jacket, Alexei looked as coolly beautiful and remote as a classic bronze statue.

'Tia is on the way out,' Natasha forecast knowledgeably. 'He's bored.'

'Maybe,' Billie responded, watching the way Tia's fingers were smoothing across Alexei's shirtfront with the familiarity of a lover. It hurt her to look, yet some awful fascination prevented her from snatching her gaze away.

As the hostess drifted off to relocate her husband

Damon crossed the floor to greet Billie. 'You owe me a dance.'

Billie tensed because Damon's wife, Ilona, was the possessive type. She had visited the site on several occasions and had made it clear that she wanted to be sure that any interaction between her husband and his former school friend remained strictly related to business. 'Do I?'

'Sorry, Damon, you missed the boat a long time ago,' Alexei breathed sardonically, stepping between them without warning and closing an arm round Billie to sweep her straight out onto the dance floor.

'What on earth are you doing?' Billie gasped, thoroughly taken aback by his sudden appearance and that crack that harked back nine years to her first crush as a schoolgirl.

'Saving your good name,' he censured with a curled lip. 'Damon's wife took the kids and went home to her parents last week. His marriage is over. Damon making a beeline for you is a bad idea as you'll get the blame for breaking them up.'

'You couldn't care less about my good name,' Billie riposted.

Hooded dark golden eyes dropped to her tense heart-shaped face. 'Damon's looking for consolation, so give him a wide berth. Remember the guy who cut you dead on the ferry all those years ago. You look sexy in green—'

'Out of line, Alexei,' Billie framed, wildly aware of the strength and power of his tall, well-built body against hers and the hand splayed to her taut spine. She was barely able to breathe for nerves. 'Where's Tia?'

'With her friends. She's drunk and angry I won't go to the races with her next week. Organise a flight home for her tomorrow.'

'Yes.' So, Tia was yesterday's news. However, the effervescent blonde had lasted six weeks, which was a good month longer than many did.

The hand at her spine eased down to her derrière. Heat curled in her pelvis, her breasts stirring within the confines of her bra, the nipples distending in response.

'Oh...look at your parents out on the terrace!' Billie suddenly exclaimed, and she stilled to watch the older couple dancing outside alone. 'They're really enjoying their party.'

Alexei lowered his arrogant dark head, his breath fanning her cheek. The familiar scent of him, a specific aroma composed of warm husky male and the designer cologne he wore, assailed her nostrils and sent an arrow-sharp dart of longing through her. If he came too close she suffered that instinctive response half a dozen times in her working day. The awesome physical awareness he could inflict on her was terrifying.

Alexei held her back from him the better to look at her. Simmering dark golden eyes roamed over her like caramel melting on a hot day, burning everywhere his gaze touched. 'Stop trying to change the subject,' he husked. 'The way that fabric clings to your breasts is indecent and very flattering.'

And she glanced down and saw that her prominent nipples were clearly visible beneath her frock. Mortification engulfed her like a tidal wave. A hot pink flared up below her fine skin and washed her face with colour. Turning on her heel, she walked off the floor, furious with him, furious with herself. He was baiting her. He knew she was still attracted to him and he used it like a weapon against her. But she shouldn't have reacted.

The party, Billie decided ruefully, would be fine without her. She smiled at the touching recollection of Alexei's parents wrapped in each others' arms as they danced alone outside. It did not occur to her, nor indeed to anyone else that evening, that this image might be one of the last she or they would ever have of the older couple...

CHAPTER FIVE

THREE WEEKS LATER, the news of the tragic accident came in a devastating phone call. Helios, the head of Alexei's security team, phoned Billie. It was the middle of the night and she was half stupid with sleep when she answered. He repeated the details slowly and with great sorrow. After a stunned pause, she asked him why he had not rung Alexei direct.

'You know him well. You are a woman—you will break the news better,' Helios opined heavily. 'It is a terrible thing.'

'I'll go and speak to him.' Finger-combing her hair off her brow with a shaking hand, Billie got out of bed and pulled on the wrap lying on the chair. She did not dare wait to wash and brush up because time was of the essence. She literally ran down the passageway to his bedroom and knocked loudly on the door before opening it.

The light went on by the bed, Alexei lurching up against the pillows, black hair spiky and tousled, a heavy shadow of stubble obscuring his jawline, while a tangle of black chest hair rioted across his superb masculine torso. She suspected that he wasn't wearing a stitch of clothing.

'What's up?' he asked thickly.

'Helios phoned. Your parents…'

'My parents…*what*?' Alexei rasped at her as if some sixth sense had already kicked in to forewarn him that she had bad news to break.

'They were involved in a motorway pile-up. They're in hospital in Athens. It's very serious,' she told him carefully.

She watched his bright eyes darken and the sudden spread of pallor below his bronzed skin now pulling taut with tension across his high cheekbones. He thrust back the bedding in a violent movement. 'Are they alive?'

Hastily she spun away and turned her back to him before he could cross the room naked in front of her. '*Just*. There are no details yet. I'll contact your pilot—'

'Make the arrangements,' Alexei bit out.

'Do you want me to come with you?' she prompted.

'Of course, I bloody well want you to come!' Alexei launched back at her rawly.

Tears of shock and compassion ready to overflow from her eyes, Billie sped back to her room, tore off her night gear and yanked out a business suit to wear. It was only forty-eight hours since they had arrived at the chateau Alexei owned in the South of France. While Alexei toured the vines and the state-of-the-art winery he had created and enjoyed long technical discussions with the vintner he had hired, she had relaxed from formality and worn cropped linen trousers and a casual T-shirt to wander around the lavender-edged borders in the idyllic garden that thrummed with visiting bees and hummingbirds. Just hours earlier that combination of sunshine and scented flowers had struck her as the purest taste of heaven but now those feelings were being utterly swept away…

Alexei was unusually quiet during the flight, his dark mood weighting the atmosphere. There was a mention of the accident on the news but no names were released. Somehow word of the high-profile victims had escaped, however, for the hospital was already under siege by the press when they arrived. For the first time ever, though, a path through the crush of paparazzi that led all the way to the entrance cleared in front of Alexei. In the foyer they were greeted by the chief administrator and a doctor who answered Alexei's questions about Constantine and Natasha's conditions. Alexei's mother had sustained a serious head injury and was on life support. Constantine had already had emergency surgery and remained very weak. The prognosis was not good for either of them.

Reluctant to intrude, Billie hung back as it slowly sank in that Alexei's mother was in a coma from which she was unlikely to recover. She was shocked by the sight of the vivacious older woman lying so still in her hospital bed. After sitting by Natasha and talking to her for a while in an effort to revive her, Alexei hurried on to his father's bedside. Constantine roused and gripped his son's hand and words were exchanged but within the hour the old man suffered a massive heart attack and passed away. Mid-morning, Alexei was present when his mother's life support was switched off. Billie's heart bled for him but he remained fully in control. They left the hospital by a back entrance and drove out to a pri-

vate airfield to board a helicopter. His mobile phone
was ringing incessantly by then. He answered the first
few calls from relatives, explained what had happened
and then he gave the phone to Billie to look after. By
the time they landed back on Speros, he was grey with
grief and exhaustion.

The household staff, some of whom were openly
crying, awaited Alexei's arrival in the hall of the villa.
Alexei talked to all of them. By then, Billie was field-
ing calls from chief executives and lawyers, wanting
to know what was going to happen in a hundred different areas. She told them all that they had to wait.
Alexei needed peace in which to grieve and while he
wandered round the huge rambling villa like a lost soul
Billie made the funeral arrangements.

The following few days were very stressful. Great-
aunts, great-uncles, aunts, uncles and cousins travelled
from all over the world to the island, packing out the
villa just when Alexei would have preferred time alone.
Television channels were running documentaries based
on old grainy newsreel coverage of Constantine's life
and various marriages. The media was responding with
a similar slew of articles. Although the funeral was to
be strictly private and for family and close friends only,
several of Alexei's former lovers arrived uninvited. It
was Billie's job to send them packing again and after
being treated to a fit of hysterics by Brigitte, a French
singer, that left her ears ringing, she was desperate to
escape the hothouse feel of the villa and went off to visit
her mother for a couple of hours.

After the Dean episode the previous year, Lauren

had spent quite a few weeks in London staying with her sister, Hilary. Once off the island, Lauren's relationship with the toy boy had disintegrated fast. She had phoned her daughter several times to say sorry and although Billie fully believed that she had forgiven Lauren she now saw less of her mother and avoided her altogether when she had a man in tow.

'I had a walk up to see how that fancy new house of yours was coming on,' Lauren told her. 'It's going to be quite something—no wonder the locals are talking!'

Billie tried and failed to resist her curiosity. 'What about?'

'What do you think? We all see the fancy women in Alexei's life in the newspapers and the magazines, but you're the only one to get a building site within walking distance of the Drakos villa. Everyone knows you work very closely with Alexei and enjoy a lot of privileges—naturally some people think that you're earning the extras on your back!' Lauren supplied with a crudity that made her daughter grit her teeth together.

'It's not like that between us.'

'But not for want of you wishing,' Lauren needled, casting a shrewd eye at Billie's pink cheeks. 'I'm not so stupid that I haven't noticed how you feel about him.'

It was not a conversation Billie wanted to have with Lauren, who had never been very good at keeping secrets. Her mobile phone rang and she answered it as a welcome distraction, wandering to the other side of the room and switching to English when she recognised the upper-class English vowel sounds of Alexei's great-aunt, Lady Marina Chalfont, his father's half-sister. Lady

Marina was stranded in Athens. Billie was happy to sort out transport for her, not only because the older woman was in her eighties but because she was Alexei's favourite relative.

'You're on duty twenty-four-seven,' Lauren complained.

'It's not quite as bad as that,' Billie declared, pressing a kiss to her mother's cheek before leaving an hour later.

But nonetheless that was how it felt when Billie returned to the villa and discovered that chaos had developed in her absence. Alexei strode into the entrance hall, lean darkly handsome face hard with anger and frustration. 'Where the hell have you been?' he demanded rawly. 'I'm trying to work and the phone is ringing off the hook. Your assistant is an idiot and my cousins are doing a conga through the house!'

'I went to see my mother.'

Like a storm cloud, Alexei shrugged his dismissal of that as an acceptable excuse and strode back to the office suite in high dudgeon. A moment later, the conga crew passed Billie by and she intervened. Alexei's cousins, many of them just teenagers, were keen to treat the funerals as an excuse to enjoy some sun, sea and sand and were striking a very wrong note in the grieving household. It took all of Billie's tact to soothe everyone down before a major row broke out. Chastened, the young people went down to the beach in pursuit of more acceptable entertainment.

Her assistant, Kasia, was swallowing back tears when Billie joined her and she confessed that in certain moods Alexei scared her. Everyone on the business team kept their head down when Billie arrived and she knew that Alexei had been letting everyone feel the rough edge of his often sarcastic tongue. Alexei's great-aunt arrived soon after in the helicopter Billie had despatched to pick her up.

'Go and see Marina settled,' Alexei commanded her.

'It's you she will want to see.'

'I'm not in the mood right now.'

Billie breathed in deep to restrain herself but still couldn't hold back the words bubbling into her mouth. 'Maybe it's time you got in the mood. Lots of people badly want to speak to you. Tomorrow will only be more difficult if you don't make time for some of them now.'

An unearthly silence spread like a cloaking cloud of poison gas through the large office. There was a palpable air of shock. Alexei lifted incredulous dark eyes of hauteur to Billie's unrepentant face. Ducking his searing gaze, she spun on her heel to leave the office.

An instant later he was walking by her side. 'Don't you ever speak to me like that again,' he warned her icily.

'You know perfectly well what you should be doing.'

'You have no idea what I'm going through,' Alexei condemned.

'Oh, yes, I have,' Billie fielded ruefully, for nobody who had witnessed the camaraderie between Alexei and his parents could have failed to notice how very close the trio were. Like many only children, Alexei had spent a great deal of time with adults and his childhood as such had been short-lived. His father had been taking him on guided tours of supertankers and oil refineries by the age of five. Independent though Alexei was, his parents' deaths had left him like a ship without a rudder.

Billie showed Lady Marina, the tall and imposing daughter of a countess, into the most spacious guest suite. 'How is my nephew?' the old lady asked fondly.

'He's coping very well—'

'Which for a Drakos male means he's not coping at all,' Marina interposed with a shake of her elegant white head. 'Constantine always froze too when an emotional response was demanded. Is Alexei using work as an escape?'

Billie folded her lips and nodded.

'Alexei's in shock. Drakos men aren't used to problems that they can't solve, situations they can't fix. He needs to go wild for a while, get it all out of his system. Holding it all in is unhealthy.'

Billie almost smiled at that unlikely idea because, while the tabloids might once have depicted the fabulously wealthy Drakos heir as a wild, undisciplined playboy, Billie had learned that even though Alexei might break the rules and flout the conventions he always acted with forethought and he never, ever relinquished control. He also rejoiced in nerves of steel and the sensitivity of a granite block.

But what she saw later that evening when Alexei had abandoned his social mask shook that conviction. Unable to find him to pass on news of an unexpected movement on the New York Stock Exchange, she finally ran him to ground in the special conservatory that housed his mother's prized collection of tropical orchids. She hovered outside, watching him through the glass as he stood there and trailed a long lean finger down the stem of a white waxen bloom. He had never had any interest in the flowers that had fascinated his Russian mother, and neither had his late father. Indeed both men had regularly teased Natasha about her obsession. But, for all that, a year ago Alexei had financed an Amazonian plant collectors' trip, which had resulted in his mother having a newly discovered orchid named after her. Natasha had been thrilled beyond belief at having such an honour conferred on her.

Billie's gaze flicked up to Alexei's bold brown profile and froze at the sight of the glisten of moisture highlighting his hard cheekbones. Silent tears were rolling down his face. She could *taste* his sadness, his regret for times past never to be regained. Her throat thickened, her own eyes wet, and she looked hurriedly away, feeling that she could not possibly intrude on so intensely private a moment in which he believed himself alone and unobserved. But, oh, how she longed for the right to push open that door and hurry to his side to offer him comfort! But freedom of expression was not part of her role and she reluctantly walked away while scolding herself for having underestimated the depth of Alexei's loss and his feelings. His tough self-discipline had fooled even her, persuading her that he was totally in control and that business would pretty much go on as usual. Why else had she chased him down to talk about his US Stocks? She left a note on his desk but it was a long time before she got to sleep that night because she was far too busy wondering when Alexei had last slept.

The following day was an extremely busy one for Billie. The security precautions to ensure the interments remained private were rigorous. Constantine and Natasha were laid to rest in the walled cemetery behind the village church. Alexei, who always rose highest to a challenge, shook off the moodiness and silences of the day before to act as gracious host at the villa. Special travelling arrangements had been put in place to enable the guests to leave in good time for their flights home.

Once everyone was gone, an unearthly silence spread through the house because most of the staff was now off duty as well. Billie went off in search of Alexei because after working so many hours at a stretch she was keen to have some time that was her own. After all, tomorrow would bring an early start, the reading of the will and a return to business, which promised to be even more challenging than anything that had gone before. But who could tell what mood Alexei would be in? Only since the motorway pile-up had she truly appreciated just how volatile he could be

Alexei was on the terrace with a drink in his hand. He had gone through most of the day that way and the sight of that ever-present glass struck a wrong note for her because overindulging in alcohol was not the norm for him. She recalled her painful glimpse of him with his mother's orchids the night before and compressed her mouth. He had discarded his tie and unbuttoned his shirt but he still wore his black designer suit with striking panache. As she looked at him, taking in the grim gold of his stunning eyes and the rough shadow of stubble darkening his jaw line, her heart skipped a beat and she felt horribly guilty for reacting to his sexual allure on such an unhappy day.

'You need a drink,' Alexei drawled.

'No, thanks...er—'

Alexei strode past her into the house. 'What would you like?'

'I don't drink when I'm working—'

'If I'm not working, you're not working either,' Alexei traded and slowly the stiffness in her bearing eased.

'Rosé wine...'

'Rosé? You've got no class,' Alexei groaned from indoors.

'I only like sweet drinks,' she confided.

'Relax, take off your jacket,' Alexei told her.

And she did because she was too warm. Her sleek grey silk T-shirt complemented her tailored skirt. She had learned how to put together an outfit for work and was satisfied that she looked elegant, while being less confident of what she wore outside working hours. A moisture-beaded glass clasped in her hand, she studied Alexei, long dark lashes veiling her anxious green eyes from the disturbing penetration of his.

'You put on a hell of a show for my family today. I appreciate it.'

Her cheeks warmed. 'Thanks.'

'I just wish I felt a little happier about having left my mother in her final resting place down by the church.'

Billie frowned. 'Sorry, I don't understand.'

'I'd always planned to take her away travelling once my father was gone,' Alexei confided with a raw, roughened edge of emotion to his voice. 'I waited too long. It never occurred to me that they might die at the same time. When she married my father she gave up her youth. She spent thirty-odd years withering with boredom and frustration on this island. Speros was her cage, her punishment for marrying a man in his fifties who was afraid that she would meet someone else if he let her have more freedom. She deserved better.'

'Your mother always seemed happy.'

'She was a great wife and mother.' Alexei downed the contents of his glass in a salute. 'But she got very little pleasure out of being a Drakos.'

'You and your father—her family—meant everything to her,' Billie responded softly, and then she set down her empty glass. 'I'm going to turn in now.'

'You have to be the only woman in my life who continually tries to walk out on me,' Alexei remarked with a wondering shake of his handsome dark head. 'Any idea why that is?'

And all over again Billie felt the intense charismatic pull of him tugging at her senses. He was gorgeous and she would have had to be bereft of her senses not to appreciate him. His high-voltage sensuality was like a honey trap, she reasoned feverishly, and not one she could afford to fall into again.

'Working for you is tiring,' she fielded awkwardly.

'What a drab description of being in my employment,' Alexei countered, his Greek accent and possibly the amount of alcohol he had consumed making the words slur together.

Meeting his brilliant golden gaze, Billie felt like a

rabbit caught in car headlights: paralysed, trapped and befuddled by the blinding brightness.

'It's never boring and I enjoy the travel and all the different people I meet,' she conceded in a small tense voice. 'Perhaps you should have allowed Brigitte to stay on today to keep you company.'

'The French one who screamed abuse at you when you told her she couldn't stay? You've got to be kidding!' A familiar pulse of arousal was making Alexei uncomfortable. There was something about Billie that turned him on and he had long since given up trying to work out what it was. Yes, she had beautiful green eyes, clear fine skin and a peach of a mouth, but she wasn't in his class and he knew it. She had nothing in common with his other lovers either—that would be a ridiculous comparison to make. Yet, somehow, he was always aware of the movements of that small, delightfully curvy body when it was in his vicinity. He never failed to notice the luscious curve of her breasts and the firm feminine swell of her bottom below a fitted skirt. And, just at that moment, with his blood running insanely hot and making him hard as steel, he wanted to strip off her clothes and sink hard and long into the silky welcome of her virginal body.

'You shouldn't be alone tonight.'

Alexei reached out and closed his lean brown hands over hers to tug her closer. 'Ah-h-h, that's sweet, Billie. Do you really think I need emotional support from anyone?'

'Well, you're unlikely to find it at the foot of a bottle,' Billie told him with unhesitating disapproval.

Lounging back on the edge of a stone table with his long, lean, powerful thighs spread wide, Alexei flung back his handsome dark head and laughed with rich appreciation of that reprimand. His hands tightened over hers swiftly when she made a move to break free. 'Only from your lips, *moraki mou*. The unblemished truth.'

'Don't call me "my little baby",' Billie urged with complete seriousness. 'It's that sort of talk which gives people the wrong idea about our relationship.'

'But you *are* very small,' Alexei riposted with dark amusement, his rich drawl running the syllables of the words together as he thought it was funny that she never seemed to notice the effect she had on him. 'I'm not accustomed to little women.'

'That's not the point.' Lifting her head, Billie encountered scorching golden eyes framed by luxuriant black lashes and registered that looking at him directly was seriously unwise. She felt the heat of that appraisal right to the very core of her, setting up a string of little sensual shocks that tightened her nipples and made her uncomfortably conscious of the uniquely sensitive area between her thighs.

'The point here...' Alexei breathed silkily as he flexed his strong hands and inexorably drew her closer still '...is that I want you and you want me and we've been dancing round that fact for far too long.'

Billie was as unyielding as a cliff face being buffeted by a high wind. 'That's not true.'

'Stop being stuffy,' Alexei urged, his intonation soft and sibilant, black-lashed stormy golden eyes threatening to reel her in like a fish on a line.

'I'm not being stuffy. I'm just stating a fact,' Billie told him tartly. 'Last year I got a bit of a crush on my boss but I got over it—I'm sure you've had loads of female staff who over time became attracted to you.'

'But none who tasted as hot as you,' Alexei slotted in dangerously. 'So you got over me?'

Billie nodded vigorously, glad he had made that very basic but crucial connection. *'Totally.'*

Alexei leant forward and slowly, sensually captured her lips, suckling their ripe curves before sliding his tongue moistly into her mouth in an explicit thrust. And she couldn't breathe for excitement and felt her legs wobble like crumbling supports. He caught her to him with strong arms, hands splaying across her bottom. Trembling she came up for air and gasped, 'We *can't—*'

'Ne, ne, we can,' Alexei asserted thickly. 'No more games.'

Resistance had hitherto been ingrained in Billie, but, although she dug deep, this time she couldn't find a trace of her usual caution. Games? The very word offended her. Was that what he thought? That saying no had merely been an exercise cynically staged to increase his desire for her? She refused to believe that he could see her in that light because her own feelings were so different. In his arms she ironically felt ridiculously safe. There had been no other man in her life for three years. She loved him and he would never need her more than he needed her now. Like a battery-operated doll able to go in only one direction, she let her swollen mouth brush back across his, her entire body tingling with sexual longing. Being touched by him, even having the right to hold him close, lent a whole new exciting dimension to her feelings for him that went to her head like strong drink.

He carried her past the swimming pool terrace to the guest suite she was occupying until her house was ready for her. Automatic lights flashed on at every step to illuminate their progress.

'What about tomorrow?' Billie asked with sudden urgency.

'Who knows?' Alexei breathed in a tone of dismissal. 'Right now I don't want to think about today or, for that matter, tomorrow, *moraki mou.*'

Her slim fingers brushed his cheekbone in a soothing gesture of tenderness. 'Then don't think about them,' she whispered softly...

CHAPTER SIX

'IF YOU ONLY knew how long I have dreamt of doing this with you...' Alexei groaned, settling Billie down on the bed and pausing only to shed his jacket and shoes before joining her there.

Billie was mesmerised by his intrinsic poise, for he seemed as at home in her bedroom as in his own. Indeed, lounging back against her pillows, Alexei was a beautiful fantasy that didn't seem quite real to her. His black hair and sun-darkened olive skin were an eye-catching contrast against the pale bedding. It was a challenge for her to drag her gaze from the exotically high cheekbones, dramatic deep-set dark eyes and arrogant nose that gave such strength and character to his lean, handsome face. The sensual side of her nature had finally run away with her, she acknowledged in a rush of dismay. Did that mean that she was more like her highly sexed mother than she had ever appreciated? That fear tormented her but one kiss had mown down her defences and turned her into a pushover.

'You don't believe me,' Alexei accused.

'Does it matter?' Billie wouldn't look at him. Thoughts of her mother's chequered love life had cast a sleazy shadow over her. Perhaps Lauren had also thought that she loved the first man in her life. Would Alexei simply think she was cheap and easy if she slept with him? With a past like his, she could hardly expect to stand out from the crowd.

'With you? *Yes*,' he told her bluntly in English for emphasis.

'I don't need empty words and promises.' Billie made a valiant attempt to suppress her insecurity and turned towards him, green eyes darkened to emerald by her yearning and the terrible guilty sense that she was breaking every one of her rules. Yet when she met those heavily lashed golden eyes, it struck her that rules were made to be broken and that, for her, Alexei Drakos would always be an exception. He laced long brown fingers slowly into the tumbling fall of her red hair, smoothing and fanning the vibrant strands across his palm in the lamplight in a move that accentuated the different shades.

'I never found red hair attractive until I saw yours glowing in the sunlight with all those crazy streaks of copper and gold and bronze,' he admitted, before he jerked her head back and took a hungry driving kiss that exploded through her wound-up body like a depth charge.

The renewed taste of him was a wake-up call to her slumbering senses. That kiss was insanely stimulating. Indeed the probe of his tongue sent a spasm of fierce sexual need spearing right to the heart of her, releasing a feverish energy that pulsed through her receptive flesh in a sensual wave. Alexei pulled back from her to remove her T-shirt, an action that left her blinking in surprise like an owl suddenly thrust into bright light.

'You're always wearing too many clothes, *moraki mou*. I can't wait to get them off,' he confided thickly, one lean hand already engaged in unzipping her skirt so that he could slide it off her as easily as if she were standing up.

Uneasily conscious of her body's semi-clad state in a serviceable black cotton bra and panties, Billie went stiff and self-conscious. She was hopelessly convinced that he was sure to notice his mistake now when he discovered that—shock! horror!—her garments did not miraculously conceal a designer-thin body with dainty breasts and legs as long as a giraffe's. She knew that though there was nothing wrong with her figure it was very ordinary, and while she might be undersized in the height department she certainly wasn't in her bust or hip measurements. Her face was scarlet with self-consciousness.

'I have a huge sense of anticipation,' Alexei revealed, reaching for her bra, his attention welded hungrily to the snowy hillocks firmly encased in black cotton.

'But anticipation often leads to disappointment,' Billie warned him worriedly, pushing his arms back so that she could start unbuttoning his shirt and occupy her trembling hands. She was desperate to conceal her nerves and her sheer embarrassing ignorance of such intimacies. 'It's my turn.'

'Always the pessimist and so democratic,' Alexei mocked.

Billie was very well aware that she was dealing with

an autocrat, who had learned in the cradle that he had no need to share anything with anyone. Her fingers were clumsy on the buttons of his shirt and to complete her task she daringly yanked the garment free of his belt. Deep down inside her head, a frightened voice was wailing, 'What on earth are you doing?' over and over again. Black hair curled over Alexei's powerful pectoral muscles and arrowed down over his taut abdomen to vanish from view below his waist. He was a hot but sexually intimidating vision and he took her breath away.

With an unhurried hand he unhooked her bra and trailed it off. Billie had to fight a powerful urge to try and cover her breasts with her hands like some shocked maiden from an old comedy film; her skin had never felt so naked or exposed.

'You're magnificent,' he told her in Greek 'Lush...'

And the taste of that word resonating in the silence made her tremble, while his almost reverent finger brushed the prominent bud of a pouting pink nipple adorning her voluptuous blue-veined flesh. He bent his dark head and closed his mouth to that tantalising peak, rolling the unbearably tender bud between his lips while he used skilled fingers to administer similar pressure to its neglected twin. Pushing her back on the pillows, he cupped and squeezed her plump breasts, stroking them while he suckled ever more strongly. Swiftly he plunged her straight into a storm of new and almost painful sensation. Her nipples throbbed from his attentions and tugged internal strings that seemed to be connected to even more intimate places. Her hips lifted, her thighs pushing together to contain the tension between them. Little animal sounds escaped low in her throat. All of a sudden she was in a place she had never been before and feeling things she had never dreamt she might feel. That it should be Alexei taking her to that place blew her away.

'You're so different from the women I'm used to, *moraki mou*. And differences are always exciting,' Alexei husked, tugging up her knees and skimming off her panties in one easy movement before dispensing with his trousers and casting them aside.

That statement had unsettled Billie as much as the all-male bulge of arousal defined by his silk boxers. 'How am I different?' she pressed in a small voice.

In the midst of an assessing visual sweep of her body, Alexei suddenly smiled down at her with the wicked charisma that was so much his own. He made no attempt to hide the hungry appreciation in his dark golden eyes. 'Everything about you is one hundred per cent real…the colour of your hair, your breasts. Nothing is fake and nothing has been remodelled.'

Beneath that powerful appraisal, Billie could still only blush and she was so painfully uncertain and shy that that betraying tide of colour even engulfed the pale upper slopes of her breasts. 'Here I am, flaws and all,' she said valiantly. 'I can only assume I take after my father for, let's face it, I inherited none of my mother's genes!'

'Your attributes are much more subtle,' Alexei interrupted, discarding his boxers.

'But I really would have loved the blonde hair and long legs,' Billie confided shakily, using humour to try and hide her vulnerability while trying not to stare fixedly at his manhood, which was of more threatening masculine dimensions than she had expected.

'Blonde hair and long legs are easily found. I prefer you just as you are,' Alexei husked, running a forefinger down between her breasts and over her quivering stomach to the triangle of dark red hair at the junction of her legs.

Billie stopped breathing while her heart hammered at a frantic rate. He found the sensitive swollen bud below the curls and gently massaged it, releasing a rolling tide of sweet sensation that stole the breath from her lungs. She could feel her insides dissolving to honey even while a burn of greater need flamed into being. Her slender thighs parting, she shifted against his knowing hand, her hips developing a motion all of their own because she could not contain the intensity of what he was making her feel. As he explored the delicate pink folds of flesh she had exposed and pleasured the hidden opening to her womanhood she writhed, out of control and breathless.

'You're so tight and wet,' Alexei growled with raw satisfaction. 'Are you still a virgin?'

Eyes wide and green and feverish against the hectically flushed oval of her face, she nodded confirmation. 'Does it matter?'

'Oh, yes. It matters to me, *moraki mou*,' Alexei told her in Greek. 'A more honourable man would walk away, because I'm not making you any promises.'

'I know that.' Billie was quick to dispel any suggestion that she had such expectations, yet the denial was like a stab at her heart.

Simmering golden eyes fringed by inky black lashes assailed her. 'But, for what it's worth, I feel more of a connection with you than I have ever felt with a woman. Somehow we fit, *khriso mou*. I respect you. I like you. Everything feels natural with you, nothing forced or false.'

'It's just all the emotion of the last few days,' Billie protested, fearful of allowing herself to believe that anything was happening between them that could mean something to him, because she thought that such a conviction could only lead her to the madness of false hope and disillusionment. 'And the alcohol.'

'The...*alcohol*?' Alexei carolled in disbelief. 'Are you suggesting that I might not know what I'm doing?'

'I don't want to take advantage of you,' Billie said deadpan.

Laughing uproariously, Alexei pulled her to him and held her close to kiss her with a hungry passion that was passionately free of restraint. The sexual heat flowed through her again while he strung a line of provocative kisses down the extended length of her throat and across the alabaster slopes of her breasts. She was boneless, breathless even before he returned to the hot dampness between her legs. With exquisite skill, he toyed with the satin flesh, probing the delicate entrance where she ached for a fulfilment she had never known before. His sensual onslaught was a sweet torment, lighting up her every nerve-ending with longing. Her excitement built and built to a towering height and she couldn't stay still or silence the tiny gasps and whimpers breaking from her lips.

He put a pillow below her hips and came over her with practised ease. 'I'll try not to hurt you,' he promised thickly. 'But I want you so much I'm in agony.'

Feeling him nudging at the entrance to her body, she tensed. He urged her to stay still and as relaxed as possible before he sank his engorged shaft slowly into her tight inner channel. She was lost in the extraordinary feeling of his erotic invasion. A flicker of discomfort came as a warning before the main event, when he plunged deeper into resisting flesh, and she yelped at the flash of pain, only to be mortified when he stopped.

'No, don't stop…just get it over with,' she mumbled through gritted teeth.

'How can I resist such an invitation?' Alexei groaned, pausing to brush his lips across her brow in a comforting motion before driving deeper until her body yielded and sheathed him completely. Becoming accustomed to that sensation of fullness, she shifted her hips and as swiftly savoured the flood of intense erotic feelings roused by his slow, steady movements. She brought up her knees, lifting her hips to accommodate his thrusts and crying out her pleasure in encouragement. He abandoned his control, sliding his hands below her to lift her even higher and deepen his penetration, his heart labouring against hers. He ravished her with long driven thrusts and sent her excitement climbing so high she screamed when she tipped over the edge into an explosion of ecstasy and wild ripples of sensual delight gripped her quivering body in the aftermath.

'Bliss…for the first time I see the point of your name, *khriso mou*,' Alexei breathed from the rumpled depths of her hair, slowly lifting his tousled head to gaze down at her with wondering appreciation. 'That was amazing, but—'

'*But?*'

'We have just had sex without precautions. I can assure you that I'm clean. I have regular check-ups and I have never until this moment made love without a condom.'

Billie was much more tense than Alexei, whose big powerful frame was comparatively relaxed against hers. '*Without?*'

'We should have gone back to my room. What part of your cycle are you in?'

Embarrassed by the enquiry and rigid with apprehension, Billie had to think and then they had to count, a pastime that Billie was much better at than Alexei, whose unusually slow mental arithmetic only reminded her that he was very far from being sober. Although she was in the second half of her cycle, he decided that there wasn't much to worry about. Billie was, however, less sanguine, momentarily picturing the horror of conceiving a child by a male who revelled in his freedom and who wouldn't want an illegitimate kid or its mother.

Claiming a hot, driving kiss, Alexei coaxed her out of that pensive mood. He shifted against her, cupping her hips to bring her into contact again with his renewed arousal. Billie was startled, not having realised that he might be ready again so quickly or even that he might want to repeat the experience. 'It was so good I can't wait to do it again,' Alexei told her raggedly, his hands straying to more sensitive places to lessen any reluctance she might be suffering from.

Billie was astonished by how fast he could make her want him again even when she was a little sore. She melted below his urgent kisses. He put her in a different position on her side and made love to her slowly and provocatively, driving her to an even more earth-shattering climax the second time.

'This is crazy,' he acknowledged lazily in the aftermath. 'I'll have to go and get some condoms. I don't want to get you pregnant.'

'We're being very irresponsible,' Billie agreed breathlessly, so limp, weak and mindless after that last wave of pleasure that she could barely speak.

'That's what I like about you, *khriso mou*,' Alexei husked, brushing aside the dark red damp hair at the nape of her neck to kiss the tender skin there. 'You bring out another side of me, an irresponsible side. I'm different with you.'

The mattress gave as he slid out of bed and she flipped over with anxious eyes. 'Where are you going?'

'The shower, then to my room to take care of the contraception.'

For a couple of minutes, Billie lay on the bed as though she were welded to it. Shock was sinking in fast and filling her with apprehension and doubts. Although she had sworn that she would never be foolish enough to sleep with Alexei, she had just done so. In fact she had taken part in a shameless sexual romp that was indefensible for, while she might love him, he did

not love her. What price now her long-held secret belief
that she was somehow morally superior in her restraint
to her mother? That she was different? More sensible,
more steady? Shame drenched her in a tide of drown-
ing regret. As far as Alexei was concerned now, she
would just figure as one more in a long line of willing
bed partners...

'Billie?' Alexei called, startling her.

'What?'

'Come and join me,' Alexei urged impatiently.

In the shower? In no immediate hurry to extend her
sexual education, Billie slid uneasily off the bed and
padded into the en suite, snatching up a towel from the
doorway and holding it against herself.

'Drop the towel,' Alexei exclaimed, making her jump
as he rammed back the glass door to survey her with a
raised brow of enquiry.

Her heart was beating frantically fast as her fingers
released the towel and he smiled, a slow burning smile
that turned her heart inside out. Later she had no recollection of moving forward to join him in that glass
cubicle. He soaked her hair and ran the soap over her
voluptuous figure with lascivious thoroughness. As he
teased her she became less self-conscious and was still
giggling when she watched him pull on trousers over
his boxers.

Alexei extended a lazy hand. 'Want to come with
me? We could spend the rest of the night in my room.'

Thinking of all the women he had entertained there
and the household staff who would soon register her
presence in their employer's bedroom, Billie shook her

head, her amusement killed stone dead in its tracks. It would be like announcing their intimacy and the news would go round the island faster than the speed of light. Lauren would smirk at her as if she had known all along that her daughter was a fool. 'I'll wait here for you.'

'Lazybones,' Alexei mocked, tugging on his shirt and thrusting his feet into his shoes.

Bare-chested, his hair spiky from the shower and with a heavy growth of black stubble on his handsome face, Alexei resembled a very sexy pirate. Her heart pounded as hard as if she were running a marathon. The instant he stepped out of the bedroom into the adjoining reception room that formed part of the guest suite she was gripped by a strong sense of loss. Soon it would be dawn, soon the night would be over—would what they had just shared die along with the night hours? Filled with dismay by that enervating suspicion, Billie scrambled out of bed, pulled on her wrap and went after him.

As she left the bedroom she heard Alexei vent a startled curse in Greek and then there was a noise she didn't recognise, followed by silence. She hurried to the door that opened out onto the pool area and stared in horror at the sight of Alexei lying flat on the concrete, apparently having fallen down several steps. Her handbag lay on its side just outside the door. Oh, dear heaven, he had tripped over it!

'Alexei! *Alexei?*' she cried, kneeling down beside him and registering that he was unconscious.

Rising swiftly, she went to phone for help when a groan emanated from Alexei. Quick as a flash, she rushed back to his side. He was sitting up, clutching his head.

'Alexei? Are you all right?'

'Billie?' He focused on her with clear difficulty, a dazed aspect to his eyes. 'What happened?'

'You tripped and fell.'

Alexei levered himself upright, brushing down his clothes, and even though he was swaying he began walking back in a wavering line towards the main house.

'You should lie down for a minute.' She hurried ahead of him to open the door he was heading for and rested her hand on his arm before he could pass her. 'Let me call the doctor.'

'The doctor? What are you talking about?' Alexei countered flatly, frowning down at her restraining hand. 'I don't need a doctor.'

'You knocked yourself unconscious for a couple of minutes and it's always advisable to consult a doctor in those circumstances,' Billie pointed out anxiously, withdrawing her hand after the look he had given her. Only minutes ago he might have been sharing a bed with her, but her gesture had clearly struck him as too familiar by far. 'A head-scan might be a good idea as well.'

'Stop fussing, Billie. I'm not in the mood.' Alexei raked the black hair back off his face in a gesture of exasperation. 'My hair's damp and I'm not wearing any socks. I must have gone for a swim. That'll teach me to drink—I don't remember and I might have drowned myself.'

Billie frowned and looked down at her bare feet. He

thought he had gone swimming? He didn't remember. 'What's the last thing you recall?'

'Talking to Marina after the funeral,' he breathed tautly. 'I don't want to think about all that right now.'

'I know, but the fact that you can't remember everything means there's something wrong. You're confused,' Billie stated tightly.

'Don't be ridiculous,' Alexei derided. 'I'm not a child and I'm not confused either. I had a few drinks too many and now I'm paying the price for it. No offence intended, Billie, but right now I'd prefer my own company.'

A painful flush washed her heart-shaped face as if he had slapped her. That colour slowly waned to leave her pale as she looked steadily back at him. There was nothing there in his lean, hard-boned visage: no tenderness, intimacy, or even awareness that anything might be lacking. He had forgotten her as easily as one forgot a bad dream or something trivial. And, on a Drakos male's terms, a fleeting sexual episode *was* of the utmost triviality.

'Goodnight,' she said shakily. 'But I still think you ought to see a doctor.'

Already halfway across the salon, Alexei was no longer listening. For several minutes, Billie simply stood there, barefoot and naked but for a thin wrap. For the space of that time she couldn't believe that he had forgotten her and walked away with no intention of coming back. She imagined following him into his bedroom, telling him that he had made love to her, but what use would that be if he could not even recall the incident? Wouldn't she look pathetic? As if she was chasing after him?

But wasn't it downright dangerous that he was refusing to seek medical attention? He had hit his head hard enough to lose consciousness, however briefly. Obviously he had sustained an injury. It had been early evening when she saw him talking to his great-aunt, Lady Marina. He was suffering from a loss of memory but evidently convinced that, rather than amnesia caused by a head injury, an alcoholic blackout was at fault. Was it all right to leave him alone to go to bed? Anxiety fingered down her taut spine.

Billie knocked on Alexei's bedroom door. She was about to repeat the action when it flew open.

'What?' Alexei demanded curtly.

'Are you sure you're okay? No headache? Nausea? Dizziness?' she prompted.

'Go back to bed and stop fussing round me like a mother hen!' he urged with unhidden impatience.

Tears stinging her eyes at that label, which was about as far removed from sexy or desirable as could be, Billie did as she was told. Tomorrow morning though she would ring the village doctor and tell him about Alexei's fall.

Her bedding carried his scent and she buried her nose in a pillow and cried. Was it ridiculous to wonder if his forgetfulness regarding that crucial few hours could be subconsciously deliberate? Maybe he had forgotten about going to bed with her because he didn't want to remember that it had happened. And maybe fate was giving her a second chance, for what he didn't recall she didn't have to worry about. Now she could just go on as if nothing had happened, with the added comfort of not having to fret about what he thought of her for sleeping with him in the first place. Her job was safe.

But no matter how hard Billie worked at putting a positive spin on his inability to recall their short-lived intimacy, she failed to find solace in the fact. And the fear that he might have suffered a more serious injury than he was willing to consider destroyed her ability to sleep. So great was Billie's concern on that score that she phoned the village doctor as soon as the surgery opened and Dr Melas agreed to come up to the villa and check Alexei out…

CHAPTER SEVEN

BILLIE WAS SO tense that even the shallowest breaths were rattling through her lungs at too fast a rate. Lean, strong face set in grim lines, Alexei was seething with her and every inch a Greek tycoon in his proud bearing.

'You overstepped the mark. You skirt it all the time but today you went too far,' Alexei delivered in a tone of rebuke and command that was still raw-edged with anger. 'This is your last warning. Nobody is indispensable, so, if I once gave you the impression that you were, wipe that assumption from your mind. For what I pay you, I could find someone else equally efficient—'

'Yes, yes, I'm sure you could,' Billie inserted, her skin clammy with nervous perspiration, for he had never before spoken to her in such a tone or studied her with such censure.

'Don't interrupt me when I'm speaking!' Alexei launched down at her crushingly.

Billie buttoned her mouth up tight and gritted her teeth. She could feel the tears building up behind her eyes, tears of chagrin and hurt and shock at being treated like a lowly office junior who had messed up spectacularly.

'I did not need or wish to consult Dr Melas this

morning. And even had I needed to, it was for me to make that decision,' Alexei imparted succinctly. 'You wasted the good doctor's time. You lack perspective with regard to your role as an employee.'

Billie swallowed back angry defensive words and said with a determined lack of emotion, 'I was genuinely concerned about your health.'

Alexei dealt her a cold appraisal that cut her to the bone. 'That's way beyond your remit.'

'Yes. It won't happen again,' Billie told him woodenly.

Her colour high, she walked straight-backed back through the general office past the business team, who must have heard Alexei raise his voice to her, and returned to her office. Her only consolation was that Dr Melas had called in to talk to her before he left to stress that, although he had got nowhere with Alexei either, she *had* done the right thing in phoning him. He too wanted Alexei to see a neurologist and have a scan. Of course, wasn't Alexei just being his usual nonconformist self? Too stubborn to play safe and too convinced of his superhuman health and higher intelligence to take advice from lesser mortals? So that was the end of that road. She had overstepped her boundaries. For the moment, Alexei had forgotten their hours in the guest-suite bed. Would he ever remember? And did she even want him to?

His father's sudden death had left a couple of important business deals wide open and Alexei went straight to New York with his team to handle the fallout the next day. He stayed there for over a week, putting in workaholic hours, and followed it up with a similar week in London. Being left alone on the island shook Billie, as Alexei rarely left her behind. Her assistant, Kasia, had crumpled under the pressure of working for Alexei and had used her position as a springboard into a less taxing job elsewhere. Billie had yet to hire a replacement. Convinced that a break from her usual routine would do her good, she set off on a quarterly visit to a number of Alexei's European properties, where she checked out problems, new staff and authorised essential maintenance. She was in Venice, at his ancient palazzo, when Alexei decided to take some time off and cruise the Caribbean in his yacht, *Sea Queen*. He invited friends on board and several long-distance photos of gorgeous bikini-clad women appeared in the newspapers. Billie's heart sank like a stone and when she found herself poring over those pictures with a magnifying glass to see if she recognised any of the faces, she realised that jealousy and fear were eating her alive.

Yet how could she fear losing what she had never had? There was no commitment and no security in being a one-night stand. She'd had her moment and it had lasted for even less time than she might have hoped. And even while she scolded herself for being so foolish, she recognised that she already had a much more serious issue to worry about: her menstrual cycle had stopped dead in its tracks and her period was overdue.

That reality struck horror into Billie's bones. Furthermore, there was no way she could go down to the village pharmacy and purchase a pregnancy test or visit the doctor without the fear that her movements might become public knowledge. While she trusted Dr Melas, she had less faith in the other surgery staff with access to medical records. Juicy gossip on the island had a way of bypassing all the rules of confidentiality and travelling faster than the speed of light. For that reason, Billie caught the ferry to Athens and bought her pregnancy test there, carrying it out in the privacy of the small hotel room she booked for the night. The result was positive.

In complete shock she sat on the side of the bed and studied the test wand, her green eyes darkening with panic and pain. *Now what?* Nothing would ever be the same again, she acknowledged sickly. The child of a single parent, who had often mourned the lack of a father in her life, Billie was utterly devastated by this positive confirmation. From her teen years, she had prided herself on her common sense and the restraint she had utilised to ensure that she did not make the same mistakes as her mother had. But, even so, in spite of her awareness of the pitfalls of an unplanned pregnancy, here she was, just like Lauren, alone and pregnant by a man who had made no commitment to her. Her life was suddenly going badly wrong and it was all her own fault for sleeping with Alexei. Billie was appalled by her predicament.

And practising a conveniently short memory in respect of Alexei's amnesia would no longer be possible: *he* had made her pregnant. Sitting on the edge of the bed, she rocked back and forth in an unconsciously self-soothing motion while shame, self-loathing and regret flooded her. She had thought she was so clever, but she hadn't been half clever enough when it came to looking out for herself and her own interests. They had both been very foolish that night in letting passion triumph to the extent of running the totally unnecessary risk of her conceiving. Now, unhappily, it was evidently time to pay the piper and her reputation, her entire career, were dead in the water. Everyone would think that Alexei had always used her as a convenient body in his bed between affairs and just as many would think she had contrived to fall pregnant with an eye to the main chance. Mortified by that prospect, she breathed in deep. He was due back on Speros the next week and she would have to tell him. What choice did she have?

That it might not be that clear-cut a question became clear during the subsequent days. Panos phoned her from the yacht to ask her to transfer some computer files that were required.

'Not that I really think we're likely to need them with the boss otherwise occupied,' her colleague groaned.

'What's he occupied with?' Billie prompted as her fingers flew nimbly over the keyboard while she searched out the requested files.

'Not what, *who*,' Panos corrected wryly. 'There's a new, demanding lady on board *Sea Queen* and all of a sudden business is taking a back seat. We won't be back tomorrow. The cruise is being extended.'

In response to that announcement, Billie's heart started thumping very, very fast, her skin turning clammy. Of course she had guessed that Alexei would soon find a new woman but the reality of it actually happening hurt like hell. In fact she felt as if someone had knocked her chair over and sent her to the floor with a bone-jolting crash. 'Who is she?'

'An old flame, but one from well before my time— tall and blonde, with the looks of a supermodel… Calisto Bethune, recently divorced,' her colleague supplied.

Already winded by that metaphorical crash, now Billie felt as if she were being brutally kicked. She recognised that name, recalled the gossip. Calisto was possibly the only woman alive who had ever passed over Alexei in favour of another man and now it seemed she had returned to take a second bite from the same apple. Gripped by an awful obsessive need to know more, Billie got busy on the Internet and checked out Calisto. Now the childless ex-wife of a Swiss electronics tycoon, she was truly gorgeous, with a perfect face and a perfect body and a similar heritage to Alexei's own as she was from the upper echelons of Greek society.

Back on Speros that night, Billie phoned her aunt, Hilary, in the UK and talked until she was hoarse about what she had done and how it had all gone hideously wrong. As the sad tale unfolded Hilary made sympathetic sounds and exclamations that allowed Billie to feel that she was no longer quite as alone as she felt.

'I've been worrying about something like this happening for a long time,' her aunt confessed ruefully. 'You're in love with Alexei Drakos and were probably putting out encouraging signals. An opportunistic male like him was certain to take advantage at some stage and the night of the funeral was a given…'

'I just wanted to *be* there for him…'

'Well, don't be too tough on yourself. Plenty of

women have dreamt that same dream as you.' Hilary sighed with something less than tact. 'But what's done is done. Now you need to decide what you want to do and you have to spell out what happened that night to Alexei. Embarrassment shouldn't come into it. You and that baby you're carrying need support.'

But in the days that followed, nausea began to surface when a certain smell or taste made Billie's newly sensitive tummy roll and sent her rushing to the cloakroom. She came no closer to the answer of what to do next: to try to make such a revelation to Alexei on the phone struck her as out of the question, but the prospect of flying out to the yacht to break such news with his latest lady in residence seemed even more inappropriate. Increasingly, references to Calisto Bethune began to appear in the gossip columns and were soon accompanied by photos of what was referred to as the 'loved-up couple'. Billie saw a photo of Alexei and Calisto walking hand in hand, both of them tall, beautiful and coolly fashionable, and she thought sickly that the pair looked so well together that they might have been a match made in heaven.

Barely twenty-four hours after Billie had pored with agonised eyes over that picture, wondering if she had ever seen Alexei look so relaxed, he returned to the villa, having flown himself home in a helicopter. He strode into the office, black hair tousled by the breeze, his lean, dark, devastating face intent. There she was at her desk, her bright head inclined to her computer monitor, and as she glanced up, emerald-green eyes flying wide with surprise, a faint flush of pink warmed her porcelain skin. One look and she was metaphorically on her knees, desire quivering through her slight body in a guilty surge of awareness, heat bursting at the heart of her while her breasts swelled in response to the incitement of his presence.

'I didn't intend to stay away so long. I confess that I didn't want to come back to an empty house,' Alexei admitted abruptly. 'There are too many memories here.'

'Yes, of course there are,' Billie agreed in Greek, chiding herself for not making that same deduction from his unusually long absence; it had to be a challenge for him to walk into what had been so much his parents' home and relive their absence all over again. 'But concentrate on the good times.'

Alexei studied her with shrewd dark eyes, acknowledging that he had missed that bright, optimistic spirit of hers that refused to acknowledge negative outcomes. He was equally quick to recall their less than positive parting. 'I was too hard on you at our last meeting. You meant no harm.'

Her heartbeat thudding like a heavy pulse at the foot of her throat, Billie stood up. 'No, I was out of line,' she said awkwardly.

Alexei could feel the wall of cool withdrawal in her and wondered what was wrong. She didn't hold onto spite—at least she never had before. Her candour and relaxation around him were qualities he cherished and rare indeed among the women he met and worked with. Yet, for all the fact that she looked unexpectedly small and fragile, her eyes were evasive, her stance unnaturally stiff and her voice expressionless.

'You're almost as close to me as a relative, so why shouldn't you be the first to know? I believe I've met the woman I might marry,' he told her with a sudden shimmering smile of satisfaction.

It was a body blow and the shock was so great that Billie did not know how her trembling legs contrived to keep her upright. For so long she had deemed Alexei unobtainable with the wild free spirit of a male who might never want to settle down. Yet what could be more natural than that, having lost his family, he should be set on creating a new one to fill the void in his life? She had to force her gaze to remain on him. Exotic high cheekbones sun-burnished, dark black-lashed eyes bright as bronze, he had never looked more gorgeous. Or more out of reach. He hadn't just moved on, he had jumped ship into a new galaxy.

Marriage? He was planning to marry Calisto Bethune? Her semi-prepared opening speech about the accident by the pool and the prior episode in the guest suite was just blown out of the water by that declaration. She tried to be happy for him, she tried so hard, for what could be healthier than his new desire to commit to a single relationship? But there was a silent scream of pain and rejection inside her that would not be silenced. She carried his baby in her womb and, whether she had the right or otherwise, it was an agony for her to appreciate that he had had another woman in his bed and that he had fallen in love with her. Sex she thought she could bear because she was accustomed to bearing that knowledge from the sidelines of his life, but the concept of him loving one of his female entourage was more than she could stand.

'Congratulations.' Billie was pale as milk and she spoke with a fixed smile while she fought with all her might to conceal and dampen her true feelings of bitter jealousy and resentment. 'I assume you're talking about Calisto Bethune. I'm very happy for you both. Have you set a date?'

Alexei released a husky laugh and spread his hands in an immediate silencing motion. 'I'm not moving quite *that* fast, Billie. We're back together and that happened quickly enough. That is more than sufficient for the moment.'

Billie breathed again at that evidence of native caution while he went about giving her instructions for the party he wanted organised to officially introduce Calisto to his family. With her dark auburn head bent, she took rapid notes from Alexei while he stood by her desk. The aroma of the peachy scent he always associated with her assailed his nostrils. He thought it was soap or shampoo, rather than perfume, and he had always liked it. He found himself gazing down at the pale crescent of skin exposed at the nape of her neck. That little bit of bare skin exuded an oddly erotic appeal. For a split second he was tempted to bend down and press his mouth to that delicate fine-grained flesh that never took any colour from the sun. The urge made him tense in surprise and frown.

Straightening, he strode over to the French windows overlooking the flower bedecked terrace and superb gardens beyond the glass. There was a heaviness at his

groin, a ready sexual urgency that startled him. Was
it simply a reaction against the relationship he had recently revived? Too much familiarity and proximity
could breed more than contempt, he acknowledged
wryly. What had come over him? It was a source of
pride to him that, with the exception of one weak and
curious moment when he'd kissed her, he had never hit
on Billie. He was fond of her, had always been fond of
her, and he looked out for her much as though she were
one of his youthful cousins. There was an innocence
about Billie that he had always cherished.

Long after he had gone, Billie sat there wondering
what theme the caterers would dream up for the Drakos family bash. It was to take place in London. She
would ask if she could take that weekend off to see Hilary. Alexei would definitely not want her baby now and
that conviction cut through her like a knife, sending a
shard of pure panic travelling through her. The timing
of her conception could not have been worse; it might
wreck his romance if Calisto realised that she would
not be the mother of his firstborn child.

Did that mean that she should keep quiet? Could she
rise above her jealousy enough to let Alexei and Calisto continue to enjoy their happiness in finding each
other again? She knew she wasn't prepared to have an
abortion. That option had been discarded early on, even
though she had not yet admitted it to Hilary, who had
become the safe repository for most of Billie's turbulent
thoughts and feelings. But surely her only other choice
was to give up her child for adoption? That was another

painful sacrifice she could not face. After all, she might not be able to have Alexei, *but she could have his child*.

And if he had no memory of sharing her bed, he would have no suspicion that he had fathered her baby. On the other hand, she reflected ruefully, he would be so shocked by her having a child out of wedlock that he would not rest until she had told him who the father was. He might have accused her of overstepping the line but, in truth, it had always been Alexei who was most inclined to interfere in *her* private life. Furthermore, if she wanted to keep her baby, how was she to afford to do so?

She earned a terrific salary, but she had poured every cent she earned into the building of her house, the price of that project far exceeding the original estimates. For the next year her earnings were committed to completing the house, which would be ready for occupation in six months' time. A house she could never sell except at a bargain price, for all island property had to be offered to the locals first and it would be too expensive for most of them to consider. With single parenthood staring her in the face she could not afford to write off or sell her only asset at a huge loss, particularly when Alexei's generous gift of that plot of land with panoramic sea views had to be reflected in ensuring he received a fair percentage share of any sale.

In short, Billie appreciated she was financially trapped on the island of Speros for the foreseeable future. She could not jack in her job either while she needed to settle the bills for the house. Her *dream* house, she reflected painfully, had suddenly become a burden, an anchor tying her to a place and a job that she now wanted to leave. After all, how could she stand by and watch while Alexei romanced and married his long-lost first love? Getting ready for bed that evening, she studied her still-flat stomach with anxiety and wondered how much time she had before her condition became obvious.

Hilary was not impressed by her niece's arguments against making Alexei aware of her pregnancy. 'So, he's spoken for now, well, bully for him!' she snorted the following night when Billie phoned for a chat. 'But he still has a big responsibility towards you and any other woman he impregnates!'

'Legally, yes, but I don't want or need his support...'

'Don't be so proud that you cut off your nose to spite your face,' Hilary pleaded. 'It's unfortunate that at this point he's met another woman and it seems to be serious, but that is not your responsibility.'

'He's happy. I don't want to wreck it,' Billie confided heavily. 'In addition, since he's forgotten what happened that night, telling him and convincing him will be a very undignified battle...'

'Even a Drakos can't fight a DNA test,' Hilary opined. 'Perhaps it would be as well to wait until the baby is born before making a claim.'

'I really don't want his money, Hilary. I'm more concerned about finding a way to keep my baby and stay in my job.'

'But how on earth could you do that and work at the same time? If you're thinking of Lauren helping out, I don't think—'

'Of course I'm not—'

'If only it was me that lived on the island and not my sister, the problem would be solved,' Hilary commented. 'I would love to look after your baby.'

'Well, you could if you were willing to move out here. My new house has plenty of room. Of course you couldn't leave John,' Billie realised, referring to her uncle who was living in a care home where Hilary visited him almost every day.

'John might not be here for much longer,' her aunt divulged tautly. 'He's fading away before my eyes.'

'I'm so sorry,' Billie responded, having also refused to think about the near impossibility of concealing her baby's parentage if she tried to raise her child on the island. 'I was lost in this wonderful daydream of having you here on the spot, instead of thousands of miles away. I was being silly.'

'No, if it wasn't for John, I would agree like a shot. I would just love a fresh start, new faces, new possibilities...' Hilary confided breathlessly.

The germ of an audacious idea came to Billie. 'I think I know how we could do it and nobody would ever be able to guess that it was Alexei's baby.'

And that was the moment that the plan of concealment was born, laid out at first to an unimpressed Hilary, who thought her niece was utterly crazy to suggest such a thing; there was no question of Hilary leaving her sick husband alone in the UK. 'But who would ever believe that your baby was mine?'

'Why not? You're only thirty-eight. Nobody here but Lauren knows about John's illness,' Billie argued with growing enthusiasm. 'And we wouldn't have to live the lie for ever, Hilary. Once I'd saved enough money up, I'd sell the house and find another job and we would leave the island with the secret intact. But there would be no need to continue the pretence once we settled somewhere new—'

'Even if I was ever in a position to help you, Lauren would know we were lying—'

'I'm sure we could persuade Mum to keep quiet. Hilary, if it was possible—it would allow me to keep my baby without causing a big furore,' Billie reasoned fiercely. 'Please think it over and say yes.'

'If it's what you really want, I would do it simply because I love babies and I'd love to live on the island. But not while John is still alive. He may not recognise me most of the time when I visit,' Hilary admitted painfully as she referred to her husband's dementia, 'but he does have occasional moments when he's quite lucid. I know he hasn't long left but let's not talk about the impossible right now.'

'No, let's not,' Billie said, guiltily aware of her insensitivity.

'I don't understand how you're planning to hide the fact that you're pregnant from Alexei,' Hilary declared.

'I'll conceal it for as long as I can and then I'll ask Alexei to give me a career break so that I can return to England to stay with you for a while. It's a reasonable request.'

'If you give birth here you could leave the baby with me to look after. I haven't been able to find another permanent teaching job yet and I could manage fine,' her aunt asserted. 'It wouldn't be easy for you to leave your child behind with me but I'd love him or her like my own.'

'I know you would,' Billie replied warmly.

Billie slept right through that night for the first time since she had discovered that she was pregnant. In the dawn light she wakened and ran back over the plan, worrying over the weak spots while wincing over the idea of plunging both herself and her aunt into living a lie. No solution would be perfect or foolproof, she reasoned frantically, but one that ensured her child enjoyed loving care and security would definitely be worth bending a few rules for. She splayed her hand over the deceptive flatness of her stomach. She wanted to keep her baby; she wanted her unborn child very, very much. In the short term, if nobody was harmed by her concealing her secret, surely a few lies could be no great sin?

The next day, Damon Marios asked her to meet him at the site of her new house to discuss the terrace. She had hired him to not only design her new home, but also as project manager to supervise the building, ensuring that she endured minimal disruption to her life. In the slumberous heat of the afternoon, Billie drove up the rough gravelled lane and parked at the edge of the site beside Damon's SUV, wondering how she would ever turn the baked-dry dustbowl of her surroundings into a garden.

'I thought we'd have some lunch while we talked,' Damon remarked, a smile on his handsome face as he indicated the picnic lunch already artfully arranged in the shade of a gnarled olive tree.

'Oh...what a lovely idea,' Billie said in surprise, lowering herself down onto the rug with a soft sigh. Damon offered her food while trying to persuade her to do something more elaborate with the terrace than had been planned. 'The views are so spectacular,' he pointed out.

Billie breathed in deep and shook her head at the wine he offered in favour of the bottled water. 'I'm afraid I want the house finished as soon as possible and I would prefer not to incur any extra expense. I do still have to furnish it!'

Scanning the taut pallor of her face, Damon frowned. 'You've been so stressed these past weeks, Billie. What's wrong?'

His perceptive powers were unwelcome and her face tightened and she munched busily at her sandwich, finally pausing to murmur, 'Nothing's wrong. The summer heat here sometimes tires me out—that's all.'

'Alexei does like to get his pound of flesh. I don't know how you stand the pace. And if the press are on the right track, he's got that bitch Calisto back to keep him busy.'

Billie stiffened. 'Why do you call her that?'

'If she is back in Alexei's life to stay, you'll soon find out. According to my mother, Calisto was horrible to the household staff at the villa last time around...a real diva. There's also a rumour that his parents disliked her so much they threatened to disinherit him and that that's why she married Bethune instead.'

'People change and she was young,' Billie said wryly.

Damon reached for her hand. 'We used to be close friends, Billie.'

'I hope we still are.' Billie gently slid her hand free again.

'But I'd like us to be something more than friends,' Damon was honest enough to admit as he retrieved her fingers with dogged determination.

And it was at that opportune moment that Alexei strolled out of the back of the house and stood lazily studying them from the shadows. Black hair swept back from his brow, sunglasses anchored on his arrogant nose and sheathed in a soft grey summer-weight suit, he was as stylish and sophisticated in appearance as a model on a catwalk. 'Don't mind me,' he urged silkily. 'I thought it was time I came for a look around.'

Instantly, Damon released Billie's hand and sprang up. 'Let me give you the official tour.'

'I didn't hear a car,' Billie commented.

'I walked over from the villa,' Alexei fielded, eyes framed by dark-as-midnight lashes skimming over her blushing face. 'Sorry if I interrupted something.'

'You didn't,' Billie countered flatly, tugging her skirt down to her knees and reaching defiantly for another sandwich.

The two men walked round the house while Billie sat outside in the shade, fed up with both of them as she listened to snatches of their revealing dialogue. Damon was so deferential around Alexei that he set her teeth on edge and Alexei had no business declaring that a larger terrace was a necessity, rather than an extravagant extra. And what was Damon playing at? Why did men always refuse to take no for an answer? How many times did she have to tell him that she wasn't interested now in dating him?

Alexei reappeared and asked her for the keys of the car she had driven over, which did after all belong to him. 'Come back with me. I have some calls for you to make.'

Ignoring Damon's look of disappointment, Billie scrambled up and smoothed down her skirt. Red-hot temper made her hands tremble a little. It was not that she wanted to stay and risk encouraging Damon, it was resentment at being smoothly manipulated into doing what Alexei wanted her to do.

'You're about to overstep the boundaries again,' she warned Alexei fiercely as she climbed into the hot car with him.

'He's not the guy for you. A bloody picnic on a building site…' he breathed with incredulous derision. 'How cool is that?'

'If I listened to you, I'd never get a guy! Every time one comes near me, you interfere and stick a spoke in the wheels. I'd like to know how you justify that when I'm not even allowed to call a doctor if you hurt yourself!' Billie launched back at him in an angry hail of words that she shot at him like bullets.

'You can trust me to put your interests first,' he drawled with unblemished assurance, his bold bronzed profile relaxed. 'Damon will most probably end up returning to his wife and children. Don't get caught up in their drama.'

'Working for you I've got enough drama of my own!'

Billie bawled back at him, turning up the air conditioning with an impatient hand, ignoring it when he winced at the furious rush of icy air directed at him. 'You have no right to interfere. I'm an adult entitled to make my own mistakes. Stay out of my private life!'

And she sat there thinking how ridiculous it was for her to argue with him when she was carrying his child, to be able to shout but not to tell him the truth. But he would pity her if he knew the truth and he would feel very guilty. She knew him well enough to make that forecast and although her heart ached inside her like an open wound she was painfully aware that neither his pity nor his guilt, and certainly not his money, would provide her with the smallest comfort...

CHAPTER EIGHT

IN THE WEEKS that followed, Billie began to gather unwelcome information about Calisto Bethune, a woman she had never met who, it seemed, had a way of making her mark wherever she went. Calisto trod on toes without fear, she hurt and insulted with constant criticism, she demanded and screamed abuse if she didn't get what she wanted fast enough. Sooner or later, all staff complaints about Calisto ended up on Billie's desk. It seemed to her that every employee who came into too close contact with the gorgeous blonde whom Alexei was planning to marry hated her.

'If you're not prepared to make an official complaint, there's nothing I can do,' Billie told a sobbing stewardess from the yacht. 'Mrs Bethune is Alexei's partner. You'll have to get used to her ways.'

'She's so rude. I'm not her slave! If she speaks to me like that one more time, I'm quitting!'

'You could make this complaint official,' Billie pointed out for the third time.

The stewardess grimaced. 'I don't want anything on paper…you know Mr Drakos has promised my brother a job when he finishes school. I wouldn't want to take the risk of offending him.'

Billie suppressed a sigh, for she had heard it all before too many times. Nobody ever wanted to annoy Alexei. Everyone wanted to stay on the right side of him. It meant that he sailed through life on a sea as smooth and flat as glass, protected from the ripples and storms that lesser mortals endured.

The chef on *Sea Queen* had already quit after a volley of censure from Calisto over a meal she had disliked. One of Alexei's most choice and favoured employees, the chef had long had secret offers from others keen to poach his renowned skills. When Alexei professed surprise that Billie had not contrived to dissuade his chef from leaving his employ, Billie decided to be more honest.

'Your girlfriend offended him. I tried to persuade him to stay but he wouldn't change his mind.'

'Calisto is very forthright.'

'The chef isn't the only one of your employees with a problem with that,' Billie dared.

Every inch an arrogant Drakos in his bearing, Alexei lifted a questioning ebony brow. 'Are you saying that there have been complaints?'

'Nothing official, but some employees are finding her manner hard to handle.'

Alexei compressed his wide sensual mouth into a forbidding line. 'Then they'll have to learn to be less sensitive. I won't tolerate disrespect towards her.'

'Of course not,' Billie declared, inwardly castigating herself for not having the gumption to warn him that Calisto was a demon with staff and that few would long withstand her vicious temper and verbal abuse.

No doubt when people began to leave he would get the message, but there was no way that Billie could bring herself to be more frank right now.

'How are you feeling?' he asked.

'Me?' Billie questioned in surprise. 'Why are you asking me that?'

Alexei released his breath in an impatient hiss. 'Anatalya told me that you've been unwell for quite a few weeks. I would have preferred to hear that from you.'

Billie's face flamed and then lost colour again. Her entire skin surface dampened with nervous tension below her clothing. How foolish of her to overlook the likelihood that the housekeeper would notice the attacks of nausea she had tried so hard to conceal!

'Did you consult the doctor?'

'Er...no,' she admitted grittily.

'So I'm not the only person around here who avoids medical advice,' Alexei noted mockingly.

'I caught a bug and it took a while to shake off. That's all,' Billie retorted with a jerky lift of her shoulders that dismissed the topic as trivial. 'I'm fine now.'

That weekend she flew to London to check that the events planner, Janine, had all the arrangements in hand for Calisto and Alexei's party. The ballroom of Alexei's town house was exquisitely decorated for an event that promised to be the most fashionable of the season. Billie checked her profile in a mirror, noting with relief that the loose jacket of her suit still concealed her thickening waistline and softly curving stomach. Mercifully, she had got over her nausea and at three months pregnant was now anxiously noticing that the changes in her shape were beginning to accelerate. She reckoned that within another six weeks other people might begin to suspect her secret. Within the next fortnight she would have to tackle Alexei about her proposed career break. In readiness, she had already advertised for a new assistant to be trained up to take over during her absence.

She was walking through the back door of the ballroom when she heard a woman calling Janine's name.

'Calisto…' Janine was saying in a rather strained welcome; the party planner had confided to Billie that Calisto kept on changing her mind about what she wanted.

Billie spun around and glanced back apprehensively over her shoulder. Calisto was casually turned out in a red dress, a black leather jacket and high-heeled sandals. Even at a glance the Greek woman was a striking beauty with a magnificent blonde mane of hair and amazingly long legs. Billie had only to think of those incredible legs wrapped round Alexei's lean bronzed body to feel sick and she backed away from the door before she could be seen and walked hurriedly away. Once again she had avoided a face-to-face meeting with Alexei's fiancée. She had twice sidestepped encounters on the yacht. Indeed, since Calisto's appearance on the scene, Billie had stayed very much in the background of Alexei's life and he had yet to bring Calisto back to Speros for a visit. But then, the happy couple were both very busy people who spent a lot of time on board *Sea Queen*. Calisto, whose once stalled career had taken off again on the strength of her new high profile with

Alexei and his A-list friends, was currently accepting modelling assignments across the globe.

Billie had arranged to spend the weekend with Hilary. Her aunt's husband—John—had passed away a month earlier and although Billie had flown over to the UK to attend the funeral she had not been able to stay on. But in spite of the open invitation to all his personal staff she had no intention of attending Alexei's family party. She was jealous and hurting inside and no matter how hard she fought not to feel and think that way she was failing.

'I've decided that I'm coming to Greece,' Hilary informed her niece. 'Once your baby's born, I'll put this house up for rent so that I have somewhere to come back to if I want to.'

Billie hugged her aunt. 'It'll make such a difference to my life and to the baby's. I just hope you're not only doing this for my sake.'

'Of course I'm not. I'm planning to write a book on King Henry IV and the House of Lancaster. Ever since university I've wanted to do it. I'll be able to do my research over the next few months with the help of the Internet,' the older woman told her with an enthusiasm that Billie hadn't seen her show in years.

'I'll be able to help you,' Billie added. 'I won't have much else to do while I'm getting through the rest of my pregnancy.'

But that prospect seemed a blessing once she saw a photo of Calisto in the fabulous ballgown she had worn for the party in the next day's newspaper. In every way Alexei was fulfilling his destiny. His family expected him to marry a woman as large as life as he was himself and Calisto, with her beauty, fame and connections, certainly fitted the bill. Billie felt another crack form in her breaking heart. She was beginning to marvel that she had ended up in bed with Alexei in the first place. That could surely only have happened because he was drunk and grieving, which was neither a comforting nor ego-boosting suspicion for her to hold.

Two weeks later, Billie was in Milan with Alexei when she broached the subject of her career break over the working lunch they were sharing.

Alexei glanced up to study her with frowning force. Her burnished copper streaked hair glinting in the sunshine, she tilted her heart-shaped face back and looked back at him with wide wary eyes as green as limes. 'Surely this is very sudden?' he queried. 'Where has this idea come from?'

'I've been thinking about it for a while. I'd like to spend some time back in England with my aunt. She could do with the support.'

'She lost her husband recently,' Alexei recalled, surprising Billie. 'Well, I have every sympathy, but I'm not prepared to tolerate some idiot trying to do your job for the next six months—'

'For a minimum of *eight* months,' Billie corrected before he could contrive to try and bargain down the duration of her absence. 'I need a break, Alexei… I really do *need* the break.'

'I don't understand why.'

'I would come back to work refreshed.'

From below lush black lashes that any woman would

have killed to possess, Alexei looked her over with keen bronze-coloured eyes of enquiry. He didn't think she looked in need of refreshment, although he was prepared to admit that she had got a little too thin in recent months, so that her clothes seemed to have become too big for her slight frame. He sensed that something was being concealed from him. 'What's really wrong?'

Her gaze took on an evasive slant. 'I just want a break and…' in a nervous flicker of motion her tongue crept out to moisten her dry lips as she braced herself to tell her first lie '…my aunt is pregnant and alone and she could do with my support.'

Alexei watched stinging colour warm her cheeks and wondered why she was blushing. Perhaps it was not the late husband's posthumous baby but the result of a fling with someone else since. He suppressed a sigh: Billie to the rescue. That made perfect sense to him. His wide sensual mouth flattened. 'I don't want you to take a break now. I consider you a vital member of my staff.'

'You've met Olympia. I'm training her to take my place.'

'Olympia skulks behind doors when I'm around. That isn't promising—'

'But that's better than a young woman who continually throws herself in your path,' Billie pointed out, well aware of how often that desire afflicted women in his radius and of how exasperating he found such behaviour. Yet she had never had the heart to judge a single one of those women when she herself had always been far too susceptible to Alexei's charisma.

'I can tell you now that Olympia won't cut it,' Alexei told her very drily.

Billie tilted her chin. 'She'll have to because I need you to agree to this career break.'

'I'll consider it.' Alexei's rich dark drawl carried more than a touch of ice. 'But why don't you consider basing yourself in my London headquarters for eight months instead? That would be a more sensible option and it would still give you a change of scene and new colleagues.'

Unprepared for that very reasonable suggestion, Billie stiffened in dismay. 'I would really rather have a complete break from my current employment.'

Alexei made her wait for a week for a final answer. She had thought she might have to remind him and her nerves suffered while she waited; if he refused she would have to hand in her resignation. He called her into his office shortly before he was due to fly out to Paris for the weekend. She entered the room, stiff-backed as she tried to shrink inside her jacket, lest the fabric fall revealingly against the small swelling mound of her stomach.

'I'm not in agreement with this career break as you call it,' Alexei informed her without hesitation, his dark golden eyes grim and cool. 'It'll be a nuisance, but you've worked well for me for some years now and I am conscious of that. When do you want to go on leave?'

'At the end of the month,' she told him, weak with relief but taut with guilt at the tangle of deception that she was embarking on.

But she could not see a choice. Although an engagement had yet to be announced, Calisto was already said to be consulting wedding planners. Billie could only hope that the marriage would take place before her return. The passage of time, she told herself urgently, would cure her of sleepless nights and the erotic longings that embarrassed the hell out of her.

She wasn't herself any more. It was as if Alexei had picked her up and shaken her so that nothing inside her was in the right place any more. She was at the mercy of her hormones, of passionate crying jags and, sometimes, wild crazy thoughts and hopes. Distance would cure her, give her the chance to get over him, she told herself fiercely, because if she was planning to return to work for Alexei, she needed to grow a tougher skin.

'You and my sister are thick as thieves at present,' Lauren remarked when her daughter came to say her goodbyes, her burgeoning tummy carefully concealed below a loose T-shirt and a canvas jacket. 'When are you planning to tell me what's really going on?'

Billie ducked the question and gave Lauren a guilty hug, wondering how she would ever face telling the truth to her mother, who was sure to have some very cutting comments to make when the time came. But all that really mattered to her at that moment was that, step by step, her plan was working…

EIGHT MONTHS LATER, as she'd promised, Billie made her return to Speros. She stood on the ferry with Hilary and Nikolos, who had become known as Nicky within days of his birth. She pointed out landmarks on the island to Hilary, who was glowing with enthusiasm by her side. With her short blonde hair tousling in the breeze, her aunt's brown eyes were alight with curiosity and excitement.

'So that's your house…my new home,' Hilary breathed, straining to see the small dwelling to the right of the vast Drakos compound. 'And that massive yacht out there is *Sea Queen*? I had no idea the yacht was as big as a cruise liner.'

'You'll be able to come on aboard and tour the yacht on St George's Day,' Billie commented. 'The whole island takes a holiday for the festival of *Agios Georgios* and although it's the celebration of the saint that the village church is dedicated to, there's also a lot of fun with bonfires on the beach and loads of food and drink.'

'I'm looking forward to it. I remember you talking about it a couple of years ago,' Hilary admitted. 'Isn't it typical that Nicky has finally fallen asleep?'

Billie gave her infant son a rueful look. That was Hilary's polite way of saying that Nicky had been a little horror for most of the journey from London, evidently disliking the changes in his usual routine. He had cried for most of the flight and had refused to settle in between times. Offers of bottles, changes and cuddles had made no impression on his general dissatisfaction with life.

'I can't wait to see my house. The photos Damon emailed only whet my appetite.' Billie's arm was aching and she shifted Nicky to her other shoulder, where he continued to doze, his little breathy snuffles sounding in her ear. He was a surprisingly heavy bundle for a baby of only three months old. She stroked his back, wondering how she would bear working for hours away from him every day but knowing that, like millions of other working mothers, she had no choice.

Lauren greeted them at the harbour and made a beeline for the baby, who was now in Hilary's arms. 'So this is my…nephew,' she exclaimed, and it seemed to her daughter that there was a deliberate hesitation over that designation. 'My goodness, he looks older than three months and he's rather Mediterranean in his colouring, isn't he? I wonder who he got all that black hair from—'

'Don't exaggerate, Lauren. He's not a baby werewolf.' Hilary reclaimed the sleepy baby from her sister and clambered after Billie into the village taxi.

'What colour are his eyes?'

'Brown.' Billie avoided the hard stare her mother was subjecting her to from the front passenger seat.

Mercifully the new house took over as the topic of conversation. Billie had had furniture and household effects ready in storage before she even left the island and Lauren and Alexei's housekeeper, Anatalya, had worked together to find a place for everything. The two women had done a great job, but Billie realised that the furnishings looked sparse, particularly when the wood and tiled floors and white walls were bare of any adornment.

'It's so light and bright!' Hilary carolled, walking out onto the terrace where Billie was already admiring the wonderful panoramic view of the bay. 'It's amazing, a fabulous house and so spacious. Should we put Nicky down for a nap?'

'You're his mother, darling. Surely that should be your decision,' Lauren interposed with suggestive bite.

'He's the most beautiful baby!' Anatalya exclaimed in admiration, bridging the awkward moment between the three women related by blood.

Nicky was settled in his nursery where a musical mobile was switched on for his entertainment. He watched it with wide unblinking dark eyes and then his little face creased and he began to grizzle and complain.

'I think the mobile is irritating him,' Hilary opined.

Billie switched it off.

'So the baby rules the roost,' Lauren remarked from the doorway. 'Is it, by any chance…a Drakos baby?'

'Shush!' Billie hissed at her mother in shock. 'Don't even breathe an insinuation like that!'

'I worked it out a long time ago. That's why he gave you the building plot next door—'

'Billie!' Anatalya called.

Relieved by the excuse to move, Billie slid past her mother to answer the older woman, whose plump smiling face was set in an unusual expression of discomfiture as she returned a mobile phone to her pocket. 'What is it?'

'Thespinis Calisto has just phoned me to say that she would like to see you immediately.'

Billie swallowed hard. As Lauren broke into rude comment Billie gave her mother's arm a warning squeeze. 'She's probably going to be my boss's wife, so although I don't start back to work officially until tomorrow I had better show willing.'

'I'll soon find my way around. Nicky and we'll be fine,' Hilary declared.

Billie got into Anatalya's beat-up old car. Alexei was heading home from Australia and not due back until later that night. And here Billie was finally heading for the meeting she had managed to avoid for months. 'Do I address her now as Miss Calisto or Mrs Bethune?' she asked the older woman.

'She told us all to call her the first. We all find her difficult,' the housekeeper admitted heavily. 'She has new ideas about the way we do everything at the villa.'

'Well, that's to be expected,' Billie quipped with determined good cheer. *What can't be cured must be endured* had become her personal mantra in recent months.

Calisto elected to see her in Alexei's office. She was still gorgeous, all blonde hair, white teeth and long legs displayed to advantage by a fluorescent pink dress.

'So you're Billie,' the statuesque blonde pronounced, treating her husband's employee to a head-to-toe unimpressed appraisal, her lips curling with scorn. 'There's loads of things going wrong at Alexei's properties because you've taken too much time off.'

'I'm sorry. It's unfortunate that my replacement didn't work out.'

'You're very lucky to have a job to come back to.' Calisto lifted a sheet of paper and extended it in a regal gesture of command. A whiff of her expensive perfume engulfed Billie. 'I've made a list of the most important things you need to take care of. I hope you're planning on working late tonight.'

'No, not tonight. I've been travelling since early this morning. But I'll make a start now,' Billie declared equably, glancing down at the entries on the paper. It was not a factual list of tasks, rather a long list of complaints that appeared to range from a poorly maintained swimming pool to impertinent domestic staff and finally colour and furnishing schemes that Alexei's consort wanted changed. 'I'll soon get it all sorted out.'

'See that you do. Alexei likes things to run like clockwork. He has no patience for cock-ups and neither do I. He says you're very efficient and this is your chance to prove it.'

Billie nodded and went to the door that led through to her own office space.

'I believe you organise things here for *Agios Georgios* day,' Calisto remarked in sudden addition. 'Do you think you could cancel the open house reception here at the villa?'

'It became a tradition when Alexei's father was a boy.'

'Yes, well, we're the new generation and I like my privacy. I don't fancy the local fisherfolk marching through our home. Make sure it doesn't happen.'

Billie said nothing, for it was not within her power to make such a decision. She suspected that Alexei, who had great respect for island tradition and hospitality, would insist that the usual arrangements went ahead.

That night she slept in her new house for the first time, the smell of fresh paint and new furniture in her nostrils. She wakened very early, fed and dressed Nicky, who was squirming with morning liveliness in his cot, and decided to go for a swim before getting ready for work. Hilary didn't fancy swimming at that hour and prepared breakfast to eat out on the terrace.

The beach on the other side of the narrow coastal road was a stretch of pale golden sand. Billie shed her towelling robe on a rock and waded into the water, shivering at the chill of it. The water was colder than she had expected and she realised that she had been spoiled by the temperature of the Drakos swimming pool. After a vigorous swim to warm up, she had walked back up the beach before she realised that she was no longer alone.

Alexei, casually dressed in faded jeans and a black sweater, and with dark stubble outlining his stubborn jawline and wilful sensual mouth, strode across the sand towards her. 'I saw you from the villa,' he drawled with a smile. 'England has made you hardier. That water is icy.'

'A little colder than I expected,' Billie conceded, her full attention welded to him for their first meeting in eight interminable months. And he did not disappoint her. Even fresh and unshaven from Calisto's bed, a thought that sent a sharp slicing arrow of pain through her, Alexei looked stunningly handsome. Furthermore, his aura of raw energy and white-hot sexuality hit her like a force field. A tingle of urgent heat speared between her legs and she came to a sudden halt, trying not to shiver from awareness as much as from cold.

Long before he had reached her, Alexei had noted the full lush silhouette of her breasts and hips in the swimsuit. Had her curves always been that pronounced, that spectacular? Surely not? With her Titian hair trailing in wet dark red ribbons against her white skin and her nipples protruding through the clinging fabric, she was intensely sexy, and as his body reacted his jeans grew tight. He didn't fight it either, but he was frantically striving to work out how she could have that effect on him when her hair was in a mess, she wore no make-up and her costume was as old as the hills.

Self-consciousness made Billie hurry on until she could grasp her robe, pull it on and turn back to him. Although she had lost almost all her pregnancy weight, her breasts had gained a cup size and her stomach, no matter how hard she sucked it in, now had a slightly rounded curve.

'You're never getting a career break again,' Alexei warned her. 'Things I took for granted have gone hay-wire without you.'

'I'll hit the ground running,' she promised him.

'Bring your aunt up to join Calisto and me for dinner tonight,' he told her. 'What do you think of your house?'

'It's wonderful.'

'Damon actually pulled it off.'

Her eyes gleamed emerald. 'With a lot of interference from you.'

'He's back with his wife and kids where he belongs,' Alexei told her. 'I was on target there, wasn't I?'

'I'm glad they're back together.' Billie refused to rise to the bait he offered. 'I'd better get back home or I'll be late.'

'I believe you have an understanding employer.' Brilliant bronzed eyes held hers for a long moment and her tummy performed a somersault. 'I noticed your absence, *moraki mou*.'

Without warning, hot burning tears pricked the backs of her eyes. With a forced smile and a clumsy wave, she sped off back home. She spent a busy day working and asked Anatalya's daughter to babysit for her that evening.

Hilary was very impressed by the dinner invitation and fussed over what she wore. 'We're keeping his son from him. I can't afford to like him,' she said uneasily.

'It's a lovely welcome to the island for you.'

'I'm dying to see Alexei's home, and the gilded lifestyle of a billionaire!' Hilary rolled her eyes with humour.

It was fortunate that Hilary was in an upbeat mood, for Calisto could not have made her dislike of the occasion and the guests more obvious. Alexei drew out Hilary's intention of writing a book about King Henry IV, while Calisto sighed, wrinkled her classic nose and yawned with boredom before rising to put on music at a volume that made it difficult to continue the conversation. Billie saw Alexei glance at his fiancée and knew he was annoyed. Whatever faults he had, generosity and courtesy towards guests were sacrosanct to him. His shrewd gaze rested on Billie for an instant and she reddened fiercely, hoping he couldn't sense her uncharitable thoughts.

'I'm glad I got the chance to meet Calisto,' Hilary told her niece late that evening. 'How can Alexei be in love with a woman like that? He's a clever, cultivated man and she's a spoiled brat with no manners and, I suspect, pretty dim—'

'Let's face it, you're biased. She *is* a very beautiful woman.'

'That won't be enough to sustain a durable relationship.'

'Alexei is no fool. He must see something in Calisto that we don't,' Billie responded heavily.

'Maybe you should come clean with him about Nicky—'

'No! Why are you saying that now?' Billie demanded in dismay.

'You should tell him before he gets married to another woman. It wouldn't be fair to either him or his wife if you dumped the news on them afterwards.'

'He's not planning on getting married yet.' That question settled, Billie cuddled Nicky, her son a drowsy and sweet-smelling weight in her protective arms. He was adorable. She could not imagine Alexei as a father, only as a lover, and that was a discomfiting realisation. She tucked her child back into his cot and wished him goodnight.

The minute she told Alexei that Nicky was his, her whole life would change, because she would hardly be able to continue in her job. In addition, what relationship she did have with Alexei would be destroyed. An inner chill pierced her deep at that prospect. Shorn of the memory of their sexual encounter, he wouldn't believe her story. Initially she would just seem like another one of the gold-digging women who had tried to entrap a share of his huge wealth.

No, Billie decided doggedly, having gone to such lengths to conceal her secret, she would be very careful to pick the optimum moment to tell Alexei the truth. When that precise moment came, her sixth sense would tell her...

CHAPTER NINE

TWO WEEKS LATER, the celebration of *Agios Giorgios* began with a parade to the little church down by the harbour and a celebratory service, which Alexei and most of his staff attended.

A buffet lunch for all followed at the Drakos villa, where games and amusements were laid on for the island children. As a former teacher Hilary was a great help with organising fun activities to keep the children occupied. At Calisto's request, Billie had made arrangements for a private lunch for Alexei, Calisto and their house guests, but Alexei excused himself from the meal in the isolation of the separate dining room and attended the villagers' buffet instead. That there was tension between him and his girlfriend was obvious to everyone.

Billie watched him circulate. He cut a flawless figure in a superbly tailored silk-blend grey suit while his air of command and self-assurance left no one in any doubt of his elite status. But he mixed with the villagers at a much more comfortable level than his late father, Constantine, ever had. He kicked a stray ball back to the boys playing football on his immaculate lawns.

'Tell Alexei I want to speak to him,' Calisto instructed Billie, who was watching over events from the shade of the terrace.

Billie glanced at the beautiful blonde, gloriously if impractically clad in a pure white dress that was low of neck and very short of skirt. Her mouth compressing into an apologetic line as she approached Alexei, she did as she was asked.

His lean, darkly handsome features took on a forbidding aspect and Billie marvelled at Calisto's lack of savvy about the man she was hoping to marry. In certain moods, Alexei needed lots of space. A woman who clung or demanded more attention at that point could only infuriate him. And summoning him through a third party, who was also an employee, was an absolute no-no.

'Calisto and I will go out to *Sea Queen* now,' Alexei imparted. 'I'll leave you to oversee the transfer of our visitors.'

Billie nodded, sensing the anger he was controlling, grateful she was not the target. Alexei could be so unpredictable and volatile and she sensed that Calisto had very little idea of how his mind worked. All the seething passion and power of Alexei's strong personality could suddenly ignite like a volcano and—like lava— he would burn everything he came into contact with.

When she arrived on the yacht with Hilary and Nicky, Captain McGregor got talking to her aunt and offered to act as her escort for a personal tour of the luxurious vessel. It was fortunate that Billie was able to leave Hilary in good hands because, with Calisto nowhere to be seen, Billie was forced to act as hostess and greet and organise the arrivals.

Much later that afternoon, Billie found Alexei squatting down on deck in an effort to calm a lost little boy who was crying noisily. She went to his assistance, lifting the child to comfort him and recognising him as the son of the island nurse. 'He needs his mum. I'll go and find her,' she told Alexei softly. 'He's probably overtired and high on sugar from all those treats you laid on for the kids.'

'It's only once a year.' Straightening again, Alexei gazed down at his PA with hooded dark-as-ebony eyes that were unusually serious and contained no glint of gold. The toddler was now clinging trustingly to Billie with chocolate-stained fingers and sucking his thumb. '*Efharisto, moraki mou*. You like children, don't you?'

Billie paled. 'Very much.'

His darkly handsome face shadowed and hardened as though that response was the wrong one and, without another word, he inclined his proud dark head in acknowledgement and left her to it. She restored the toddler to his grateful mother, who had assumed her youngest child was being looked after by his older siblings. When it was time for all the locals to return to dry land, Calisto finally put in a grudging appearance on deck. Her once-pristine white designer dress now bore stains and it looked as though an attempt to clean it had enjoyed little success. There was quite a breeze and seeing Billie—who had left her jacket on shore—shiver, Alexei had a word with one of the stewards, who went off and returned with a soft cream-coloured pashmina. Alexei draped the wrap round Billie's bare shoulders.

Taken aback by that considerate gesture and mortified by the angrily accusing stare she was receiving from Calisto, who seemed to be in a particularly bad mood, Billie busied herself with ensuring the guests enjoyed a smooth departure. She was hurrying off to look for Hilary and Nicky when Calisto cornered her as she walked past the main salon. 'Come in, I need to speak to you.'

Billie fell still, her anxious green eyes flying to the set of Calisto's petulant face. 'How can I help?'

'By keeping your distance from Alexei. For such a plain little thing, you're very good at attracting attention to yourself. You're far too familiar with Alexei and I won't tolerate you flirting with him right under my nose—'

Rigid with resentment, Billie lifted her chin. 'I don't behave like that. Now if you don't mind, I have to find my aunt—'

'I *do* mind. How dare you walk away from me when I haven't finished speaking to you?' Calisto launched at her an octave higher and several notches louder in volume. Billie decided that flight would be wiser than an argument with her employer's enraged partner.

'Hilary and her son are out on deck with McGregor, Billie. Go and join her. Thank you for your assistance today,' Alexei interposed from behind Calisto, his lean, strong face grim. 'I will deal with this.'

Relieved by his intervention, even though she feared that it would win her Calisto's undying hatred, Billie did as she was told. Behind her she heard Calisto raise her voice again and breathed in deep. If only Alexei hadn't made that gesture with the wrap! But Alexei was like that, prone to little random acts of thoughtfulness that people didn't expect from so rich and powerful a man. There had been nothing remotely intimate or flirtatious in his behaviour. A little old lady could just as easily have been the recipient of his consideration. Billie pressed clammy hands to her hot cheeks. No, indeed, Calisto had misunderstood what she saw. When Alexei got truly intimate with a woman, he crossed boundaries with the speed, power and high visibility of a champion racehorse.

Hilary looked unusually distracted when they finally got back to the house after the bonfires and the firework display on the beach. Billie reclaimed Nicky and urged her aunt to put her feet up for what little remained of the evening.

'I'm fine… I do like Stuart,' the blonde woman confided.

'Stuart?' Billie hadn't a clue who the other woman was referring to.

'Stuart McGregor, the captain of Alexei's yacht. He's a lovely man, quiet but very well read,' Hilary declared.

'I don't know him very well,' Billie admitted. 'The yacht crew don't mix much with Alexei's other employees, but I'm glad you enjoyed yourself.'

When Billie started work the next morning at the villa, she was surprised to discover that Alexei had already flown to New York.

'Did Calisto accompany him?' Billie asked the housekeeper.

'No. She flew back to Athens last night.' Anatalya came closer and lowered her voice. 'I think Mr Alexei has broken up with her. I heard her shouting and when she left she took everything she owned with her.'

'Probably just a tiff,' Billie suggested, less prone to jumping to conclusions than the older woman. 'They've been together for almost a year now.'

But Anatalya was right on target: the gossip columns and the celebrity magazines confirmed that the relationship was over later that week. On the cover of one glossy journal there was a photo of Alexei and Calisto together with a jagged line like lightning separating them. Alexei had refused to comment when asked why, but Calisto had given a couple of interviews and implied that Alexei's reputation and party lifestyle had given her pause for thought.

At the start of the following week, Alexei phoned Billie and told her that he needed her to fly over to his English country house. He was staging an important business meeting there and he wanted Billie to ensure that all the arrangements flowed smoothly.

'We knew you'd have to travel. It's part of your job,' Hilary reminded her niece as Billie held her baby son close and wondered anxiously how long she would be away from him. Secrecy was all very well, she began to appreciate, but there were definite drawbacks. Had Alexei known that she was a mother he would never have expected her to leave her child for days on end.

'When he left you behind here on the island, you

worried that your role was being reduced,' Hilary added. 'So, you can't complain now.'

Billie breathed in the sweet familiar scent of her baby and hugged him, loving the weight and feel of his little trusting body in her arms. 'I just don't want to leave him.'

'You can phone every hour of the day and I'll put him on the webcam,' her aunt promised sympathetically.

It was well over a year since Billie had visited Hazlehurst Manor in Kent. Although she had planned to hire a car at the airport, Alexei had sent a vehicle to pick her up. From the instant the car turned up the long stately driveway to the imposing Georgian pile, her eyes were anxiously scanning from left to right for maintenance issues that would require attention. But the verges were neat, the parkland picturesque and what she could see of the manicured hedges suggested that the gardens were just as well groomed. She was greeted by the manor's highly efficient housekeeper and taken straight off for a tour.

A suite on the ground floor, complete with a facility for tea and coffee, had already been set up as a conference centre. The bedrooms were as well prepared for occupation as any in an exclusive hotel. Billie was impressed and said so—on the accommodation front there was nothing left for her to do. Alexei arrived in a helicopter late the following morning while Billie was going over some estimates for renovations to the kitchen quarters. He strode into the office where she was working, his black hair blown back from his lean bronzed features, an unexpected smile tilting his passionate and wilful mouth. It lightened the often forbidding aspect that had long characterised the Drakos reputation in the business world.

'For the first time, I feel you're back where you belong...ensuring everything runs like clockwork.' Alexei studied her closely, wishing her vibrant hair were loose instead of tightly confined and mentally reclothing her in garments more appealing than the black pinstripe skirt suit she wore. He would like those little fingernails painted too. His sense of anticipation spiked, his body reacting with hot sexuality to the concept of Billie's lush little body clad in silk and lace lingerie, and for the first time there was no guilt, no sense that such thoughts, images and reactions were inappropriate where she was concerned. And why was that so? His intentions were wholly honourable for possibly the first time in his life.

Dry-mouthed at the full spectacular masculine effect of Alexei Drakos up close, Billie scrambled upright, her heart drumming out a disturbing tattoo behind her breastbone. 'Everything was done before I arrived. The housekeeper here is a gem.'

His beautiful smile broadened, showing a flash of strong white teeth. 'Generous to others as well. You have many sterling qualities, Billie. My guests arrive this afternoon and I would like you to act as my hostess while they're here.'

Billie inclined her bright head in acknowledgement.

'But as I imagine you didn't pack for that eventuality I ordered some clothes for you.'

Her green eyes widened. 'You ordered clothes for me?' she queried in surprise.

'I don't want you running round dressed in a business suit for the next forty-eight hours, *moraki mou*.'

In receipt of the full stunning burn of his dark golden eyes welded to her, Billie tensed as sexual awareness prickled over her entire skin surface and made heat lick in private places. 'I thought we had agreed that you wouldn't call me something like that...'

Alexei laughed out loud. It occurred to her that for a man whose recent romance had gone down in flames of invasive publicity he was in a remarkably good mood. 'No, you objected, but I made no such agreement. I'll call you what I like.'

That arrogant assurance was vintage Drakos and ironically eased Billie's tension a little, since up until that instant he had been behaving in an unfamiliar manner. With the experience of long acquaintance guiding her, she moved on to more business-orientated matters. 'I've been going over the figures for the proposed renovations here and I'll have to discuss the budget with you before I can establish—'

'No, no work for the moment. Go and put on one of the new outfits and join me for lunch,' Alexei instructed, determined to lift their relationship right out of the usual business mode.

'But your guests won't arrive until later.'

'Is there some particular reason why you need to argue with me today?' Alexei enquired in a drawl as smooth and acerbic as a diamond cutter.

Billie parted her lips and then closed them again. It annoyed her that she didn't know why he was behaving as he was. Buying her clothes, for example: what was that all about? Years ago, when he had helped equip her for her new job with him, he had known she didn't have the money to purchase smart suits and there had been good reason for his generosity. But why now, all of a sudden, should it matter to him what she wore? Was he suggesting that she was dressing badly again? Trying to smarten her up? Embarrassment claimed her until she went up to her room where she discovered that a staggering array of designer clothes awaited her attention. Not one of those outfits impressed her as being suitable for work wear. The collection of lingerie took her very much aback as it was far too intimate a purchase for him to have made on her behalf. She assumed he had instructed some personal shopper and that the lingerie was a mistake.

Mistake or otherwise, however, Billie was intrigued by the exquisite undergarments and finally succumbed to the temptation of seeing herself garbed in pastel-blue silk lingerie of the most frivolous and revealing kind. She picked a devastatingly simple royal-blue dress with a draped neckline and a short-sleeved jacket from a famous designer and put them on, posing in high strappy heels and barely recognising her reflection. She let her hair down, ran a comb through the thick tangle of coppery red strands that tumbled round her face and smiled. So *this* was how feeling you looked your best felt! She knew she should take the outfit off, go back downstairs and tell him that she could not possibly accept a virtual new wardrobe from him. Shamingly, however, and her cheeks reddened at this awareness, she badly wanted him to see her clad in her fine feathers first.

Alexei's black-lashed gaze whipped over Billie's slender elegant figure with considerable satisfaction when she reappeared. 'You don't look like my PA any more.'

'And that's not right,' Billie pointed out earnestly.

'It is if you're in line for a promotion…a major kind of promotion,' Alexei framed with teasing precision. 'I've thought a lot about you since I ditched Calisto and I have reached a fascinating conclusion. You're the shining example of the sort of woman I want to marry.'

Her eyes wide with bemusement at that far-reaching statement, Billie breathed weakly, 'I suppose I should say thanks for the compliment.'

'I know you inside out. You know and understand me,' Alexei asserted with formidable cool as he guided her into the dining room with a light hand resting to her spine. 'You have all the qualities I admire: honesty, self-respect, courage and kindness. The people who surround me like and respect you as well.'

'I just work for you. You're making me uncomfortable,' Billie reproved, shaking out her napkin and taking a seat opposite him with two high spots of colour burnishing her cheeks.

'Don't tell fibs,' Alexei derided. 'There's a strong sexual attraction between us and there always has been.'

Her face felt so hot that she honestly feared her skin was on fire. 'I don't understand what all this is about or why you're talking to me like this—'

'Then don't interrupt, and listen,' Alexei cut in with withering bite. 'I'm not a romantic man. I never have been. I never will be. Calisto was a major mistake and

I'm grateful to have appreciated that fact before I put a wedding ring on her finger. But that fiasco did make me think about what's important in a life partnership, what I want from a woman and what that woman might expect from me.'

'Well, that's very sensible but just at present I imagine you're feeling rather anti-women and not thinking quite as clearly as you believe you are.'

His lean, darkly handsome face tensed and darkened, his eyes narrowing with hauteur. 'That's where you're wrong. I have never been so sure of a decision before. To be frank, I don't spend much time thinking about my relationships with women.'

'I know,' Billie agreed feelingly, thinking of some of the appalling mismatches that had featured in his past love life.

'You know the worst I'm capable of.'

Billie wondered why he was talking to her in such an unusually intimate vein and her brow stayed indented in a frown. She was tense and uneasy.

'Let me have my say first,' Alexei urged her as if he perfectly understood her bewilderment. 'I'm bored of casual sex.'

'Well, it took you a long time to get to that point, but that you did get there finally is in your favour,' Billie informed him cheerfully to cover up her embarrassment at that blunt admission.

'If you don't keep quiet for five minutes, I may well strangle you!' Alexei groaned in exasperation. 'Right now, I'm ready to settle down and get married and *you* are the only woman I can see in that role. I want to marry you.'

Billie froze in shock and stared at him, unable to believe that he could mean what he had just said. The silence that followed came down like a crushing weight on her nerves.

'I have more faith in you than in any woman I've ever met and our relationship is not based purely on sex, or on your love of my wealth. I'm convinced that the talents that have made you a dependable and trustworthy employee will make you an even better wife,' he concluded grimly. 'So, I'm asking you the question I never got as far as asking Calisto... Will you be my wife?'

'You can't ask me that only a week after you've broken up with another woman!' Billie suddenly launched at him in helpless condemnation. 'You're on the rebound. You don't know what you're doing!'

'Of course I know what I'm doing,' Alexei fielded in dry exasperation.

Although he was offering Billie what she had most wanted in the world for several years, it was in terms that she found horribly humiliating. In addition, words like 'dependable' and 'trustworthy' tore her up inside when she recalled the game of deception she had become engaged in over a year earlier—and in which she was still up to her throat. He probably thought he knew the worst of her as well, but he *didn't*. Nor was his proposal of marriage of the type that had ever featured in her dreams. He didn't love her. He was simply fed up dating and, having been disappointed by Calisto, he had decided to settle for a woman he believed he knew inside out. A sensible woman with a good work ethic who knew him well: Billie. It was a very logical decision and very much Alexei who, for all his passion and volatility, was now focusing his remarkably practical and shrewd business brain on the institution of matrimony. Was he choosing her as the low-risk, low-maintenance option in the bridal stakes?

'You haven't even explained why you broke up with Calisto yet.'

His aggressive jawline squared. 'Nor do I intend to. Why pick over the past? There is no comparison between you and Calisto. Our marriage would have much firmer foundations.'

Of course there could be no comparison between ordinary Billie Foster and the gorgeous model, Calisto Bethune. A shard of bitter anger and pain pierced Billie at his unhesitating candour. Alexei, Billie suspected, thought that there would be no ups and downs with *her*, that she would be so quiet and eager to please that waves would be non-existent. But he was thinking that way because he wasn't allowing for the reality that how Billie behaved as an employee would scarcely be the same as she behaved as a wife. It burned a smoking hole in her heart that he should ask her to marry him because he respected her as a person and admired what he saw as her sterling character. How much would he respect her if he knew the truth of what she was capable of? If she told him the truth about Nicky, if she told him she had conceived his child and concealed the birth from him, he would hold her lies against her and he would no longer want to marry her.

'I don't want to talk about this any more,' Billie announced, planting her hands down on the table surface and forcing her slim body upright in a move that patently took him by surprise. 'I need to think about this.'

'Why?' Alexei thrust his chair back and sprang up. Bronzed eyes gleaming like polished metal, he gazed down into her troubled heart-shaped face and breathed in a raw growling undertone, 'What's to think about, *moraki mou*? I know you've always cared about me.'

Sparks of rage lit up inside Billie and fuelled the angry step she took back from the table. So that was the true deal, she reflected in raging pain. She was to supply the love in this sensible marriage of minds— only until now he had been too modest and polite to say so. He might not love her but he had no objection to being loved. At least he would make no objection as long as she made no demands. Indeed, Billie was under few illusions as to the exact nature of the marriage she was being offered: a matter-of-fact partnership based on mutual respect and sexual attraction.

'It's a very insulting proposal,' Billie told him flatly.

'Insulting?' Alexei repeated in thunderous disbelief. 'How have I insulted you?'

'Just you think about what you've said to me and then ask yourself how many women would want to marry you on those terms!' Billie flung back at him furiously as she stalked out of the room, headed straight to the front door and out into the fresh air.

Her hasty steps only slowing as she reached the concealment of the garden hidden behind manicured hedges, Billie pressed the heel of her hand to the thunderous pounding at her temples and trembled at the force of the emotions she was striving to rein back. A jumble of mortifying phrases were still assailing her and making her cringe. *A major kind of promotion. Dependable? Trustworthy? I'm bored of casual sex. No comparison between you and Calisto.* She was the safe alternative to his capricious ex-fiancée, as cosy and insipid as hot milk when compared to such a spicy cocktail. Calisto's high jinks and the memory of his father's three very costly divorces had made Alexei cautious in the matrimonial stakes. He didn't want a wife who would rock the boat with emotional outbursts and petulant demands. He wanted a wife who would do as she was told just like an employee, a wife who was grateful enough for her position to let him live his life without interference. No, such a marriage was not the stuff of which dreams were made and it never would be.

Billie sank down heavily on a bench overlooking a still circular pond that reflected the smooth green surrounding lawn. Only in a fantastic dream would Alexei Drakos ever have proposed to her in any other terms, she told herself in exasperation. Of course he wasn't in love with her. She wasn't drop-dead gorgeous or even a sensational challenge to his masculinity. She was his social secretary who had long been in love with him.

And just how long had he been aware of that crucial fact? Her face stung with shamed heat. No doubt she had betrayed her true feelings for him long ago, because he was a man who knew and understood women all too well. Never by word or by gesture, however, had he revealed his knowledge until now when, in the act of

honouring her with a marriage proposal, he had joined
up all the dots to point out how well she would suit him.

She had no doubt whatsoever that he saw his proposal as an honour he conferred upon her. After all,
what did she have to offer a young, handsome billionaire
but her very ordinariness? Yet, astonishingly, that ordinariness was suddenly what he had decided would best
suit his requirements. A humble, grateful, loving wife
would, of course, be far easier to live with than a diva
like Calisto Bethune. You had to hand it to Alexei—
even marriage had to be one hundred per cent on *his*
terms. For, really, what would be in it for her?

Billie breathed in deep as she reached the crux of the
matter. It was all very well storming off in a passion
of hurt pride and wounded feelings, but was she really
going to say no to her one and only chance to become
Alexei's wife? So, as proposals went, it had been a pa-
tronizing, humiliating insult. But he had been honest
with her about his expectations and he had evidently
never got as far as actually asking Calisto to marry him,
which could only please Billie. But then had Alexei even
loved Calisto? Indeed had he *ever* been in love? Billie
had never even heard him mention the word. Alexei had
always had a detached quality with women.

Billie thought about Alexei's own background and
acknowledged that it was scarcely the stuff of dreams
either. His parents' shotgun marriage had been, on the
face of it, a successful relationship, but Natasha Drakos
had deferred very much to her older husband in every
field. It had been a very traditional and conservative
Greek union in which Constantine had travelled while

Natasha had stayed home, dutifully fulfilling the roles of wife, hostess and mother. That kind of controlled unemotional relationship, Billie finally registered, was the blueprint that Alexei—whether he realised it or not—was applying to his own marital plans.

'The big flare-up and walk out isn't like you,' Alexei breathed coolly from several feet away. 'I expected you to be sensible.'

For a male who knew women, he was being appallingly tactless. Billie lifted her lashes to look at him, smitten to the heart by his dark male beauty. 'I am being sensible. I'm thinking over what you said.'

'What is there to think over?' Alexei fielded drily.

Billie tilted her chin, green eyes sparkling. 'You don't love me. You'll be difficult to live with. You'll always want your own way. You may not be faithful. I think there's plenty there for me to think about.'

As she spoke dark blood had coloured his high cheekbones and his sleek bone structure tightened defensively below his tawny skin. She knew it was a struggle for him not to snap back at her and cut her off at the knees for her cheek. 'I'll give you my answer tomorrow.'

'I trust you to make the right decision,' Alexei retorted.

He trusted her! Oh, dear heaven, Billie thought in a maelstrom of anguish at his careless assurance, he *trusted* her! Yet if he knew that he had a son called Nicky, his trust would be destroyed. That awareness was like a stiletto knife in her heart, yet she was convinced that she dared not come clean with him at that moment.

A lean hand closed over hers to raise her from the bench and then splayed to the curve of her hips to tilt her against his strong muscular length. Alexei lowered his handsome dark head. 'I want you—much more than you've ever appreciated, *matakia mou*.'

His lips covered hers and she literally stopped breathing, caught up in the moment of searing eroticism that pierced her body when his tongue plunged deep into the tender interior of her mouth. She shivered as if she were in the eye of a storm-force wind, hunger storming through her slight body with sudden fierce impatience, for having once tasted the heat of his passion she longed to feel it again.

The intensity of her response to a single kiss shook Alexei and aroused him even more. He backed off though, determined to take that aspect of their relationship slowly. He was convinced that he would be her first lover and was tantalised by the idea.

'As I know you're not experienced I won't expect you to share my bed until we're married,' Alexei breathed huskily. 'So, as I'm sure you will understand, I don't want to wait long for the wedding.'

Billie almost shielded her gaze with defensive lashes. He had assumed she was still a virgin, had no idea that he had already ensured that she could no longer claim such innocence. He had no fear that she might refuse his proposal either. His arrogance infuriated her.

'I might say no tomorrow,' she pointed out stiffly.

Alexei hauled her even closer and kissed her again, long and hard and sexily. His lean hands smoothed over her ribcage, tantalisingly close to the swollen sensitivity of her full breasts. Emerging breathless from that heated embrace, Billie could barely focus or breathe, never mind think and reason. The very feel of his long, lean, aroused body pushing in demand against hers paralysed her brain and ignited her to a fierce fever pitch of longing.

That night she barely slept for excitement. He didn't love her but she loved him and knew it would break her heart to stand by while he married someone else, as he inevitably would should she refuse him. Her heart ruled her, even though her head warned her that the path ahead would be twisty and stony. She joined him in his private dining room for breakfast.

'Your answer?' Alexei enquired silkily.

'Yes, I will marry you,' Billie pronounced, watching his wide sensual mouth curl with satisfaction. 'Are you surprised?'

'No, as I have already said, I have enormous faith in you, *khriso mou*,' Alexei confided, sending a sharp pang of guilt and regret through Billie's slender body. My gold, my treasure, he'd called her. But for how much longer would he see her in that idealised light?

CHAPTER TEN

TWO AND A HALF weeks later, Billie studied the exquisite emerald engagement ring on her finger.

It was a slim elegant ring mounted with a deep green stone of surpassing beauty that complemented her small hand; Billie had to keep on checking it out to convince herself that she had not accidentally stepped into a dream. When she was holding on to so many secrets, how could planning her wedding feel real? First and foremost, Alexei respected her for her ability to tell the truth. Finding out that she had lied and lied again would be a very unpleasant surprise for him.

'You have to tell him about Nicky *before* you marry him,' Hilary pronounced without hesitation.

'If I do, he won't marry me,' Billie muttered feverishly.

Unmoved by that view, Hilary shook her blonde head. 'That's a risk you have to take.'

But Billie's courage had failed her on that score. Even two weeks after the proposal, wedding bells were still pealing inside her head. She finally had the magical right to hug the guy she had fallen in love with, although opportunities to do so had been few because he had hardly been around since the day he had proposed. Billie had stayed on Speros to organise the wedding while Alexei was abroad on business. Even so, her world had suddenly become a place of infinite promise and happiness, and confessing up to the deception of the year over their son, Nicky, had little appeal. Indeed her dishonesty hung over her like a giant black rain cloud that carried the threat of imminent doom.

Her face very pale, Billie murmured tautly, 'Alexei might try to take Nicky away from me.'

Hilary frowned. 'Why would he do something like that?'

'Because he'll be so angry. He's a control freak. I'll have let him down, hidden the truth from him…and he *hates* lies. An illegitimate child will also embarrass his family. He'll blame me.'

'Of course she can't tell Alexei about Nicky until she's got that wedding ring safely on her finger!' Lauren broke in, shooting her younger sister a look of angry derision that dismissed her advice. 'He's a Drakos and as slippery in the wedding stakes as a man can be. He's very wary of marriage—of course he is…his father did have four wives! Give Alexei an excuse this big and he'll call it off!'

As her mother voiced her daughter's deepest fears Billie shifted uncomfortably in her seat because her conscience was absolutely writhing. It had proved impossible to keep the truth from Lauren once the wedding was being planned and, in some ways, her mother's understanding of Billie's predicament and mood was superior to Hilary's, whose moral compass was less yielding. Lauren totally appreciated that Billie's greatest apprehension was losing the chance to marry the man that she loved. At least if they were married, Billie thought fearfully, she would have the chance to work on the damage she had done to their relationship. Unmarried and living apart, what opportunity would she have to persuade Alexei to calm down and see her viewpoint?

In addition, Lauren saw no reason why her daughter should shoulder all the blame for the fallout caused by Alexei's amnesia. That disastrous accident could not be laid at anyone's door. But Alexei had then swiftly got tangled up with Calisto in what had appeared to be the romance of the century and it was for *his* sake rather than her own that Billie had remained silent. Her mother had deemed that decision 'plain stupidity'.

'Right now, Billie has to keep quiet and save her big announcement about Nicky for when they're married,' Lauren declared in a tone of flat conviction. 'Having carried on the pretence this long, what do another few days matter?'

'What matters is that Billie's relationship with Alexei has changed beyond recognition since he proposed,' Hilary argued vehemently. 'And if she doesn't tell him now, it'll make her look calculating.'

Torn apart by the discussion, Billie went into her bedroom where the beautiful embroidered wedding gown she had purchased in Athens hung in readiness for her wedding day, which was now only forty-eight hours away. She had prayed that Alexei would recall the night they had spent together without her interference. While she had been in Athens she had even consulted a psychiatrist about Alexei's amnesia. She had received cold comfort in response. Alexei's memory had only misplaced a few hours of the very distressing day when he had buried his parents. Some day he might recall those hours or missing fragments of them, but the longer time went on, the less likely that would be. Furthermore, filling in that gap in his memory for him was unlikely to help him to recall events for himself.

In truth, Billie didn't need anyone to tell her what she ought to do. She knew that with every day that passed she was sinking deeper into the quagmire of her own deception. She already knew what was right and what was wrong. She knew the difference. She had no fancy excuses to hide behind. *Tell him,* a little voice shrieked in her conscience, but she had seen very little of Alexei since he had asked her to marry him and what she had to say could scarcely be passed on during a phone conversation. He was due back at the villa for dinner that very evening. Once again Billie began mustering her courage in an effort to bite the bullet and confess all.

Garbed in a dark green knee-length strappy silk dress, Billie walked into the Drakos villa. Anatalya greeted her with warmth. While Billie was not quite as popular as an island girl born and bred on Speros would have been as Alexei's future bride, she was the nearest equivalent and, as far as the locals were concerned, infinitely preferable to a stranger. Billie glanced at her reflection in a tall mirror. She had done a fair amount of shopping in Athens, recognising that Alexei expected her to dress up for her new role in his life. For a young woman who had once had no particular interest in fashion or her appearance, she had made a big effort. Her hair was trimmed into a more sleek style and her nails were manicured.

Anything to make herself more attractive, anything to please, she ruminated with a frown of growing self-loathing. She had once thought that her appearance didn't matter that much. Now, instead, she thought of Calisto and her well-groomed predecessors and cringed at her naivety. A homespun unadorned woman was unlikely to appeal for very long to a male with Alexei's sophisticated tastes. His standards had to become hers.

That same week she had signed a pre-nuptial contract that ran to fifty pages of small type. She had given up on reading it about halfway through, having only registered that Alexei was promising to give her an enormous allowance every month. Lauren had urged her to consult a lawyer in Athens but Billie preferred to trust the guy she was about to marry and in any case there really wasn't enough time left before the wedding to start negotiating clauses.

As Billie recognised the sound of a helicopter flying in over the bay, she drew in a steadying breath. She was going to do the right thing: she was going to tell him and bear the consequences, whatever they were. She was not a coward. She was not by nature a liar either.

Alexei stared across the big airy salon at his bride-to-be. The green colour of the dress threw her white alabaster skin into prominence and accentuated her jewelled eyes. How had he ever believed she wasn't beautiful? How had he ever considered that vibrant coppery hair unattractive? Smooth wine-red wings of hair curving to her cheekbones, eyes bright, mouth a sultry peachy pink, she looked amazing. He extended a hand to her in invitation.

'I—I thought I should give you the chance to change your mind if you want to…about marrying me,' Billie stammered nervously as she crossed the room to his side.

'I haven't the slightest intention of changing my mind, *moraki mou*,' Alexei fielded, his wide sensual mouth flashing an amused smile as he closed a hand over hers and strode across the hall and down the bedroom corridor. 'I'm very pleased with the decision I've made. I also authorised a press release about our engagement today. We'll have a peaceful wedding day. Unless one of my relatives blabbers, which is of course possible, the press won't be expecting us to get hitched so quickly after the announcement.'

Having entered his bedroom, Alexei released her and jerked loose his tie. 'I need a shower before dinner. Tell me about your week.'

'There's so much important stuff that we haven't talked about, Alexei,' Billie said apprehensively, marooned in the centre of the carpet in the large room.

Shrugging off his jacket and embarking on the buttons on his shirt, Alexei strolled with predatory grace towards her. 'We have the rest of our lives to talk. This marriage is going to last. My aunt, Marina, sends her best wishes. She approves of you; she said she didn't know I had so much sense.'

'I'm flattered…'

'Then try to be a little less insecure,' Alexei advised drily. 'I'm not good with needy women.'

In receipt of that criticism, Billie reddened unhappily and stiffened. 'We haven't even discussed…er… having children…'

Alexei quirked a questioning brow, brilliant bronzed eyes pinned to her. 'Some day, but *not* some day soon. I don't want children for a few years yet,' he confided without hesitation.

The opening she had sought had suffered a landslide, cutting her off from that particular route. Right now Alexei didn't want to be a father, which was fair enough because he still thought that he had a choice to exercise on that score. Only he didn't have a choice, which was not a position he was used to occupying. She pictured Nicky, a healthy, livewire baby already learning to grab at objects and roll over while babbling in his own language. She adored her son, believing like all mothers that her baby was the very epitome of cuteness and appeal. It had never occurred to her that Alexei might react to the news that he had a child in a less than positive way and now as that risk did occur to her it glued her tongue to the roof of her mouth. What courage she had built up was steadily draining away.

Alexei's shrewd gaze narrowed. 'I just said the wrong thing, didn't I? Are you really gasping to reproduce?'

'No…er…no. It's not that.' Billie moved restively round the room in no particular direction.

Bare chested, his magnificent torso as well honed by his daily gym workouts as any athlete's, Alexei moved into her path, his hands closing over hers to hold her entrapped and draw her to him. 'Good. Just the two of us appeals the most to me at present. Babies cry and demand a lot of attention,' he pointed out, his breath fanning her cheek before he took her soft lips with ravishing force and urgency.

Her heart went bumpety-bumpety-bump, as if she were running up a steep hill and breathing were a desperate challenge but she didn't want what she was feeling to stop—no, indeed. His hands released hers to search out more sensitive places and she strained eagerly against him as he pushed up the hem of her dress and ran long fingers up the inside of one slender thigh.

A violent trembling seized hold of Billie. Alexei groaned with hungry satisfaction when he reached the stretched taut silk barrier of her knickers and felt the responsive dampness there. He lifted his dark head, his black hair tousled by her clutching fingers, and told her exactly what he wanted to do to her. Her eyes widened in sheer shock at that bold and graphic description.

Engaged in teasing the hot, throbbing sensitivity of the silken flesh between her thighs, Alexei stilled only when he saw her expression. He felt like a firework ready to blaze a trail. She got him hotter and harder than any woman had in a long time and denying himself satisfaction was a challenge until he saw the surprised and self-conscious look on her face. Her lack of experience touched and shamed him. He wanted to give her more than a quick lusty coupling before dinner. Slowly, he withdrew his hand from her seductively responsive flesh and dropped the hem of her dress. He held her close while the after quivers of unsated arousal continued to make her slender frame tremble feverishly against his.

'Alexei…?' she framed, weak-legged with need.

'We have an agreement, *moraki mou*,' he reminded her when she gazed up at him in a daze of confusion. 'We'll wait. It'll be better for you that way…more special.'

Flushed and still shaken when he walked away from her into the bathroom, Billie breathed in deep. She would have lain down on his bed even without an invitation. Her body was a seething mass of pleading nerve-endings, greedily seeking the pleasure that he had given her before. Her face burned with mortification. Even sex, she suddenly appreciated, would now be a risky venture for her. He believed that their wedding night would be 'special'. Did that mean that he was expecting her to be a virgin? It seemed that he did. Would he be able to tell the difference? Was she fated to have to tell the truth to him on their wedding night? *Oh, what a tangled web,* she thought miserably.

Over the meal, served out on the terrace to take advantage of the glorious view of the bay, Alexei asked her a question that startled her. 'One of my relatives asked me who your father was and I realised that I knew nothing on that score.'

Billie tensed. 'Well, you know about as much as I do. Lauren once told me I was the result of a one-night stand with a man she didn't stay in touch with. There's no name on my birth certificate. I'm not sure if Lauren even knew his name,' she admitted in a wry undertone. 'So I didn't push her for any more information.'

Alexei talked business and then, with some amusement, described the calls he had received from curious relations as word of the wedding invitations, made by telephone for discretion, began to spread round the family circle.

'I'm sure that everybody thinks that you could have done much better by marrying a celebrity or an heiress or someone more—'

A fiery glitter in his dark golden eyes, Alexei covered her clenched fingers with his. 'More...*what*? You suit me. How many other women would tolerate me being away for so long without complaint? Ask me intelligent questions about my work and then settle for a quiet dinner at home?'

A deep dark pain pierced her. 'What if I'm not who you think I am, Alexei?' she asked him sickly.

A sinfully magnetic smile slanted his beautifully modelled mouth. 'Then you'll have to work at *being* who I think you are. Stop looking for trouble.'

BILLIE KNEW THAT her wedding day was supposed to be one of the happiest days of her life.

The sky was blue, the sun was shining and the only sound apart from birdsong was the timeless beat of the waves on the white seashore far below. She had her breakfast on the terrace with Nicky in his high chair beside her and marvelled that she could have spent so long building a property that she was only actually going to have lived in for three months. Of course, Hilary planned to stay on and write her book in Billie's house.

'What a gorgeous day!' her aunt carolled, strolling out to join her niece and grand-nephew in the sunshine.

The hours that followed were incredibly busy ones.

A beautician and her assistant arrived to do Billie's make-up and her hair, which was to be worn loose the way Alexei said he liked it. Surrendering to their combined attentions, Billie sank into her own little world of thoughts. Speculative articles about her containing few actual facts had already appeared in the world's press and the media had chosen to depict her as a working Cinderella, a little office girl who had miraculously attracted the attention of one of the world's richest and most successful tycoons. Mercifully, none of Lauren's previous lovers had been dug up to tell embarrassing tales and virtually nothing was known about Lauren's and Billie's life on the island of Speros. Again, fortunately, the islanders were highly unlikely to sell stories that might embarrass Alexei.

Mid-morning, Billie paused before she donned her sleek simple gown to open the wedding gifts Alexei had sent her. A flat box opened to display a breathtaking diamond pendant and drop earrings. Lauren was ecstatic on her daughter's behalf but Billie felt guiltier than ever. The second box, a good deal bulkier, squirmed as if something inside it were struggling to get out. Eyes wide, Billie lifted the lid and scooped out a little wriggly hairy bundle with four legs and a curling tail and a pair of anxious big brown eyes that could have melted granite. It was a little black Scottish Highland terrier pup.

'What's he doing, giving you a dog?' her mother demanded, unimpressed, indeed checking out the box minutely to ensure it did not contain something more valuable than an animal.

But, of all of them, Billie understood exactly why

she was being given a very cute little puppy. It was to satisfy the keen maternal instincts that sixth sense had warned Alexei his bride was concealing. No, he definitely wasn't ready for a baby and he had decided that giving a dog to Billie to dote on as a substitute was a good idea.

'Can you take her with you on your honeymoon?' Hilary asked dubiously.

'I'll call her Skye and I wouldn't dream of leaving her behind.' But a sense of irony swiftly assailed Billie and doused her amusement. Wasn't she about to leave her beloved son behind? That was that, enough was enough, she conceded fiercely. Tonight she would tell Alexei that he was a father. There would be no more pretence, no more excuses, no more put-offs. Whatever happened, she would tell the truth. Her conscience cried that she should never have lied in the first place and she suppressed that voice.

Everything would work out, she told herself urgently. He would come around once he realised he had a son. He would understand why she had remained silent, why she had felt forced to pretend that Nicky was her aunt's child rather than her own, wouldn't he?

So, she wasn't perfect. So, maybe she hadn't done the right thing. So, maybe she had made the wrong choice, had lacked the backbone to go for the tougher option. But she could still remember the tall handsome boy she had first met on the beach all those years earlier when she was being bullied and she reminded herself that Alexei was no innocent when it came to human nature. He would be very surprised by what she had to tell him but she was convinced that he would recognise why she hadn't spoken up sooner.

The wedding ceremony was to take place at the church devoted to *Agios Georgios* down by the harbour in the village. The richly decorated building, built by Alexei's grandfather and packed with guests, was filled with white heavily perfumed flowers and glowing candles that lit the shadows. It was really beautiful and Billie's heart swelled along with the organ music when she saw Alexei waiting at the altar for her. Tall, dark and stunningly handsome with his black-lashed dark golden eyes intent on her, he sent her heart rate rocketing and stole the breath from her lungs.

The religious ceremony was as uplifting for Billie as the wonderful music. She was in love and on a high of positive thoughts. Alexei slid the slender band of gold onto her wedding finger and she rewarded him with a blindingly bright smile. He stared down into her animated happy face and believed that unlike his father he had hit the jackpot the first time around in choosing the right woman to marry. He thought of Calisto's pleading phone call the day before, urging him to change his mind. He had had no time for her interference. No male moved on more quickly from a dead love affair than Alexei.

Billie rested her hand on Alexei's sleeve as they walked back down the aisle. The deed was done: they were married. The man she loved beyond bearing was finally hers to love, her husband. She told herself that it was a day in which to glory in her good fortune and happiness. As he swung her into his arms on the steps to kiss her with breathtaking sensuality and their guests cheered that unashamed display she buried every negative thought and fear and kissed him back with all her heart. He would understand. For her sake and that of their son, he *had* to understand…

* * * * *

THE BRIDE'S SECRET

Part Two

CHAPTER ONE

THE OPULENT CLOAKROOM was adorned with stylish contemporary fittings and fresh flower arrangements and was as large as many reception rooms. At a vanity unit that was more private than any of the others on offer, the bride was touching up her smudged eye makeup with a careful hand, while scolding herself for getting so weepy and overcome at the altar. However, her green eyes also shone with happiness. She jumped when the door from the hall noisily opened to feed in a burst of animated chattering females.

'… Calisto threw tantrums, so clearly Alexei decided that life would be easier with a doormat,' a very correct English voice pronounced with a giggle. 'He will get bored *so* fast—'

'And she's just a worker from his office… Who ever would have believed that a Drakos would even have looked at her?' someone else observed acidly.

'And *so* plain—positively dumpy!' the first speaker added with vitriol. 'As for *that* dress. No train and all that fussy dated embroidery. Obviously Alexei is on the rebound—'

Gritting her teeth together and keeping herself out of view, Billie was literally trying to mentally seal her ears and stop listening to the bitchy comments. She reflected in disbelief on the exquisite hand-embroidered heirloom dress that she had fallen madly in love with, feeling affronted and hurt by that criticism of her gown. She could have put a face to every voice though. All three women featured on Alexei's impossibly long list of former lovers, each of whom had gone on to marry or move in with one of his wealthy friends or business colleagues and thus contrived to stay within his social circle.

'Calisto must have really screwed up—a billionaire on the rebound. If I'd known that miracle was on the horizon, I'd have gone for a divorce and made myself available!' the Englishwoman confided in a petulant tone that implied her outrageous suggestion was far from being a joke.

'But Calisto was a one-off,' her companion returned crushingly. 'She's the only one of Alexei's exes that he's ever revisited.'

'What's that worth now when he's just married right out of his class and culture? I give this mismatched union three months, four if she plays her cards right and ignores it when he strays,' the Englishwoman forecast. 'Then Alexei will ditch his homely little bride so hard and fast her head will spin!'

That was the exact moment when a glint of defiant green flared in Billie's eyes. Pride would not allow her to skulk out of sight somewhere in the splendid villa that was now her home. As she moved into view three female faces froze in a rictus of almost comical discomfiture. Sidestepping their stilled figures, her bright auburn head held high, Billie left the cloakroom.

Hilary, her aunt, was walking in circles in the hall while she rocked the sobbing baby in her arms. Her eyes settled on Billie in some relief. 'I've been looking everywhere for you. Nicky just won't settle for me. I think he's getting another tooth—'

'Let me take him.' Billie sped over immediately to grasp the little but solid, squirming body of her baby son. Her *secret* son, she reminded herself guiltily, gazing down worriedly into his cross little face. She adored him, wanted to show him off, not behave as though he were Hilary's child and her infant cousin. But that masquerade had been forced on her when she chose to bring Nicky and her aunt back with her to the island of Speros, for she had yet to tell the man she had just married that morning that she had conceived a child by him on the night following his parents' funeral. Unhappily, Alexei, having suffered a fall and a blow to the head shortly afterwards, had no memory of their brief intimacy. Their son's face was flushed below his spiky shock of silky black hair. She hugged him close in spite of her aunt's exhortations for her to be careful of her wedding gown. The scent and feel of the baby in her arms was a comfort to her frayed nerves and the charm seemed to work both ways because Nicky started to simmer down and indeed began to snuggle into his mother's soothing embrace.

A tall, devastatingly handsome, black-haired, olive-skinned male strode across the echoing hall towards Billie and Hilary. Instantly, all Billie's senses went on red alert and she sucked in a ragged breath to steady herself. She collided with Alexei's dark-lashed exotic bronzed eyes and her surroundings became immediately invisible: his effect on her was that shocking and intense. Her mouth ran dry because she could still barely credit that she was now his wife. That was a dream so long held and suppressed by her that even on her wedding day it could only seem to her to consist more of fantasy than fact. Alexei, blithely ignoring the greetings of those who would have sought to deflect him from his bride, drew level with her.

For a split second he seemed to stare at the sight of Billie cradling a child in her arms and his attention lingered on the striking contrast of the baby's tawny complexion and black hair against Billie's white dress, auburn hair and naturally pale skin. It struck him as surprising that the kid bore not the slightest resemblance to any one of his female relatives. A slight frown line forming between his sleek ebony brows, he dismissed that fleeting thought and snapped an imperious set of long fingers to bring a manservant running, at which point he addressed him in a low-pitched aside.

'You keep on disappearing like mist, *khriso mou*.' He inclined his handsome dark head in approval as one of the team of nannies hired to take care of the guests' children joined them and put out her arms to take Nicky.

'Oh, no… I'll take care of him,' Hilary said straight away.

'Nonsense. That is why the nannies are here, so that our guests can relax and enjoy our day with us,' Alexei pointed out lazily.

Billie passed over Nicky with pronounced reluctance. He began to complain but the nanny swept off again at speed and her son's muted cries of protest soon disappeared into the distance. Her cheeks pink, Billie gave Alexei a glance that spoke of reproach. With the cool intolerance of an autocrat, he had banished Nicky from their wedding celebration for the simple sin of crying. She folded her empty arms, shaken by how protective she felt of her child and of how much she longed for the nerve to chase after the nanny and retrieve him. Alexei had to be told the truth about Nicky's origins soon… he *had* to be!

'You shouldn't have interfered,' Billie remarked as her aunt drifted off at a signal from her sister—Billie's mother, Lauren.

'As a good hostess you should have taken care of the problem for your aunt,' Alexei admonished smoothly. 'Hilary can't even dance with a baby in tow. I should imagine she'll be glad of a break from the incessant demands of so young a child.'

At that rebuke, the colour drained from Billie's face, leaving her pale while her soft brown curling lashes screened her discomfited gaze. She was shaken by the awareness that Alexei had spoken the truth and that it was a truth that she had ignored in her eagerness to keep her son within reach. Nicky should have been passed over to the nanny team earlier in the day along with all the other young children, leaving her aunt free to take full relaxed advantage of a rare day out. More and more she was appreciating just how complex and challenging her deception had become. She was no longer being fair to Hilary. Although Hilary had agreed to look after her great-nephew and behave as though he were her son, neither woman had foreseen just how onerous and complicated that responsibility might become.

From the doorway, Billie regretted their combined naivety about Nicky while she watched as the captain of Alexei's yacht, Stuart McGregor, boldly swapped place cards at the top table to ensure that he got a seat beside her attractive blonde aunt. The older man had been keenly pursuing their acquaintance from the first day that he had met Hilary. He had already visited Billie's house on several occasions, calling in on the pretext of books he wanted to loan her aunt and then inviting her out to lunch or for a walk. Although Stuart had yet to suggest that he was seeking anything more than platonic companionship from Hilary, the recent widow seemed to like Stuart and might well already be wishing that she could come clean and admit that Nicky was not actually her child. Billie realised that the pretence that Nicky was Hilary's son had put her aunt in a very awkward position. For the first time it occurred to Billie that a lot of people other than Alexei would condemn both women when the truth finally came out. After all, nobody liked to be lied to and deceived.

'You're very fond of Hilary's baby, aren't you?'

'Of course, I am,' Billie responded, almost wincing at the unnecessarily defensive note in her reply.

Alexei laughed softly. 'And the compliment is returned. The child was clinging to you with both hands like a little limpet.'

'The child's name is Nicky,' she told her bridegroom.

'Whatever.' Alexei had already lost interest in the topic and without further comment he curved an arm round his bride's slender body to direct her back into the airy room where their guests were already taking their seats for the meal.

The world-famous and very beautiful singer whom Alexei had engaged to entertain them while they ate rested her huge sultry brown eyes on the bridegroom and aimed every lovelorn passionate note she sang in his direction. Steadily growing as rigid as a concrete post in her seat, Billie watched the byplay and registered that something much more important than good business was prompting the entertainer's behaviour. Evidently there was, or had been at one time, a much more intimate link between her husband and the artiste, the existence of which Billie had never suspected.

Before she could even think of what she should or should not say on that score, Billie found herself leaning closer to her new husband and saying in an acid undertone new to her repertoire, 'You've slept with her, haven't you?'

Alexei quirked a satiric brow. 'I won't dignify that question with an answer.'

'Well, it's pretty obvious to everybody here,' Billie declared, refusing to heed the voice of caution chiming to be heard inside her head. 'I'd have to be stupid not to see the way she's looking at you.'

'I don't see a problem—'

'Well, I expect you wouldn't,' Billie agreed, thinking bitterly that he was too accustomed to receiving languishing looks and flirtatious smiles from women to appreciate that his bride might find such displays particularly offensive on her wedding day. Just for once she would have enjoyed the absence of that kind of blatant behaviour in his radius. Just for once she wanted to take pole position and shine more than any other woman around him. As the juvenile quality of her wishes pierced her, she almost laughed. Since when had she wanted to show off? And just when had she forgotten that she owed the ring on her wedding finger to qualities that Alexei deemed superior to mere sexual attraction? It was a sobering acknowledgement.

'I don't expect you to fuss about such trivialities,' Alexei told her drily.

Billie bridled, as she very much disliked the suggestion that she had no right or excuse to experience feelings of resentment and disapproval when other women went out on a limb to give an unashamed sexual come-on to her new husband. Feverish colour highlighted her cheekbones and enhanced the bright emerald sparkle of her eyes. 'If it was an ex-lover of mine parading the fact in front of you, how would you feel?'

'I'd knock his teeth down his throat,' Alexei conceded with a softness that was all the more chilling for its assured cool and conviction. 'But then I'm the only lover you'll ever have, so, in our case, that situation will never arise. You're exclusively mine, *khriso mou*. I like and appreciate that.'

That macho response sent Billie's teeth flying together with a snap and she bit back a stinging response. It infuriated her that he was right, that he would never know the slightest discomfort on her behalf in another man's radius. She had no past, no sexual history to challenge his indefensibly sexist and hypocritical attitude, but then she *was* holding back on enough secrets to sink the *Titanic*, she reflected with a belated shiver of foreboding. It worried her even more that he was so confident that she was a virgin. It was a little too late to disabuse him of that notion now. She had allowed too many comments in that line to flow past her unchallenged. But after that night following the funeral when he had swept her off to bed with him, she was no longer intact. Would he be able to tell the difference? She very much hoped not.

She had already decided to wait until the next day before making a clean breast of events with regard to that night. She was praying that they could enjoy their wedding day and hopefully their wedding night as well without the daunting necessity of a confessional session that would shatter all harmony between them. Even one night of intimacy would surely make Alexei a little more understanding and approachable? After all, nobody would be less tolerant than Alexei when he suddenly discovered that he was *not* in possession of all the information there was to know about her, or indeed that she had gone out of her way to conceal certain facts about herself. Her troubled eyes resting on his hard classic profile and the fundamental strength and obduracy that were etched there, Billie struggled to stay calm despite the daunting challenges that lay ahead of her. With an idle thumb she massaged the new ring on her wedding finger as if it were a talisman that would protect her.

'The only problem I can see right now *is*...your mother,' Alexei delivered in a stern undertone. 'She's getting out of control.'

Billie's startled gaze followed his across the room to where Lauren had risen from her seat to begin dancing with a man, even though the rest of the guests were still sitting. Her mother cannoned clumsily into another table and then a chair while continuing to laugh and talk very loudly, all her attention predictably pinned to her male partner. Lauren, who had obviously imbibed a fair amount of alcohol, was impervious to the dirty looks she was attracting as those around her tried to concentrate on listening to the world-class performance the singer was putting on.

'Oh, for goodness' sake!' Billie framed between gritted teeth because she was mortified by her mother's rude behaviour. A thousand times and more, when she was younger, Billie had suffered similar squirming moments when her parent made a spectacle of herself in public. But today of all days was special! Already very conscious of her humble beginnings, Billie had prayed beforehand that, just this once, Lauren would not embarrass her by doing anything to draw attention to herself in polite company. But her mother, it seemed, would always be as irresponsible as a defiant teenager, particularly if there was an attractive man within her radius. In the background Billie saw Hilary rise from the same table and advance on her giggling, swaying sister.

Lauren paid heed to Hilary in a way she wouldn't have to her daughter. Within the space of a minute the dancing display was over. Lauren returned sulkily to her seat while the man she had been dancing with returned to his at an adjoining table.

'Thank goodness for Hilary,' Billie remarked with relief. 'Who's the man that Lauren was with?'

'One of my cousins, who is old enough to know better.'

'Age doesn't necessarily make people wiser,' Billie retorted half quietly; the supposed wisdom of experience and maturity had made little mark on Lauren, who remained as giddy as an adolescent. What was more, Billie thought ruefully, men always seemed to quickly shed their inhibitions and behave badly in her mother's company.

'Don't make yourself responsible for Lauren any more,' Alexei urged Billie, surprising her with that unwelcome recommendation. 'She's not going to change. Just let her live her life.'

Billie thought that it was all very well for him to hand out such advice, but he had never had to cope with the hard reality of Lauren's problems when an affair broke up and she was abandoned once again. At such times, her mother would sink into depression and self-pity and use alcohol as a crutch and it was then that she needed her daughter or her sister. Without such support Lauren did not have the resources to pick herself up again.

'Of course, I will always support her financially,' Alexei added. 'You don't need to worry about that.'

Billie reddened. 'She's pretty much fine since I bought her the house. She doesn't need to hang on your sleeve—'

'I have plenty of relatives of my own who do,' Alexei fielded evenly. 'It makes sense.'

That Alexei was making a point of spelling out his intentions towards her feckless parent surprised Billie and made her smell a rat. 'What do you know that I don't know?' she prompted, wondering if her mother had got into financial trouble again and if it was possible that Lauren had made a direct request to him for his help.

'I don't want to talk about this now,' Alexei answered coolly.

And Billie found herself thinking of all the many occasions when, as an employee, she had had no choice but to respect such arrogant embargos. 'She's my mother. I have a right to know what's going on.'

Alexei dealt her a dark look of exasperation. 'Do we really have to discuss your mother's debts on our wedding day?'

Hot colour ran up like a banner below Billie's fair skin and her slender spine stiffened. It was news to her that Lauren had run up debts again and she was furiously embarrassed by the revelation. 'You should've told me—'

'Why?' Alexei sent her an impatient glance. 'Your problems are my problems now.'

With effort Billie overcame the sense of humiliation that was threatening to overpower her. She grasped that he'd had no prior intention of telling her and regretted her own persistence. 'Just one more question—how did you find out that Lauren had such problems?'

'Speros is a small place.'

That revealing assurance ensured that Billie's sense of mortification and shame lingered. The awareness that some islander, probably either a tradesman or a shop-keeper, had clearly approached Alexei on the score of an unsettled bill cut her to the quick. For years she had been proud of the fact that the financial help she'd given her mother had prevented such embarrassing situations from arising. She remembered too well how it had felt as a child when Lauren had owed money everywhere in the village.

'It's time for us to dance,' Alexei breathed, closing a hand over Billie's and raising her from her seat.

Unmercifully conscious of being the cynosure of attention when she was much more accustomed to playing the role of a backroom girl, Billie found it impossible to lean into the strong, hard support of his tall muscular length. Lean fingers splayed across the curve of her hips and sexual heat flared through her in jagged response.

'Why are you so tense?' Alexei censured in a rough-ened undertone. 'You feel like a little steel girder in my arms.'

Billie had to force her slender body to yield into his. She was quivering with tension and the sudden on-slaught of a sexual awareness that was almost painfully strong. Memories of their short-lived intimacy on the night that Nicky was conceived were sizzling through her and her body was awakening again, shedding the taut suppression of feelings and tight self-discipline that she had practised for so many months.

'That's better, *khriso mou*,' Alexei told her thickly, shifting against her so that even through the barrier of their clothing she could feel the unmistakable urgency of his arousal.

And a kind of heavenly satisfaction enveloped Billie at that instant, for she had never truly managed to see herself as a sexually appealing woman in Alexei's eyes. After all, what they once briefly shared had been unreservedly forgotten by him and she had found it hard to equate that cruel hard fact with the idea that their intimacy had been in any way special on his terms. But now, in the most primitive way of all, she could enjoy the proof that Alexei wanted her as a man wanted a woman and as a husband wanted a wife. *Her*, miraculously; not one of the more beautiful and sophisticated women present who had entertained him most successfully, though if only for a little while. And what if she came to the same end? The thought struck like a dagger in Billie's vulnerable heart. What if those gossiping exes of his were right and Alexei got bored and swiftly realised that he had made a mistake in marrying her?

Anxious green eyes screened, she luxuriated in his embrace while her mind teemed with rampant, fearful thoughts that dismayed her. Since when had she been so scared? But all too often in recent months Billie had appreciated that loving Alexei and having Nicky had changed her in a fundamental way: she was much more at the mercy of her emotions than she had once been.

And, of course, she was nervous about the future. After all, Alexei wasn't in love with her. He had married her on the rebound after breaking off his relationship with Calisto Bethune. That particular taunt, overheard in the cloakroom, had not been without foundation.

Alexei had chosen Billie as a wife because he believed
he knew her well and considered her to be thoroughly
sensible and trustworthy. He had *not* chosen her because she was gorgeous, exciting or fantastic fun. He
had picked her with his head, not his heart, deeming her
perfect for the role of a conservative, low-maintenance
wife. How would he react tomorrow when her revelations forced him to appreciate that she was as flawed
and imperfect as any other woman?

They left the floor to circulate among their guests.
Later, in the early evening, Hilary, her eyes full of dismay, sped over to her niece and whispered urgently,
'Lauren's talking in the room next door. She's drunk
and saying silly stuff. She wouldn't listen to me—'

'I'll come with you.' Sliding free of Alexei's hold,
Billie hurried in her aunt's wake.

Lauren was easily spotted. The table in front of her
was littered with empty glasses. With a cigarette in one
hand and another burning in the ashtray beside her,
Lauren was revelling in being the centre of attention.

'Billie!' Lauren exclaimed with enthusiasm when she
laid eyes on her diminutive daughter. 'You know that's
not her actual name. That's what Alexei christened her
when she was a kid—her real name is Bliss…'

'What else can you tell us, Lauren?' an eager brunette prompted.

'Obviously, I know where all the bodies are buried!'
Throwing back her shoulders in emphasis and exposing rather too much bosom in her low-cut dress as she
did so, Lauren widened suggestive eyes, only to start

coughing violently as the smoke from her cigarette wafted up into her face.

'There are no bodies,' Billie interposed firmly, finding her way to the bedraggled blonde's side and slapping her on the back.

'Don't listen to her...there's lots of bodies!' Lauren carolled rebelliously loudly. 'And one of them is very little. In fact, I warned my daughter to keep all her secrets until she was safely married. At least that way even if the marriage crashes and burns, she'll be rich and secure—'

Losing all patience in the wake of that outburst, Hilary grasped one of her sister's arms and hauled her bodily from her seat. 'It's time for us to go home now, Lauren—'

'I don't wanna go home,' the middle-aged blonde slurred as she swayed. 'I'm enjoying the party.'

A horrible little silence fell and only as she assisted her aunt with her stumbling, angrily muttering mother did Billie register that Alexei had joined them. Her face burning, her tummy twisting with fear, she clashed with blazing golden eyes.

'I've organised a car for you,' Alexei told Hilary in a gentle undertone as a nanny appeared to pass over Nicky into her care. 'I'm sorry that you have to leave early.'

Lauren, who, for all her outspokenness, was intimidated by her son-in-law, had turned an ashen colour and was now avoiding both his gaze and her daughter's. Billie was wan and uncomfortable as she watched her aunt leave with Nicky and her mother.

'I think Lauren may well need professional help,' Alexei breathed with icy cool.

'Sorry. I know she's an embarrassment...but professional help?' Billie echoed, finally working up the courage to look directly at him.

'A stint in rehab might at least cure her of looking forward to our marriage crashing and burning,' Alexei countered sardonically, brilliant golden eyes cutting as lasers. 'Clearly she hasn't read the terms of our prenup. But what the hell was she talking about? Buried bodies? *Secrets?*'

Pale as milk, Billie trembled as she registered how close her mother had come to exposing Nicky's parentage in public. 'She was drunk and getting carried away with all the attention she was getting—that's all. But I don't think she needs to be packed off to rehab just yet—'

'Leave me to deal with Lauren,' Alexei interrupted with ruthless cool. 'I understand her better than you do.'

And Billie, accustomed to her mother's single-minded obstinate egotism, reckoned that he very probably did.

CHAPTER TWO

IT WAS AFTER MIDNIGHT. The bride and groom had stayed with their guests until late, then had then taken a motor launch out to Alexei's yacht, *Sea Queen*. But lights in Billie's own little house were still twinkling brightly back on shore, Billie registered as she stood on the private deck beyond the incredible luxury of the stateroom suite. Hilary, at the very least, was still awake. Was Lauren still with her sister and behaving badly? Or was Nicky reacting poorly to his disrupted routine and preventing her aunt from getting the rest she needed? Billie's arms felt horribly empty. Her heart ached at once again having to face the prospect of leaving her infant son.

Only for a week, though, Alexei had sworn. He was no big fan of honeymoons or indeed any enforced break from business, but he was also too astute not to recognise that to neglect any show of intimacy and togetherness after their wedding would attract the kind of comment that might embarrass his bride. And tomorrow Alexei would finally know everything there was to know about her, Billie reminded herself doggedly. The pretences, the lies would mercifully end there. There would be no more secrets. He would understand her attachment to Nicky, but how would he feel about suddenly and without any preparation at all becoming a father?

Billie shivered in the cool crisp late spring air. A light step sounded behind her and Alexei closed his arms round her from behind, drawing her back into the heat and shelter of his tall, muscular body. 'That was one very long day,' he sighed above her head. 'How the hell did my father manage to go through with marrying four times over?'

'I suppose the fact that he kept on trying to find the right wife says a lot about his optimistic outlook,' Billie remarked, her voice wavering as her bridegroom pressed his mouth sensually to the tender skin where her shoulder met her neck. She was not aware that it was a sensitive spot, but it sparked a surprising burst of heat low in her pelvis and she trembled, straining back against him in response.

Alexei laughed softly. 'Don't be so naïve. He only married my mother because she was carrying me. He wanted a son and heir more than he ever wanted any woman—'

Cooler air brushed Billie's spine while he unhooked the back of her gown with the lazy pace of a gourmet contemplating a six-course banquet. 'You're so cynical!' she returned.

'The marriage might have been a success on your terms, but even my mother knew that he would never have married her had she not conceived. She was a nobody from nowhere...'

'Like me,' Billie could not resist commenting in receipt of that arrogant opinion.

'No. You're a local girl with a clever brain and a colourful background,' Alexei teased, sliding his hands below the loosened bodice of her dress to find the firm thrusting softness of her breasts. 'And now you're my wife, my perfect wife, *khriso mou*.'

Her breath caught in her throat as he expertly massaged her swelling nipples between thumb and forefinger, sending sharp arrows of desire darting to the very centre of her restive body. Helpless in the grip of those sensations, she leant back against him and he swept her up into his arms and carried her back into the stateroom. Setting her down he peeled her out of the gown he had undone and lifted her clear of the foaming swathe of petticoats.

'Full marks for surprising me,' Alexei quipped, pausing to take in the full effect of her turquoise satin and lace lingerie and the lacy hold-up stockings she sported on her slim legs.

Although rosy colour warmed Billie's face beneath his lingering appraisal and her breasts shimmied in the turquoise satin cups as her breathing increased in rapidity, she countered, 'I'm a bride…what did you expect?'

'White cotton, no frills,' he told her frankly, resting her down across his long powerful thighs while one strong arm supported her spine.

Billie gazed up into brilliant golden eyes and her heart felt as if it were bouncing up onto a positive high of love. 'Oh, you'll see plenty of white cotton on the other three hundred and sixty-four days of the year.

This is a one-off,' she warned him deadpan. 'Enjoy it while you can.'

And Alexei laughed and kissed her, framing her face with spread fingers, delving into the moist tender interior she offered long and deep until her heart was thumping like a piston and she was kissing him back hard, revelling in the wicked pleasure of being crushed against him. He released the catch on her bra and moulded the lush fullness of a rose-tipped mound with reverent appreciation. 'You can have no idea how many times I've fantasised about your breasts...'

'In the office?' Billie gasped, taken aback by that candid admission.

'You look so shocked.' Alexei was laughing again, both hands now fully engaged in massaging the swelling bounty of her creamy flesh.

'Well, it's not very professional, is it?' Billie complained, embarrassed for herself in the past.

'But I only looked and imagined. I didn't touch,' he reminded her. '*Of course* I looked. I'm a man and the more you covered up, the more I noticed and wondered. Modesty is a great turn-on. If you'd sunbathed topless I'd have satisfied my curiosity long ago.'

As his skilled fingers found the distended tips of her nipples her eyes slid shut in an instant of intense arousal that made heat bloom like a yearning flower between her trembling thighs. But even as her body reacted she was thinking over what he said, registering that her discreet clothing and apparent reluctance had heightened his desire for her and immediately wondering whether constant marital availability would swiftly convert his interest to boredom. He bent her back over his arm and closed his mouth over first one throbbing reddened peak and then the other, laving her sensitised flesh with his tongue and grazing the beaded peaks with his strong white teeth. She gasped out loud, her body catching fire and flaming as fast and hotly as bone-dry straw. Rational thoughts fled her head like fallen leaves blown by the wind.

'I never thought I'd be so excited by my wedding night,' Alexei confided huskily, setting her aside and springing up to begin carelessly shedding his clothes. 'Congratulations, Billie. Experienced as I am, you make even sex feel fresh and new.'

Awesomely conscious of the stinging sensitivity of her nipples and the lush heat at the heart of her, Billie was dry-mouthed and all of a quiver, while wondering if she would ever be able to match his cool…or, for that matter, his evident expectations. So many women had tried and failed to hold his attention. Why should she be any different? Even to lie there half naked without rushing to cover up her exposed flesh was a challenge for Billie. Impervious to such insecurities, Alexei cast off his shirt, revealing the tightly honed muscular magnificence of a torso sprinkled with dark whorls of hair, a narrow waist and a stomach as flat as a rock slab. Physically he was just pure perfection, she acknowledged, her gaze riveted by his sheer spellbinding masculine impact. He discarded his last garment and the very boldness of his towering erection washed colour over her face, for her memory—unlike his—had no missing gaps and she was recalling the velvet-sheathed-in-steel feel of him beneath her fingers and moving inside her. Something clenched deep in her stomach.

He lay down beside her and pulled her back to him, crushing her mouth hungrily below his with a hot sexual urgency that thrilled her. He slid long fingers in a bold trail below her panties and groaned with earthy satisfaction, 'You're so wet and ready for me, *khriso mou.*'

Feverishly aware of that betraying damp heat, she trembled beneath the confident touch of his hand, raising her knees to assist him as he skimmed off the final barrier between them. 'I can't help wanting you,' she breathed shakily.

'And isn't that only as it should be?' Alexei husked, golden eyes glittering over her with virile approval even as his fingers came into contact with a roughness to the skin of her lower stomach that surprised him. 'What is this I feel?'

Billie froze, belatedly realising that he had found her Caesarean scar. 'Just a gynaecological thing—some surgery—I had,' she answered as casually as she could.

'You never mentioned it,' Alexei commented.

'Some things women like to keep to themselves.'

He shifted his hand back to a more sensitive spot and every skin cell in her quiveringly appreciative body seemed to leap. She was feeling too much to feel comfortable because her responses were already breaching the boundaries of her self-control. The exquisite pleasure of his skilled exploration of the slick folds of tender tissue between her thighs was almost more than she could stand without crying out aloud. She twisted and she turned until he stilled her and then she gritted her teeth together, her slender neck extending while he delicately teased the tiny erect bud of her clitoris and right then her concept of what was unbearable was re-written from inside out. Her hips shifted and jerked upwards in a pleading motion and he lowered his dark arrogant head to the distended rigidity of her nipples, sucking them into his mouth and toying erotically with her wildly responsive flesh.

'Please...*please now*,' she framed brokenly, tormented by the burning heat of an excitement too much to be borne.

He came over her and into her in an almost simultaneous movement. With a sinuous shift of his hips he positioned his long powerful body and sank into her inner warmth with a low, melodious growl of sensual pleasure. For a split second, fear pierced the veil of her excitement and her inner muscles clenched hard round his swollen shaft. His golden eyes caught the momentary look of concern and unease she couldn't hide and then his hands closed round her hips and he drove into her again with hard, sure sensual force as if he knew the intensity of her need. The feeling of pressure low in her belly increased until all she was conscious of was the remorseless intrusion of his strong body into hers and the ravishing irresistible force of a physical stimulation so extreme it came close to pain. Tingling sparks of her impending release shot through her stomach and she writhed and gasped, her body arching as the most intense orgasm gripped her and sent wild sensation flooding through her in an uncontrollable and explosive tide.

The feeling of release from her earthly body was so

powerful that for long moments after that climax Billie was in a daze. Only slowly did she regain awareness again, register the weightiness of her limbs, the heavy cocoon of sweet satisfaction that was reluctant to let her go, and even more slowly did she notice that Alexei had pulled away from her when she most wanted to cling to him. And then there was the silence…thrumming and taut as only a male as volatile as Alexei could make it. Her bright head swivelled on the pillow, green eyes very dark and wide flaring to Alexei.

He looked levelly back at her and a lump of dismay formed in her throat, for she read the challenge in his appraisal. The silence lay like a claustrophobic blanket threatening to stifle her ability to breathe. A whoosh of alarm ran down her spine like a cold warning hand. 'What's wrong?'

Thrusting the pillows back against the headboard, Alexei sat up. Brilliant golden eyes rested on her with all the extraordinary force of his fierce temperament. 'I'm amazed you have the nerve to ask me that. You lied to me, and you know how I feel about lies.'

Fear cut Billie as deep as a knife wound and a kind of panic raced like a wrecking ball through her more usually calm thoughts, creating mental havoc. Her blood ran cold, her skin turned clammy. 'L-*lies*?' she queried, playing desperately for time.

'That certainly wasn't the very first time you had sex. You weren't a virgin before I married you, yet you were determined to make me believe that you were. What is that other than a lie?'

He was disappointed, she assumed, realising just

what a pit she had dug for herself to fall into. How could she tell him the truth without telling him the *whole* truth? The few hours of grace she had believed she still had had suddenly vanished, depriving her of any control over the situation.

'Of course it would be downright hypocrisy for a guy of my experience to expect or demand a virgin bride in this day and age,' Alexei drawled in glancing continuance. 'I may have made a false assumption but you lied by omission. Lying by staying silent when you should have contradicted me is *still* a lie.'

'I didn't know how to tell you,' Billie framed uncertainly. 'When you made that assumption I felt trapped by it—'

'No, don't make the mistake of trying to lay your dishonesty at my door,' Alexei cautioned her, his lean handsome face hardening into grim lines at her response. 'I also want to know who your first lover was: Damon Marios, your spineless first love?'

The instant he flung that arrogant demand and that name at her she froze, wondering whether she really had to trail out all her secrets there and then, if there was no escape, no other way of deflecting him. And then she marvelled at her own reluctance to speak, her terror of breaking free of the cosy bridal bubble of happy-ever-afters and fantasy. 'You're not going to believe me when I do tell you who it was.'

As he stared at her from below the dense dark screen of his luxuriant lashes Alexei's handsome mouth took on a sardonic quirk. 'Try me. At least you have the wit not to persist in the lie.'

Billie no longer felt comfortable in the bed. She was no more comfortable under his intent scrutiny when she slid out naked from below the sheet to move a few steps away and reach for the light silk robe draped in readiness for her use over a chair. Enveloped within its concealing folds, the sash tightened round her waist with unsteady hands, she felt curiously more in control again.

'How did you know? How did you guess?' she suddenly pressed, unable to resist asking that question.

'You told me. You betrayed yourself by the expression in your eyes, your face, your very responses. You looked and acted guilty.'

'Because that's how I feel and it's really not fair because not all of this is my fault,' Billie reasoned with a defensive edge of defiance. 'You can't be so judgemental about lies. Not everything is that black and white.'

'Spare me the moral philosophy speech,' Alexei derided. 'You may be my wife but one thing hasn't changed: I still expect a straight answer to a direct question.'

'You asked me who my first lover was but, quite honestly, you have no right to ask me that question!' Billie dared, flashing that answer back to him in retribution.

Alexei dealt her an arrested appraisal, her insubordination clearly coming as an unwelcome surprise to him.

Billie was trembling. 'I mean, how do you even dare to ask me that question?'

His golden gaze was splinteringly hard and unyielding. 'I dare because you're my wife and nothing in your life should be hidden from me.'

Billie tried and failed to swallow at that bold, star-tlingly idealistic expectation. A tiny pulse at the base of her throat was flickering wildly. The tip of her tongue snaked out to moisten the taut dryness of her full lower lip. '*You* were my first lover…but you don't remember the time we spent together—'

His ebony brows drew together. 'What the hell kind of nonsensical claim is that?' Alexei demanded, his raw impatience unhidden.

'It may sound like nonsense to you at this moment, but it's still the truth. On the night of your parents' fu-neral, when everyone else had gone home, you had been drinking and you went to bed with me,' Billie recounted, her agitated fingers knotting into the too long sleeves of her robe and tugging in a restive motion at the cuffs.

'Any moment now you'll be telling me that you were abducted by aliens! Are you crazy?' Alexei jibed, tossing back the bedding and springing from the bed, a tall, pow-erful figure all the more daunting unclad. 'Or are you drunk? That's the only explanation I can come up with!'

'We made love in the guest suite where I was staying at the time. We had no contraception. You were heading back to your own room for condoms when you tripped and fell down the steps by the swimming pool. When you came round, you didn't remember that you'd been with me…' Billie's taut voice quivered with tension as he came to a halt, wheeled round and stared at her with frowning questioning force: she had finally won his full attention. 'You thought you'd been in the swim-ming pool because your hair was damp but you'd only been in the shower…'

Dark eyes blazing wrathful gold, he studied her, his lean, strong visage clenched into forbidding lines. 'No, Billie,' he cut in icily. 'You're very ingenious but I won't fall for a story like that. You tell me that we slept together on the one night of my life that I can't fully recall and you expect me to believe you? How stupid do you think I am?'

In a growing state of confusion, Billie gazed back at him. She had known it would be a challenge to make him believe her, but it had not crossed her mind that he might suspect her of fitting fictional facts to an actual event to provide back-up for what he deemed to be lies. 'But we really *were* together that night.'

'So, according to you, unlike every other woman I have ever met, you gave me your body and expected nothing in return—not even an acknowledgement from me?' Alexei slashed back at her with incredulous scorn. 'At least come up with lies that make some sense!'

Anger licked like a hungry flame out of her bone-deep anxiety. She felt as if she were fighting for her life and certainly for the love of it. Not so very long ago they had enjoyed an instant of perfect harmony out on deck and she had been so happy. 'When have I ever lied to you?' she queried emotively.

'What about those weeks before our wedding when you were playing the innocent little virgin charade? You need to fine-tune those principles I mistakenly thought you had. It's not the lie you allowed to stand, it's the fact that you were dishonest that disgusts me.'

Every word Alexei spoke flailing her like a whip, Billie had lost colour. Her body, so lately hot and damp from the vigour of his lovemaking, suddenly felt cold and shivery. Her green eyes dominated her heart-shaped face but the anger that had awakened inside her was already climbing higher and growing stronger in her defence. How dared he say that she disgusted him after all she had gone through on his behalf? She had stood by in silence while he romanced Calisto and slept with her. She had endured her pregnancy and the birth of his child without his support. *How dared he judge her?*

'Don't you dare tell me that I disgust you!'

Hard-as-granite dark golden eyes raked over her slight figure before finally condescending to meet her incensed gaze. 'It's the truth and that's all I've ever wanted or expected from you: the truth,' he told her insistently. 'If you can't even give me that, what have we got?'

That harsh question assailed her like water dripping incessantly on stone, for no matter what excuses she gave and no matter what words she spouted she would still be faced with the reality that she had lied to him. And just then, as he stepped into the shower and switched on the controls, Alexei was a formidable presence, terrifyingly immovable in his stubborn conviction. Rigid with tension, she went back into the stateroom. She quailed at the prospect of telling him about Nicky right there and then. If he couldn't even credit her claim that he had once made love to her, how likely was it that he would accept that he was the father of the child he didn't yet know she'd had?

Her slender hands clenched into fists as she attempted to will greater strength into herself. Hilary

had insisted that her niece should tell Alexei the truth
before the wedding, and Hilary had been right, Billie
acknowledged with fierce regret over her own weakness. Instead of respecting the sound ethical base of
her aunt's argument, Billie had listened to Lauren, her
self-serving and avaricious mother, who had never let
notions of what was right and decent come between her
and anything that she wanted. Billie had wanted that
wedding ring at any cost, and now that she had it on
her finger it felt like an own goal, a mockery, an empty
promise...*why*? They had only been married for a matter of a few hours and Alexei had just told her that she
disgusted him.

Billie sat down on the richly upholstered chair and
surveyed her extravagant surroundings with blank eyes.
Although it was warm, she felt cold. Shock was setting
in and hitting her hard. He was the guy that she loved
and she had burned her boats so thoroughly that she
did not know how to go back and retrace her steps. Just
then, damage control seemed an impossibility. Nothing
that she could say or do would alter the fact that she had
lied. And in the same moment she recognised just how
much falling in love and having a child had altered her,
for she was so much more emotional than she had once
been. That made her feel so vulnerable and she longed
to slide back into the practical, less sensitive shell of
the young woman she had once been.

TOWELLING HIS WET body roughly dry with impatient
hands, Alexei listened to the silence from the adjoining
room. The silence only inflamed him more. He should

have had the truth out of her by now, not those ridiculous lies! Discarding the towel, he strode into the communicating dressing room to pull out clothes. He was
so angry that there was a tremor in his lean muscular
hands. He stared down at them with brooding dark eyes
and clenched his teeth together hard. Billie, whom he
had trusted. *Ise Vlakas!* Stupid, he called himself angrily. Why had he placed such faith in her when he had
long known that precious few women could be trusted?
He had long accepted that many women would do virtually anything to get close to a man as hugely wealthy as
he was. But that for her own ends Billie should attempt
to make use of that particular night when he had drunk
too much was an act of even more serious subterfuge
and one that he considered unforgivable. To add more
lies to the lies she had already allowed to stand between
them was inexcusable. To think that he had thought her
intelligent, worthy of being his wife, *perfect*....

Although in one sense, she had been perfect, Alexei
conceded grudgingly as his mind roved back to their
brief intimacy. A prickling heat at his groin and the stirring heaviness of renewed arousal assailed him while
he recalled his bride's surprising wildness between the
sheets. Her eager responsiveness and complete lack of
control when he touched her had excited him—*she* had
excited him more than any woman had in a long time.
Any man would have rejoiced in receipt of such fervour.
That passionate receptiveness had not been what he expected from a woman who was well known for her rigid
self-discipline and old-fashioned notions.

Old-fashioned? His handsome mouth curled with

renewed derision. What was truly real about Billie? And what was fake? Only hours earlier he would have sworn she was genuine one-hundred-carat gold, the real article, a woman he could actually respect…and *now*? He wondered if Damon Marios had taken her virginity, or whether it had been one of his other employees, or even whether the identity of Billie's secret lover lay far back in her youth. But why should the man's identity even matter to him? He had never been a possessive man, particularly when it came to sex. He was too practical to be otherwise. The crux of the matter was that Billie had lied.

Distaste filling him afresh, Alexei strode out of the dressing room, across the spacious stateroom and out of it again without even acknowledging her presence. He would give Billie time to consider her options before he left *Sea Queen*. He was already considering his own: he had no intention of staying married to a woman he couldn't trust.

CHAPTER THREE

FRESH FROM THE SHOWER, Billie tackled her tangled and damp hair until it dried in a heavy silken swathe across her shoulders. She breathed in deep and set off to find Alexei. She was not a coward, she had *never* been a coward; he would listen to her, he *had* to listen to her. That was the only hope of salvation that she had left. Yet she knew how hard Alexei Drakos could be, how uncompromising, how very cold-blooded when his own interests were at stake...

Alexei was working at his laptop in the office just as if it were the middle of his working day rather than halfway through his wedding night. His luxuriant blue-black hair gleamed below the discreet down-lighters, lush dark lashes casting crescent shadows across his exotically high cheekbones. It was a pose she had seen him in a thousand times before and she had known exactly where to find him—at times of stress, Alexei always took refuge in work. But she could read the tension still etched into the lineaments of his classic profile and the warning flare of his straight aquiline nose as he lifted his proud dark head and saw her in the doorway and his grim golden eyes hardened.

'I know you're angry with me but I have to talk to

you,' Billie said with low-pitched urgency. 'I have to tell you what I've done—'

'What you've *done*?' Alexei repeated drily, a slanting brow quirking in emphasis. 'Does this relate to Lauren's loaded comments about knowing where the bodies are buried?'

That was a question that Billie would have preferred not to have to answer just then. But the awareness that she could not afford to play with the truth even just a little froze her in place. Slowly she nodded in reluctant affirmation of that point and watched his lean strong face darken in angry acknowledgement.

'Even your mother knows what I do not?' Alexei demanded.

'Yes. I did try to keep it all private but I'm afraid she worked out what I didn't tell her for herself,' Billie confessed quietly.

Alexei let his gaze roam over her small straight figure. For once what she wore enhanced rather than concealed her body and it was obvious that she was naked below her robe. The lush curves of her breasts were clearly delineated by the thinly draped silk and the tip-tilted swollen nipples that had thrilled to his attention were still tantalisingly prominent below the fine material. The heaviness stirring at his groin forced him to shift position in his seat while he wondered cynically if that revealing wrap had been chosen purely for his benefit.

Regardless of that suspicion, desire slivered through him and the strength of his sudden heated arousal took him aback. Just for once, satisfaction had not led to

satiation. But then the very force of what he was feeling, that pungent mass of anger, bitterness and disillusionment, required a physical response; he was far
more comfortable with his body's natural appetites than
he was with words or emotions. Determined to ease
himself in the most effective way of all, he extended
a lean hand to her in silence and with a wary look of
surprise in her green eyes she was quick to grasp his
fingers. Banding his arms round her slight length, he
crushed her to his big powerful frame and claimed her
soft mouth with hot, driving hunger.

'Se thelo.' Alexei told her bluntly that he wanted
her in roughened Greek and as the heady combination
of yearning and relief at that invitation gripped Billie
it left her infinitely weak. His embrace had blown her
vague expectations out of the water and with every
erotic plunge of his tongue her legs felt more boneless
and less able to provide independent support. So keen
was she to bridge the gulf between them at that moment
that he could have done virtually anything with her and
she would have offered no objection.

With a bold tug on the sash of her robe so that the
edges fell apart, Alexei lifted her up onto the desk. He
moulded the lush, creamy swell of her breasts, tugging
at her swollen nipples, before he lowered his dark head
to close his mouth urgently to a pouting peak while he
pushed her legs apart so that his fingers could slickly
massage the tiny bud of her arousal and probe the ex-
cruciatingly tender pink flesh beneath. She whimpered,
excitement shrieking through her in a great rampant
roar of heat, her body eager for release from the ter-

rible tension. That fast, she could think of nothing but the urgent craving that his skilful caresses had induced.

Her arms linked round his neck and she trembled as he settled his hands below her hips and pulled her closer to stand between her spread thighs. There was a split second when she was aware that he was donning protection and sanity almost came back to her but, an instant later, he drove his rigid shaft into her hot velvety depths and her slim body bucked and writhed in ecstatic response. He pushed her flat and raised her thighs to pound into her tight wet channel with ravishingly forceful thrusts. Sounds she couldn't control escaping from her throat, she was at the mercy of intense sensation and extraordinary pleasure. She was flung to a height and then the pressure and tightness in her pelvis broke and fireworks exploded inside her in a wild, jerking, totally uncontrolled release.

'*Efharisto*…thanks. That took the edge off my temper.' Alexei lifted her off the desk and deposited her in a bemused heap in a nearby armchair.

Blinking rapidly and still all of a quiver from the raw passion he had unleashed on her, Billie watched blankly as he strode into the washroom. She looked down at her naked breasts and, with a stifled exclamation of shock, reared upright to tie the robe securely closed again. That seeming necessity did, however, make her think of that well-known saying that talked of bolting the stable door after the horse had already bolted. She was so shocked by what had just happened between them that she was trembling.

She had not known that it was possible to make love

like that, for everything to be so intense and wild that it overwhelmed every other thought and decent consideration. Nor had she ever suspected that she might have the capacity to enjoy such an encounter and that new knowledge shamed her in her own eyes. Indeed she was devastated by his demonstration of savage sexual power over her, because even though no such intimacies had even been on her mind he had taken her from cool passivity to the hottest orgasm without the slightest hesitation or difficulty. *That took the edge off my temper*, he had said, as if the taking of her body was on a par with a good gym workout. Her face burned scarlet at the recollection.

Across his desk as well, she recalled in consternation, mortified by the awareness that in spite of the chasm between them she had let him do exactly as he liked. Even so, it was still their wedding night, wasn't it? Saying no to her highly sexed husband would not be the wisest path to take if she wanted to heal the breach between them. And, of course, anything that could reduce the tension between them was sensible and good, she reasoned, raking her tangled hair back off her damp brow with an unsteady hand. After all, she still had to talk to him, but the prospect of doing so while her body still hummed, tingled and downright ached from the sexual *Blitzkrieg* of his was a major challenge.

Only the dark shadow of masculine stubble roughening his strong jawline and sensual mouth marred Alexei's visual perfection when he rejoined her. His cream linen chinos and sweater were as expensive, tailored and sophisticated in style as any more formal wear.

Black hair brushed back from his brow, Alexei looked startlingly handsome but worryingly untouched by the emotional vulnerability threatening her equilibrium. All over again she longed for the detachment and self-control she had once been able to call on around him, for it had protected her from pain.

'I believe you said that you had something to tell me,' Alexei drawled cool as ice, as if that episode of hot breathless sex had taken place only in her imagination.

Locking pained green eyes to his angular bronzed face, Billie said quietly, 'You *were* with me on the night of your parents' funeral. After your fall I knew that you'd lost a couple of hours and were actually suffering from concussion, even possibly a form of amnesia, but I couldn't persuade you to seek medical help.'

Alexei straightened his broad shoulders, his imposing height of over six feet casting a long forceful shadow across the dimly lit room. His entire attitude was detached, even businesslike. 'I can't accept any part of your story. I would never have slept with you in such circumstances, and as for that tale you told about sex without contraception? I'm afraid that could only have happened in the fictional realms of your brain because, drunk or sober, I don't ever take risks in that line.'

In her eagerness to persuade him, Billie leant forward. 'I'm not lying and maybe you'll understand that better once I've told you everything—'

Dense ebony lashes screening his stunning eyes to a dangerous gleam of gold, his lean dark features were a mask of disdain. *'Everything?'* Alexei repeated with a saturnine look of mockery that sent the blood drumming heavily into her cheeks. 'What other strange fantasies have you dreamt up for my amusement?'

That piece of ridicule made Billie want to slap him hard. Her fingers clenched tightly together on that dangerous impulse. 'Maybe I was wrong not to tell you the truth months ago, but once you met Calisto the whole situation changed and I didn't feel I had any choices left. I assumed you were in love with her—you pretty much told me you were going to marry her. I had just discovered that I was pregnant. I was planning to tell you but you couldn't even remember sleeping with me—'

Black brows pleating together, Alexei cut boldly into that recitation. 'You were pregnant? By whom?'

Billie flung him a fevered glance of frustration. 'You're not that slow on the uptake—I conceived on the night of the funeral; I fell pregnant by you. You may not remember it but we made love twice without precautions.'

Alexei released his breath in a sharp exhalation, his instant dismissal of that possibility clear by his expression.

'Hilary's son is actually *my* son,' Billie spelt out, refusing to be daunted by that discouraging silence. 'He's my baby. I gave birth to him while I was on my career break in London. The only reason I asked for the leave was so that I could conceal my pregnancy.'

His brilliant eyes suddenly shimmered like a firework display, his outrage at what she was saying etched into every harshening angle of his lean darkly handsome features. 'Hilary's child is yours? You are telling me that you have actually given birth to a baby? That you deliberately concealed that fact from me and let me go ahead and make you my wife?' he roared at her in a sudden wrathful attack that made her shrink back momentarily into the shelter of her seat, shaken by his vehemence. 'And now you dare to try and pass off some other man's child as mine?'

Rigid with tension and with perspiration dampening her brow, Billie faced him. 'It's not like that at all. Nicky *is* your son. I've never been with another man.'

Alexei wasn't really listening. What he had learned was sufficient for him to make a judgement. A red mist of rage was burning through his brain while he struggled to put together what she had told him. His bride was a mother...she had a *child*? Appalled by that revelation, he remembered the seam of scar tissue low on her abdomen, which only hours earlier she had passed off as 'a gynaecological thing'. A Caesarean scar, he guessed, for the first time seeing a solid foundation to what had initially struck him as incredible claims. He could not at first get over his sense of shock that she could have concealed so much from him and even the most cursory appraisal of the past year or so warned him that Billie must have spun him an elaborate ongoing pack of lies in an outrageous attempt to pass off her child as his. Of course, she was anything but stupid. She knew that that was the only circumstance that might give her the hope that he wouldn't divorce her.

Golden eyes steadily chilling to the temperature of a sunlit iceberg, Alexei surveyed her. 'What a devious little schemer you are! You have the nerve to sit there looking me in the eye while you confess that you lied and cheated your way to the altar knowing that I would never have married you had I known the truth about you!'

Billie leapt up, her long, thick, wine-red hair rippling like bright ribbons across her shoulders and sliding across her cheekbones to highlight her pallor. 'That's not how it was, Alexei. There were lies and I'm sorry for that, but there was no cheating. Nicky is your son. How was I supposed to persuade you of that fact when you couldn't even recall being with me?'

'I assume you have heard of DNA testing?'

Hotspots of pink deepened the hue of Billie's cheeks in reaction to that unexpected taunt.

'This kid is...what age?' Alexei queried.

'He's four and a half months old. But when he was born you were still with Calisto and thinking about marrying her.' Billie referred to his ex-girlfriend, Calisto Bethune, with a heavy heart. 'I didn't want to cause trouble. I saw no benefit to anyone in doing that. It seemed to me,' she continued painfully, 'that you didn't want to remember being with me, and that probably everyone concerned would be happier if that night remained a secret.'

'I don't believe for one moment that your child is mine,' Alexei declared with icy conviction. 'I refuse to believe it. I hope you don't plan to take these insane stories into court with you. You will make a laughing stock of yourself—'

'Into...court?' Billie echoed shakily. 'What are you talking about?'

'Do I really need to spell out the fact that what you've just told me is grounds for divorce?'

Billie turned as cold as though he had just plunged her into an ice bath, consternation and shock gripping her hard. 'I know that you're shocked by what I've told you—'

'Of course I'm shocked by the image of you, your mother and your aunt plotting against me like Macbeth's three witches!' Alexei derided with ferocious bite.

Billie's temper flared and she flew upright. 'It's ridiculous to talk like that. Nobody *plotted* against you! When I persuaded Hilary to pretend that Nicky was her child, my only motivation in doing so was to hide Nicky's parentage and protect you.'

'*You* wanted to protect *me*?' Alexei exclaimed harshly, his contempt for that claim unconcealed. 'Even now in the midst of your attempt to palm off your bastard child on me, you can't tell me the truth! My proposal of marriage was what motivated your lies and deception—'

'How could it have been?' Billie flung back fierily, standing her ground to challenge him. 'My pretence that Nicky was my aunt's child began when I first told you that she was pregnant and asked for a career break. And that was months before you even considered marrying me!'

Stumped by that inescapable fact, Alexei studied her with enraged hauteur, his glittering gaze bright against his superb bone structure. 'You lied to me and you deceived me over a very long period—'

'But not with any malicious intent!' Billie rushed to

interpose, desperation racking her with a level of fear that did nothing to clarify her state of mind. 'I admit that I should have told you about Nicky before the wedding but I didn't have the guts—'

'Naturally avarice and ambition won out over honesty. Why? Only because you knew there would be no wedding if you told me the truth about yourself.'

'The very last thing I have ever wanted from you is money!' Billie launched back at him, angrily objecting to that base accusation. 'And don't refer to my son as a bastard ever again. However he was born, whoever he is, I love him and I'm proud of him. If you think so badly of me, how could you make love to me again?'

That emotive demand made Alexei's jaw square and he sent her a flashing look of scorn. 'That was just sex, a primitive urge for physical release, nothing more complex.'

Her face flamed and then slowly paled as his response sank in and trampled her pride into the dust. She wished with all her heart that she had said no, pushed him away, stuck to the business of confession and blame. But what was done was done and she could not change it. In spite of that sophisticated façade, Alexei had a primal streak that ran through him like tempered steel and powered his volatility and his ruthlessness. He was a Drakos through and through. His father, Constantine, had not hesitated to divorce the blameless third wife who'd adored him, and replace her with his pregnant mistress. Alexei, it seemed, would be equally quick to discard her now that she had disappointed his expectations.

'Nicky is your son,' she swore one last time, desperate to convince him of that crucial fact before he could tear their marriage apart.

'Nothing can excuse your lies and trickery,' Alexei drawled in a tone of finality. 'You cheated your way into our marriage and deserve nothing but my contempt. Naturally I'll order DNA tests, but only to ensure that you can't continue to allege that I fathered your baby.'

Humiliated by the threat of such testing being carried out on her child, Billie flung him a seething glance of condemnation. 'That's an insult! You're the only man I've ever slept with.'

Alexei rested forbidding dark golden eyes on her. 'I can't believe a word that comes out of your mouth and whose fault is that?'

He strode out of the room. Billie lingered in the shadowy office and struggled to cope with her unwieldy emotions. Their marriage had barely begun and she had wrecked it by keeping secrets from him, a little voice warned inside her aching head. She had lost his trust and it would not be easily regained. He was angry with her, very angry, but she had known he would be, she reminded herself dully. She heard the racket of rotor blades and unfroze to rush over to the desk and snatch up the phone. Captain McGregor informed her that Alexei had filed a flight plan for Monaco and had taken off in the helicopter with his security team. She thanked him for the information and replaced the receiver with a trembling hand and a heart racing like an overworked piston.

Alexei had just left her, walking out on her and their

marriage. That realisation was a body blow that hit Billie very hard. She felt sick with the pain and trauma of that bold move and knew she had seriously underestimated his reaction to the secrets she had kept. It would be virtually impossible to influence a man who was determined to put an ocean between them. Few brides, however, were abandoned within hours of the wedding and Alexei's activities never passed under the media radar. The press would pick up the story of his unbridegroomlike behaviour and run with it for weeks.

Tears choking her and stinging her heavy eyes, Billie went back to the opulent stateroom in order to get dressed. It might not be dawn yet but the wedding night was well and truly over. She would take the motor launch back to Speros and go home to look after Nicky. What else could she do? Her presence on *Sea Queen* had driven Alexei off his beloved yacht.

Was this it? Was their marriage over as well? Over even before it got past the beginning? She tried and failed to imagine Alexei giving her a second chance. Why would he do that when he had never loved her? Without love, what hold did she have over him? She had screwed up so badly that she hated herself at that moment. It seemed just then that keeping quiet about her pregnancy had cost her any hope of a happy future

CHAPTER FOUR

DURING THE LONGEST two weeks of her life, Billie followed Alexei's every move across the globe, for the pursuit of the paparazzi ensured that everything he did was reported in the tabloid press.

So, Billie got to know that Alexei stayed up two nights in succession at a Monaco casino gaming with a bunch of male friends. Then, after he went out to a fashionable nightclub in London she lay awake wondering whether, even though he had arrived and left alone, he had been with other women inside? Or indeed if at some more discreet location a woman had waited patiently for his visit. For the sake of her own sanity she tried not to read any more of the humiliating articles that speculated about the state and nature of the Drakos marriage.

All too many gossip columnists decided that Alexei had married his PA only because he would retain his sexual freedom with a wife who would appreciate her good fortune in marrying him too much to make unreasonable demands; a practical wife who didn't expect her gorgeous predatory tycoon to become as domesticated as a tabby cat. And, as another columnist quipped, Alexei Drakos was not the sort of guy likely to welcome rules. Alexei had always done what he wanted when he wanted without apology.

Old Drakos history was also dredged up, with Constantine's worst womanising exploits, even while married, spicily presented to entertain the readers even more. Billie felt doubly humiliated when far from flattering wedding photos of her, evidently taken with one of their guest's phones, appeared in print. Looking mousey and squat as she did in those horrible snaps she had felt that she was being shown up as the bride any self-respecting Greek tycoon and modern-day sex-symbol would desert.

'I just can't believe the way you're behaving!' Lauren snapped with angry irritation, studying her daughter, who was playing with her son and Skye, the puppy. 'What were you thinking of when you moved back into this stupid little house? You're a Drakos now, you belong at the big swanky mansion next door! Of course people are talking when you're trying to act like the marriage never happened.'

Billie prevented the little black terrier from sinking her teeth into one of Nicky's toys, setting the item aside to be washed. 'I have no intention of moving Nicky into Alexei's house until he acknowledges that he is his son—'

'Oh, don't be more stupid than you can help!' Lauren hissed, her attractive face unattractively lined by her annoyance. As her shrill voice rose in volume the puppy fled behind the sofa. 'Leave the brat here with us and take possession of what's yours. You have the right to live in that villa—you're Alexei's wife!'

Billie glanced coolly at her mother. 'Don't call my son a brat!'

'You know I didn't mean it nastily,' her mother argued. 'After all, Nicky—bless his little heart—is your golden goose. I mean, good grief, getting yourself pregnant was the only thing you did right! Alexei can do and say what he likes, but at the end of the day you will still be the mother of his son and heir and nothing can change that!'

'That kind of offensive talk isn't helping anyone, Lauren,' Hilary interposed, sending her a sister a reproachful look while she soothed and petted the puppy who had crept over to her feet. 'Billie is more interested in saving her marriage than in making a profit. I think she's right to stay here rather than up at the villa, particularly while Alexei believes that Nicky is not his child.'

At that moment, Nicky gave a chuckle of satisfaction. His big brown eyes looked up to his mother for approval and she told him what a beautiful boy he was. Anatalya, having firmly placed herself in Billie's support camp, arrived with the day's newspapers. While the housekeeper bent down to give Nicky her attention, Billie spread the papers across the dining table.

'You shouldn't look at them,' Hilary warned her in the tone of a woman who knew her advice would be ignored. 'They twist the truth and print lies, and it upsets you.'

'I'm not upset and I won't get upset,' Billie vowed, only for the blood to drain from her features while she studied the latest photo of Alexei. There was no chance that what she was looking at was a lie, she reflected wretchedly. *If only it had been.* With a stunning lack of discretion for a married man, Alexei was seated at a fashionable pavement café on an elegant Parisian boulevard with a very beautiful blonde companion, a woman whom Billie had never expected to see in his company any more. 'Alexei's meeting up with Calisto again!' she cried strickenly before she could think better of that revealing outburst.

'I don't believe you,' Hilary breathed in disbelief, only to stare in dismay at the newspaper pages that her niece spread across her lap.

'I told you that you should have chased after him when he left the yacht,' Lauren sniped, staring over her sister's shoulder, unmoved by that shocking photo. It was obvious that her cynical expectations of her son-in-law had just been fully vindicated. 'Never let an angry man go if you want him back. Left to their own devices, they get up to all sorts of mischief!'

Billie was incapable of response. Just then, looking at Calisto with Alexei in Paris and thinking of them being together, she was living her every nightmare come true. Who had contacted whom first? Who had made that crucial first move? After being disillusioned by Billie, had Alexei turned straight back to the glamorous Greek divorcee for consolation? Was he already thinking that breaking off his relationship with Calisto had been a mistake?

A smart rat-a-tat-tat on the rarely used front door of her home made Billie jerk in surprise. 'Who on earth is that?' she muttered.

'I'll go and see.' Hilary was already out of her seat,

keen to bury any further discussion about Alexei and Calisto Bethune in Paris. A minute later, however, Billie's attractive blonde aunt stuck her head back round the door and asked Billie to join her.

Billie was taken aback to find a trio of men standing in her hallway. Two of them were known to her and their appearance dismayed her a good deal: Baccus Klonis, the head of Alexei's legal team, and his second-in-command. Her face coloured with embarrassment. The third man was the doctor entrusted with the task of taking a DNA swab from the mouth of Nicky. Billie was stunned by their arrival without prior notice and the clear expectation that she would agree to the testing being carried out. While Hilary moved ahead of her to shepherd Anatalya, Lauren and the dog into the small seating area off the kitchen, Billie showed her visitors into the spacious lounge.

'Did Alexei ask you to do this?' she prompted tautly.

'Naturally I'm following Mr Drakos' instructions,' Baccus informed her with scrupulous politeness.

Billie felt as if she had just been slapped in the face and her cheeks reddened afresh. Even though Alexei might appear to be wandering without purpose around Europe he had still contrived to consult his lawyers and it cut her even deeper to learn that he had instructed them to have their baby son DNA tested in spite of the fact that he knew that Billie was against it. A tense silence settled while Billie considered her options. Of course she could withhold her consent to the test. Possibly Alexei even expected her to refuse and he would undoubtedly consider a negative response as yet more evidence that she was lying. It might be humiliating to agree to her son being tested, Billie conceded angrily, but at least it would prove his identity. That at least would force Alexei to accept that their intimate encounter had actually happened somewhere other than in her imagination.

The doctor explained the simple procedure. Billie scooped up Nicky. A swab was taken from inside her child's mouth. Although it was accomplished in seconds and without causing her child the slightest annoyance or discomfort, the whole scene felt unreal to Billie and very much like a nasty invasion of their privacy. Had she and Alexei truly reached such an impasse that he had to treat her like this? And communicate with her only through his legal representatives? She watched the men leave and shivered as Hilary came up behind her and squeezed her taut shoulder in a quiet gesture of support and understanding.

'It had to be done,' her aunt said quietly. 'When Alexei realises that that little boy is his, everything is sure to change for the better.'

It was typical of Hilary to cherish an optimistic outlook. Billie was less confident. Was Alexei ready to be a father? She didn't think so. Would he begin to understand why she had behaved as she had? Or was she to be for ever condemned as a disgusting liar by a guy who had never had to adjust his black and white take on ethics for anyone's benefit?

'I think I'll go for a walk on the beach—'

'I'll put Nicky down for his nap,' Hilary cut in, well aware that her niece was eager to escape listening to what her mother would have to say about the DNA testing Nicky had just undergone.

A slender elegant figure in cropped brown trousers and a gold T-shirt, Billie paused at the roadside to allow a car to drive past. She gave a weak smile when the car stopped and Damon Marios lowered the window to greet her. 'I was just about to call on you—'

'I'm going down to the beach.'

With a nod as if she had issued an invitation, Damon parked his car on the broad verge and got out to join her.

'I don't think that us being seen together is likely to do either of us any good,' Billie remarked, secretly squirming with the anxiety over her marriage, which was urging her to exercise a rare kind of extreme caution. But when Alexei was being seen out and about with Calisto, what was she worrying about?

Damon cupped her elbow to steady her as she stumbled on her descent of the sloping ground that led down to the beach. 'Well, don't worry on my behalf. I'm getting a divorce…'

Billie turned dismayed eyes on him. 'But I thought you and Ilona were back together again.'

Damon released a rueful laugh. 'Yes, we were, but only briefly. I'm afraid the reconciliation didn't work out. Two years ago, Ilona fell for a colleague at work and had an affair and now that she's finally prepared to come clean on that score with her family and mine, we are both free to move on.'

Taken aback by that frank explanation, Billie spun and rested a sympathetic hand on his sleeve. 'I had no idea, Damon… I'm truly sorry.'

'It's most sad for our daughters. They don't understand why their mother is now bringing another man into their lives,' Damon replied heavily as he reached for her hand and squeezed her fingers. 'Ilona and I tried really hard to make a go of our marriage for their sake but we failed.'

Billie squeezed his arm. 'How are your family taking it?'

Damon rolled his eyes and grimaced. 'Like it's the end of the world, like nobody ever got a divorce before; like Ilona has suddenly become the most wicked woman on Speros.'

'I thought that was me!'

'Your husband's reputation goes before him. Everyone suspects Alexei of double-dealing.'

'In this case they would be wrong.'

'But not if the rumour that your aunt's child is in fact yours is actually true,' Damon chipped in, curious dark eyes settling on her flushed face.

'That is true,' Billie confirmed, since she had insisted that that deception was dropped the day after her wedding when she travelled back to the island alone. She could see that Damon was dying to ask who Nicky's father was and that only good manners were restraining him, but she dropped the subject. She had no intention of sharing her innermost secrets with the son of one of the biggest gossips in the village.

Forty-eight hours later, having stayed in London long enough to secure the purchase of several oil supertankers at a fantastic price, Alexei flew home. The sun was going down over the island of his birth in a blaze of

fire on the horizon. Full of all the splintering energy
and impatience that characterised him, he sprang out of
the helicopter and strode towards the villa whose many
windows were reflecting the vivid skies. Most of his
staff greeted him in the front hall. His keen gaze narrowed, for the one person he had expected to see was
nowhere to be seen. He strolled down to the master suite
to check out his suspicions and glanced into the dressing room. Thirty seconds later, he summoned Helios,
his head of security, and asked a question. The answer
he received infuriated him.

BILLIE WAS ALONE in her house when Alexei arrived. He
walked straight through the back door, noting and disapproving of the fact that it was unlocked as it facilitated
his entry. 'Billie?' he called out, frowning at the silence.

The kitchen was tidy, the living area empty. A black
fluffy puppy peered out from behind a sofa at him,
uttered a tiny tentative little bark and then hurriedly
disappeared again, duty evidently done. Alexei's attention dwelt briefly on the basket of colourful toys
and arrowed away again. Hearing music playing, he
glanced into a bedroom and then noted the triangle of
light showing to the side of the bathroom door, which
had been left ajar.

Billie was enjoying a rare moment of self-indulgence
and relaxation in the bath. Hilary had taken Nicky down
to the village to see Lauren. She had not heard Alexei
arrive because of the music and when the door opened
she gasped in dismay and sat up in a sudden movement,
water sloshing noisily round her. When Alexei appeared

she was thunderstruck because he was the very last person she had expected to see.

Alexei focused on Billie in her sea of bubbles. Her creamy skin was wet and slick, the rounded globes of her rosy-tipped breasts invitingly pert and moist. His reaction to her was instantaneous; his body, which had been infuriatingly indifferent to the presence of other women, stirred into a rampant erection. Her generous pink mouth fell open on his name and, looking at the soft pink cushiony proportions of her lips, he knew for the first time in days exactly what he wanted and marvelled at the strength of his craving.

'Alexei…' Billie whispered unevenly, her bright head falling back and her green eyes widening to take in his tall muscular length with a sense of disbelief. His pearl-grey Italian suit had the sheen of silk and it hugged his broad shoulders, lean hips and long powerful thighs with the fidelity of the most expensive tailoring. Brilliant dark golden eyes gleaming from below the ebony screen of his luxuriant lashes, he looked spectacular enough to take her breath away.

'What the hell are you doing in here?' Alexei demanded in a wrathful undertone. 'Do you realise that I was able to just walk into this house? I could have been anyone…'

'You're probably the only person I know on the island who wouldn't bother to knock on the door and wait for an invitation,' Billie contradicted without hesitation.

'Where's your brain? I could have been a bloody paparazzo! Don't you realise how aggressive the press are now? You're not safe here without security. Get out of the bath,' he instructed her, extending a towel. 'I'm taking you home.'

'This *is* my home,' Billie protested, sitting firm and resolutely resisting a modest urge to cover her bare breasts, which she knew would provoke his scorn.

Alexei dealt her a splintering appraisal, his tough jawline clenching at her defiance. 'You're my wife— you don't belong here any more.'

'You told me I was a disgusting liar and you walked out on our wedding night,' Billie reminded him tightly. 'I don't feel like your wife any more.'

'I've got the perfect cure for that.' Alexei strode forward and sank his hands below her arms. Before she could even work out what he was doing he had scooped her wet, resisting body out of the bath, set her down and enveloped her most efficiently in the folds of the towel.

'Stop it!' Billie shouted at him full throttle, trying to clumsily slap away his hands at the same time as she kept hold of the towel.

'If I walk out of here without you, I'm not coming back, *yineka mou*,' Alexei swore between clenched white teeth.

Billie froze as if an avalanche had suddenly engulfed her, stopping her in her tracks and depriving her lungs of oxygen. 'You can't threaten me like that!'

'It's not a threat, it's the truth,' Alexei countered harshly. 'Either you're with me, or you're not. I won't play games.'

In mute frustration, she watched him tug her wrap from the hook on the back of the door and extend it to her. He had the subtlety of an army tank on a battlefield. He had walked out on her and she longed to take a rebellious stance and defy his warning. But life just wasn't that simple, she acknowledged, digging damp arms into the sleeves of the wrap while letting her towel drop to her feet. She didn't know how to behave with him now, but he knew so well how to cut through all the aggravation to what really mattered. And what really mattered now was that she cared about him and loved him with all her heart, she reflected painfully. In his defence he was trying to bridge the gulf between them and their living in two separate houses would scupper any attempt to achieve that end.

'This isn't where you should be,' Alexei told her, his husky accent roughening his vowel sounds into a sexy growl as he backed her into the corner, wrenched the ties she was fiddling with from her grasp and knotted the sash with deft hands. 'You're coming home with me.'

And those words sounded so unexpectedly good to her that tears prickled at the backs of her aching eyes. The past fortnight of stress, gossip-column headlines and wild speculation had drained her strength and awakened her worst fears for the future. He contemplated her down-bent head and tipped up her chin so that he could see her triangular face again. The anxiety in her expressive eyes disturbed him but it didn't put a lid on the seething desire he was struggling to restrain. He had no idea why he wanted her so much at that moment. He only knew that her absence from his home where he had expected to find her had enraged and unsettled him to a degree that he was deeply uncomfortable with. Half-formed thoughts and jagged responses he didn't like were travelling through him, giving him an edgy and unfamiliar out-of-control sensation that he despised.

The atmosphere was so thick that Billie could taste it. He was frowning down at her, lean hands settling down on her shoulders with authority, the heat of him burning through the fine fabric of her wrap. She collided with scorching golden eyes and the quickening awareness low in her pelvis made her press her thighs together on the ache stirring between her legs. Uneasy with that piercing arrow of sheer wanton lust, she pulled away from him. 'I'll get dressed.'

'No.' Alexei closed a hand over her arm, pulling her back. 'There's no need. The car's outside. Someone will come over and pack for you.'

On the threshold of her bedroom, she stilled. 'What about Nicky?'

Alexei's big powerful body was resting lightly against hers, but when she posed that particular question he went rigid and his handsome dark visage set hard. 'He stays here.'

She twisted round, anguished eyes seeking his. 'I can't do that. He's my son, *my* responsibility.'

'You can visit…when I'm not around,' Alexei breathed with a raw note in his rich dark drawl. 'I'll cover his every need. He can have round-the-clock nannies, every luxury…'

'You can't ask me to choose between you!' Billie exclaimed wretchedly, suddenly grasping the devil's bargain he was laying down for her like a cruel gin-trap for the unwary foot.

Remorseless golden eyes struck her disbelieving gaze head-on. 'That's the deal for now and it's your choice.'

'I'm so sorry to interrupt,' another quiet familiar voice intervened and Hilary stepped into view in the living area, her face flushed with discomfiture. 'But you needed to know that you weren't alone any more. I'll take care of Nicky, Billie. You don't need to worry about him.'

Alexei thanked her aunt with grave courtesy and Billie flung a questioning glance at the older woman, wondering why she was encouraging Alexei in his callous conviction that the obstacle of Nicky's very existence could be neatly set aside. And then it dawned on her that, within a few days at most, her son's paternity would no longer be in doubt. 'I don't want to leave him,' she admitted shakily.

'You and Alexei should have time alone as a couple. There's no harm in that,' Hilary murmured soothingly as if the situation were the most natural thing in the world.

Alexei directed Billie towards the back door as if the last definitive word had been spoken and was now etched in stone.

'I'm in my bare feet!' Billie objected jerkily.

'You don't need shoes!' Alexei countered, unwilling to countenance spending even five more minutes in what felt like the enemy camp. He bent down and swept her up off her feet into his arms.

'Please put me down,' Billie urged between compressed lips while her aunt opened the door to smooth the progress of their departure.

Wearing a beaming smile, Helios stepped out of the huge black SUV outside to flip open the passenger door in readiness. Alexei stowed Billie into the rear seat and climbed in beside her. She gritted her teeth, horribly conscious of the reality that she was wearing neither make-up nor proper clothes. Impervious to any sense of awkwardness, however, Alexei made use of the brief drive to instruct Helios to organise a separate security team to watch over his wife.

'That's really not necessary,' Billie argued as the SUV swung up the driveway to the villa's imposing entrance.

'I know what's necessary,' Alexei asserted, settling a large domineering hand over hers where it rested on the seat. 'Whether you like it or not, you're at risk now as my wife and I want to know that you're safe, regardless of where you are.'

The presence of Helios and the driver made Billie restrain her snort of disagreement as she could not imagine what possible harm could come to her on Speros. Anatalya already had the front door open wide, and the housekeeper's eyes shone with satisfaction when she saw Billie inside the vehicle. Alexei scooped Billie out and strolled up the front steps into his home as if it were an everyday event to walk in carrying a wife clad in a dressing gown. He had always had that kind of ultimate cool, even as a boy, she recalled, and a sharp little pain stabbed through her as she thought of all that she stood to lose if their marriage broke down. Oddly enough, until that moment it had not occurred to her how deeply embedded Alexei was within even her life memories. Pausing only to instruct Anatalya to have Billie's clothes removed from her home and ask when dinner would be ready, Alexei took Billie into the master bedroom suite.

Billie sucked in a steadying breath as Alexei set her down on the carpet. 'We can't just act like these past two weeks never happened.'

Alexei swung round, his keen dark gaze grim. 'For the moment, why not? Of course, you could cut a lot of the **** out of this by just telling me the truth now. I would rate you higher for that than if you force me to drag the truth out of you *after* the DNA-test results.'

With a rueful sigh, Billie sank down on the side of the stylish big bed. 'It would have been easier if you had just left me where I was for now. Why did you insist on bringing me back here tonight?'

Doffing his jacket and wrenching off his tie, Alexei sent her a darkling glance of warning as though she had strayed into a conversational no-go area. Muscles rippling through the fine silk of his shirt, he bent to remove his shoes. 'I want a shower before dinner...'

Billie tried to avoid the temptation of watching him undress, but she learned that she hungered for even that small intimacy. Black hair tousled, strong jaw shadowed by blue-black stubble, he was stripping off his clothes without a hint of self-consciousness. 'I've nothing to wear here,' she pointed out. 'I left half my clothes on *Sea Queen*.'

Alexei laughed. 'I would be quite happy for you to dine with me naked.'

'It's not going to happen.' Billie knotted her hands together and watched him lift the house phone by the bed to issue a command and then discard his shirt and shoes. Every lithe movement of his lean bronzed body mesmerised her: he was utterly gorgeous. A knock sounded on the door and he strode over to answer it and accept the garment bag and boxes he was handed. He dumped them on the bed.

'That's the clothing problem solved,' he said with distinct satisfaction.

'These are for me?' Astonished, Billie unzipped the garment bag and pulled out a flamboyant, strappy scarlet dress. 'You bought this for me? But when?'

'I saw it in a window in Paris. You wear drab colours. I thought that I would enjoy seeing you in something bright for a change.'

Once again, Alexei had contrived to confound her expectations. He might have met up with Calisto in Paris, but while he'd been there he had also contrived to go shopping on his wife's behalf. She pulled open the other packages and her complexion warmed when she saw the zingy red lingerie and high heels, which carried a much more sexual message.

'Those items were pure self-indulgence,' Alexei agreed without a shade of remorse.

'Why did you bring me back here?' Billie pressed uneasily, utterly disconcerted by his unpredictable behaviour.

His ebony brows drew together. 'That's a silly question. You're my wife. Until I decide otherwise, this is where you belong, *yineka mou*.'

He was a Drakos and possessive of what was his. But he was talking as though she were a prized car or some other item that he owned and he would keep her close... *until I decide otherwise*. Those words of cold warning sent a cold shiver down her sensitive spine and she was no longer so certain that staying at the villa with him was the right thing to do. 'I felt more comfortable in my own home,' she told him tautly.

'Sleeping alone? Get over yourself!' Alexei quipped with daunting disbelief, striding like a bronzed naked statue brought to life into one of the twin en suite bathrooms.

She remembered that picture of him with Calisto in Paris and discovered that she didn't want to ask him about that just at that moment. Not right now when everything felt so fragile and uncertain between them that she feared the wrong word or query might lead to a quarrel that could end their marriage for good. Her lies, her silence when she should have spoken up, had already put them on that dangerous slippery slope. Living in separate houses would not mend their differences and get them back together again, she recognised ruefully.

Even so she was walking on eggshells and could hardly bear the knowledge that to see Nicky she would have to leave the villa. It had proved a relief rather than a sacrifice to end the pretence that Hilary was Nicky's mother and, after all, she'd had only two weeks to luxuriate in the joy of being a full-time mum again for the first time since she had left London after her son's birth. And even though that fortnight had been a strain because of the situation between her and Alexei, Billie had adored having the comfort of her child within reach at all times.

Before Alexei was even out of the shower, two maids arrived with suitcases from her home. While they got busy in the dressing room, Billie went into the other bathroom with the outfit Alexei had bought for her. Thirty minutes later, she was ready for dinner and far from happy with her appearance. The scarlet dress was much more revealing than what she usually wore, cut away at the bust to make the most of what she had and very short, showing off her legs to well past mid-thigh. She checked her reflection, her brow furrowing while she wondered if the dress was a gift with a sting like a scorpion. Was this how Alexei saw her now? As a sexually provocative and available woman? As yet another in a long line of women prepared to wear whatever he bought and behave however he wanted if it pleased him?

Alexei watched Billie walk into the dining room with keen attention. He shifted an authoritative hand to make her twirl for his appraisal and his brilliant gaze shimmered gold because he very much liked what he saw: Billie, as he had always wanted to dress her for his own private enjoyment, no longer the efficient office machine in her crisp buttoned-up blouses and low sensible pumps. Scarlet looked amazing against her porcelain redhead's skin and the cut of the dress enhanced the curves of her ripe rounded breasts and slender thighs. The reaction at his groin was instantaneous and he suppressed a groan as his trousers tightened. In that moment, he knew exactly why he had come home to reclaim his deceitful bride. Lust that powerful had an appetite and a drive all of its own.

The chef had put on a spread worthy of a banquet for the reunited couple. Nervous as a cat on hot bricks, Billie wondered how on earth she could match Alexei's stubborn refusal to acknowledge that anything was wrong between them. But, in fact, conversation flowed freely as Alexei told her about his latest deal and the changes he had decided to make in the command structure at his London headquarters. Intrigued, Billie asked eager questions, made a couple of suggestions and was duly impressed by the deal he had cut on the supertankers.

A couple of delicious mouthfuls into the dessert she was savouring, Billie discovered that Alexei's gaze was positively welded to her. 'What?' she prompted, her face warming.

'You're a very sensual woman, *mali mou*.'

Lashes veiling her gaze, Billie shook her head in instinctive disagreement. 'I don't think so.'

Brilliant golden eyes glittering, Alexei sprang upright. 'But you just don't see yourself the way I do.' He reached down to tug her up out of her seat and bent his handsome dark head to kiss her.

Her heart was thumping so loudly she was afraid he would hear it and guess that she was a total pushover when he got that close to her. The familiar scent of him sent shivers down her spine and warmed the hollow in her tummy, leading to a shower of sharp spiky little longings in an infinitely more private place.

'I was enjoying the dessert,' she dared before his sensual mouth could connect with hers.

Eyes gleaming, Alexei threw back his head and laughed with appreciation. 'Is this your idea of playing it cool?'

'Why would I act like that?' she traded.

'Maybe because you know how much I want you,' Alexei husked, rubbing his cheek against the extended length of her throat as he bent her head back. 'But it won't work because your heart is racing and I can feel you trembling against me, *mali mou*.'

As his lean, muscular body shifted against her, she registered the forceful swell of his erection and the heat of her desire intensified. She turned her face under his and found his mouth hungrily for herself and didn't begrudge the male satisfaction in the growling laugh that vibrated low in his throat. Suddenly all the seething emotion of the past weeks was welling up inside her with explosive effect and the glory of his mouth on hers set her alight.

Stepping back from her, Alexei closed a lean hand over hers and walked her out of the dining room. Her troubled thoughts warred against her intentions. Yet in spite of everything that had passed between them, Alexei had come home to her and he still wanted her. Wasn't that some cause for celebration? Didn't that prove that she had more of a hold on her bridegroom than she had dared to hope? But how could he simply ignore the fact that he believed she was trying to palm off some other man's child on him? She just wanted him with her...*but she wanted her son too*. She also felt guilty that she had dressed up and dined in state while Nicky was being put to bed for the night by his great-aunt.

'Shouldn't we be talking about more serious stuff?' she asked Alexei abruptly.

As if jolted by a sudden flash of lightning, Alexei swung round to rest silencing fingers against her soft mouth, preventing her from saying anything more. 'No,' he breathed harshly. 'I don't want to talk about any of it because if I have to stop and think, I would know that I shouldn't be here with you.'

That blunt admission unnerved Billie and shook her to her very core. Generally, Alexei was decisive, disciplined, tough and immovable regardless of how difficult situations became. He had never got into the emotional aspect of events. But right now she felt rather as if she were trying to deal with a split personality, a stranger. He *knew* he shouldn't be here with her? Yet here he *was*? It was as though he had built a wall between the revelations on their wedding night and the present, spelling out the fact that only his ability to blank out and suppress those revelations allowed him to be with her again now. She gazed up at him with wide green eyes full of dismay and, in a move that suggested that her vulnerable look disturbed him, Alexei lifted her up against him and crushed her berry-tinted lips beneath his with a hungry impatient fervour that put her troubled thoughts to flight.

Billie gasped as Alexei blazed a trail of kisses across her shoulder, tugging the straps down on her dress and burying his face in the warm valley between the full

globes of her breasts as he urged her down on the bed.
She kicked off her shoes while his fingers slid up her
thigh to the narrow band of her thong. In a swift movement, he wrenched the tiny garment off and tossed it
aside. Her breath caught in her throat, channelled in
urgent gasps of helpless anticipation.

Alexei was standing over her shedding his clothes
with a seething impatience that thrilled her. Lean strong
face taut, he viewed her with scorching golden eyes.
As he cast aside his shirt, he bent down and raised her
up to pull her dress off her without unzipping it. She
heard the rip of material, for it had been a neat fit. He
flicked loose the catch on the balconette bra that had
merely acted as an extra line of suspension and, with it
gone, she was naked.

'No, don't you dare try to cover a centimetre of that
beautiful bare flesh,' Alexei censured huskily, lifting
her up the bed to settle her in a pose that concealed
nothing from his burning gaze. 'This is what I wanted
from the moment I saw you in the bath earlier. Within
seconds I was hotter than hell for you, *moraki mou*.'

A high-voltage smile of extraordinary sexual power
tilted his beautiful mouth and it was just as if he lit a
fire inside her. In a flash Billie went from feeling hideously awkward in her unadorned skin to lying back
in quivering readiness and acceptance. He wrenched
off his silk boxers and came down to her. All rock-hard
muscle from his magnificent torso to his flat stomach
and long powerful thighs, he was hugely aroused. He
brought her hand to the virile shaft rising from the thick
dark curls at his groin.

Feeling the pound of the pulse at the heart of her and the moisture there, she closed her fingers round his hard male heat and watched his thick dark lashes sweep down with an uninhibited sensual pleasure that sent the blood pounding at an insane rate through her own veins. With a new boldness she drew him down to her and used her mouth to caress his straining masculinity.

Within the space of a minute he pulled back from her. 'I can't take too much of that,' he confided, his dark deep accented drawl rough with erotic meaning. 'I want to be inside you too badly.'

And he touched her then with infinite skill, his thumb teasing her swollen bud and making her release an abandoned little cry and shiver even as a lean finger probed the slick wetness of her lush opening. As her hips bucked in a movement as old as time he entered her all too willing body with a single driving thrust. Her spine arched and her teeth clenched on the extraordinary tide of sensation as his engorged length stretched her tight inner depths.

'You feel like hot silk,' Alexei ground out, rising over her while gliding into her tender flesh with strong, stirring strokes that fuelled her growing excitement to ever greater heights.

He wanted to make it last but her sheer abandonment to pleasure and the frantic urgency of her movements pushed him to the edge very quickly and created a chain reaction. As Alexei surged into her with ever greater power, it was too much for Billie and she soared into a convulsive orgasm, writhing and crying out with the bittersweet pain of release. While she was still struggling to surface from the incredible intensity of that climax, Alexei's magnificent body shuddered over hers in the grip of the same overwhelming finale.

Afterwards, Billie felt emptied and adrift, totally shattered by the intensity of what she had just experienced. But this time, Alexei did not pull away from her, making her feel alone and uncertain at a most vulnerable time. Still trembling from the explosive force of his own release, he kept her in the circle of his strong arms and kissed her brow in a surprisingly gentle salutation.

'Alexei…' she whispered softly in acknowledgement, her body surrendering to her exhaustion, her eyes sliding closed.

'You're worth going to hell and back for,' he murmured with growling carnal satisfaction. 'Nobody has ever given me that much excitement, *moraki mou*.'

And Billie drifted off to sleep in his arms, happier than she had ever dreamed she might be after that awful nerve-racking two weeks apart from him. The sex was amazing, she was willing to agree, but that tender kiss and his relaxation with her in the aftermath meant a great deal more to her. She wondered if she would ever fully understand the man she loved. He was so complex, volatile and in every respect unpredictable. And on that frustrated acknowledgement she sank into the deepest sleep she had enjoyed in many weeks.

She awakened, befogged by drowsiness and bewildered, to the bright light of an island morning. Alexei, fully dressed, was standing over the bed.

'Is there no end to your deceptions?' he demanded of her in savage condemnation.

Astonished by that attack, Billie pushed herself up clumsily against the pillows, suddenly conscious of her nudity and holding the sheet to her breasts. Running trembling fingers through her wildly tousled red hair to rake it back off her face, she mumbled, 'What are you talking about? What's wrong?'

'*This*…this is what's wrong!' Alexei bit out rawly, flinging a newspaper down on the bed for her to look at. 'You and Damon Marios holding hands on my private beach!'

Her face stiff with shock, Billie glanced down at the page and froze, her skin turning clammy, her throat closing over. It was not the best photo she had ever seen and it seemed to have been digitally enhanced for clarity, but it did show her and Damon on the beach, clearly engaged in intent conversation, her hand in his, her face turned up to his. She was dismayed to recognise that even though her dialogue with Damon had been entirely innocent of even flirtation the photo was misleading, as was the closeness of their bodies.

She flung her head back, green eyes very bright. 'This is not what it looks like,' she whispered shakily.

CHAPTER FIVE

'IT WAS TAKEN by a telephoto lens. The paparazzo must've been in a boat,' Alexei grated between clenched teeth, and then he swept the newspaper off the bed again in an angry gesture of repudiation. 'What the hell is going on between you and Marios? Is he the father of your baby?'

'No, he is not. We're friends, nothing more. All that happened between us was a rather emotional conversation. Damon was telling me why his marriage had ended.'

'Exchanging sob stories, were you? Getting all touchy-feely?' Alexei glowered at her unimpressed, his lean dark features hard with angry denunciation. 'I don't believe you. Damon was your first love and you've always had a thing for him. I can well understand too why you would want to conceal your child's identity on Speros after Damon chose to reconcile with his estranged wife last year.'

At that crack, Billie turned very pale, for it struck her as terrifying that it could take only one piece of misinformation to provide a foundation for a seemingly convincing case against her. 'I've never been intimate with Damon. He is *not* the father of my child,' she intoned afresh, desperate to make Alexei listen to her.

Alexei swore only half under his breath. '*Na pas sto dialo!* Go to hell,' he told her roughly. 'I'm leaving. In a couple of days the DNA results will be available and I refuse to see you again until then.'

In consternation, Billie watched him stride towards the door. 'Where are you going?'

'London. I'll see you at Hazlehurst in forty-eight hours,' he spelt out grimly.

He didn't even have to pack, Billie acknowledged limply, because Alexei kept capsule wardrobes all over the world at the properties he used the most. He was walking out on her again. After a night that had filled her with a crazy burst of hope for the future, he was leaving and she was devastated by that development.

It was the work of an instant to run to the door and shout furiously down the corridor after him, 'You're a total coward, Alexei Drakos!'

She knew that hurling that accusation at a proud Greek male was like waving a red flag in front of a maddened bull and, sure enough, her tall, muscular husband wheeled straight round in his tracks to throw her an outraged look of incredulity from fierce golden eyes.

'I mean it…every word!' she flung in provocative addition, only belatedly becoming conscious that she was stark naked, and closing the door hurriedly to seek something to wear.

And true to the arrogant Drakos tradition of fearless confrontation, Alexei powered back down the corridor again and thrust the bedroom door back open so violently that it crashed back against the wall. Halfway into his discarded shirt, Billie faltered. She had never seen him so irate, his eyes blazing above the patrician cheekbones showing prominent and pale beneath his bronzed skin, his lean hands clenched into fists. 'How dare you accuse me of such behaviour?'

'Because you've been running away ever since I told you the truth about our child. You left the yacht on our wedding night and you're leaving me now, walking out all over again,' she condemned bitterly. 'How does that solve anything? Last night you wouldn't even talk. You won't discuss anything with me!'

'What the hell is there to discuss?' Alexei raked back at her in a lion's roar of intimidation that made her tremble, his powerful stance as aggressive as it was dogmatic. 'You've told me nothing but stupid stories that a child could tear apart.'

'Those were not stupid stories!'

Alexei came several steps closer. 'You've lied and lied and lied again to me,' he derided. 'Why do you think I would want to listen to more of the same?'

'I *had* to lie… I didn't know what else to do,' she shot back at him shrilly. 'Why does everything have to be about you? What do you think it was like for me when you took up with Calisto and told me you were thinking about marrying her?'

Alexei stretched out his arms and then dropped them again in a volatile gesture of frustration and impatience. 'I'm not listening to this nonsense again. Nothing you have told me justifies your behaviour. You've got nothing left to say. Lies are lies, no matter what the circumstances. I won't live with them or forgive them.'

White with anger, he studied her standing there in

his half-buttoned shirt, her tangle of colourful red hair spread round her shoulders. He dealt her a bitter look of cynicism. 'We're over, we've got to be. Sizzling sex isn't enough to keep me with you,' he delivered with harsh emphasis, and this time when he turned to leave she said nothing and she made no attempt to bring him back.

THAT EVENING AFTER Billie had tucked Nicky up for the night in her own home, she found herself engaged in a bitter debate with her mother.

'Your marriage is already over bar the shouting,' Lauren told her daughter sourly.

'Of course it isn't,' Billie reasoned. 'Once Alexei realises that Nicky is his son…'

'He's not like his father who was desperate for an heir,' the older woman pointed out bluntly. 'You're so naïve, Billie. Men aren't driven to be fathers the same way women are driven to be mothers. It's different for them, so wise up. Alexei has already told you that the marriage is over and in my opinion the discovery that he has a kid isn't going to change that.'

'You're such a pessimist,' Hilary scolded her sister from the lamp-lit corner where she had been trying to read a book.

'Billie has to look out for her own interests now,' Lauren argued forcefully. 'Alexei consulted his lawyers when he organised that DNA test. Billie should see a good divorce lawyer while she's in the UK. Hilary, stop looking at me like I just took an axe to Santa Claus! Alexei is a Drakos—let's face it, her marriage was always going to end in tears. His father only finally settled down because he was getting too old to stray and you can't hope for that with a guy who's only thirty-one.'

Billie breathed in deep. In truth she was finding her mother's ominous predictions more than she could comfortably cope with just at that moment. She offered to make some supper and went out to the kitchen, for she had already learned that the only way to keep a grip on her worries was to physically *do* something. Idleness while she had nothing but anxious thoughts whirling inside her head had become a torment. Much as she loved Nicky, she missed the buzz of working.

She was taking Nicky to Hazlehurst with her and had already arranged for Anatalya's daughter, Kasma, to travel with her and help her look after her son. After all, unlike Alexei, Billie already knew the results of the DNA test and she was convinced that she and Alexei would have a lot to talk about. She was praying that Alexei would find himself more interested in being a parent than her sceptical mother had forecast. A child could bring them together again, couldn't it? Unfortunately she remembered reading somewhere that a child only made matters worse in a failing relationship and she could only hope that Nicky would have a more positive effect on their marriage. Surely Alexei would not divorce her for being the mother of his only child?

The following day while she was engaged in packing for their trip to England, Anatalya brought her a letter, addressed to her as Alexei's wife but heavily marked private and confidential. Opening the missive, she sank down on the bed to read it after her eyes flew wide on the first shocking sentence, 'I believe it is possible that I may be your father...'

Slowly and carefully, Billie read the letter. For all its startling opening, it was a remarkably sensible and far from dramatic communication in which its writer, Desmond Bury, explained that he had fallen in love with her mother, Lauren, when she'd come to work as a teenage receptionist at his father's vehicle-repair garage. An engagement had followed during which Lauren had fallen pregnant. Sadly, by then, Lauren had decided that she no longer wanted to marry Desmond and, having told him that she intended to seek a termination, she had dumped him for another man. He'd had no further contact with Lauren until he'd come upon a newspaper article about Billie's engagement to Alexei, which had also featured a picture of her with Lauren. Ever since he had been wondering if Billie could be his daughter, for her age and colouring fitted that scenario. The letter concluded with a small paragraph on Desmond's history. He had eventually married and was now the widowed owner of a flourishing chain of garages. If Billie believed that she might be his daughter, he would like the opportunity to meet and get to know her.

Five minutes after her third reading of the missive, Billie drove down to the village with Nicky to see her mother and handed her the letter. 'Is there any truth in this? Is it possible that this man could be my father? Were you once engaged to him?'

Lauren grimaced and rolled her eyes theatrically several times while she read the letter. 'Yes to all those questions,' she said grudgingly. 'But he's got no right

telling you that I considered a termination while I was
carrying you...'

'I think he may only have mentioned that because he
wanted me to know that he would have taken an interest
in me sooner had he known I existed,' Billie responded
mildly. 'And I don't blame you for considering it...'

'Well, you can thank Hilary for the fact I didn't go
ahead with it!' Lauren fielded tight-mouthed. 'But I've
got no regrets where Desmond was concerned. He was
a bore, middle-aged at twenty-five, a pipe-and-slippers
man, not my type at all.'

'So why, when I was a teenager, did you tell me that
I was the result of a one-night stand?' Billie asked painfully. 'That upset me and I honestly thought you didn't
know *who* my father was.'

Lauren laughed heartily at that candid admission.
'I thought you would blame me for not marrying Desmond and giving you a more conventional childhood.'

'I'm glad you didn't marry him just for the sake of it,'
Billie told the older woman truthfully. 'It would never
have worked out if you were so different.'

'Will you get in touch with Desmond?' Lauren
prompted with a frown. 'You know, he's really not an
exciting person.'

'If he is my father, I would like to meet him.'

'Oh, he is definitely your father,' Lauren confirmed
with a sigh, as if she was more embarrassed than anything else by that.

The next day Billie arrived in London and climbed
into the limo that would waft her, Nicky and Kasma to
Hazlehurst. She had dressed with care in a beautifully

elegant dark purple suit, rescued from looking like office apparel by a short skirt, high heels and snappy
accessories. Kasma, who had only been abroad once
before, was excited by everything she saw while Nicky
looked adorable in a practical blue-striped playsuit and
little jacket. The closer they came to their final destination, the more nervous Billie became.

Basking in early summer sunlight, Hazlehurst looked
idyllic. The house wore its Georgian beginnings with
style and elegance. The redoubtable housekeeper looked
surprised when Billie arrived with a child in tow but
wasted no time in calling another member of staff to
escort Kasma and her charge upstairs to the nursery
floor. Even before Billie was directed into the drawing
room to see Alexei, her tummy was rolling and her skin
dampening with nervous perspiration.

The tall front windows had a wonderful view of the
lawns that ran below beech trees clad in the fresh green
of their seasonal finery. Poised to one side of that view,
Alexei looked formidable, sheathed in a dark pinstripe
business suit of flawless cut and tailoring. His lean,
darkly handsome face was taut and unrevealing, but
his brilliant eyes glittered with a light that warned her
that appearances could be deceptive, and that he was
by no means as calm as he might seem on the surface.
Alexei was, after all, studying her as if he had never
quite seen her before.

'You...*know*,' Billie guessed immediately, her voice
emerging strangely squeaky and insubstantial from her
lips. Even when he intimidated her, he could still take
her breath away with his stark male beauty and high-

voltage sexual magnetism. No matter what thoughts ran through her anxious mind, at the back of those thoughts she was recalling the hard driving rhythm of his lean powerful body on and inside hers and the ecstasy of release that had allowed her, for such a brief time, to feel close to him. Was it any wonder that her throat was dry and her lungs reluctant to give her more oxygen?

'I received the DNA results early this morning. At first I couldn't credit it,' Alexei imparted between compressed lips, more than a hint of ferocious self-discipline still etched in his tense stance and forbidding aspect.

'You should have known I wouldn't lie about something that was so easily proven one way or other,' Billie dared, lifting her chin in challenge. 'Of course, Nicky is your child.'

'But I remember nothing,' Alexei growled in a driven undertone, his incapacity in that field evidently now a source of deep resentment. 'Although I now know it obviously happened, it's still a challenge for me to accept that I slept with you that night and that I was so careless that I got you pregnant.'

Dismayed by that punishing choice of wording, Billie flinched. 'All I can say is that we were both upset and vulnerable that evening and when we were together it didn't feel wrong or out of place.'

His intense stare made her feel as though he would like to get inside her memory of that evening and take it from her rather than simply share it with her. She sensed his duality in the strong current of aggression that still ran beneath his self-disciplined surface and wondered at it. He was not reacting to the revelation of Nicky's paternity as she had hoped or expected and yet she could not have said precisely what was wrong with his attitude.

'I don't want platitudes from you. I want to know exactly what happened between us…'

Unsure as to what he meant by that statement, Billie worried at her lower lip with her teeth. 'The *obvious* happened—'

She collided with unrelenting dark golden eyes. 'I want to know what I did, what I said, what you did—every detail,' Alexei told her flatly.

Embarrassment swallowed Billie whole and glued her tongue to the roof of her mouth. 'I don't remember much,' she fibbed in desperation.

Alexei dealt her a gleaming look of contempt. 'Just another forgettable shag, was I?'

'I wouldn't know about that—I don't have anyone to compare you to!' Billie snapped back at him furiously. 'I was a virgin.'

Alexei nodded acceptance of that fact. 'Okay, so talk…'

Billie wandered restively over to the window and turned her narrow back to him in self-defence. In truth she had near-perfect recall of their time together and she repeated snatches of conversation and mentioned the sharing of the shower and the reason for his departure. 'I think you fell down the steps because you tripped over my handbag… I'd dropped it on the floor by the door on the way in,' she completed woodenly.

The silence stretched and gnawed at her nerves. Throwing back her head, vivid coppery hair falling back from her pale cheeks and brow, Billie straightened her stiff shoulders and spun back to him. 'So, now you know that Nicky is your son—'

Her husband's lean powerful visage hardened from the reflective look he had worn. 'And I so easily might never have known,' he interrupted. 'Had I married Calisto, you would *never* have told me—'

She was alert to the renewed tension in the atmosphere. Billie's spine went rigid and a smidgeon of colour warmed her cheeks. 'I don't know what I would have done if you had married her,' she contradicted.

An ebony brow quirked, for he was unimpressed by that claim. 'Don't you? You would have deprived me of my son, denied my son his father and disinherited him of his Drakos heritage,' he condemned, taking her breath away with those hard-hitting charges. 'Both he and I would have paid a very steep price for our ignorance of our bond. Were you planning to lie to him when he got old enough to ask who his father was?'

'I hadn't got that far, for goodness' sake. I hadn't even thought about stuff like that!' Billie disclaimed in a tone of unconscious appeal. 'Nicky's only a baby—'

Alexei raised his head high, dark golden eyes hard with censure. 'Nikolos is my son and you passed him off as someone else's, even brought him into my home in that false guise. As a mother, you failed in your duty to him.'

Shaken by those accusations, Billie felt her cheeks grow hot. 'And as a wife?' she chipped in helplessly.

'You leave more than a little to be desired,' Alexei delivered without hesitation and he swung open the drawing-room door and stood back with contrasting courtesy for her exit. 'Now I would like to see my son. At least you had the good sense to bring him here with you.'

Billie felt rather as if a whip had somehow contrived to lash her skin below her clothes. Anger sparking, she tried to defend herself. 'In my position some women would have opted for a termination and your son would never have been born.'

'Maybe you saw his existence as money in the bank for a future power play. Certainly that is how your mother thinks and don't try to tell me otherwise. Lauren is always out for what she can get.'

At that cruel taunt, her delicate facial bones tightened below her fair skin and her fingernails bit sharp crescents of restraint into her palms, because she truly wanted to shout and scream at him for daring to make that humiliating comparison. He had never in his life before compared her to her feckless and avaricious parent, and that he should do so now hurt like the sharp slice of a knife in already tender flesh. 'I'm not like my mother and you know I'm not.'

Crossing the big echoing hall on his passage to the grand staircase, Alexei skimmed a cool glance at her taut profile. 'Once I would have agreed with that statement, but not any more. I don't know you the way I thought I knew you.'

A lump formed in her throat. 'I don't feel I know you either just at this moment.'

'I'm still very angry with you,' Alexei responded with succinct bite. 'Of course I am. I've already missed out on months of my child's life and I'm a complete stranger to him.'

Mounting the stairs by his side, Billie murmured, 'I thought you weren't ready for a child.'

'He's *here*, ready or not!' Alexei quipped with derision.

'I didn't realise you'd feel this way.'

'Until I found out about Nikolos, neither did I,' Alexei admitted in a raw undertone. 'But he's the next generation of my family and his beginnings couldn't have been worse! He's my responsibility and the buck stops here.'

Ouch, Billie thought at that far-reaching assumption of responsibility but she said nothing, recognising that he had to have a lot of conflicting feelings to work through and that in many ways he was probably still in shock at the result of the DNA test. All of a sudden he had been plunged into fatherhood and the smokescreen with which she had surrounded Nicky's birth and paternity only complicated that state of affairs.

Kasma was playing with Nicky on the floor of the well-appointed nursery. Alexei told the nursemaid to take a break and the young Greek woman had barely crossed the threshold when he bent down to scoop his son up off the carpet. Taken by surprise, Nicky loosed a startled yell of complaint and scowled at his father.

'He can be a bit strange at present; he's not comfortable with anyone he doesn't know,' Billie warned him reluctantly, mentally willing Nicky to be compliant and friendly at this crucial first meeting with his father.

Alexei drew his son awkwardly closer and Nicky

burst into noisy floods of tears and wrenched his little body dramatically sideways in his mother's direction.

Billie reached out to take her distraught son into her arms. 'Try playing with him first,' she suggested.

'I've never played with a kid in my life,' Alexei said flatly. 'Is he always this jumpy or is it just me?'

'Babies can be very sensitive to atmosphere and we're both fairly tense.'

Alexei studied his son's truculent little face with intense interest. He scanned the baby's tousled black hair, his olive skin tone, his big dark accusing eyes and the manner in which he was clinging to his mother. Alexei wondered how he hadn't guessed that Nikolos was his child for, in his opinion, the physical resemblance was marked. How come some sixth-sense prompting hadn't urged him to take a closer look at Billie's supposed cousin? How come he hadn't tied together the evidence of her unexplained sickness as reported by Anatalya and her months-long career break, which had come out of nowhere at him? But he knew exactly why he hadn't put it all together.

He had had no recollection of their sexual encounter and he had trusted her absolutely while she had gone to extraordinary lengths to deceive him: there was no getting round that unpleasant truth.

Billie lifted up a picture book and pushed it into Alexei's hand. 'That's Nicky's favourite. I'll put him in the baby seat and you can read it and show him the pictures.'

'Surely he's still too young for stories?'

'He always looks interested and stays quiet while I read to him. Babies like familiar rituals.'

With a strong air of reluctance, his lean dark features tense, Alexei sank down in the armchair beside the baby seat and leant down to Nicky's level. 'You don't have to stay,' Alexei told Billie. 'I don't need an audience for this.'

Billie would have preferred to stay to act as a buffer and a source of advice, but then Alexei had always been very self-sufficient in the face of a challenge. She walked out of the door and closed it, listened outside as her son started to sob at her departure and heaved a sigh as she moved away again. If there was a lesson to be learned, Alexei would only learn it the hard way and at his own pace.

Alexei had never had to entertain a child before, but his quick intelligence soon came to his aid. In no time he had the box full of toys by the wall emptied and he was demonstrating the different items for his son's amusement. The tears dried on the little boy's face as he slowly responded to that stimulation. He smiled when Alexei got him out of the baby seat and sat him on the carpet instead. He gurgled with pleasure when Alexei showed him the different noises one toy made and stretched out his hand for it, pummelling it with a chubby fist, only to start complaining when he couldn't get the same sound to emerge. Alexei showed him again and took a little fist and showed him where to press. Nikolos chortled with satisfaction, thumped the toy energetically several times with his clenched hand and then suddenly held out his arms to Alexei to be lifted.

Kneeling on the carpet in front of his son, absently wondering when he would be old enough to appreciate mechanical toys, Alexei froze at that unexpected invitation. The baby gave him a huge grin and, ending his hesitation, Alexei moved forward and lifted him. Nikolos grabbed his father's tie and yanked it, and then put it in his mouth to chew. Alexei deprived him of the tie, sprang up to find a source of distraction and found it in the view from the window. While he was showing his son the trees, the tractor and the sheep that were visible, the little boy laughed and tried to copy him and point his own fingers, brown eyes full of life and fun.

And, for Alexei, that unstudied moment of shared relaxation suddenly became one of the most important and emotionally gripping of his life. Only a few hours earlier he had decided that he was still too young and selfish to be a parent. At the speed of light he had worked out all the drawbacks of parenthood, swiftly recognising the boundaries that would now be imposed on his once free and untrammelled lifestyle. He might have had no experience of young children but he certainly knew enough to know that a child was major baggage.

But now memories were surfacing of his own father and with them a rich appreciation of the fact that *he* was still young enough to fully understand what his child would enjoy and to actually play with him. Constantine Drakos had never, ever played with his son and had treated him like a miniature adult. Their relationship had always been sedate and a little detached with

Alexei's mother cheerfully supplying the glue of family affection and all the fun.

Ten minutes later Alexei was sitting with Nikolos on his lap and he was reading the few words in the picture book and, what was more, he was bringing an excitement to that familiar pastime, for Alexei mimicked the noises the different animals made when Billie had merely read them.

When Billie reappeared an hour after her departure, all was quiet in the nursery. Alexei moved a silencing finger to his mouth; their son was fast asleep in his arms, as relaxed as if he had known his father from the day of his birth. Both surprised and pleased by that discovery, Billie smiled warmly, relief uppermost. She had no idea what Alexei had done to win the little boy's trust but, whatever it was, he had clearly done it well.

'I am grateful you had him,' Alexei admitted outside the door and as she gazed up at him, a vulnerable light in her emerald-green eyes, his handsome mouth compressed. 'But he deserved that you should have told me the truth right at the beginning of your pregnancy.'

Her eyes veiled. 'Maybe so.'

His lean, strong face clenched hard. 'You know better than that. I have work to catch up on before dinner,' he responded, heading for the stairs, making no attempt to hide his exasperation with her.

Grovelling didn't come naturally to her, Billie recognised ruefully as she entered the master bedroom to decide what to wear for their evening meal. He remained angry with her, while refusing to accept that she had grounds for being angry with him as well. There were two sides to every story. He needed to acknowledge that his partial amnesia had put her in an untenable and humiliating position and then Calisto's arrival on the scene had proved to be the last straw. She had given birth to their child without his support and the deep unhappiness and loneliness that she had endured during the long months of her pregnancy still haunted her. Hilary had been marvellous but her company had also made Billie feel that she had to act as if she were a good deal happier and more positive than she actually was. For months she had lived behind a false face and had maintained that she was feeling fine.

Desperate to escape the circuitous anxiety of her thoughts, Billie took out her father's letter and read it again. She decided to phone Desmond Bury there and then, have a chat and see how she felt about him without making a major production out of establishing contact. After all, Desmond might be her father but he was also a stranger with whom she might have nothing whatsoever in common. At the same time, however, she and her mother were so different that she could not help hoping that she might find something of her own nature reflected in her other parent.

Her heart was in her mouth when she made the call and a crisp businesslike male voice answered on the fourth ring. She heard his surprise when he realised who she was and then, with an endearing warmth and enthusiasm that touched her, he aimed a flurry of eager questions at her. He was surprised when she told him that she had a son and marvelled that there had been no mention of Nicky's existence in the newspaper article he had read. When she admitted that she was actually in England, rather than Greece, he asked if she would like to meet him and in receipt of a positive response immediately offered to get together with her in London. She arranged to meet him the very next day for lunch.

Proud that she had had the courage to make that phone call, Billie showered and set out black silk trousers and a sapphire-blue evening top to wear, before lifting a magazine she had bought at the airport to read. She frowned with distaste when she came on a little newsy segment on Calisto, photographed looking every inch a top model dressed in the latest fashion and talking about how much she loved living in Paris. Billie stilled and studied the building in the backdrop of the photo, which struck her as familiar. It dawned on her that she knew that street, knew it really well because she had on several occasions visited the splendid town house that Alexei owned there. Just as suddenly she was recalling that photo of Alexei with Calisto in Paris and appreciating that the pavement café they had been patronising could well be the one she recalled being just round the corner from the town house.

Could Calisto currently be living in Alexei's Parisian home?

Or were the photos just a ghastly coincidence? His town house was, after all, situated in a very trendy and photogenic part of Paris. Was insecurity making her suffer from increasingly paranoid suspicions? Billie grimaced. Suspicions about the fidelity of a male whom every paparazzo in Europe nourished suspicions about? A guy to whom fidelity was a dirty word, if it came between him and a woman he wanted? *Of course,* she was suspicious. Alexei might have married her, but he hadn't come with any cast-iron guarantee of loyalty and there was every possibility that he saw her lies and deceit over Nicky as an excuse to stray. Hadn't he already told her that they as a couple were *over*?

Just how had she contrived to overlook that fact? *We're over, we've got to be,* he had said before flying to London. Her mother, Lauren, who rarely suffered from rose-tinted glasses when it came to the male sex, had believed her daughter's marriage was already over as well. Only Billie had been naïve enough to arrive at Hazlehurst, groomed within an inch of her life, in the foolish hope that Alexei, having discovered that Nicky was his son, might greet her with apologies, understanding and forgiveness.

CHAPTER SIX

LATER, BEFORE DINNER that evening, Alexei called Billie on the house phone, told her that two of the business team were off sick and asked her if she would mind helping out for a while.

Billie was quick to agree and stayed only long enough in the bedroom to dress in casual clothes. In the ground-floor office suite, she stepped into the working role she had given up as if she had never been away and although the other staff were now somewhat over-awed by her new position as Alexei's wife she very much enjoyed being kept busy.

'I miss working,' she told Alexei when she joined him later for dinner, having finally donned her slinky evening trousers and blue top.

Supremely handsome in his dark suit, Alexei surveyed her slight figure and the bright hair flaming round her pale heart-shaped face and his wide sensual mouth compressed. 'But you're a mother now.'

'Surely I could still work part-time with you?' Billie prompted, longing for the closeness of that working relationship to be restored.

'Not when I'm travelling,' Alexei pointed out drily. And Billie *had* overlooked that necessity when she'd come up with her proposition. While she was ready to allow her son to be cared for several hours a day, she was not prepared to leave him for several days at a time or to disrupt his routine by taking him travelling round the world with her.

'But your talent for efficient organisation and working well under pressure is much missed,' Alexei conceded wryly.

'I think I could still work several hours a day from the villa without Nicky suffering any deprivation,' Billie responded with quiet determination.

His brilliant dark eyes lingered on the obstinate set of her small face and his lush lashes screened his gaze. 'I'll think it over.'

'When you talk to me like that—as if I haven't a brain or self-will of my own and I'm a possession—I want to slap you hard!' Billie confided in a rush, pushing her chair noisily back from the table and leaping upright in a temper.

Refusing to rise to the bait, Alexei surveyed her steadily with his stunning dark golden eyes. 'With reference to most of the decisions you have made over the past year and more, I cannot be impressed.'

Billie gritted her teeth and shot him a look of frustration. 'Did you think Calisto was more impressive?' she dared in a driven voice.

His strong jawline clenched. 'I have no intention of discussing Calisto with you.'

Her angry flush receding at that wounding snub, Billie muttered, 'I'm tired. I'm going to bed.'

Coward, she scolded herself once she was lying in

the lavish marital bed. Why hadn't she mentioned that photo of him with Calisto in Paris? Asked where Calisto was staying over there? Yet without proof of anything untoward, what would be the point of questioning Alexei? He would very much resent an interrogation. And with their marriage hanging in the balance did she really want to take the risk of heightening the conflict between them? Of making counter-accusations that might well have no basis in reality? Alexei had still to apologise for suspecting her of a secret affair with Damon Marios, she reminded herself doggedly. She tossed and turned while she swung between angry defiance, fear of losing Alexei and self-loathing. She loved him too much, still wanted him too much in spite of the way he was treating her, and that made her despise herself. Oh, how she longed to reclaim the sensible wall of detachment she had once been able to protect herself with around Alexei!

Alexei was considerate enough not to put on the lights when he came to bed after midnight, but when he swore after colliding with a solid piece of furniture in the darkness Billie stretched up with a sigh to switch on the bedside lights. 'It's all right… I'm not asleep,' she told him.

She tried to go to sleep then, but when the mattress sank beneath his weight, she said abruptly, 'Did you really think I'd got involved with Damon?' That demand came to her lips before she even appreciated that she needed to ask him it.

'I was with Calisto. How do I know what you did during that period? Or whether you would turn to him for sympathy when our marriage was in trouble?' he fielded stonily.

'Well, you could start by trying not to assume that everything I say is a lie,' Billie pointed out gently. 'Just because I found Damon attractive when I was a teenager doesn't mean I still feel the same way as an adult—'

'Why not? He so obviously *does* still find you tempting,' Alexei retorted drily.

That response filled her with impatience over his obstinacy. She was damned if she did, damned if she didn't. 'There's just one flaw in that view. I'm in love with you,' she said boldly.

'If hiding my child from me is your idea of love, I can live without it. Trust is more important and we've lost it,' he delivered bluntly, turning out the lights again.

As his lean powerful body brushed up against hers Billie froze like an icicle; his take on their marriage chilled her to the marrow. He didn't love her, he didn't even want her love and he didn't trust her either. Did that leave anything left for her to hope for? Any bond with which they might rebuild their relationship? Alexei closed an arm round her and tugged her up close in a movement that took her totally by surprise and reminded her of a potential fringe benefit of matrimony that she had overlooked. The sensitive tips of her breasts swelled and tightened in contact with his hard muscular torso and a sensation like hot liquid lightning snaked through her pelvis, creating moisture on the tender flesh between her slender thighs. His mouth brushed her cheek, his breath fanning her lips, and the musky male scent of him flared her nostrils and left her

weaker still. But her defences conjured up that photo of
him seated with Calisto in Paris and somewhere down
deep inside herself she was able to switch off the current of responsive heat and turn colder than a winter's
day in his arms.

'No,' she breathed in fierce rejection.

Alexei tensed. *'No?'*

And a part of her that she didn't like very much glo-
ried in his lack of familiarity with that negative word
between the sheets. She pushed him away and retreated
to the far edge of the bed. 'No. Feeling as you do about
me, I don't think you should be touching me,' she extended in blunt clarification.

Without warning the lights went on again and she
blinked in astonishment. Alexei sent her a seething appraisal, his lean dark features hard as iron. 'You're not
going to punish me with celibacy, *glikia mou*!'

'That's not what I'm trying to do!' she snapped back,
even while she wondered if it actually was and if sometimes he saw her more clearly than she saw herself.

Alexei flung back the sheet and strode naked and still
heavily aroused into the bathroom. Seconds later she
heard the shower running and she lay there very still for
quite a while until he finally reappeared, a towel negli-
gently knotted round his narrow hips. Green eyes wide
with consternation, she studied him over the top of the
sheet. She could feel his anger like a physical force in
the atmosphere and was already wondering if she had
made a mistake in refusing him what she wanted herself. But she was ashamed of the fact that regardless of

what he said and how he behaved he only had to get close for her to crave him with every fibre of her being.

'We can't make love with everything so wrong between us,' she muttered in urgent appeal.

A sardonic expression stamped to his darkly handsome features, Alexei shot her a harsh narrowed glance of condemnation. 'Who said anything about making love?' he repeated the expression with silken derision. 'I was talking about sex. You think separate beds are likely to help us?'

'Sex isn't the answer to everything!' Billie slung back in frustration.

Alexei looked grim as he walked to the door. 'No, but it's important to me, to *any* man!'

'Where on earth are you going?' Billie gasped.

'I don't want to run the risk of waking up tomorrow morning and treating you as if you're my wife,' he derided. 'So I'll sleep elsewhere.'

Tears stung her eyes at the prospect of that cold physical separation. She wasn't at all sure about what she had just done but his refusal to even countenance the term 'making love' for their intimacy had hit hard and had bolstered up her defences. At the same time she just couldn't get Calisto out of her mind and his refusal to talk about his ex-fiancée only increased her doubts about the nature of his continuing relationship with the other woman. In one way Alexei had been very right: the trust they had once shared had gone and without it she felt lost, scared and out of control.

When she awakened early the next morning, Alexei had already left the house. She had to phone Helios to discover that her husband had flown out to France, a revelation that shook her inside out. As soon as she heard it she was convinced that he would be staying in Paris with Calisto and spending the night with the gorgeous blonde. That conviction killed her appetite for breakfast and made it a major challenge for her to feed Nicky and play with him with her usual light heart. Worry stoked her growing anger. Possibly freezing Alexei out of the marital bedroom the night before had been unwise, but he had blocked all her efforts to bridge the mental gulf between them. If he imagined, however, that she planned to close her eyes to his infidelity as so many other women had in the past he was in for a huge shock! Determined to discover the truth at first hand, Billie booked a late afternoon flight to Paris. If Alexei had resumed his affair with Calisto, she would confront them and see the evidence for herself before she gave up hope on their marriage.

After all that drama and agonising over what to do next it was an effort for Billie to get into the right frame of mind to go and meet her long-lost father for the first time. When she realised that a security team was to accompany her to London, she swiftly appreciated that if she accepted their presence she would never be able to surprise Alexei with Calisto in Paris as he would immediately be informed if she was flying into the same city. So, when Petros joined her in the hall to request exact details of her planned itinerary in London, she told him that she was sorry but that she did not wish to be accompanied.

'I'm following your husband's orders, *kyria*,' Petros

replied in some surprise. 'It is the wish of Kyrios Dra-kos that you enjoy protection whenever you leave home.'

'But I'm afraid it is not my wish,' Billie replied firmly. 'You may tell my husband that I refused to allow you to come with me.'

Feeling guilty at having put the bewildered Petros in that awkward position, Billie left Hazlehurst without any further ado. Just before Billie got out of the limo at the rural station where she was to catch a train to the city, Alexei called her on her mobile phone.

'What the hell are you playing at?' he demanded without any preliminary chat. 'You *need* a security team—'

'I don't need anyone following me every place I go. I like my privacy.'

'Privacy in which to do what?' Alexei queried in a glancing challenge that startled her.

Billie released an angry laugh. 'So now we're getting to the truth of the matter. It's not my personal safety you're concerned about, but what I might be doing. You want me to have bodyguards so that you can spy on me and I won't accept that!'

Buoyed up with a sense that she had to stand up for her rights before Alexei's powerful personality and con-trolling nature steamrollered her bid for independence flat as a pancake, Billie switched off her mobile phone and plunged it back into her bag. She caught the train to London and walked to meet her father in a quiet res-taurant that lay not far from the station.

Her first impressions of Desmond Bury were good and her tension slowly began to drain away. She found unexpected pleasure in the fact that she had evidently inherited her father's small stature, auburn hair and green eyes. Smartly dressed in what was obviously a new suit, the older man felt familiar from the first moment he joined her with a rather shy smile at her table. He asked her a great deal about her childhood experiences on Speros and she wrapped up the truth as best she could, while suspecting that he had known Lauren well enough to deduce that her daughter might well be glossing over some disagreeable realities. In turn Desmond answered Billie's questions about his side of the family tree and his business. His marriage had been childless and his parents were long dead so, with the exception of a couple of elderly great-aunts in Scotland, there were no other close relatives for her to discover. Billie asked him if he thought they should get a DNA test to confirm their relationship and he looked taken aback momentarily. Then he grasped her hand firmly to assure her that she was the very picture of his late sister and that he was already fully satisfied that she was his flesh and blood. His unquestioning faith in their bond warmed her heart as much as Alexei's distrust had chilled it.

Lunch lasted much longer than Billie had originally planned and she parted from her father only after accepting an invitation for her and Nicky to spend a weekend at his home in Brighton. She was grateful that he had not asked awkward questions about her marriage and only realised afterwards that having confided that Alexei knew nothing about their get-together had probably revealed more than she would have preferred to have admitted about the state of her marriage.

IN EARLY SUMMER, Paris was packed with tourists and the traffic from the airport was heavy. Desperate to escape the stuffy cab and calm her frantic thoughts, Billie chose to be dropped a block from Alexei's elegant eighteenth century town house on Ile St-Louis. The tree-lined quai could not have looked more attractive in the sunlight but Billie had never been less aware of the beauty of the ancient buildings because she was a bag of nerves beset by doubts and insecurities.

As she approached the steps to the imposing front door, she asked herself what she was most afraid of. Was it of what she would find, or of having to deal with the fallout from a husband's extra-marital affair? That latter discovery would mean the death of hope and the end of their marriage, but she could not live in fear; she had to know one way or another if Alexei had resumed his affair with Calisto. She rang the doorbell before she could think better of it.

Calisto answered the door. Luxuriant blonde hair waving round her slim shoulders, her big dark eyes haughtily enquiring, her tall slender body was sheathed in a stretchy miniskirt and top ensemble that was provocatively tight and short. Her gaze hardened as she recognised her caller. 'What are you doing here?' she demanded baldly.

'As this is Alexei's house, I think I could more easily ask you that,' Billie dared to reply in Greek, trying not to be intimidated by the reality that the beautiful blonde towered over her like an adult beside a small child. 'I would like to come in.'

Calisto dealt her a scornful glance and, turning on her heel, walked away from the door, leaving it open. 'If you feel you must…'

'I do,' Billie replied, closing the door behind her with a trembling hand. 'Alexei isn't here, is he?'

Calisto cast her a maddeningly amused smile. 'He will be soon. Feel free to sit down and wait. I would enjoy being a fly on the wall at that meeting.'

Icily calm on the surface, Billie lifted her chin. 'I'm not afraid of you.'

Calisto released a scornful and unimpressed laugh. 'Of course you are—why else would you be here?'

As the other woman's laugh echoed eerily in the cool marble hallway with its high ceiling nausea stirred in Billie's stomach. She felt lost and hopeless and the very thought of being found in the town house with Calisto by Alexei made her blood run cold. All of a sudden she had no very clear idea why she had decided that she had to confront Calisto face to face, or of what she had come to Paris to say. *Leave Alexei alone? Stay out of our marriage?* She was, after all, fairly certain that Calisto didn't have a good side to which she could appeal.

Calisto raked her imperious gaze over Billie from her head to her toes and with a contemptuous toss of her head made it clear that she could not see what the source of her attraction was. 'Alexei and I were in love. You stole him from me. Did you really think it was going to be that simple? He's a Drakos and you're just a little office girl who got herself knocked up—oh, yes,

I *know* about the kid,' she confirmed as she saw Billie's eyes widen in surprise.

'Alexei and I are married,' Billie heard herself say rather desperately, for she could think of no stronger verbal comeback.

Calisto just laughed again, a six-foot-tall Amazonian blonde of spectacular beauty and shining confidence. 'That may be so but it doesn't change the fact that Alexei is my lover—'

'Alexei broke off your engagement,' Billie reminded her, struggling not to flinch at that bold claim that pierced her heart like a knife.

'He got cold feet—you must know the feeling well. After all, he abandoned you within hours of the big wedding. The press had a ball with that little detail, didn't they?' Calisto sniped with her perfect white-toothed smile. 'Alexei was on the rebound. He and I belong together but I should really thank you for having the all-important son and heir for me…'

'Thank me?' Billie frowned in bewilderment. 'What on earth are you trying to say?'

'That I'm not remotely kiddy-minded or interested in the idea of breeding babies, but that Alexei would have insisted that I have at least one child. I'm quite happy for that child to be *your* child. I'm not into stretch marks and saggy bits. I'm very proud of my perfect body. I'll be much happier as a stepmother than I would ever have been as a mother.'

'There is no way that I will ever let you near my son!' Billie snapped back in shaken retaliation, anger surging through her in a sudden adrenalin rush.

'Famous last words—do you really think that Alexei will give you a choice?' Calisto purred in a poisonously sweet response. 'He's very taken with the kid, isn't he? The next generation of the family dynasty and all that… when he divorces you, you'll be very lucky if he lets you keep custody of him.'

'Nobody is going to take my son away from me!' Billie shot back shakily and, whirling on her heel, she sped back to the front door because she recognised that the confrontation had gone beyond the stage where she could hold her own. She had also learned what she would rather not have known: Calisto knew way too much about Alexei and Billie's marriage, and about Nicky, whose very existence and paternity Billie had fondly imagined was still a secret known to only a precious few off the island of Speros.

Indeed the level of Calisto's information told Billie first and foremost that the gorgeous blonde enjoyed Alexei's complete trust. Clearly, Alexei had returned to his former lover as soon as he'd become disillusioned with his marriage, Billie registered sickly. He had to be sleeping with the Greek fashion model again.

Jealousy and despair assailed Billie in a dizzy wave. He had already discussed Nicky with Calisto, yet he had only found out that Nicky was his son early the day before. That Calisto should already know so much was uniquely revealing and her assurance in speaking as though she was to be Alexei's next wife was even more menacing.

As Billie walked with a down-bent head along the pavement to hide the tears spattering her cheeks in the fading light of evening a man straightened from the railings he had been leaning against and signalled the driver of the car parked further down the road. 'Kyria Drakos?'

Billie was shocked to recognise that it was Helios, the head of Alexei's security team, standing in her path. 'Helios?' she queried with a frown of surprise.

'Your husband asked me to collect you and convey you to the airport,' the older man told her with a caution that warned her that Helios was well aware of her obstinacy over her personal security at Hazlehurst earlier that morning and of Alexei's anger at her behaviour.

In a daze after her upsetting encounter with Calisto and truly appalled by the suspicion that Alexei might already be aware that she had tackled his former girlfriend, Billie climbed into the waiting limousine. While the luxurious vehicle struggled through the traffic she wondered how on earth her movements had been tracked all the way to her destination in Paris. She laid her mobile phone on the seat beside her and waited for Alexei to ring her with a heart sinking like a stone but it stayed mercifully silent. Her heart was hammering with nervous stress, her skin clammy with perspiration.

Had Alexei and Calisto already discussed future living arrangements for Nicky? It had sounded to her very much as though they had and her courage was failing her in the face of such a cruel, unfeeling threat to her love for her child. She felt sick and scared, while she inexorably recalled all the many times that she had stood back and watched while Alexei utilised every ruthless, clever and unemotional Drakos gene to come out on top. He was remorseless, determined to win every battle.

Helios took her to a private room at the airport and plied her tirelessly with magazines and refreshments as if he sensed her growing feeling of terror at her predicament. How could she be scared of Alexei? But she had never crossed him before to such an extent. It shook her that he had had her tracked down and retrieved like a wayward child even though she was in a foreign country. But in truth her own behaviour shook her even more. In one catastrophic move in facing up to Calisto she had fallen off the straight, narrow and sensible path she usually followed. But she had *needed* to know about Calisto, had needed to know that there were genuine grounds for her self-humiliating suspicions. She freshened up in the cloakroom, studying the pale drawn triangle of her face and seeing only Calisto's glowing physical beauty superimposed over her own. There was no contest; never had been and never would be.

Helios told her when it was time to board her flight home. 'Where is Alexei?' she could not help asking, for she had spent over an hour in that silent room, flinching every time she heard footsteps in the passage outside.

'Already on board,' the older man confirmed.

Shivering a little in the cool of late evening, Billie mounted the steps to the private jet and looked straight past the assembled flight crew greeting her to see Alexei seated with his laptop at a desk. The instant he saw her he lifted his arrogant dark head and vaulted upright. Blazing golden eyes struck hers and she almost reeled back from the force of the corrosive anger he was struggling to contain while they still had an audience. Walking down the aisle between the cream leather seating towards him felt as dangerous and daunting as walking a pirate's plank above shark-infested seas.

CHAPTER SEVEN

THE THRUMMING POWER of the jet as it took off sent vibrations rippling through Billie's taut slender length. As soon as they were airborne the crew served drinks and snacks, after which Alexei dismissed them. As the tension in the atmosphere took on an explosive edge, Billie gnawed at the soft underside of her lip until she could no longer bear the silence.

'What were you doing in Paris today?' she demanded thinly.

'The Drakos foundation was staging a charitable lunch,' Alexei answered, referring to the global charity set up by his father. 'I had a speech to make.'

She had a vague recollection of the luncheon benefit and compressed her lips. 'How did you know where I was?' she asked tautly.

'Helios only tracked you down when you arrived at the airport for your flight out to Paris.' Alexei's cool, controlled diction unnerved her and merely increased her wariness. 'So where did you go in London beforehand and who were you meeting? You were very keen to ensure that there were no witnesses.'

Billie turned her head and finally focused on him. 'I didn't want you to know that I was planning a trip to

Paris as well,' she admitted baldly. 'I had no other motive and no reason to hide where I was going or what I was doing. Actually, I had my first meeting in London with my father over lunch today—'

That announcement certainly did grab Alexei's attention and his expressive brows drew together. 'Your father?' he exclaimed in disbelief. 'But I thought you had no idea who he was!'

Billie dug into her bag to retrieve the letter Desmond had written and leant across the aisle to pass it to Alexei.

His bold bronzed profile set hard while he scanned the comparatively brief communication. 'And until now you never even thought to mention this man's approach to me?' he ground out.

Billie reddened, for he sounded so astonished that she could have neglected to share the contents of that letter with him sooner. 'There was so much else going on between us at the time—'

'But you still just went ahead and arranged to meet this guy, taking him on trust?' Alexei thundered in interruption, springing upright to stare down at her in frank disbelief. 'You didn't even have a background check done on him! Have you any idea what a risk you took?'

'There was no risk,' Billie disclaimed. 'Desmond is a perfectly ordinary middle-aged businessman.'

'But this letter could have been a con trick to lure you into a vulnerable position.' His striking cheekbones prominent below his dark skin, golden eyes blistering, Alexei slowly shook his handsome head in angry wonderment. 'You could've been kidnapped, robbed, *any-thing*!' he spelt out angrily.

'Don't be so melodramatic—'

'Don't be so stupid,' Alexei retaliated with icy bite. 'You're part of my world now and worth more money as my wife than most people could earn in a lifetime. People maim and kill others for a great deal less. Round-the-clock protection is a necessary precaution to ensure your safety.'

A good deal paler than she had been after receiving that graphic warning, Billie nodded acceptance of his concern, which did ironically have the side effect of briefly lifting her mood. Alexei could be so cold and unemotional that it was good to know he cared enough to worry about her well-being to this extent. 'I promise that I won't be so trusting with anyone again, but my father is a very agreeable man.'

'That doesn't mean that he couldn't also be a fraud-ster on the make,' Alexei proclaimed with crushing cyn-icism. 'I'll have him thoroughly checked out before you see him again.'

Quietly convinced that her father was exactly who and what he purported to be, Billie made no comment. It struck her as deeply sad that she had had to look to Alexei's anger to find solace in the idea that he cared about what happened to her. Had their relationship al-ways been so one-sided, so empty? Then he did not reciprocate her feelings, nor had he ever pretended to. She sipped her cold drink to moisten her dry mouth. 'Please don't let's talk about what I was doing in Paris,' she urged him in hasty appeal.

'How can I ignore what you did? What the hell were you thinking of when you went there?' Alexei responded with censorious golden eyes. 'You're my wife. I expect you to behave with dignity. That does not mean confronting Calisto in one of our homes and accusing her of having an affair with me.'

Her face burning at that rebuke, Billie lifted her chin. 'I wasn't sure that you still regarded me as your wife. Most of our conversations since our wedding have ended with you walking out or talking about us being over as a couple...'

Golden eyes gleaming, Alexei loosed a harsh laugh of challenge. 'You make me sound *so* unreasonable. Nobody would credit that you spent more than a year lying to me and then produced my son like a rabbit out of a magician's hat the same day that I married you!'

Having paled at that accurate if acerbic summing-up of her sins, Billie swallowed hard. She registered that in his eyes she was never going to live down her past and concentrated on what mattered most to her at that moment. 'I'm still entitled to ask you what's going on between you and Calisto.'

'Nothing sexually.' Alexei's wide sensual mouth took on a sardonic twist. 'It's business now. Her father died during our relationship and in his will he placed me in charge of her inheritance. As she was one of three children the legacy was not particularly large. But when I parted from Calisto it was on poor terms and it was easier for me to ignore the responsibility her father had given me. While I was doing that, she got into considerable debt.'

'*Debt?*' Billie leant forward to question in unabashed surprise at that statement. 'I thought Calisto was a wealthy woman in her own right.'

'So did she, but she didn't get a big divorce settlement because of the pre-nuptial agreement she signed with Bethune,' Alexei informed her wryly. 'And as the wife and then the girlfriend of two very rich men there was never any need for her to watch her expenditure. But once she was living on her own income, she quickly got into trouble.'

'And because of this, she's now living in your town house in Paris?' Billie had already worked out the direction his cool explanation was going in and she was not overly impressed by it. So, poor Calisto had finally been forced to live as an independent woman and settle her own bills! She could see that such an obligation would have been uncomfortable for Alexei in the aftermath of a broken relationship, but she did not accept the need for him to have got involved again with Calisto on such a very personal basis. He could easily have brought in an accountant or lawyer to take charge of the Greek woman's financial affairs and have kept Calisto at arm's length.

'If I had done my duty by Calisto as her late father expected of me, her finances would never have got in such a mess,' Alexei reasoned as if his involvement and sense of guilt were the most natural and understandable reactions in the world. 'As she's currently working for a Parisian fashion house, it made sense for her to use my property as a base and reduce her outgoings.'

Billie wondered why he hadn't just settled his ex-fiancée's debts in compensation for his neglect of her affairs. Billie could not help thinking about the amount of very private information about their marriage that Calisto had apparently had full access to and she reckoned that she was only receiving part of the truth from her volatile husband. Alexei and his former lover were clearly on very close terms again. It was possible that that intimacy had not yet stretched to accommodate a renewed sexual relationship, but it could only be a matter of time until it did. Perhaps Calisto was also being given a second chance to prove herself and Alexei was biding his time before reaching any firm decision about his future plans. After all, he had dived at uncharacteristic speed into their marriage and what had that gained him? A son she'd dragged like a rabbit out of a magician's hat?

'You shouldn't have gone anywhere near Calisto,' Alexei breathed grimly, his hard gaze cutting into her like a laser beam. 'Today, when you subjected her to a jealous scene, you embarrassed me. I expect more from you than that kind of gutter behaviour.'

While inwardly cringing at that rebuke, Billie perfectly understood how Calisto had delivered her into Alexei's hands, gift-wrapped and tagged, and as a jealous vengeful witch. Calisto must have got onto the phone within minutes of Billie's departure to get her version of events in first. Alexei believed she had gone to fight over him with another woman and, as she had never really known how she planned to tackle Calisto or indeed what she would say to her, she could not have come up with a more dignified explanation for her visit.

Alexei surveyed her steadily, lush black lashes screening his gaze to the hot gleaming gold of a hunting animal, while his dark accented drawl took on a husky deep note that shimmied down her sensitive spine like a caress. 'Before today, I would never have dreamt that you would act in such a primitive way, *moraki mou*. I've always admired your restraint and intelligence.'

'Well, it just goes to show that you never really know anyone,' Billie quipped unevenly, marvelling at the stunning beauty and power of his eyes and feeling her treacherous body quicken in a physical response as natural to her in his presence as the feel of her own skin. Her nipples peaking into straining buds, she wondered whether she should shout at him for calling her 'primitive' or revel in his evident fascination because something equally basic in him clearly liked the idea of her fighting for him. And nothing had ever illustrated for her so clearly the innate dichotomy of Alexei Drakos the man, censuring her behaviour while reserving the right to sexually savour it.

Billie closed her eyes tight on temptation. And he was the ultimate temptation for her and always had been. But the time for that kind of behaviour was past, she told herself firmly, crushing the inner quivers of desire that would have destroyed her self-respect had she let them linger. Unlike him she refused to take refuge in sex when their relationship was falling apart and she could not accept his current intimacy with Calisto Bethune either.

Maybe he hadn't yet got back into bed with his ex-fiancée but that did not make his betrayal of their marriage any easier to bear. He had shared *their* secrets and evidently even discussed who would get custody of their son. She could not forgive him for that disloyalty. He had been right on one score though. Until she had spoken to Calisto, Billie would have fought for their marriage with whatever weapons came to hand. But loving Alexei was no longer enough and she *had* made some terrible mistakes, she acknowledged painfully. Now, however, she felt alienated and on the brink of being discarded, a humiliating sensation that did not sit well with her pride. It was really time for her to look out for her own interests and those of her son and prepare for a future that did not include Alexei. Furthermore, rather than wait to be pushed she was discovering that she would very much prefer to jump.

'Billie…' Alexei murmured thickly.

'No, don't look at me that way, don't talk to me that way either,' she told him tautly. 'It's no longer appropriate.'

Alexei frowned at her evasive eyes and cool intonation, the sensual heat dying out of his intent gaze. 'What are you talking about?'

Billie breathed in deep. 'Marrying you without telling you about Nicky was a huge mistake,' she admitted heavily, lifting her head to study her husband with pained eyes. 'But fortunately we don't have to live with that mistake for ever.'

Alexei had fallen very still. 'Meaning?'

'You were right. We should get a divorce,' she extended flatly, pinning her tremulous lip line firm as she voiced that ground-breaking decision.

'I only entertained that idea *before* I knew we had a child!' Alexei raked back at her with disdainful force. 'Now that I do know, a divorce is out of the question.'

'But we're not working out as a couple.'

'And whose fault is that?' Alexei raked back at her.

'It's not *all* my fault,' Billie told him, green eyes flaming back at him like highly polished jewels. 'Your renewed intimacy with Calisto—'

'There *is* no intimacy!' Alexei broke in angrily.

Billie gave him a stony look. 'Well, there's a closeness that I find unacceptable.'

'You find it…unacceptable?' Alexei framed in a raw undertone of wrath.

'As you said, trust is gone,' Billie reminded him tightly. 'Calisto was a major part of your life for many months while I was pregnant and I refuse to stand by on the sidelines again while you entertain her.'

Black-lashed bronzed eyes brilliant with fury at her daring to lay down the law to him, Alexei spread his arms wide in an angry movement of dismissal. 'You are my wife,' he growled between compressed lips. 'That should be enough for you.'

'But it's not enough. I feel like an accidental wife, not a real one. You said I cheated you. You regretted marrying me within hours of the ceremony.' While Billie grimaced, she also held her head high as she reminded him of those facts. 'I can't rewrite our past and neither can you.'

A screaming silence that flared along the edges like an inflamed wound fell in the opulent cabin.

'I won't give you a divorce,' Alexei delivered in sardonic challenge.

'I don't mind waiting a bit longer to get the legal stuff over and done with,' she said wearily, a thumping headache beginning to pound behind her temples. 'But while you can hold things up you can't stop me getting a divorce. I know enough about the law to know that.'

Bronzed eyes shimmering like polished metal, Alexei set his even white teeth together.

Billie sensed his brooding dark fury and watched his long brown fingers tighten to show the white of bone round the glass in his hand. He was a Drakos, an Alpha male with a very powerful personality, and he was outraged that *she* should talk of divorcing *him* when he blamed her for the disintegration of their marriage. She understood that, she understood that perfectly, but she was fed up of eating humble pie, turning the other cheek and staying quiet when she wanted to demand answers and felt she deserved more understanding. As yet she could not even imagine a life without Alexei in it, but in time she would get stronger and she would get over him...*oh, yes, she would*! She had more than enough strength and resolve and courage, she told herself fiercely.

A barrage of paparazzi awaited them at Heathrow Airport. Cameras flashed to catch the first sight of Alexei Drakos together with his English-born wife since a single official wedding photo had been released. Questions were shouted and, certain someone had asked her about her child, Billie shied away, wondering if Nicky's existence had now become public knowledge.

Alexei stopped dead so suddenly that she almost tripped over him.

'I have a son,' he announced with considerable pride and satisfaction. 'His name is Nikolos.'

And with that Alexei turned to close an arm round Billie and herd her onward out of the airport. 'You might have warned me that you were planning to do that!' she exclaimed.

'It had to be done,' Alexei fielded without a shade of apology. 'I will not tolerate speculation about my son's paternity when a simple acknowledgement from me will protect both you and him from spurious rumours.'

So, everyone would think that Nicky was the reason why Alexei had married her. He had laid bare the fact to the world that she had conceived his son before he had even got together with Calisto Bethune. His relations would be shocked, but then they were very well used to being shocked by Alexei and would probably honour him for marrying the mother of his firstborn son, just as his father had once done a generation ago. Billie asked herself why she should still be so sensitive to those facts when she had already reached the decision that their relationship had no future. Obviously she needed to grow a much tougher skin.

'We'll fly back to the island tomorrow,' Alexei told her smoothly as she slid into the waiting limousine.

Billie turned startled eyes on him and he closed a hand over hers. 'No...' she began.

'You can't run out on our marriage after three weeks,' Alexei drawled with a soft sure sibilance that filled her with disquiet.

'Why shouldn't I?' Billie dealt him a defiant glance and snatched her hand free of his. Sometimes she thought she had spent half her life waiting for Alexei to return after he had walked away from her. As an employee madly in love with her boss, she had been defenceless. Even when pregnant with his baby she had contrived to be powerless because she had not stood up for her rights. She had been too sensitive, too proud to face her fear of being a burden and an embarrassment to him. But her days of martyrdom and victimhood were now at an end. This time around she would do what was right for her and what suited Alexei wasn't going to influence her, she promised herself, having stoked up her anger with him to a fine burning heat.

'As for me running out on our marriage, *you* didn't even last the length of our wedding night,' Billie completed in provocative addition.

'That is past. We're not children. Indeed, we have a child to consider. We have to work this out,' Alexei informed her grittily.

'I've already worked out what is best for me and I'm not going back to live on *your* island, to stay in *your* house to be surrounded by *your* people!' Billie rounded on him to respond with ferocious resolve.

'What has got into you?' Alexei bit out with a roughened edge of incredulity in his dark deep accented voice.

Staring out of the windows at the dark lamp-lit streets of the city and the ever-present surge of traffic, Billie dropped her head to study the hands she had linked together on her lap. 'I'm thinking of me for a change, not of you.'

'Try thinking about our son instead. He would be more relevant.'

'No, don't you dare try that maternal guilt trip on me!' Billie flared back at him in furious rebuttal, her small face stiff with resentment. 'You seduced me, you got me pregnant, then you conveniently lost your memory. I did the best I could for my child in a rotten situation and I don't owe anyone anything, least of all you!'

Bemused by the positive violence of her response, Alexei studied her fixedly, his bold bronzed profile taut, his piercing gaze assessing her hectically flushed face. 'Forget about me. I'm actually asking you to put the needs of our son first.'

Billie flung up a hand in a silencing motion, angry that he could dare to attack her on that front. 'I've made enough sacrifices and I'm not in the mood to make any more!' she warned him.

'You're being totally irrational. Only today you flew over to Paris to confront Calisto—that's not the behaviour of a woman who wants a divorce.'

Billie glued her lips together in a mutinous line. As far as she was concerned taking part in any further discussion concerning Calisto would be humiliating for her and she had no intention of going there.

'I want a divorce,' she repeated steadily. 'I want my life back and my new life will naturally be here in England.'

'Is that a fact?' Alexei interposed with a scantily leashed savagery of tone that made her turn back to stare at him.

'Well, why would I want to live on Speros any longer? At least I can get a job here,' she pointed out squarely.

'You're talking about taking my child away from me as if it means nothing,' Alexei condemned in an aggressive undertone.

'But we can't stay married just for Nicky's sake,' Billie protested helplessly. 'I want more, I *need* more than some empty charade of a relationship. I'm not prepared to spend the rest of my life paying for the mistake I made on the night of the funeral.'

'If you live in England, I will see very little of our son. I consider my role in his life to be as important as yours. You're being unreasonable and unfair. Nikolos needs both of us.'

Billie could hear his continuing surprise at the way she was behaving and she wondered why he expected her to be reasonable when he had been so very judgemental and inflexible since she had fallen off her pedestal with a crash on their wedding night. Right at that moment, after enduring all the stresses and strains of an inordinately long and eventful day, she was at the end of her tether. She was too tired to argue with him, for he would keep up the pressure and refuse to quit until he wore her opinions down and she knew that she could not afford to allow that to happen this time around.

It would be a ghastly joke to divorce Alexei and end up living as his ex-wife on the island of Speros. What life would she have there? Once again she would be living on the edge of *his* life, watching him with Calisto or some other woman, and for the sake of her sanity she just couldn't *do* that any more! A fresh start far away from Alexei and his influence was what she needed, not a rehash of the past when constant exposure to him had enslaved her and ruined her for any other man. So as far as where she lived was concerned she was fully convinced that she had no choice but to be unreasonable as he called it.

A huge weariness that encompassed Billie's entire body was gaining on her steadily. She let her heavy eyelids slide shut and thought longingly of having Nicky in her arms again. The love of her child would surely fill the giant black hole where her heart used to be. Without Alexei around to upset and distract her, she would be able to concentrate on being a mother. That thought was the very last thought she would later remember.

BILLIE WOKE UP slowly the next morning. It was just after eight and a twinge of guilt assailed her because Kasma would already have given Nicky his morning feed. The pillow beside hers was pristine and untouched and she knew that once again she had slept alone. Alexei had put her to bed in her unexciting white cotton underwear. She wondered with a sudden savage pain if he had smiled when he saw what she wore underneath her clothes and recalled her warning on that wedding night that had gone so terribly wrong. No, Alexei had probably not been any more in the mood to smile the night before than she had been, she acknowledged unhappily, sliding out of bed and heading into the bathroom for a quick shower.

In fact Alexei, she conceded ruefully, was much more concerned for Nicky's future in the event of a divorce than she would ever have believed. His own parents, of course, had maintained a stable relationship, setting their only a child a good example. She pictured Alexei as she had seen him with Nicky only two days earlier, their son lying trustingly asleep in his father's arms. Alexei had proved to be much more hands-on with his son than she had expected as well. Indeed he had accepted Nicky straight away and had immediately wanted to get to know their child.

Of course she recognised the importance of a father in her son's life! She wasn't stupid, nor was she so selfish that she wanted to keep Nicky all to herself. She would make every reasonable effort to share their son with Alexei, but he was primarily based in Greece and she was not prepared to continue living abroad for his benefit. Was that so heinous a crime?

As Billie got dressed she was still rationalising the decisions she had reached the day before. Alexei no longer respected or trusted her. They had no relationship left to save. A quick divorce would be a better solution to their predicament than a long dragged-out marital breakdown. Why shouldn't Alexei spend more time in London? Was that so much to ask of him? Surely they could both be good and effective parents even if they lived far apart?

Still stressing about the serious conclusions she had made after the trip to Paris, Billie went up the flight of stairs to the nursery, which was traditionally and inconveniently sited on the top floor of the house. She walked into the room, which was empty, and crossed it to knock on the door of the bedroom that Kasma was using. When there was no answer she opened the door. There was no sign of Nicky's nurse or of her belongings. Indeed the bed had been stripped. Her brow furrowing, Billie went back out onto the landing. The housekeeper was emerging from her self-contained flat on the other side of the gallery.

'Did Kasma take Nicky out for a walk?' Billie asked the older woman.

The housekeeper looked surprised at the question. 'Mr Drakos flew out at dawn with Kasma and the little boy...' Her voice faltered as Billie went white and closed her hands tight round the stair rail. 'Is there anything wrong, Mrs Drakos?'

Billie didn't know what she said, but afterwards she went back into the empty nursery to get a grip on herself and on the shocking news that Alexei had simply taken their son out of the country with him without her permission. She looked down into the cot and finally noticed that, strangely, her mobile phone was lying on top of the disturbed bedding. She lifted it and registered that it was flashing because it had an unopened message.

'Call me,' ran the text, and it was from Alexei. He must have deliberately placed the phone there for her to find it.

Call him? She wanted to throw the mobile through the unopened window, tear the room apart and scream her fury loud enough to be heard in Greece! Call him? She was so shattered by what he had done that she could barely think straight. He had kidnapped Nicky and taken him abroad without her knowledge, indeed knowing that she had other plans. How dared he? *How flipping dared he?* Denied her son when her arms ached for him, Billie was overwhelmed by the sudden fear that Alexei was already making a bid for custody of their child. Her heart seemed to skip a beat and she felt sick as she pelted downstairs to check her handbag for Nicky's passport. As she had expected, it had gone.

CHAPTER EIGHT

'WHAT THE HELL have you done?' Billie yelled down the phone the minute her call was answered. 'Where is Nicky?'

'Here at our house in the South of France with me. He's about to have lunch. He's fine.'

That Alexei and her son were in France took Billie aback and she could only dimly assume that there was some advantage to that location that she had yet to work out. 'You kidnapped him…how could you do that to me?'

'My jet is waiting at Heathrow for you. I'm sure it won't take you long to pack,' Alexei countered without remorse.

Barely able to vocalise, never mind think, Billie was trembling with rage and distress. 'If you were standing here in front of me, I honestly believe I would kill you!' she hissed at him and she flung the phone down on her bed, folded her arms and stared at it with rampant loathing.

Arrogantly ignoring everything she had said the previous day, indeed clearly impervious to her wishes, her opinions *and* her feelings, Alexei had removed his son from his mother's care and taken him to another country. It was a shocking move that filled Billie to over-flowing with dark, fearful foreboding for the future. As a gesture it was uniquely effective, for in that one outrageous act of aggression Alexei had contrived to jerk all her strings at once as though she were nothing but a puppet he was able to control.

Billie was truly shattered. It honestly had not occurred to her that Alexei might fight dirty from the word go. She had assumed they could be civilised—at least in the initial stages of a separation. She had most definitely not been prepared for a war in which no holds were barred to break out so fast. Why had Alexei taken their son to France? Was there some legal advantage in doing this? For the first time in her life Billie regretted not following her mother's guidance and approaching a divorce lawyer. In business, Alexei always took keen advantage of legal advice and she was convinced that Alexei would have sought a professional opinion of what he had just done before he did it. She wished she could have grabbed at the comfort of believing that he was too stupid to appreciate that such behaviour might be held against him in a divorce court when it came to discussing his access to their son. But having worked for Alexei for so long and seeing at first hand how in touch with events and boundaries he always was, she could find no consolation in that line of thought.

Dressed in a yellow shift dress, Billie watched her luggage being stowed in the silver SUV that had come to collect her from the flight to Nice. The sun was warmer and brighter than it had been at Hazlehurst and the sky was a great bright arc of endless blue above her head.

Alexei's idyllic chateau in the unspoilt Luberon Valley had always been her favourite Drakos property so it struck her as especially ironic that he should have taken Nicky there. As they travelled deeper into the countryside hills the colour of ochre gave a dramatic edge to the scenery and fields of purple lavender stretched as far as the horizon. Stands of woodland, peach orchards and the serried ranks of highly productive vines that belonged to the chateau surrounded the little medieval settlement of Claudel that was perched high on a rocky cliff like so many other fortified villages in the area. On the uphill climb the SUV traversed the narrow streets with care, snaking across the sleepy village square past the beautiful old church to take a steep cobbled lane lined with medieval dwellings and terminated by the elaborate turreted entrance to the chateau. The electronic gates whirred shut in the vehicle's wake.

In front of the ancient stone bulk of the chateau, which had, over the years, been burned down and ruined many times only to be rebuilt to survive another century, Billie sprang out of the car. She didn't take the time to admire the magnificent view of the village and the valley below and she paid no heed at all to the lovely peaceful gardens where she had so often sat basking in the sunshine. Indeed she barely paused to greet the maid who opened the solid oak front door, and sped down a corridor walled with rough stone to thrust open the door of the room Alexei used as an office…and there he was: her quarry! Impervious to the warmth of the day in the air-conditioned room, he was very elegantly clad in a dark blue designer suit fashionably cut to define every sexy, virile line of his long powerful thighs, muscular chest and broad shoulders. Her heartbeat kicked up speed, her breathing straining in her throat. She hated his guts like poison at that moment but there was no denying that he was gorgeous.

Alexei surveyed her with glittering golden eyes and there was neither apology nor remorse in that bold challenging appraisal. 'No shouting,' he warned her.

But Billie was so violently angry to discover that he had relaxed and simply got on with working while she agonised over the disappearance of her son that she sought the nearest heavy object, swept it off the side table and threw it at him with all her strength. Alexei ducked in the nick of time and the metal paperweight she had lifted sailed over his shoulder and smashed through the window behind him.

Just a little shaken by the hail of broken glass noisily showering the floor, which Alexei hastily stepped back from, Billie breathed bitterly, 'I wish I'd hit you.'

'Mercifully you missed—your French isn't good enough to handle a murder charge in a court here, *mali mou*,' Alexei quipped, and as the door burst loudly open to frame an anxious Helios he smiled and dismissed his bodyguard with a fluid movement of a lean brown hand. 'An accident, Helios. My apologies for disturbing you.'

Billie set her teeth together so hard she was surprised they didn't splinter. 'I don't have the words to tell you what I think of you. Have you any idea how I felt when I learned that you had taken Nicky abroad? Do you know what it felt like when I saw that empty cot?' she launched at him in a shaking voice of rage once Helios had withdrawn again. 'He's my son and you had no right to take him away from me.'

Alexei rested steady dark golden eyes on her angry troubled face. 'Yet you were prepared to do the exact same thing to me,' he said silkily.

For a split second Billie was transfixed by that unexpected comeback. 'You can't compare my choosing to live in England to what you did today!'

'Can't I?' A well-shaped black brow lifted. 'Speaking as someone who knows my commitments as well as I do, how often do you think I was going to get to see my son?'

Billie lost colour and compressed her lips, refusing to be drawn on that score.

'But you were quite happy to impose that loss on me,' Alexei declared with a raw edge to his deep voice. 'And do you know why? You've spent the past five months ignoring my rights as a father and you see no reason why that can't continue.'

'You're twisting things—I'm not that selfish!' Billie protested.

'You are where our son is concerned,' Alexei contradicted in Greek. 'And that's why I took him today, knowing that you would follow us.'

'Never in my life have I heard anything more reckless or irresponsible!' Billie fired back at him furiously. 'I was so scared when I realised you'd taken him…it was wicked and unpardonable to put me through that.'

'You knew he would come to no harm in my care and Kasma's. I would consider it equally wicked were you to deprive our son of his father,' Alexei drawled with a steely sibilance that cut through her defences.

'Message received!' Billie flung back at him angrily, her complexion reddening. 'But you didn't have to go to such lengths to make your point!'

'Didn't I?' Alexei replied, unimpressed. 'You're even more stubborn than I am when you get the bit between your teeth.'

'What you did was *wrong*.'

'I agree, but you didn't give me a choice,' Alexei reasoned, having astonished her with that initial admission of fault. 'I have no intention of being an occasional father. Our son will need my guidance as a child and as an adult, and if we don't forge a close relationship now you can kiss goodbye to me having any influence with him when he's older.'

For just a moment, Billie recalled how wild Alexei had been as an adolescent, with unlimited wealth and two very indulgent parents. Constantine Drakos had only ever interfered in Alexei's life when he believed his son might be in physical danger. It dawned on Billie that one day Nicky might be just as rich, wilful and careless of his own safety as Alexei had once been, and when that day came it very probably would take a personality as forceful as Alexei's to exercise control over their son.

Billie stiffened. 'I *do* appreciate that you have an important role in Nicky's life as well.'

'But until this moment you weren't prepared to make any allowances for the fact.'

The pink tip of her tongue slid out to moisten her

dry lower lip. She was beginning to feel like someone pinned between a rock and a hard place. 'Maybe I was a little hasty in some of the things I decided.'

Lush ebony lashes fanned down low on his electrifying golden gaze, and as he stared at the glistening curve of her voluptuous lower lip a nerve ending pulled taut in her pelvis. She shifted uneasily off one foot onto the other. Alexei strolled towards her as lithe as a hunting cat on the prowl. The atmosphere hummed with sexual awareness and she fought her responses with all her might. Alexei made no such attempt, closing his hands to her hips to urge her close. As she parted her lips to object he brought his sensual mouth down hungrily on hers, his tongue delving into the tender interior between her lips with an erotic heat that made every nerve ending in her treacherous body sit up and take notice. A trembling started low down inside her, her bra constricting her swelling breasts, a snaking burn and surge of moisture tingling between her thighs. And in that fiery instant she learned that she could hate Alexei but still want him with a remorseless, bone-deep craving that was terrifyingly strong.

'No!' she told him fierily, striking her fist against a broad hard shoulder and when he didn't immediately draw back doing so again.

He lifted his arrogant dark head. His bronzed gaze burned her like honey heated to boiling point, unbearably sweet and tempting. 'Even if it's what we both want, *glyka mou*?'

Billie threw back her head, jewelled green eyes

bright as rapier blades. 'I don't do *just* sex, Alexei. You should know that by now.'

'You have impossible standards.'

'Only to someone like you.' Deep inside, she was squashing a wealth of pain and regret that it should be that way. She didn't do just sex but he didn't do love or for ever and, even worse, she wasn't even sure that he knew *how* to do them. For a little while she had assumed he loved Calisto, but nobody witnessing the smooth, un-emotional way he had moved on from that affair could have believed that he was nursing a broken heart. If he had decided that he wanted Calisto back, it was most probably because she suited him and his lifestyle bet-ter than Billie could.

'I've always enjoyed a challenge,' Alexei riposted, a strong hand on her spine trying to urge her back into his arms.

'Right now, I just want to see my son,' Billie an-nounced, hectic colour in her face but sincerity shin-ing in her clear gaze.

And the darkening of Alexei's beautiful eyes, the tensing of his stunning dark features, would have sig-nified annoyance had she been naïve enough to believe that his responses could be that human. He freed her, thrust open the door and escorted her in silence up the sweeping staircase, which would have looked more at home in an antebellum mansion than in a hilltop cha-teau with the core of a medieval fortress. But then it was exactly that endearing quirkiness that she had al-ways loved about the Chateau Claudel. Each new owner

had added personal touches, few of which were histori-
cally accurate.

Nicky was lying in his cot, Kasma busy tidying away
toys. As Anatalya's daughter moved to greet her Billie recognised the relief the younger woman couldn't
hide and knew that Kasma had been uneasy about her
charge's removal from his mother's care. Her son kicked
up his bare toes and gave her a wide gummy smile,
which told her that while her world might have been
rocked on its axis, all was right in his. Her heart beating
very fast, Billie reached down into the cot and scooped
the baby up, loving the weight of him in her arms and
the sweet familiar smell of his skin as she cuddled him
close. Alexei was watching and she gave him a fierce
warning look before she gave her attention back to the
child she adored.

'Where are you going?' he enquired as she headed
for the stairs.

'I think I'll sit in the garden for a while…before I
pack his things,' she tacked on as casually as she could,
for she refused to reward Alexei's cruel manipulation
of her attachment to her child by staying on in France.

His lean dark face shadowed, dense ebony lashes
fanning down on his stunning eyes as he absorbed that
unapologetic statement. 'I can't let you do that,' he murmured very softly, but she was not taken in by that softness of tone because she knew that the cooler and the
quieter Alexei was, the more dangerous he was.

She didn't reply. She walked with Nicky in her arms
outside into the afternoon heat and sought the bench in
the shade of the ancient oak tree in the walled garden.

There she had often sat to enjoy the magnificent view. *I can't let you do that.* Did he mean to physically prevent her from leaving with Nicky? Or was he planning to flex his muscles in some other way?

'Your father is so, *so* tricky,' she sighed into her son's tousled black hair.

The tranquillity of the garden and the silence enclosed her, soothing her anxious thoughts. But she could not escape her recollection of her dialogue with Alexei. At first she had been so angry with him that she couldn't think, but then he had *made* her think of what her plans would mean to him. Regardless of what happened between them, she had never wanted to shut him out of his child's life or to damage their chances of developing a normal father and son relationship. But she was only beginning to get used to the concept of sharing her son with his father and she knew that the concept of sharing anything was a worryingly alien concept to any Drakos male.

If she insisted on living in England she would be making it very difficult for Alexei to develop strong ties with his son. Yet the alternative of living on the island would cruelly restrict her life in every way and make it virtually impossible for her to move on as an independent woman. She supposed the bottom line ought to be what would most benefit her son, not herself. Perhaps there was no happy-medium solution that would be beneficial to both her and her son. But enabling Nicky to enjoy a close relationship with both his parents would be the wisest, kindest option, she acknowledged ruefully. It was just unfortunate that that might well have to come at the price of her freedom.

Hearing a step, she glanced up and saw Alexei with Kasma and a pushchair in tow. Nicky had drifted off to sleep and when the nursemaid offered to take him, Billie passed him over. As Kasma wheeled him away Billie glimpsed the momentarily tender and unfamiliar expression on Alexei's lean strong face as he gazed appreciatively down at his son and her heart stabbed her. Alexei, who had all his life been adored but who, as far as Billie was aware, had never truly responded to any woman after his mother, had somehow and in a very short space of time contrived to become deeply attached to his infant son.

'We have to talk,' Alexei delivered as soon as Kasma had headed back indoors with her charge.

Billie viewed his tall, powerful figure with pained eyes. 'You didn't need to steal him to make me understand how much he meant to you as well. You could just have told me.'

His hard jawline clenched as if her candid reference to his obvious attachment to Nicky had embarrassed him. 'You weren't willing to listen.'

Billie didn't want to plunge them back into an argument by referring to all that had passed between them since their wedding. She had done wrong but so had he. Yet he was still the guy that she loved with all her heart, she acknowledged unhappily. No matter how angry or frustrated he made her, she never lost sight of what he meant to her. 'I was very shocked that you just took Nicky's passport and whisked him away from me,' she admitted tautly. 'What would you have done had I called in the police?'

Alexei froze, his lean powerful face washing clean of expression, his eyes glittering dark as night in the shade of the tree. 'I would have informed them that I have legal custody of my son.'

Her smooth brow indented. 'What the heck are you talking about?'

The blankness of his features was put to flight as he bit out a rare curse in Greek before saying, 'You didn't read the pre-nuptial agreement, did you? I couldn't credit you would be that trusting, but obviously you were...'

Billie leapt upright, all her attention locked to him. 'Why? What was in the agreement?'

'If you gave me a child you signed away all rights over that child to me.'

Billie stared back at him in disbelief, her flush in the heat of the day fading to be replaced by pallor. 'That's not possible.'

'Billie....' Alexei spread fluid brown hands in instinctive appeal to her natural intelligence '...when you only hire the very cleverest lawyers in the world, *anything* you want is possible.'

CHAPTER NINE

FOR THE LONGEST period of her life, Billie stared at Alexi in horror. 'But you didn't even know we had a child when we got married.'

'But I hoped there would be one eventually and, after my father's various costly excursions into matrimony, my legal team naturally sought to protect me against every possible threat in the future. If we break up, I retain custody of our children.'

Her legs wobbling, Billie slowly sank down on the bench again. 'I would never have knowingly signed such a contract. It's immoral. I trusted you and you cheated me…'

'There was no deception. You signed the document without reading it,' he pointed out drily. 'How wise was that?'

'You actually thought that I would be willing to give up all rights over my own children just to marry you?'

Alexei shook his dark head with wry amusement. 'You know better than that. There are women in this world who would give their last pint of their blood to marry me.'

'Possibly not if they're sitting where I'm sitting,' Billie tacked on helplessly. 'Do you honestly think that something like that would stand up in court?'

'I don't want to take you to court. I don't want to remove my son from your care. I don't want a divorce either,' he completed with measured emphasis.

Billie got up again on knees that felt shaky. 'I wish I had never slept with you and never had your child. But my worst mistake was marrying you.'

'I'm grateful that you did all those things. I don't want to turn the clock back. I would very much like to remember the night our son was conceived—' Alexei sent her a gleaming glance of rampant curiosity that made her bridle '—but in the absence of that, I am delighted and proud to have a son.'

And he didn't want a divorce. Now she was beginning to wonder if she did either. In a divorce he might well exercise the legal right to take charge of their son and what would that do to her? Would he win if she fought him in a court? Was that a risk she was prepared to take? If she lost the right to be the primary carer of the child that she loved, what would her freedom be worth to her then? Her blood was already chilling in her veins at the very idea of such deprivation.

'You're blackmailing me,' she condemned in disgust.

'I want you to give our marriage a chance.' Alexei held her angry gaze with level cool and considerable force of will. 'That's why I took Nicky and why I brought you out here to join us. I was playing for bigger stakes than making some stupid point!'

'I don't like being manipulated and intimidated into doing what you want. I don't think the end justifies the means,' Billie argued forcefully. 'Do you want to know what you've really achieved? You've made me appreciate that I couldn't bear to stay married to someone like you!'

As Billie attempted to walk past him Alexei closed a hand like a steel cuff to her arm and held her back. 'I won't let you go.'

'I'm not giving you a choice!' she blazed back up at him, wrenching her arm violently free of his hold.

'What the hell has come over you?' Alexei bit out, staring down at her with hard questioning eyes. 'I'm willing to fight for you and our marriage. How is that blackmail? How is that something to be ashamed of? What's right and what's wrong doesn't come into this. You and Nikolos are my family now and I'm not going to lose you!'

Family. It was a word with very deep and important connotations for Billie. She had had an unhappy childhood and a difficult adolescence with a mother who was incapable of putting her child's needs before her own. She had grown up envying schoolmates with two parents, longing to be a part of family rituals like birthday parties and lunches when their whole families, young and old alike, would get together. She had always blithely assumed that some day she would create that family backdrop to nourish her own children's need for love, support and security. Now as an adult she was learning that life was not so simple and that being part of a family demanded personal sacrifices. Did she stay married to a man who didn't love her? Did she walk in eyes wide open and settle for that kind of marriage because it was the best she was likely to get and because she loved him?

Alexei surveyed her grimly as she settled back down on the bench, turning her face away from him and returning to studying the view.

'I feel like the real you is locked up inside, somewhere I can't reach you,' he admitted in a roughened undertone.

'It's only because I'm not behaving like an employee any longer,' Billie murmured ruefully. 'I'm standing up to you and you don't like it.'

'You always stood up to me,' Alexei contradicted.

Her mobile phone was buzzing like an angry wasp in her pocket and with a look of apology in Alexei's direction she pulled it out and moved away a few steps to answer it. It was Hilary, but her aunt was so upset and talking so fast that Billie had to beg her to calm down and talk more clearly.

'Mum's…*where*?' Billie pressed in dismay. 'Doing what?'

'It's too late, Billie. I'm upset on your behalf but there's nothing you can do. Lauren signed a contract, took the money and is now living it up in a London hotel. I don't know when the article will be published. And I think Lauren handed over photos of Nicky as well,' Hilary revealed unhappily. 'I'm so sorry. If I had had the slightest idea of what your mother was planning to do, I would've tried to dissuade her, but the first I knew of what she was up to was when she called me from London to boast about how rich and famous she was going to be!'

'What's wrong?' Alexei demanded, alerted by the consternation on Billie's face and the growing anger.

'This is not your problem, Hilary. Which hotel is she in?' Finally, Billie finished the call and turned back to Alexei. 'You're not going to believe what Mum's done—she's talked about us to some British Sunday newspaper and they've paid her a fortune for it. She's even given them private photographs of Nicky!' she exclaimed furiously.

'It was an accident waiting to happen.' Alexei shrugged a broad shoulder. 'I did consider paying her to keep quiet about us but I knew you would be annoyed if I intervened with that kind of an offer.'

'Why on earth should she be bribed to keep quiet? How could my mother *sell* pictures of her own grandson?' Billie gasped strickenly.

Alexei was a good deal less surprised by Lauren's perfidy than Billie was. Over the years several lovers, acquaintances and even minor relatives of his own had profited from selling stories about him and his family to the tabloid press. He had long appreciated that Lauren Foster would be vulnerable to such an approach.

'I'll have to go back to London to see her!' Billie announced, so angry with her scheming parent that she was trembling with the force of her feelings. Lauren's efforts to prevent her sister from finding out what she was planning to do proved that Billie's mother had known perfectly well that she was doing something very wrong.

'It won't change anything. If she signed a contract, what's done is done,' Alexei pronounced. 'Leave Nicky here. The press could well be lying in wait for you to visit.'

'Why aren't you furious?' Billie demanded with incomprehension.

'I've always had to live with media intrusion. That's why I like the privacy laws here in France. The paparazzi have to follow the rules here.'

Almost grateful to have to deal with a problem that did not relate to her marriage and its uncertain future, Billie went back into the house to change. It was ironic to discover that she didn't want to leave France or her son. Nevertheless, she did feel an overriding need to confront her mother because all too often in the past she had turned a blind eye to Lauren's greed and dishonesty for the sake of peace.

'I don't think you should do this,' Alexei told her bluntly before she got into the SUV to head back to the airport. 'I should come with you.'

The thought of Alexei standing by listening, while Lauren brandished her unashamedly rapacious take on how to live life and make a profit, only made Billie cringe. 'No, of course you shouldn't. I'll fly back here tomorrow,' she promised abruptly and watched the sardonic tightening of his handsome mouth ease into a more relaxed line.

In the limo that wafted her through the London streets that evening towards the hotel where her mother was staying, Billie was rigid with tension. Clearly feeling flush after the money she had earned from selling the story to the newspaper, her mother was staying in a plush suite. When she opened the door to Billie, her tangled blonde hair and the skimpy purple dress she wore, not to mention her unsteady gait, made it clear that she had been drinking heavily.

'Even when we were kids, Hilary could never wait to tell tales on me,' Lauren complained sulkily. 'I suppose you're here to read the Riot Act.'

'No, it's a little more basic than that. All my life I tried not to be too much of a burden to you and since I started earning, I've always been generous with money as well,' Billie said quietly. 'So why is it that the minute you get the chance, you stick a knife in my back?'

Lauren pulled a face. 'You're such a goody-goody, Billie. There's nothing of me in you, not in your looks, not in your nature either. How could you ever understand what it feels like to be me? I've had a lousy life because I had you when I was too young to know any better. Most men don't want a woman with another man's kid.'

'I don't recall that holding you back much,' Billie responded drily, refusing to listen to the self-pitying emotional blackmail that had been coming her way since she was very young. 'You had loads of boyfriends when I was a child but you never seemed to want to hang on to one in those days because I think you always thought there might be someone better round the next corner.'

'That was a damned sight healthier than falling drearily in love with my boss and spending years pining for him while living like a vestal virgin!' Lauren sneered at her daughter.

'Is that a little taste of what you've put in this newspaper article?' Billie demanded fiercely.

'Wouldn't you like to know?' Lauren taunted, throwing her daughter a smug look of superiority. 'But you'll have to wait a few weeks to read it like everybody else.'

'A few weeks…why a few weeks?' Billie questioned.

Her mother shrugged. 'How should I know? Maybe they wanted to check all the details out first.'

'You don't even care that it was my privacy which you sold, do you? But to make use of photos of *Nicky*…'

Lauren laughed out loud at that rebuke. 'He's a gorgeous baby—you should be proud of him. Anyway, why are you here fussing? Haven't you got what you always wanted? So why be so mean when it comes to me? After all, you've got Alexei Drakos and that ring on your finger and pots and pots of money.'

'I've also got a mother who embarrasses the hell out of me,' Billie admitted painfully. 'How could you do this to us? You know how much value Alexei sets on privacy. You know our marriage is…rocky right now. I'm ashamed that you would sell our secrets and not even care how much distress you cause.'

Her mother was too busy topping up her glass of wine to pay much heed to that reproach. She gulped down a couple of mouthfuls and then glared at her daughter, who was watching her. Lauren spluttered angrily, *'What?'*

Billie realised that the older woman didn't care about what she'd said or about what she had done. She wasn't feeling guilty and she wasn't apologising either. Billie lifted her chin, determined not to show weakness or the engrained forgiving spirit that she had always employed with her feckless parent. 'I don't want anything more to do with you,' she declared sickly.

'Is that Alexei's order? I wondered how long it would be before he made you cut me out of your life,' Lauren framed, drunkenly gesticulating with her glass so that drops of wine spattered the pale carpet. 'But I don't care… I don't need any of you. All you've ever done is hold me back like deadweight. I want to be free. I want to do as I like without someone always raining on my parade.'

'Fine.' Billie walked to the door, shaken and deeply hurt by the older woman's complete lack of emotion. She loved her mother; she always had. Looking out for Lauren had been a need and a duty etched on her soul even as a child, yet with hindsight she finally had to acknowledge that her mother had never shown her affection and had more often made her feel like a burden whose very existence had prevented Lauren from enjoying the freedom she craved.

In a daze Billie got into the lift and travelled down to the hotel foyer. It was a moment before she recognised Helios, ostensibly browsing tourist brochures at the concierge's desk, but she was quick to recognise the movement of his head, which sent her away from the front exit towards a side entrance. A limousine, different from the one she had arrived in, was by the kerb. Only as Helios swept open the door for her did she see that Alexei was in the vehicle waiting for her.

'What on earth are you doing here?' she gasped in complete surprise, running her attention over him to note that he was still wearing the same suit he had worn earlier and, what was more, in defiance of his usual perfect grooming, was badly in need of a shave. 'And how did you get here so quickly?'

'It was a last-minute decision. I came by helicopter— I flew myself,' he advanced, searching her wan, tight face with an intensity that was unwelcome to her in her fragile emotional state. 'How was Lauren?'

'A-awful.' Billie stammered out that one word and feared that the tears would fall if she tried to say more. 'Drunk,' she finally added a minute later in grudging explanation.

Alexei skimmed a reflective knuckle down over the trail of a tear stain on her cheekbone. 'And she's a nasty drunk, isn't she?'

Billie gulped and nodded jerkily, and as she quivered like a tuning fork set on high vibration Alexei closed a comforting arm round her slim body to pull her close. Her eyes overflowed and she buried her wet face in his shoulder, drinking in the wonderfully welcome familiar smell of him, composed of an exclusive designer fragrance, essential masculinity and a unique hint of a scent that was simply him. She wanted to cling and sob but she wouldn't let herself drop her defences to that extent. Yet it meant so much to her that he had made himself available, had somehow understood how traumatic it would be for her to confront her mother. 'She wasn't even sorry!' she gasped strickenly.

'She needs rehab,' Alexei told her afresh. 'But that decision has to come from her to do any good.'

Billie snorted disbelief of that ever happening, although she was beginning to come round to his conviction that her mother did have a serious problem with alcohol. 'Where's Nicky?'

'Still in France. I thought it would be cruel to trail him back to London for the sake of one night,' Alexei confessed above her head, the dark, sexy timbre of his deep drawl quivering down her taut spinal column. 'Have you eaten yet?'

'I'm too tired to feel hungry.'

As she tripped up clumsily over her own feet in the smart hallway of the town house Alexei bent down and scooped her up into his arms. 'You're shattered,' he censured and paused only to speak to the housekeeper about dinner before carrying Billie upstairs.

It was quite a while since she had had cause to go upstairs in the town house. For the long months of his engagement she had regarded the upper floor as Calisto's territory and she still felt that way now when Alexei took her into the magnificent master bedroom. When she gazed at the big bed, opulently draped in rich purple and olive shades chosen by the Greek woman, she could imagine all too well how good Calisto's blonde mane of hair, sparkling white smile and long leggy limbs would have looked against such a backdrop.

'I've ordered some food for you. After you've eaten get some sleep,' Alexei urged, settling her down on the bed and flipping off her shoes for her.

He settled down on the edge of the bed. A meal arrived on a tray and she discovered that she was hungrier than she had realised. 'You don't need to stay with me,' she told him.

Keen dark golden eyes rested on her. 'You're still upset…'

'I'm dreading what Lauren might have told the newspaper,' Billie parried with a rueful grimace.

'Sticks and stones,' Alexei quipped lazily. 'Don't read it. Nothing that's printed should have the slightest impact on us.'

At that assurance, Billie shot him a wry glance. 'That wasn't your attitude when you saw that photo of Damon and me on the beach.'

Alexei's big powerful frame tensed. His strong jaw line clenched, his brilliant gaze veiling. 'That was different.'

'How?'

'Damon Marios has always had the hots for you.'

'That's nonsense. For goodness' sake, he married Ilona.'

'Only because he blew his chances with you as a teenager. You were his first love and he was yours. For a lot of people that creates a bond that's hard to shake off.'

'I could never see him the same way after that day he pretended not to be with me on the ferry,' Billie confided. 'I was always the outsider on the island, but he made me feel like dirt when he ignored me that day.'

Alexei curved an arm round her slight shoulders. 'He was an idiot. I was pleasantly surprised when you didn't forgive him for it.'

'I didn't like what you said about him that day but it was true and that's why you should know that I would never get involved again with Damon.'

Alexei compressed his wide sensual mouth. 'I just

don't like him around you. You're my wife now. He should respect that. He shouldn't be so familiar with you. An honourable man respects those boundaries. You're a woman, you don't understand.'

Setting aside the tray because she was full, Billie released a drowsy laugh of disagreement. 'Oh, I understand you perfectly. You'd like a tag on my ankle engraved with your name.'

'This is serious. It's got nothing to do with possessiveness or jealousy,' Alexei hastened to declare in a tone of authority. 'It's simply a question of what's right.'

'I know. I can be serious too. I don't like this bed because Calisto picked the bedding and once slept here with you,' Billie confided chattily. 'But I'm not expecting you to drag the bed out and burn it for my benefit. It's simply a question of what's reasonable.'

Perplexed by that unexpected turning of the tables and that particular comparison, Alexei turned his stunning dark golden eyes on her. 'I'll have all the beds changed.'

'But that would be unreasonable and extravagant,' Billie pointed out gently to underline her point. 'Some things we just have to live with.'

Alexei sprang off the bed and looked down at her with brooding dark-as-night eyes. 'I'm not living with you holding hands with Damon Marios. The next time I find him with a hand anywhere near you I'll *kill* him!' he intoned in a raw undertone. 'And I don't care if that's unreasonable.'

With a sleepy sigh as the door snapped shut on Alexei's hot-headed exit, Billie rested her head back on the pillows and contemplated the reality that she was married to a guy who was infinitely more possessive of her and her affections than she had ever properly appreciated. Her friendship with Damon was perfectly innocent but, clearly, it really did get under Alexei's skin. Lying there thinking about it, she realised that even when she had worked for him Alexei had always acted as though he had a prior claim to her and a right to interfere in her private life. She should never have allowed him to behave that way, but until that moment she had never quite seen the extent of his possessiveness.

Now it brought a pained smile to her lips to recall the number of women she had watched swan through his life to pass through his various beds round the world. She had writhed with jealousy and envy and had cried herself asleep more than once over Alexei's volatile love life, but nobody had caused her to shed more tears than Calisto Bethune, who she had once believed had his heart as well as his body. But at that point Billie took a pause for more considered reflection. She was beginning to recognise that, now that she was Alexei's wife, it was time for her to exercise more sense and control her jealousy and her suspicions.

To be fair, Alexei had followed her to London purely to be there for her when she emerged in distress from her meeting with her recalcitrant mother. She was astonished that he had made such an effort on her behalf, and that he had understood her strained relationship with Lauren well enough to grasp that she would be upset and in need of support. But there had been other occasions in her long acquaintance with Alexei when he had shown himself to be equally thoughtful, she reminded herself ruefully. When had she chosen to forget that? That Alexei, without any prompting from her, had shown up to offer her that support and sympathy meant a great deal to Billie, particularly when sixth sense warned her that he had no time for Lauren at all and even less patience with her shenanigans.

Billie dozed off for several hours and wakened after midnight to find that she was still wearing her clothes. Suppressing a sigh, she got up, stripped off and dragged a nightdress out of her case before taking a shower to freshen up. Through the communicating door with the adjoining bedroom, she could hear distant strains of the television news playing and realised that that must be where Alexei was sleeping. Of course, after she had refused him that night at Hazlehurst, she mused wryly, he was unlikely to share the same room with her. After drying off her damp hair, she got back into bed and doused the lights. For half an hour she tossed and turned, thinking about Alexei, wishing he were with her, missing him, feeling deprived. And then suddenly she sat up, asked herself if she was a woman or a mouse, and got out of bed again.

She didn't knock on the communicating door and when she opened it the room was in darkness. 'It's only me,' she announced, feeling horrendously self-conscious.

'I didn't think it was a burglar,' Alexei murmured huskily.

In the faint light seeping round the edges of the blinds, she picked out the dim shape of the bed and headed for it like a homing pigeon. Pushing back the duvet, she slid beneath it and wriggled across the cool expanse of the mattress until she found the hot, hard heat of him.

'You do realise that there will be consequences if you stay, *yineka mou*?' Alexei prompted thickly, one lean hand splaying across the feminine swell of her hip to press her into suggestive contact with the insistent swell of his growing erection.

Dry-mouthed and breathless, Billie snuggled into him, her heart pounding like an overwound clock. 'I was hoping so,' she admitted with a wanton little squirm of her hips in encouragement. 'I mean, I am returning to France with you tomorrow.'

Alexei rolled her under his lean powerful body and kissed her breathless. He tasted of wine and sex and the urgency pulsing through him lit her up like a blazing fire inside. 'So that we can enjoy the honeymoon we never had,' he breathed in a voice full of erotic promise.

'That's not the only r-reason I'm coming to France,' she stammered as he carried her fingers down to his hard male heat and the need in her leapt like a flame fanned into a blaze by the wind. She quivered, plunged her other hand impatiently into his luxuriant black hair and dragged his mouth back down onto hers. Her excitement licking out of her control, she trembled with hungry longing and it was long past dawn before she finally slept again.

CHAPTER TEN

OVER FOUR WEEKS LATER, Billie awakened in the glorious illuminating light that Provence was famous for and didn't waste any time in checking the other side of the big bed, because she knew she would be alone. A lie-in for Alexei was staying in bed past dawn and it was now after ten. Stifling a drowsy yawn, she stretched with voluptuous pleasure, a smug smile tilting her mouth when the movement made her aware of all the little aches and pains of a woman enjoying an active and adventurous love life.

In that department, Alexei was incomparable, she reflected with helpless satisfaction. It also seemed to her as though every time they made love she felt closer to him. Did he still think of their intimacy as just sex? She didn't know, hadn't asked, and had no plans to enquire or pick holes in the happiness she had found with him. What did the words matter anyway? What really mattered was how Alexei behaved and the connection between them was very strong. With Nicky thrown into the mix and fully shared, that bond had definitely deepened.

It had been a relief that, as yet, no tell-all revelations had appeared in print following Lauren's interviews with a journalist. But the threat of what her mother might have said still hung over Billie's head and bothered her in uneasy moments. After all, intelligence warned her that no newspaper would have paid Lauren a lot of money for information that they had no intention of publishing. She hadn't heard a word from the older woman, who was still in London living it up on the proceeds of her betrayal, according to Hilary.

As Billie laid out clothes after a quick shower she marvelled that she and Alexei had been staying at their rambling comfortable chateau for almost five weeks. Their days had slowly fallen into a pattern: mornings, Alexei usually worked and often she worked with him. Alexei had, on average, only left the South of France once a week for important meetings and was delegating all that he could.

Dressed in a blue sundress, Billie walked out onto the stone balcony to survey the timeless landscape of vineyards, lavender fields and distant cliffs. The views still enchanted her. Sometimes she and Alexei walked down the cobblestoned street to have coffee and a croissant in the village square. Occasionally they dined at the quaint little restaurant built into the fortified walls that surrounded the village. And what she loved most about the area was that, aside of the attention Nicky attracted as he smiled out of his buggy, nobody took the slightest bit of notice of them. By common consent they had stayed away from the Côte D'Azur and the exclusive resorts where Alexei would be instantly recognisable and constantly approached.

An exquisite ruby-and-diamond ring in the design of

a flower shone on Billie's finger in the glorious sunlight. Alexei had given it to her on the memorable night they went clubbing in a funky old warehouse in Marseille and he'd taught her to dance the salsa.

'What's that for?' she had asked when he gave her the ring.

And Alexei had laughed. 'You're not supposed to say that. It makes a gift sound like some sort of payment and although I have given many gifts in that line in the past you don't come into that category. Of course I could tell you it's because you're great in bed, or because you're beautiful, or because you're the only lover I've ever had with hair the colour of a sunset.' At that point in his teasing little speech, Alexei had suddenly frowned and his gaze had taken on a curious abstracted quality. 'I saw the true attraction of your hair the first time I saw it in sunlight…and I told you,' he had completed with sudden harsh emphasis as he frowned. 'I told you that on the night after the funeral.'

'You've finally remembered something!' Billie had exclaimed with pleasure. 'Do you remember how you felt that night? What you were thinking about?'

Alexei had tensed. 'Oh, yes,' he had confirmed, but he had not gone on to share any revelations on that score, although it had seemed to her that he was rather distant for the rest of that day and, indeed, the days that followed. Her elation that he had at last recalled some facet of that evening had gradually dwindled when he'd failed to mention it again.

Sometimes they played at being tourists, going further afield to sleepy hilltop villages where they wandered round market stalls piled high with fresh produce in dazzling colours and bought home-made bread, olives, honey and also armfuls of lavender that Billie loved to use to scent the chateau. To Alexei's amusement, Marie, their housekeeper, never failed to point out that produce just as good, indeed most probably superior, could be bought right on the doorstep.

Billie had learned a lot more than she had thought she needed to know about the running of an organic vineyard. Alexei took a knowledgeable interest in every step of the process and was currently teaching her to differentiate between an acceptable wine and a superlative one. Only the previous year the Domaine Claudel label had won an award and Alexei was eager to build on that success. Billie was less interested in the wine than she was in Alexei's enthusiasm in the face of a challenge.

Now she descended the stairs and frowned when she heard Nicky howling. She followed the source of his cries to the library where Alexei had abandoned his attempt to work to pull his son out of the wastepaper basket he had knocked over.

Having learned to crawl early, Nicky had rapidly become a little menace. Suddenly he couldn't be depended on to stay where he was put any more and if there was anything dangerous within reach he seemed to home in on it. He had trailed out the contents of drawers and cupboards, shredded books and burrowed into potted plants. He was a baby on a demolition mission, set on causing the maximum possible destruction to his surroundings.

'No, you can't do that,' Alexei was telling his son as

he lifted him, and as the little boy snatched a pen off the desk added, 'No, you can't have that either.'

From the doorway, Billie watched as Nicky breathed in deep and bawled in bad temper, his lower lip jutting with baby-rage at the restrictions being put on his freedom.

'And that's not going to get you anywhere either,' Alexei asserted, dropping down to lift one of the toys on the floor and hand it to his enraged son.

Nicky flung the toy away and howled even louder.

Alexei sat down and let his son claw his way upright by holding onto his jacket. Nicky jumped and his temper cleared like magic, for there was nothing he liked more at present than the ability to stand upright and bounce with energetic thoroughness.

Arms wrapping round Nicky to support him in a hug, Alexei cast languorous dark golden eyes across the room to Billie's slender blue-clad figure and he smiled his heartbreakingly beautiful smile. 'I thought you were never going to surface today.'

'And whose fault is it that I'm so tired?' Billie fired back readily before she could think better of that comment.

Alexei raised a sleek ebony brow in surprise at that question. 'I distinctly remember being woken up in the early hours by a very demanding woman.'

Billie turned hot pink at the memory. Sometimes she just stretched out and found him in the bed and desire would roar through her like an express train. She just couldn't quite believe that Alexei was now hers to touch and love. Proximity to him had made her greedy and sexier than she had ever thought she could be. The knowledge that he always seemed to want her had lifted her confidence. She wore lingerie that would have made her blush just months earlier; occasionally, she wore very little at all.

Nicky rested his little dark head down on Alexei's shoulder and sagged, long lashes sweeping on his cheekbones.

'I'll put him down for a nap,' Billie said.

Alexei slid lithely upright and led the way up the staircase. Billie changed her son and made him comfortable in his cot in the room next to their own. Kasma was out for the day and, although a local girl took over in her absence to ensure that the young Greek woman didn't have to work too many hours on the trot, Alexei and Billie regularly took charge of their son and saw to his needs without help.

Alexei stared down into the cot where Nicky was half-heartedly trying to reach for his little pink toes and then he glanced across at Billie. 'I'd like another child.'

Astonished by that abrupt confession and unprepared for it, Billie frowned.

'I wasn't part of it when you were carrying Nikolos. I missed out on everything,' Alexei pointed out levelly.

'You know why I didn't tell you,' Billie reminded him defensively.

'I know you decided that my girlfriend was more important to me than my unborn child,' Alexei countered. 'But that was *your* mistake. I would have put my child's needs first, just as my father once did. It's a shame that you didn't give me the chance to prove that to you firsthand.'

A frisson of fierce annoyance washed away all the warm feelings that Billie had experienced watching Alexei handle their son with such patience, common sense and warmth. But his skill as a parent aside, wasn't she entitled to have some pride? To want a man who was not simply *with* her because she had fallen accidentally pregnant? With hindsight, Billie now recognised that it was the fear of Alexei feeling responsible for her because she was pregnant rather than freely choosing to be with her that had made her stay silent after she had conceived. Calisto had been more competition than Billie had felt up to taking on and challenging. She needed to be wanted for herself, not for her son's benefit. But just how deep did that attitude of Alexei's go? Was he only set on showing her what a wonderful guy he could be in retrospect? Or was their honeymoon ninety per cent fake as he made a very clever and rational attempt to give their marriage sound and lasting foundations? That suspicion sent a shiver down her sensitive spine.

'I think one child is enough for us right now,' she responded quietly.

Stunning golden eyes as bright as sunlight raked over her tense, uneasy expression. 'You still don't trust me. Do you think I'm so selfish that I would suggest having another child *without* the intention of our marriage lasting?'

'It's not a matter of trust,' Billie reasoned hurriedly. 'I just need more time with you to believe that.'

'Nicky has roused emotions in me that I never realised I could feel,' Alexei volunteered, startling her with that admission. 'You're surprised… I'm surprised. But I was bored with my life as it was. I'm much more ready to be a family man than I ever appreciated, *yineka mou.*'

'That's great,' Billie told him, but she was not convinced enough to risk a second pregnancy on the strength of that declaration. When she lost her figure, he might not find her as attractive, she reasoned uncomfortably. He was and always would be a male to whom a high-voltage sex life meant a great deal and pregnancy would definitely make a difference to their relationship. That was not a chance she wanted to take.

'You saw far too much of my life as a playboy,' Alexei groaned, folding her slim, curvy body into his arms. 'That's where the problem lies.'

'I'm not prejudiced—'

'How can you lie to me like that?' Alexei censured. 'You disapproved of my sex life from the day you met me.'

'I'm not lying,' she said uncomfortably.

'You never could hide how you felt either,' Alexei continued with sardonic cool. 'You'd get a stony look on your face and go all stiff and prissy, and your voice would go cold.'

Billie was thoroughly disconcerted by that recital of her reactions.

Unexpectedly, Alexei's lean bronzed features broke into an unholy grin of amusement as he pulled her closer. 'You really were a jealous little cat from the word go!'

'That's not true,' Billie mumbled, refusing to meet his shrewd gaze, as she had not once mentioned love since her return to France, had wrenched the very word from her thoughts and buried it deep. In Alexei's radius she could only feel that the less said about love and all such sentiments, the better.

'And there I was leading a perfectly normal life as a single man,' Alexei lamented.

'You were...*wild*,' Billie rebutted without an instant of hesitation.

'But in some dark little corner of your head, you *love* wild,' Alexei murmured huskily, shifting against her in a lithe movement to acquaint her with the hard male heat at his groin.

Loving him as much as she thrilled to that wildness, Billie trembled, feeling the surge of heat and moisture between her legs, wishing she had more control over her responses. He pressed her slender length to him and bent his head to kiss her with a raw, urgent hunger that left her struggling to breathe. He had made love to her for half of the night but now he wanted her again and she rejoiced in that knowledge, which made her feel secure and needed. She let him back her into their bedroom on legs that felt as weak as cotton-wool supports. But she was no passive partner, for she dragged his jacket off him and embarked on his shirt buttons while exchanging passionate kisses that made her heartbeat race.

'I think you should just stay in bed all day,' Alexei confided, letting his teeth graze a particularly tender place on her neck and suppressing a groan as she wriggled against his long powerful thighs. 'Getting dressed is hardly worth your while. I can't get enough of you, *yineka mou*.'

He was pulling down the straps on her shoulders, accessing the scented hollow between her breasts and the pale upper slopes before he found the zip and the dress fell to her waist. He dealt with the light bra that merely uplifted the ripe swell of her flesh and he caught a straining pink nipple in his mouth to ravish it, even as he pushed up her skirt, ripped her delicate chiffon panties out of his path and found the sweet damp warmth of her silken flesh. A moment later, he braced her back against the wall, hoisted her against him and brought her down on him. She cried out in shivering excitement as he sank deep into her slick wet heat and after only a few strokes he moved her, tumbling her down on the bed and plunging into her tight depths over and over again with an erotic dominance that excited her beyond belief. She hit a shattering high of pleasure and she arched up to him and cried out at the convulsive strength of the climax gripping her. Dizzy satisfaction engulfed her as Alexei reached the same peak and shuddered in her arms.

'Did I hurt you? Was I too rough?' Alexei queried, breathing heavily.

'I'm fine…better than fine…on another planet,' she mumbled, struggling to find the right words to encompass her wonderful sense of well-being.

Alexei gave her a wicked smile that tilted her heart on its axis and crushed her close to his bare chest. 'It just gets better and better with you,' he sighed, dropping a kiss on her parted lips. 'You're an amazing find, *moraki mou.*'

A slew of phone calls disrupted dinner that evening. When Billie asked if there was a crisis of some kind Alexei fended off her questions with a shuttered look on his lean dark features. Bemused by his behaviour, she went to bed alone. In the morning she wakened to the sound of a text reaching her mobile phone and, before she reached for it, noticed to her surprise that the pillow beside hers was untouched. The message was from Hilary. It informed her that Lauren's story had appeared that morning and Hilary had faxed a copy of the piece to the chateau. It also urged Billie not to pay heed to what her aunt termed 'spiteful drivel', but Billie's apprehension about the unsavoury nature of her mother's revelations rose to new heights.

A knock on the bedroom door heralded the arrival of a breakfast tray that could only have been ordered for her by Alexei. Striving to remain calm but, for once, impervious to the stunning view, Billie sat out at a table on the wrought-iron girded balcony and ate fresh fruit. She shredded her croissant and then lost interest in eating it while she wondered what tales her mother might have shared with the press. Who would dare to disbelieve stories told by her own flesh and blood? And the answer to that was: anyone who had ever enjoyed a personal acquaintance with Lauren, who was always willing to stretch the boundaries of the truth to make a good story.

The sound of the bedroom door snapping shut made her turn her head. Alexei strolled out onto the stone balcony, a lean powerful figure sheathed in close-fitting beige chino pants and a black T-shirt. Luxuriant black hair glinting in the sunlight, stunning golden eyes semi-screened by spiky dark lashes, he looked jaw-droppingly beautiful to her attentive gaze. Her heart seemed to jump behind her breastbone and her mouth ran dry, but neither appreciative response prevented her from noting that he was pale and tense with just the suggestion of gritted teeth behind the set of his stubborn, passionate mouth.

'You've been reading Lauren's interview with the *Sunday Globe*,' Billie guessed in a hot-cheeked rush. While Hilary had assumed that their location abroad would make it difficult for them to gain easy access to that article, Billie knew that Alexei had the British newspapers flown in every day.

Alexei sent her a questioning glance.

'Hilary texted me and then faxed a copy here—'

'It came through but I chucked it in the bin,' Alexei admitted. 'It'll only upset you.'

'She's my mother. I have every intention of reading it.'

His brilliant eyes veiled as if he had been prepared for that response. 'Then you might as well know the worst now. Lauren has accused me of having an affair with Calisto...'

The numbness of shock possessed Billie's lower limbs and the colour bled from her cheeks. For several deeply unpleasant seconds she felt physically sick and in the act of rising from the chair she dropped down again and gripped the arms with clenched fingers. 'That may be my fault,' she muttered with a sudden groan. 'Before the DNA results arrived and I saw you at Hazlehurst, I saw a photo of you with Calisto in Paris and I have to admit that I *was* suspicious...'

'If I had still wanted Calisto, I would never have dumped her in the first place or moved on to marry you,' Alexei spelt out, his arrogant head held high, his jawline at an uncompromising angle. 'You have to learn to trust me, Billie. There will always be allegations of that nature made against me. Like my father, I'll often be a target and I won't have that kind of nonsense causing trouble between us. I've already called in my lawyers. I intend to sue on this occasion.'

It was at that point that Billie realised that Alexei had sought her out quite deliberately to tell her what was in that article before she could read it. A pre-emptive strike and very much in the bold, buccaneering Drakos style, she reflected painfully. How did she trust a male so clever and manipulative that he even knew how best to sidestep claims of infidelity?

Billie pushed away her plate and got up. Alexei was regarding her with expectancy. Was he expecting an apologetic hug and the assurance that of course she believed him? It hurt that her mother could have plunged them into such a confrontation, but at the back of her mind she couldn't help thinking that had Alexei been willing to be more frank with her she would never have cherished such qualms about Calisto.

'I'll get dressed,' she said without any expression at all.

'If you go outside, stay away from the front gates—
a bunch of paps are conducting a stake-out.'

'Oh…' Biting her lip, Billie looked away, finally
registering that Lauren had clearly managed to create quite a splash with her revelations. Her mother, she
thought sadly, would be revelling in the limelight. She
only hoped that the story Lauren had already sold would
be the one and only time she talked about her daughter's marriage in public. And that when the dust finally
settled there would still *be* a marriage to conserve, she
thought painfully.

When she finally held the relevant newspaper in her
hand, she felt as if a cold hand were trailing down her
spine. 'I don't need you hovering!' she told Alexei, who
was poised by a tall window with Nicky clasped in his
arms. 'Certainly not with Nicky in tow. I don't want
him to hear us arguing.'

Level dark golden eyes held hers with fierce determination. 'Then don't read it…'

And so intense were his look and tone that she almost succumbed, until common sense warned her that
she would not be able to live with her ignorance. The
fine bones of her face taut below her skin, she shook
her head in urgent dismissal of that advice and walked
out to the garden in search of the privacy in which to
read. The hot golden light of noon drained the borders
in the walled garden of their vibrant colour and the
blessed shade below the oak tree beckoned like a long
cold drink in scorching temperatures.

The whole focus of the newspaper article was encap-
sulated by a devastating photograph of Alexei kissing

Calisto in a Parisian street. In total shock at the sight of their two bodies plastered together and so close, Billie flinched and speed-read through the claim that Alexei had plunged back into an affair with Calisto within days of walking out on his bride the previous month. So, it *was* true, she reflected sickly. There were Calisto and Alexei captured together in black and white, the ultimate proof of infidelity, which even Alexei could not dispute. Evidently all her worst fears had been right on target.

Her heart thudding sickly inside her, she skimmed over the pictures of their son and read on. Surprisingly, Lauren had not overly embroidered the tale of how Billie had come to fall in love with Alexei while she worked for him. She'd described how the stressful hours of Billie's busy working days had been punctuated with the constant procession of gorgeous women with whom Alexei had amused himself and Billie's growing heartbreak while she'd watched. Lauren had had a thoroughly cynical take on Alexei's behaviour and had accused him of having 'used' her lovesick daughter for comfort in the wake of his parents' deaths and then cruelly ditching her when Calisto had reappeared, divorced and available again. Lauren had also implied that he must have known Billie had fallen pregnant and had sent her off on a supposed career break to deliberately conceal the fact.

A slight noise made Billie's head fly up, green eyes wide and pained when she saw Alexei standing on the gravel path staring at her with a curiously raw expression in his dark eyes.

'That photo of me kissing Calisto is almost two years old,' he breathed harshly. 'There *is* no affair.'

Unwilling to even listen, Billie turned her bright head away. Whichever way she looked at the problem, Alexei had betrayed her with the other woman, because in forgetting their intimacy after the funeral he had been unfaithful. Was it unjust of her to feel that way when he had given her no promise of commitment or exclusivity that night?

'Billie...that is an *old* photo, taken long before our marriage,' Alexei repeated determinedly.

'How do I believe that? I mean, I know Calisto was more than willing to renew your relationship, regardless of the fact that you had married me,' she argued helplessly. 'She was even grateful I had given you a son because she didn't want to run the risk of spoiling her figure with a pregnancy—'

Alexei was frowning, ebony brows pleated. 'When did she tell you that?'

'When I saw her in Paris. She said you wouldn't leave me with custody of Nicky, that you would take him off me and that she was willing to help you bring him up!'

Alexei stared at her in frank disbelief. 'Why didn't you tell me that before? How could you listen to such ridiculous lies?' he demanded accusingly. 'I *know* how much you and my son mean to each other. No matter what happens between us, I would never part you from him—'

'You parted us a month ago,' Billie reminded him.

'For a matter of hours, and only to get you here in order to give our marriage a fighting chance!' Alexei protested in heated disagreement. 'You're a wonderful mother and our son will always need you. How could you have listened to Calisto's poisonous claims?'

'How could you put her in your house in Paris and expect me to accept it?'

His dark gaze gleaming golden, Alexei flung up lean brown hands in a furious show of frustration. 'Because I *owed* her! I was the one who changed my mind about our relationship. She didn't change, I did. In the name of God, Billie, how could you not have told me about what happened between us after the funeral? Didn't it occur to you that I might have forgotten but that I might feel that I had *lost* something, even if I didn't know what that something was?'

Wide-eyed and shaken by that countercharge, Billie watched him stride closer. 'Lost something?' she repeated uncertainly. 'I'm not sure I know what you mean—'

'We forged a connection that night deep enough to haunt me when I lost it again,' Alexei argued. 'But I had to remember how I felt that night to realise why I'd ended up charging into a rebound affair with Calisto.'

'You're saying you remember being with me that night now?' Billie questioned weakly. 'If that's true, why didn't you tell me?'

Alexei released a shaken laugh that carried more bitterness than amusement. 'Why did it never occur to you that I would be ashamed of what I would remember of that night?'

Her brow indented. *Ashamed?* She almost bleated out the word again in dismay, but she was fed up of trying and failing to guess what he meant and this time she said nothing.

'Of course, I was ashamed,' Alexei grated in a low driven voice. 'I took advantage of you.'

Tenderness touched her frantic thoughts, slowing the flow of them. 'No, you didn't. You were lonely, shaken up, vulnerable...'

'And I took advantage of you just like your mother has accused me of doing,' Alexei completed resolutely. 'But on the same night while I was with you I realised that I was very probably in love with you and that I had been for some time.'

Blinking rapidly, Billie gazed back at him with frowning force. 'But that's not possible!'

'You got under my skin...you infiltrated me and I didn't even know it was happening to me,' Alexei bit out with annoyance at his lack of self-knowledge on that score. 'Suddenly I was always comparing other women to you and you were winning hands down in every comparison—sex was just the next natural step that night but that shouldn't have been how it happened between us.'

'You weren't in love with me,' Billie told him flatly. 'And how else should we have become intimate? One doesn't always plan these things.'

'You deserved more from me than what you got that night when I was drunk and confused and more than a little spooked by the weird way I was feeling,' Alexei extended wryly. 'When I was willing to wait until we were married—that respect and patience was a better demonstration of how I should have treated you from the first, *agapi mou*.'

My love, he'd called her, and Billie could hardly get her head around the staggering declaration engrained in that endearment. Her attention locked to his lean darkly handsome features, she breathed uncertainly. 'I just don't believe what I'm hearing from you!'

'When I fell down the steps and hit my head outside the guest suite, I forgot more than what we shared in your bed that night,' Alexei continued vehemently. 'I forgot how happy I was, how convinced I'd become that I had finally found the right woman for me. Why the hell do you think that I took the risk of making love to you without contraception? That was so out of character for me, it should have screamed at you and convinced you that I was planning a lot more than a brief sexual encounter with you!'

And there was so much truth in that contention that Billie finally allowed herself to listen. In truth, she had noticed that he was not quite himself that night and some of the stuff he had said to her had seemed to indicate a greater degree of involvement with her than she might have expected. But she had been quick to dismiss any such hopes, even quicker to assume the worst of a male who had apparently so often treated sex like a takeaway meal—cheap and disposable and forgettable. Her own cynicism and low expectations, she recognised ruefully, had combined to ensure that she was reluctant to confront him with the facts of their intimacy. In the expectation of disillusionment, she had ironically ensured that disillusionment was exactly what she had received.

'I just assumed it would mean nothing to you and that maybe you forgot because you didn't *want* to remember it.'

Alexei compressed his lips. 'There may be some truth in that angle, but not on the score of what happened between us. A few weeks ago, I did consult a psychiatrist about those hours I couldn't remember and he suggested that my mind could be reluctant to recall my grief for my parents that night. He was of the opinion, however, that since I had already contrived to recall one moment of those missing hours, I would eventually remember more. I did consider having hypnotherapy...'

'I had no idea you were that bothered about not having those memories,' Billie confided.

'Of course I was bothered. That encounter was central to our marriage and your attitude of distrust. I had to remember what I did that night to understand how horrific the experience must have been for you. One minute we were together and then the next, it was like it had never happened—'

'Yes, it was very painful,' Billie acknowledged unhappily, grateful he understood and astonished that he had seen a psychiatrist in an effort to deal with the issue and find a solution. 'But I really didn't know what to do about it. Staying quiet seemed the most sensible move on every count—of course I didn't think of what might happen if I fell pregnant. When did you remember it all?'

'I had a couple of small flashes and then, one morning, I woke up and the whole recollection was just there,' he revealed. 'I was shattered when I realised how I'd felt that night with you.'

'And you truly think you got involved with Calisto because you were on the rebound from me?' Billie whispered doubtfully.

'Didn't it ever cross your mind that Calisto and I had as much in common as a dog and a cat?' Alexei enquired drily. 'What drew me back to her was familiarity—my recollection of how I felt about her as a teenager and the fact I couldn't have her. Of course what I wanted then from a woman is not at all what I want now. It took me a while to appreciate that Calisto only married Bethune because at that time he was a better financial bet than I was, as a son still dependent on a father for support.'

Billie was afraid to have faith in what he was telling her. It was true that he and Calisto had appeared to have nothing in common. She had wondered what he could see in a fashion model who shared none of his interests. But she had also known that love was reputedly blind and had feared that beauty and sex appeal had won out over common sense. Now when he told her otherwise she wanted so much to believe that message but she was afraid to.

'I thought you were so happy with her,' Billie framed.

'The first fine flush lasted…oh, all of five minutes,' Alexei confided, his handsome mouth forming a sardonic twist in acknowledgement. 'I refused to listen to my doubts because, as I told you, I was ready for something more, something deeper, and when Calisto reappeared it felt like fate.'

Billie winced. 'Fate can be cruel.'

Alexei frowned and nodded agreement. 'If only you had told me about us, at least I would have stopped and listened.'

'If you were infatuated with her, I don't know that you would have.'

'You didn't give me the chance,' he reminded her. 'In fact you assumed the worst of me at every stage and expected nothing. That was the real problem. That was what kept us apart.'

Billie reckoned that she had spent too long on the sidelines of Alexei's life watching him live up to his bad reputation to credit that he might behave differently with her. And yet, even as she recognised that fact, she also recognised that Alexei had always treated her with a lot more respect and kindness than he'd employed with the other women in his life. She had never been just an employee, forced to respect strict boundaries, and in the same way he had always looked out for her interests.

'Why did you really break up with Calisto?' Billie finally asked.

'She wasn't right for me. I don't want to do her down,' Alexei confessed ruefully, his strong jawline hardening, 'but I saw her as she really was the day I found her screaming abuse at a toddler on *Sea Queen*.'

'On St George's Day, when you were entertaining the islanders on the yacht?' Billie questioned, referring to the saint's day when everyone who lived on Speros celebrated the holiday. 'What toddler?'

'The little boy you took to find his mother. Before that, he had bumped into Calisto and put chocolate handprints on her skirt. I found her shouting at him and the poor little chap was sobbing his heart out. I couldn't stay with a woman who could treat a young child like that, and when she turned her attention on you that same afternoon that was the last straw,' he admitted grimly. 'She has a vicious streak I can't accept.'

Well aware of how that vicious streak had offended and wounded other employees, Billie said nothing. Naturally she had known that Calisto had had character traits wholly at odds with Alexei's engrained sense of fairness and courtesy, but that Alexei could have found Calisto's verbal attack on her that same day intolerable touched her heart. Calisto had accused her of flirting with Alexei. Now all of a sudden Billie was appreciating that Alexei had cared even then about her, even if she hadn't realised it.

'I didn't love her,' Alexei breathed, reaching down to close his hands round Billie's and draw her upright. 'I never loved her. Why would I risk my marriage to sleep with her again?'

Her hands quivered in the warm hold of his and she lifted fearless eyes to him. 'You didn't care about our marriage when you walked out on me. You didn't believe that Nicky was your son either...'

His ebony brows drew together. 'Be fair. You took me by surprise and I was devastated by the fallout on our wedding night. You are the one woman in the world whom I've always totally trusted,' he reasoned urgently, and pink discomfiture coloured her upturned face with regret. 'And it did all sound crazy at the time.'

'You didn't love me when you married me...'

Long brown fingers framed her cheeks to hold her troubled eyes steady. 'I didn't *know* I loved you when I married you. I thought I was being so sensible choosing you when, all the time, you *were* the only choice. Because, right then, you were the only woman I wanted,' he told her ruefully. 'Then it all blew up in my face. I didn't know how I felt. I didn't even realise why it all hurt so much. I just felt betrayed.'

Her fingers stroked over his and gripped tight in apology. 'I know. I know how impossible I made it for you but there was no easy way to go about telling you.'

His lean hands held hers tight. 'Telling me the truth upfront,' he countered. 'Trusting me the same way I trust you—'

Sentenced to stillness by the tender look in his dark golden eyes, Billie breathed in deep. 'So, you're not chasing Calisto again?'

'No, and she's already called me to let me know that she has issued a public rebuttal to that effect,' Alexei incised and then, with an unexpected touch of amusement, 'Along with the news that she's got engaged again and she doesn't want rumours of an adulterous association with me to spoil that.'

'Engaged again? But to whom?' Billie prompted in astonishment.

'A very wealthy Parisian banker. He's a lot older than she is, but she says older men are more reliable and, since he already has adult children, he's not expecting her to have a child with him,' Alexei completed.

'But when I saw Calisto in Paris, she made it quite clear that she wanted you back.'

'But I didn't want her and the banker was obviously her back-up plan. I'm relieved she's found someone,' Alexei said wryly. 'I can hand over her affairs to an accountant with a clear conscience.'

And seeing his relief, Billie finally believed that only his sense of responsibility had urged him to go to Calisto's assistance after their relationship had ended. It was as if a weight fell off her shoulders and a dark shadow was jerked from her thoughts. With a sigh she leant forward and rested her head down on his shoulder. 'I'm relieved as well.'

'But you didn't need to be. I love you,' Alexei pointed out doggedly. 'The minute you started talking about divorcing me, I wised up fast. That was a really sensible move of yours—it brought me to my senses.'

'It wasn't a move!' Billie exclaimed in stark disconcertion at the charge. 'It seemed the only solution if you couldn't forgive me for keeping you in the dark about Nicky.'

Alexei bent his arrogant dark head and claimed her mouth with hot, hard brevity that left her breathless, her slim body curving into his and alight with the desire for more. 'The moment you threatened me with a divorce I got off my high horse. It brought me to my senses and I stopped wallowing in your sins. I didn't want to lose you, *agapi mou*,' he murmured, rubbing his knuckles down over her cheekbone in a tender gesture. 'I couldn't *bear* to lose you. I've spent the last few weeks trying to show you that but sometimes I feel like I'm banging my head up against a brick wall.'

'I was so jealous and insecure about Calisto that she came between me and my wits,' Billie confessed in a rush, finally allowing herself to believe that she was loved and revelling in the adoring intensity of his gaze on her face. 'You have been making me very happy, but I was so hurt when you didn't seem to feel anything when I told you how I felt about you.'

'I'm sorry. For a while I didn't think I could trust anything you said,' he confided candidly. 'I was angry, bitter and disappointed in you and it was a while before I could move on from that to concentrate on what's really important. And what's really important is that you *had* our son and now we have the rest of our lives to spend together.'

The rest of our lives. The warmth of his gaze, the buoyancy of his dark deep drawl wrapped round her vulnerable heart like a blanket of reassurance. She hugged him close, a pulse of happiness pounding through her as she let go of her fears and insecurities and finally felt free to claim her happy ending.

'I love you,' she whispered.

He drew her out of the shade of the oak tree into the bright sunlight and on into the dim cool of the chateau. But it was Billie who headed straight for the stairs and the privacy of their bedroom while throwing a half-embarrassed, half-teasing glance over her shoulder at him. Before they got there, however, another concern stole the lightness from her mood. 'We haven't even talked about Lauren, or what we're going to do about her,' she reminded him heavily.

Alexei swung her back to face him. 'We'll deal with her together,' he murmured with quiet resolve. 'She needs to respect our privacy as a family. But it's only thanks to that article that I know how long you've cared about me.'

Billie reddened and screened her eyes. 'I didn't want you to know that.'

'I cared about you too, *agapi mou*,' he traded softly. 'And in ways I couldn't count or explain. I never liked seeing you tired or cross or unwell. I always wanted to make you happy. I hated seeing you with another man. When I had no right to be, I was very possessive of you. Your friendship with Damon Marios really got to me and made me angry and jealous.'

'But it never was anything but a friendship.' Billie shivered as he ran down the zip on her dress and eased it down her arms, pausing to claim a hungry, driving kiss that went on and on and on because she was clinging to him with a heart that was pounding as hard as a road drill inside her chest.

'I love you like crazy,' she told him breathlessly as he tugged her down on the bed with him, finally accepting that he loved her and he was hers in every way that mattered. Suddenly she finally grasped why he had stealthily instructed that all the master-suite beds in his various homes were renewed. He was thinking about her feelings and doing what he could to acknowledge them.

'And you believe me about Calisto? I am suing the

Sunday Globe over that photo of me with her,' Alexei breathed. 'I know now why Lauren's story wasn't published immediately—the paper was waiting and hoping to get proof that I was having an affair with Calisto, but when they couldn't they dug out an old photo instead.'

'I know you're not having an affair.' Billie gazed up at him with her heart in her eyes and his smile felt like sunshine on her skin. 'And if you're still in the mood, I have reconsidered: I would like to have another child soon.'

'That's a very sexy invitation, Mrs Drakos,' Alexei purred, disposing of his shirt with careless grace and baring a hair-roughened muscular torso that seemed to beg for the touch of her appreciative hands. 'Are you sure?'

'More sure than I've ever been about anything,' Billie confessed, regretting the hurt she knew she had inflicted when she was unable to give him her trust. There was love and tenderness in his expressive golden eyes and, although it felt as if it were the first time she was seeing those emotions, she knew they had been there in recent weeks as well, only she had been too blind to recognise them for what they were. She had been equally thick-headed when it came to acknowledging that the average boss didn't treat his PA to hot chocolate topped with melted marshmallows at the end of a difficult day, or send her off on a spa break. Nor, if he was Alexei Drakos, did he offer to cut down on the other women for a mere fancy. But she had not read those signs, had thought too little of herself to recognise that she was special to him.

'I'll never stop loving you,' he swore with all the passion and intensity of his powerful temperament.

'Well, I did try to get over you lots of times, but it just never worked,' Billie admitted more prosaically.

And Alexei laughed with considerable appreciation...

EIGHTEEN MONTHS LATER, Billie tucked her infant daughter, Kolena, into her cot.

Dark-eyed and red-haired, Kolena was a delightful mixture of her parents' genes. Nicky hung over the side of the cot watching his sister and pushed a stuffed toy at her hand. The little starfish fingers closed round the bear, but then the baby's eyes slid drowsily shut.

'Kolena's sleeping again,' Nicky complained, his little boy's restive body humming with suppressed energy.

'It's been a long day for her.' Billie smiled as she thought back on a day of great enjoyment at the christening party held at Hazlehurst Manor. For the first time in her life she had contrived to have both of her parents in the same room. It was true that at the outset of laying eyes on her former fiancée and daughter's father, Lauren had merely nodded frostily across the room at Desmond, but her resistance had crumpled when Desmond complimented her on her continuing youthful good looks. Billie had last seen her mother and father chatting companionably at the buffet and was relieved that her parents could now meet without any awkwardness.

Of course, the past eighteen months had proved more than usually eventful for her mother and had led to a much-changed lifestyle. Lauren had stayed on in London to paint the town red and, within six months of the publication of the story she had sold, she had spent all the money she had earned from it and the hotel where she'd been in residence had contacted Alexei, just before throwing Lauren out onto the street for unpaid bills. At that point, Hilary had persuaded her sister to go into rehab for, by that stage, there had been little doubt that Lauren had a problem with alcohol. But, unhappily, the treatment hadn't worked on that occasion, probably because Lauren had merely surrendered to Hilary's arguments rather than acting on a genuine need to seek help for herself. It had been Billie who'd taken charge of her mother the next time that her lifestyle had got her into trouble—because, by then, Hilary had been abroad on her honeymoon. Now Lauren herself was willing to acknowledge that she had a serious addiction problem.

This second stay in rehab, followed by regular attendance at AA meetings, had helped Lauren to stay off the booze and she and her daughter were getting on much better since then. Sobriety had softened Lauren's sharp tongue and lessened her dramas, while happiness had made Billie more accepting of her mother's weaknesses.

The previous year, Hilary had married Stuart McGregor, the captain of Alexei's yacht, in a quiet ceremony. Still working on her history book, which had since found a publisher, Hilary was—to her astonishment and delight—now four months pregnant with her first child. Up until then the little terrier, Skye, which Alexei had given to Billie on their wedding day, had been the apple of her aunt's eye. Skye had, after all, lived with Hilary while Billie and Alexei were enjoying their extended honeymoon in France, and by the time the couple returned Hilary had confessed that she couldn't face giving the puppy up because she had become so attached to the little animal.

Billie currently worked several hours a day in Alexei's company and occasionally accompanied him abroad. These days he travelled less because he was keen to take an active role in his children's daily life. Billie had found her husband wonderfully supportive during her pregnancy and it had wiped out all the memories of her lonely sense of isolation while she'd carried Nicky. She had enjoyed her second pregnancy and had also been blessed with a straightforward delivery. It would be a long time before she forgot Alexei's eyes shining with tears of pride and fascination when he saw his daughter for the first time.

As Nicky pelted out of the nursery and greeted his father at the top of his voice Billie turned to greet Alexei.

'Your mother's flirting like mad with your father. He's mesmerised,' Alexei revealed with a wicked grin.

'Oh, dear, I do hope she doesn't hurt his feelings.' Billie sighed.

'I think Desmond is mature enough to look after himself,' Alexei told her with quiet assurance. 'How's our daughter?'

'Fast asleep. I think all the attention she got this afternoon exhausted her.'

'You got plenty of attention too,' Alexei reminded her, scanning her slim shapely figure in the sapphire-blue dress and jacket she wore. 'You look amazing, *agapi mou.*'

He closed his arms round Billie and eased her up against his tall, powerful body. He stared down into her shining eyes and the ready smile of welcome already tugging at her ripe mouth and murmured softly, 'Every time I see you, it's like coming home and like no other feeling I've ever had. I love you, *moraki mou.*'

Billie whispered the same sentiment back with similar intensity and gave herself up to the pleasure of his mouth on hers, happiness singing through her every skin cell…

* * * * *

We hope you enjoyed reading this special collection from Harlequin®.

If you liked reading these stories, then you will love **Harlequin Presents®** books!

You want alpha males, decadent glamour and jet-set lifestyles. Step into the sensational, sophisticated world of **Harlequin Presents**, where sinfully tempting heroes ignite a fierce and wickedly irresistible passion!

Enjoy eight new stories from **Harlequin Presents** every month!

Available wherever books and ebooks are sold.

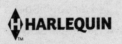

THE WORLD IS BETTER
WITH
Romance

Harlequin has everything from contemporary, passionate and heartwarming to suspenseful and inspirational stories.

Whatever your mood,
we have a romance just for you!

Connect with us to find your next great read, special offers and more.

f /HarlequinBooks

🐦 @HarlequinBooks

www.HarlequinBlog.com

www.Harlequin.com/Newsletters

⬧ HARLEQUIN®

A *Romance* FOR EVERY MOOD™

www.Harlequin.com

JUST CAN'T GET ENOUGH?

Join our social communities
and talk to us online.

You will have access to the latest
news on upcoming titles and special
promotions, but most importantly,
you can talk to other fans about your
favorite Harlequin reads.

Harlequin.com/Community

Facebook.com/HarlequinBooks

Twitter.com/HarlequinBooks

Pinterest.com/HarlequinBooks

Love the Harlequin book you just read?

Your opinion matters.

Review this book on your favorite book site, review site, blog or your own social media properties and share your opinion with other readers!

Be sure to connect with us at:
Harlequin.com/Newsletters
Facebook.com/HarlequinBooks
Twitter.com/HarlequinBooks

HREVIEWS

HARLEQUIN®

A *Romance* FOR EVERY MOOD™

Stay up-to-date on all your
romance-reading news with the
Harlequin Shopping Guide,
featuring bestselling authors, exciting new
miniseries, books to watch and more!

The newest issue will be delivered right to you
with our compliments! There are 4 each year.

Signing up is easy.

EMAIL

ShoppingGuide@Harlequin.ca

WRITE TO US

HARLEQUIN BOOKS
Attention: Customer Service Department
P.O. Box 9057, Buffalo, NY 14269-9057

OR PHONE

1-800-873-8635 in the United States
1-888-343-9777 in Canada

Please allow 4-6 weeks for delivery of the first issue by mail.

HSGSIGNUP